The Adventures of
a Parisian Aeronaut
in Unknown Worlds

The Adventures of
a Parisian Aeronaut
in Unknown Worlds

by
Alfred Driou

translated, annotated and introduced by
Brian Stableford

A Black Coat Press Book

Visit our website at www.blackcoatpress.com

ISBN 978-1-61227-067-8 First Printing. January 2012. Published by Black Coat Press, an imprint of Hollywood Comics.com, LLC, P.O. Box 17270, Encino, CA 91416. All rights reserved. Except for review purposes, no part of this book may be reproduced or transmitted in any form or by any means, electronic or mechanical, including photocopying, recording, or by any information storage and retrieval system, without permission in writing from the publisher. The stories and characters depicted in this novel are entirely fictional. Printed in the United States of America.

Introduction

Aventures d'un aéronaute parisien dans les mondes in-connus, à travers les soleils, les étoiles, les planètes, leurs satellites et les comètes, by Alfred Driou, here translated as *The Aventures of a Parisian Aeronaut in Unknown Worlds* was originally published in Limoges in 1856 by Barbou Frères. The novel was reprinted by the same publisher in 1880, and reprinted again under the title *En Ballon, voyage fantastique dans les mondes inconnus* [In a Balloon; a Fantastic Voyage in Unknown Worlds] in 1888.

Little seems to be known about the author of the work, save for his dates (1810-1880) although he was a very prolific author from the 1850s until his death. He is credited with well over a hundred titles under his own name and the pseudonyms Alfred Villeneuve, Valentin Fréville, Alphonse d'Augerot and Charles de Folleville, although he sometimes reprinted the same text under different titles and different signatures, so the exact total is hard to determine. One biographical detail of which we can be sure is that he was the nephew of Jean-Baptiste Driou (1761-1830), who was the curé of Montier-en-Der in the Haute-Marne (to whom *Aventures d'un aéronaute parisien* is dedicated). A history of *Les Moines de Der* [The Monks of Der] (1843) by R. A. Boullevaux states that a mo-nument to Jean-Baptiste Driou was erected by his nephew "M. l'Abbé Alfred Driou," which implies that the delay in the commencement of Driou's literary career was occasioned by his being in holy orders beforehand—which fits in well enough with the strident religiosity of his work, and with his drastic misconceptions regarding the mores of tribal societies, which seem to be derived from missionary propaganda. Al-though he apparently decided, a trifle belatedly, that he had no clerical vocation he evidently remain devout, at least until *Aventures* was published.

Driou's first-published literary work appears to have been a four-page pamphlet, *Récits historiques et pittoresques sur l'ancien monastère de Montier-en-Der* [Historic and Picturesque Stories of the Ancient Monastery of Montier-en-Der] (1842), although that does not necessarily mean that he was a resident of the monastery at the time. It was followed up, however, by the must weightier *Études littéraires, ou Introduction à la littérature* [Literary Studies; or, An Introduction to Literature] (1843), a textbook specifically designed for use in girls' *pensions* (boarding schools). Although few of his subsequent works carried a similar explicit advertisement, it is obvious that many of them, including *Aventures d'un aéronaute parisien*, were written with young readers in mind, and many of them had a straightforwardly didactic purpose. He might well have begun *Aventures d'un aéronaute parisien* as a didactic work, but it is by no means a straightforward exercise in popularization and is best regarded as a curious kind of intellectual self-portrait, mapping the territory that he was later to cover in detail in dozens of other books.

If the attribution of Driou's pseudonyms can be trusted, his first work of fiction was *Les mystères du cloître* [The Mysteries of the Cloister] (1846), signed Alfred Villeneuve, a two-volume novel very much in the vein of the *feuilleton* fiction that was then becoming enormous popular thanks to the efforts of Eugène Sue, Alexandre Dumas and Paul Féval. The same pseudonym appeared on two other books from the same Parisian publisher, Calot: *Les Étoiles animées* [Animate Stars—probably referring to flowers] (1850) and *Une Niche de Tartuffes* [A Nest of Tartuffes] (1854); and two more from Chappe, also based in Paris: *La Soeur de Moïse* [Moses' Sister] (1859), a novel whose second volume was padded out by the melodramatic novelette "Le Mort vivant" [The Living Corpse], and *Les Chevaliers du Temple* [The Knights Templar] (1861) but by the time the other volumes appeared, Driou's literary career was in full swing under his own name. For reasons that are unclear, the slightly variant signature "Alfred de Villeneuve" was subsequently attached to a number of publications issued after Driou's death, many, if not all, of which had previously been published under his own name or other pseudonyms; "Charles de Folleville" was another posthumous pseudonym apparently invented on his behalf by a publisher.

Driou began to publish regularly, if not yet prolifically, under his own name in 1850, beginning with the novel for younger readers *Alphonse et Lucie ou l'école de malheur* [Alphonse and Lucie; or, The School of Ill-Fortune] and continuing with *L'Enfant du choeur ou impressions et confidences* [The Choir-Boy; or, Impressions and Confessions (1851). These books were very different in kind from those bearing the Villeneuve signature, and it would not have been surprising had he decided that they should not appear under the same name as the conventional melodramas, but it is also worth noting that, although all the Villeneuve titles were published in Paris, those signed Driou were mostly issued by publishers in Limoges, to which city he might well have relocated. Two Limoges publishers, Barbou Frères and E. Ardant, issued the great majority of his subsequent books.

In 1851, Driou published two works that set a pattern for a significant fraction of his work: *Splendeurs et désastres, chroniques de France* [Splendors and Disasters: Chronicles of France] and *Les Fleurs du moyen-âge, légendes nationales* [Flowers of the Middle-Ages: National Legends]. He produced numerous other popularizations of episodes in French history, aimed to make history more entertaining for younger readers, although his endeavors did not meet with universal approval; one reviewer of *Souvenirs de la vieille France, Fragments mérovingiens* [Souvenirs of Old France: Merovingian Fragments] (1853) argued that his style as "distinguished by affectation and bizarrerie" and chided him for anachronism as well as a certain irreverence for matters of fact. Alongside such exercises in popularization, Driou continued to produce non-fiction of others sorts—including *Lis, roses et violettes; ou, le moisson des anges* [Lilies, Roses and Violets; or, The Angels' Crops] (1953, notable as an early exercise in the use of printed color plates—and to write fiction, including Les *Drames de l'esclavage* [Dramas of Slavery] (1853) and *Les Pièces d'or de Lucette* [Lucette's Gold Coins] (1854), sometimes mixing popular non-fiction and fiction, as in *L'Ange du matin et l'étoile du soir, légendes historiques* (1855), which includes the novelette "Les Démons de la nuit" [The Demons of the Night].

It appears that *Aventures d'un aéronaute parisien* might have originated as a similar hybrid exercise; it has a companion volume, *L'Album merveilleux, épreuves d'un daguerreotype aérien, ou Scènes historiques, monuments, moeurs, coutumes et costumes de tous les temps et tous les âges* [The Marvelous Album, Prints of an Aerial Daguerreotype; or, Historical Scenes, Monuments, Mores, Customs and Costumes of All Time and All Ages], similarly issued by Barbou Frères in 1856, which might have been extracted from the manuscript of the former work for separate publication, as the text of *Aventures* implies, but is more likely to have been written first, with the *Aventures* effectively written "around" it as a kind of advertisement. At any rate, *L'Album merveilleux* was evidently the less successful of the two, being one of the few works by Driou that appears never to have been reprinted.

It seems probable that *Aventures* did not work out as had been originally intended; it certainly fails to live up to the promise of its extended subtitle to deal in some detail with the other planets of the solar system and their satellites, as well as comets and the fixed stars. Instead, having failed to make much of a job of describing life on the Moon—supposedly a stereotype of all the worlds in Creation except Earth—the narrative returns to Earth, perhaps cravenly, but probably because the author had changed his mind, as a result of his imaginary sojourn on the Moon, as to what he wanted and needed to do, not merely with his narrative but with the rest of his life.

At any rate, *Aventures* marked something of a watershed in Driou's career; there was a distinct hiatus in his original publications between 1857 and 1860, when he might well have spent a good deal of time traveling—effectively, practicing what he had preached in the *Aventures* and actually going to see some of the places that he had described therein (on the basis of secondary sources that were sometimes far from reliable). Writing the summary of his world-view that is contained in the *Aventures* might well have made him aware of the extent of his ignorance as well as that of his knowledge, of himself as well as the world; at the very least, it seems to have given hum an appetite for first-hand experience, rather than the book-learning with which he had previously been content. The pattern of his publications expanded noticeably in 1861, when he began to churn out travel books in some quantity.

Driou published an account of an excursion to the Alps and Pyrenees in 1857, but that endeavor paled by comparison with the flood of such works launched by his 1861 account of Venice; accounts of Naples, Rome, Lombardy and Constantinople were only a few of the similar books that followed in 1862. Another hiatus followed, however, when he presumably went off on his travels again, this time getting slightly further afield—including the Holy Land—although he never did get around to correcting the appalling misconceptions regarding America, Africa and the Far East that he displayed so blithely in *Aventures*, and he seems to have spent more time touring the regions of France than venturing beyond its borders. He seems, however, to have settled down for good in 1870 or thereabout, and spent the last ten years of his life producing works in amazing quantity for his two Limoges publishers, the majority of them under the names Valentin Fréville and Alphonse d'Augenot.

Driou had first used the Fréville pseudonym in 1860 on the novel *Édouard et Mélanie*, but it did not appear again until it was attached to half a dozen books issued in 1872-3. Alphonse d'Augerot made his début in 1870 with *Histoire de la peinture* [A History of Painting] before being attached to two or three books per year from 1872 onwards, effectively becoming the author's usual signature thereafter. Some of the books issued under these names were reprints of previous works issued under the Driou signature, not always with new titles, so their true authorship was only partly concealed. The logic of the strategy is unclear, although it might simply have been the case that the two publishers issuing the bulk of his work wanted to disguise the extent to which they were both dependent on a single writer. It might be worth noting, however, that in the second edition of the *Aventures*, published in 1880, although the text of the novel remains largely unaltered, the signature on this dedication is changed to "A. d'Augerot." It is difficult to imagine why the author would have done that—if it was, indeed, the author and not the publisher who did it—unless he had actually adopted Alphonse d'Augerot as his name rather than simply using it as a pseudonym.

In the midst of this hectic but mostly rather pedestrian production, *Aventures d'un aéronaute parisien* stands out as a markedly anomalous item, not merely for its imaginative extravagance but also for its keen interest in technological progress. An interest in ongoing scientific discoveries was reflected in a handful of his other works, most notably the popularization *Les Cieux, la terre, les eaux et les secrets de l'univers* [The Heavens, the Earth, the Waters and the Secrets of the Universe] (1870) and the novella *Le Secret de M. le Curé, ou les vertiges de science* [The Curé's Secret; or, The Intoxications of Science] (1878), but for the most part, Driou set such matters aside. In a way, this is odd, because Driou might be reckoned a pioneer in a major boom in the popularization of subjects previously left to academic specialists, and the 1860s became the first Golden Age of the popularization of science in France. Louis Figuier, another of the pioneers in that boom, who is a major source of the information relayed in *Aventures*, was later to provide a major source for Jules Verne, who became the principal model for the writing of fiction based on and overlapping popular science. Perhaps, having read Verne's *Cinq semaines en ballon* (1863; tr. as *Five Weeks in a Balloon*), with which *Aventures* has a certain amount in common, Driou realized that he simply could not compete in that arena and would look foolish if he tried, or perhaps he became disenchanted with science when its ongoing discoveries blatantly failed to fulfill the hope and conviction expressed in *Aventures* that true science would never contradict Holy Scripture; either way, *Aventures* remained a unique anomaly.

The novel is, in fact, just as anomalous in the history of imaginative fiction as it is in the context of Driou's literary career; there is nothing else like it. That is partly to do with its exceedingly awkward hybrid status, uneasily suspended between religious fantasy and travelogue, and between wild imagination and vulgar popularization, but it is mainly a product of the author's own manifest uncertainty as to what on Earth he was trying to do. Like many works of imaginative fiction, *Aventures* became an endeavor in pure exploration in the course of being written; it was neither the first nor the last such work in which the author blithely followed his whims as they occurred to him, casting off the constraints of whatever plan he had made before starting. Although it poses as an exploration of the material world—and some contemporary readers must have been as disappointed as modern ones will be to learn that the "unknown worlds" to which the title refers eventually turn out to be the continents of Earth rather than other planets—it is actually nothing of the sort; what it really explores is its author's subjective notion of the world, with far more emphasis on judgment than description. What the narrative gains from its quasi-speculative status is not so much visionary scope, in which department it is somewhat lacking, but a license to inquire into the broad significance of the world's misfortunate history and cruel bizarrerie.

I had occasion to point out in my study of *Scientific Romance in Britain 1890-1950* (1986) that an unusually large proportion of early English writers of speculative fiction were the sons of Protestant clergymen who had lapsed from the stern and narrow faith of their fathers and were using their fiction to explore alternative world-views, in which the God of the scriptures was either absent or greatly transfigured. That pattern is not reproduced in the parallel history of the French *roman scientifique*, because lapsing Catholics tend to follow a different psychological trajectory, but if—as seems highly likely—Driou's literary career was the sequel to a forsaken religious vocation, that would help greatly, not merely to explain how he came to write *Adventures d'un aéronaute parisien* but why it is such a deeply peculiar book. Although it refuses, very determinedly, to give up on a restrictive quasi-fundamentalist form of devout Catholicism, there is no doubt that the protagonist's adventures, which are supposed to confirm that faith, actually put a enormous amount of stress upon it, often giving him the appearance of protesting far too much, and somewhat hypocritically. The author often seems to be well aware—although he never permits his protagonist to realize the fact—that his sub-Miltonic quest to "justify the ways of God to men" does no credit at all to God, or to stubborn belief. Ostensibly a work designed to shore up faith, it is difficult to believe that *Aventures* did not have the opposite effect on the majority of its readers, perhaps revealing more about its author than he had previously known about himself.

We can see now, although contemporary readers of the text probably could not, that if Driou really did want to glorify God and excuse his shabby treatment of humankind, then it was a mistake to place the history of technology at the forefront of the human story, and the history of aeronautics at the forefront of the history of technology. One of the few authentic works of scientific romance that Driou might have had an opportunity to read, Samuel Berthoud's "Voyage au ciel" (1841; tr. as "A Heavenward Voyage") could have made it very clear to him that the history of technology, and aeronautics in particular, makes much more sense if it is seen as a challenge to divine parsimony rather than a testament to divine bounty, and that trying to represent it in the latter light is a doomed endeavor.

Driou can, of course, be forgiven for thinking otherwise; Louis Figuier was still a staunch believer in the word of scripture in 1856, and Driou could not know that he would desert the cause decisively in the mid-1860s, when his decision to produce a revised and corrected edition of *Le Monde avant le déluge* [The World Before the Deluge] in 1867 immediately prompted Jules Verne to issue a revised version of *Voyage au centre de la terre* (initially 1864; revised 1867; tr. as *Journey to the Center of the Earth*—all translations use the revised edition rather than the earlier one) that would celebrate evolutionism rather than carefully avoiding the issue. Nor could Driou suspect, in 1856, that Figuier would eventually become the most important champion of the genre of the *roman scientifique*, publishing *feuilletons* under that heading for more than a decade when he took over the editorship of *La Science Illustrée* in the late 1880s. Nevertheless, Driou's colors were firmly nailed to the mast of the ship that got stranded and left behind, not the one that sailed on.

It cannot any longer qualify as a spoiler to reveal in advance that Driou's protagonist's partly-extraterrestrial balloon flight turns out to be a dream; it could hardly have been otherwise, given the literary conventions of the day. That fact is, however, far more important to the story than a mere matter of supplying it with a bathetic pretext; indeed, it is the story's free indulgence in "dream logic" that both permits and encourages it to be so revealing about the author's interests, opinions and (if only covertly) doubts. Had *Aventures* not been a dream-story, not only could the protagonist not have set out to explore the Moon, but the author could not have confronted himself with the practical problem of trying to imagine a material Paradise—a challenge that no author has ever been able to meet successfully, but whose dimensions of failure are frequently interesting. The images of transport in Paradise by balloon and railways, which are central to Driou's description, may seem irredeemably quaint to modern readers, but they are both revealing and rather touching. The truly telling point is not that Driou was able to imagine a Paradise inhabited by enthusiastic aeronauts, but that he found himself no longer capable of imagining one that was not.

To modern aficionados of speculative fiction, it might well seem that everything that happens in the novel after the visit to the Moon is anticlimactic and uninteresting, but it might be as well to remember that, whatever Driou's original intention might have been, the whole purpose of the lunar odyssey became an attempt to provide a kind of conceptual frame for the subsequent survey of the Earth: a survey whose results, by virtue of the moment of the story's writing and setting, had been compromised in advance, if not torn apart. Before the protagonist's aerostat reaches the Moon, the content of the novel is essentially forward-looking, anticipating the continuation of technological progress, but when it returns, the narrative looks back relentlessly on the past, with a particular and rather peculiar kind of regret, only bringing the present into focus—despite its inevitable eclipse of lost glories—in order to highlight appalling cruelties (most of them imaginary) in a sadistically indulgent fashion. That was not where the narrative's trajectory initially seemed to be headed, but as the paradoxical logic of the dream gradually dug deeper into the layers of Driou's subconscious, that was probably where it was always bound to end up.

It cannot be said that *Aventures d'un aéronaute parisien* is a good novel, and it would be easy enough to argue that it is a truly terrible one, but, like many of the misshapen classics of imaginative fiction, it is interesting precisely because of its imperfections, its frustrated ambitions and its self-skewering awkwardness. It fails because it never had any chance of success, not because its author was stupid or incompetent, and that is what makes its failure intriguing rather than ignominious. Of its sincerity, there is no doubt at all; there is not a single topic raised in it, save for aeronautics itself, that Driou did not take up again, in order to address in more detail and with a greater measure of sophistication. It really did provide a kind of mental map, not only of his past and present interests, but also of his future concerns and endeavors; however unseriously he intended it when he began it, it really did become a pivotal work within his career and his life—and if its patchwork quality makes his career and life look like an utter mess, in terms of their composition and ultimate achievement…well, let him who is without sin cast the first stone; my hands are empty.

This translation has been made from the version of the first edition of the text, as reproduced on the Bibliothèque Nationale's invaluable *gallica* website. The extraordinary multiplicity of proper names rendered the translation and annotation something of a nightmare, but I have done my best to clarify the historical and (mostly obsolete) geographical references without resorting to too much footnoting. As part of this clarification process I have added forenames to many of the surnames that I have not footnoted, in order to make the individuals concerned more easily recognizable or researchable.

Brian Stableford

To the Memory
of
JEAN-BAPTISTE DRIOU
Curé of Montier-en-Der
Haute-Marne
de 1805-1830

What homage would be worthy of your virtues, the good deeds you have done and the noble memories you have left behind? Let me, however, dear soul in Heaven, place on the tomb where your last remains lie this poor symbol of the information you have given me, and of the sacred memory that will burn in my grateful heart forever.

A. Driou
Paris, 20 January 1856

PREFACE

I was told that one day, there arrived in Paris, bravely come to get to know it and talk about it on long winter evenings, the most naïve of the worthy inhabitants of Champagne. Once in the midst of the capital's beauties, he was spoiled for choice. Hazard brought him, open-mouthed to the Musée d'Artillerie, where the fellow expected to encounter the inventor of gunpowder. To console him for his absence, an obliging cicerone showed him the celebrated suits of armor, especially the panoply of François I. And as the loquacious guide, proud of his superiority, rambled on about Marignan, Cérisoles and Pavie, the Champenois, ecstasized by the great deeds of the hero, exclaimed:

"Under what king did the fellow do all that?"

Amazed in the face of such robust innocence, the guide responded, with superb phlegm: "François I, my good man, did all that under himself!"

Reader, what I am going to tell you in this book happened under the Emperor Napoléon III—may God protect him!—in the year 1856 A.D., the 1267th year of the hegira of Mohammed,[1] the 2604th of the foundation of Rome, the 2nd of

---

[1] 1856 A.D. actually corresponds to 1277 A.H. The former date was presumably inserted by the publisher, in order to make the story seem contemporary at first glance; all the other dates given in the text locate the events very specifically to May 1854. The second edition altered the figure of 1856 to 1855 (without changing the supposedly equivalent dates), which makes no sense at all. Having the book issued by Barbou might well have been a fallback option on the author's part, as the opening of the narrative seems deliberately calculated to appeal to a Parisian publisher, so it might well have been written in 1854.

the 593rd Olympiad and the 5855th since the creation of the world, in the most beautiful sunlight...no, I'm mistaken, in the most beautiful moonlight in the world.

Before I get to the point, let me play the pedant, and allow me to address a few words to you by way of a preface.

A few years ago, a man—an Englishman, alas—took it into his head to search for a passage for his nation's fleets through the polar ice, in the north-western sector, which, from the Bering Strait to the Davis Strait, connects the Pacific Ocean to the Atlantic. A high rank crowned the long maritime endeavors of Sir John Franklin and, although charged with sixty winters, he still combined the prudence of maturity with the fire of youth. The intrepid mariner therefore let England heaped with the good wishes of his anxious family, furnished with the instructions of the Lords of the Admiralty, ready to meet any challenge. But where did he go? What has become of him? God alone knows...[2]

In 1789, our France had seen a similar devotion. Jean-François de La Pérouse had courageously quit his fatherland in order to obey Louis XVI, who had given him the mission of circumnavigating the world. Two frigates accompanied the skilled navigator: the *Astrolabe* and the *Boussole*. Of the ships and the illustrious admiral there has never been the slightest news. And while hoping for so long to see them reappear, what adventures have been credited to that hero of the sea, what tales have been told of his sojourn among the savages! It required Captain John Dillon, sailing in 1827 to the north of the New Hebrides, to find wreckage and equipment under the water beating the reefs of the Vanikoro Isles, which he recog-

---

[2] In 1854 Inuits reported to expeditionaries searching for Franklin that he had his crew had died on the ice in 1847 after abandoning their icebound ships, but the tale was widely doubted at the time, and materials found more recently have cast further doubt on it; there is, however, no doubt that he was dead. The real tragedy is that more ships and lives were lost searching for him than made up his original expedition.

nized as having belonged to La Pérouse's crews, finally to persuade everyone that the unfortunate man was asleep forever beneath the waves, the victim of a shipwreck.

What will be learned, eventually, about the fate of Sir John? I cannot say. But what can be said, at present, is this: Commander Robert McClure, on the corvette *Investigator*, and Captain Edward Inglefield, on the steamer *Phoenix*, for nearly five years, have been plowing every sea, visiting every island, exploring every coast, traversing every prairie, fathoming every forest and questioning every tribe—and those men, animated by a noble zeal, have not found the slightest vestige of Sir John's passage.

Nevertheless this patient research revealed two facts.

Firstly, the channel supposed by Franklin, opening between the polar ice-fields and connecting the two Oceans was found.

Secondly, a Frenchman, Lieutenant Joseph-René Bellot, attached to the expedition by love of the unknown and, more especially, love for his fellows exposed to misfortune, having ventured on to the ice in search of them, fell into one of the gaping fissures in the Arctic Ocean and disappeared forever.

Glory offered two crowns on that occasion: England took one, as she was entitled to do—but, generous this time, she gave the other to France. In fact, as I write these lines, the English, in admiration for the devotion of young Bellot, are eternalizing his memory by erecting a column to him on a rock in the sea that separates the two nations.

That event, among others—especially the alliance of the two peoples in the war in the Orient, on which every gaze is fixed—has made a powerful contribution to the retightening of the bonds between the English and the French. Henceforth, the dictum proclaiming that we hold one another by *la Manche*[3] will therefore be the truth.

---

[3] *La Manche* [the sleeve] is the French name for the body of water that the English modestly call the English Channel.

I admire the intrepidity of Bellot, to be sure, but I understand better still the emotional thirst, the need to search and discover that the expedition embodied. You will not be surprised, therefore, my young readers, if I confess to you that the great and numerous examples of audacity and curiosity that adventurous spirits offer us gave me, a poor wretch somewhat deprived on the gifts of fortune, the odd idea of inventing, discovering or giving birth to something. That soon became the strangest obsession, an incessant obsession that gave me no peace or remission. If only I could distinguish myself by the revelation of something unknown, the exhibition of some singularity or other—I had no idea what. It was an illness—the malady of the age, I think—that had infected me.

Around us, in fact, everyone is running after marvels and desirous of prodigies. Everyone is trying to produce his own phenomenon. A wind of eccentricity is blowing. There is no originality for which no one has taken out a patent. It is a veritable and furious steeplechase of discovery. It is driving people mad. Everyone is racking his brains, getting hot under the collar and contracting a fever imagining, searching and producing, eager to fecundate the absence. In their eyes, Robert-Houdin is a great man; they envy his hypnotic talent.[4] Like Philippe, like Hamilton and Giovanni Bosco, people ask him to draw some new creation from the void. There are people who would don the smock of Albertus Magnus or the apron of Nicholas Flamel without hesitation if they thought there was any hope of finding the elusive philosopher's stone in a flask, an alembic or a crucible.

I am only mentioning all these fantasies of the present day to excuse my own; for, in view of what I have just told you about everyone's manias, is it not true that it is entirely

---

[4] Jean-Eugène Robert (1805-1871), who combined his surname with that of his wife when he married, was the great pioneer of modern stage magic, but did not pose as a hypnotist.

excusable that I too had the caprice of mounting some hobby-horse and, once astride it, of riding forth on a whim?

Newly exhumed from the debris of a Roman tumulus lamp buried in the thickets of an ancient Gaulish forest, a lamp lit for nearly eighteen hundred years has been brought out, still filled with the incombustible oil about which Pliny wrote. Monsieur Poitevin,[5] arm-in-arm with his intrepid spouse, rises high into the air, lost to sight, in order to propel his phaeton harnessed to vigorous chargers, or even to gallop over the plains of the ether with one foot on a pony and the other on an ox—yes, an ox. We may presume that electrical telegraph wires will one day extend to the planets. Why should I not have my fantasy in my turn? Except that I had to hurry—there was no time to lose.

Thus, taking my head in my hands, I thought hard...

What an uncomfortable position it is to take one's head in both hands in order to reflect, especially when reflection is slow and ideas are torpid instead of springing forth! I stayed like that for a long time, wrapped up in myself...

Having done things conscientiously, not once but ten or twenty times, I got up again. I had not come up with any-thing—nothing at all!

It was enough to drive one to despair. Was the sacred fire extinct within me, then?

I needed air—fresh air—to revive me. I went out and walked uphill toward the Arc-de-Triomphe at the Étoile, through the Bois de Boulogne.

While climbing the Allée de Longchamps, I ruminated. How could I not ruminate, having invested my entire future in the success of my discovery, only to find myself so deeply disappointed! In addition, I had nothing in my pocket. My family was wealthy, but it was honest and virtuous; it wanted, above all else, to see me get a real job. Now, until that mo-

---

[5] Madare Poitevin was one of the great pioneers of aerial showmanship, who turned balloon ascents into a kind of circus performance.

ment I had preferred absurd scientific reveries to a regular life of hard work—to the extent that, to bring me down to earth, my father had judged it appropriate to let me suffer hunger. It was then that my rebellious pride had insinuated the idea of achieving a fortune without any help from my family, by some invention or other due to the power of my genius.

Poor genius! I had found nothing; now my back was to the wall. Such was my situation.

Must I abandon myself to despair? Must I bend my pride to the paternal will, so just and so rational? In order to persevere in my rebellion and to have the independence of my character demonstrate Horace's great assertion *Impavidum ferient ruinae!*[6] was it not better to die? That is how the serpent, that ancient hypnotist, subtly insinuated its horrible paradoxes into my heart.

To die! I thought. *To take the sad path of suicide in order to spare myself misfortune? Oh, no! I am a Christian before anything else, and religion is my guide, happily. If I go astray momentarily, its divine torch will not permit me to get lost. Who has the right to be a deserter from life? It is not a deposit that God has placed in our care? Can a sentinel quit the post entrusted to him without dishonor? Get away! It is an atrocious cowardice, for the sake of a few troubles, however bitter they might be, to escape from pain. Courage makes heroes; a man must be able to confront suffering and not yield to its blows. Deplorable malady of the age, cruel monomania, how many victims you claim every day! And how many, to avoid some evils, throw themselves into greater ones? For once the threshold of life is crossed, will the vengeful Lord not hold one to account for the desertion and the flight?*

I thrust away the sinister temptation that had showed itself momentarily at the door of my heart, and, in turn, grace

---

[6] "The ruination [of the world] would cause him no emotion"—Horace's characterization of the unshakable firmness of the just man.

speaking to my Catholic soul, I resolved to go straight to my family and say, with regret in my heart:

"I am yours henceforth; make of me what you please. I renounce my love for science, technology, geometry and algebra. Guide me; I will obey."

It was the month of May. Winter was giving way to a magnificent spring. Strengthened by my new resolution, I went up to the top of Arc-de-Triomphe in order to give my eyes the pleasure of contemplating the magnificent panorama of Paris, which extends so splendidly over the banks of the Seine.

Having arrived at the summit of the monument, at the exit of the dark stairway, one is immediately inundated with light and air. It is an impression that conveys some slight idea of the passage from death to a new life—and, as my dark ideas were still dogging my footsteps, my gaze immediately went toward the Bois de Boulogne, and I thought automatically, as if following my train of thought, that it was the rendezvous of those wishing to die. Yes, those whom fortune, by virtue of the rigors and privations of poverty and cruel human passions, by virtue of their tyranny, had led astray and rendered victim to mental disorder, came there—and who could count the number of victims slain there by the rope, fire, iron or poison? Like the wandering shades of Taenarum, one see them roaming, talking to themselves, and struggling against the phantoms obsessing them. Then, soon, in an increase of fever, they forget the vengeful God to whom they will have to account for their crime; they lose sight of their soon-to-be-desolate family…and fall, only to rise again in confrontation with eternity!

How one goes astray when one loses sight of the true goal of life, and makes material enjoyment the preoccupation and sole object of one's labor, one's leisure and one's thoughts!

Contrary to my expectations, there were few people on the platform of the Arc de Triomphe; it could not have been easier for me to look out in all directions. How delightful nature seemed from the height at which I was admiring it, and how richly Paris was framed by an immense crown of verdant hills!

Suddenly, a loud *hurrah*, emerging from a thousand throats, drew my attention toward the Hippodrome.

A gigantic balloon was rising majestically from the middle of the arena, while the crowd stamped their feet to the chords of a joyful band. Inscribed in large letter on the aerostat was the name *Eole*. By means of a network of ropes, the frail machine, inflated by the gas, reminiscent of an enormous bronze sphere as it reflected the sunlight, carried a man precariously seated in the gondola, who, clutching a parachute, was preparing to slide into empty space to satisfy the curiosity of the spectators.

It must be realized that the *Eole*, the only god of the winds that the country has made, had scant empire over the fluid element, for it lacked the power to steer itself, and a southerly wind, devoid of respect for its lord and master, caused the feeble vessel to incline toward the Arc de Triomphe. I trembled for the man it bore, who was risking his life in that fashion for the pleasure of his fellows.

In addition, the man occupying the gondola seemed to me to be very inexperienced. He was absolutely ignorant of the elementary rudiments of the maneuver. I understood is awkwardness and, suddenly enlightened by the instinct that leads a learned man to deduce, at the moment of danger, the means of getting out of difficulty, I slapped my forehead. Technology revealed one of its prodigies to me. Light dawned in my brain; at that very moment I discovered the key to a great enigma. I finally had a secret of my own, mine alone. I was able to steer the most rebellious aerostats through the air.

Yes, I had grasped a marvel—a marvel that would dazzle the world. People would surely proclaim a miracle when my discovery was announced, published and advertised. Obviously, by comparison with me, Christopher Columbus would no longer be anything but a pedestrian, James Cook and Jules Dumont d'Urville mere acrobats, and Franklin a pauper!

Except that, to bring the endeavor I wanted to undertake to a successful conclusion, I would need money...and I didn't have a sou!

However, an inventor, the author of a prodigy as valuable as he one I had within my grasp, cannot allow himself to be stopped by such minor difficulties.

I therefore came down from the Arc de Triomphe, transformed into the pedestal of my own glory, and, without paying any more heed to the *Eole* and the fellow with the parachute, I went in the opposite direction along the great Avenue des Champs-Élysées, no longer with my head bowed like a man ruminating but held high, my eyes proud, my mouth bold, resolved not to go back to my entresol until I had found a benevolent moneylender and obtained the benefits of his golden goose.

The sacred aureole of victory surely crowned my forehead, for that same evening, having knocked on the door of my family's banker to ask for two thousand francs, I was handed six!

Masterpiece of Creation, beloved woman, my dear mother, angel of the infant, treasure of the son, delight of the man, it was to you that I owed that surprise. You had feared that I might fall on hard times and in your anticipatory tenderness, mysteriously hidden, you had set aside resources for your rebellious child in his poverty, and given life to him for a second time. O mothers, I love you with all the love of which certain ingrate sons deprive you! But you, my mother, oh, I love you, you alone, with the love that all mothers inspire in me!

I thus found myself rich; it was enough to make me jump for joy, or to go mad! The very next day I had workers of all sorts in the courtyard beneath my entresol: textile-cutters, designers, tailors, rope-makers and mechanics; and they were all working with an unparalleled zeal that reminded me of my Virgil: *Fervet opus redolentque thymo fragrantia mella.*[7]

---

[7] "Fervent labor [and] fragrant honey scented with thyme." The quotation is from the *Georgics*.

They were making the envelope, fitting together its broad black and red strips, making the threads, weaving the cords, fitting out the gondola and arranging the rigging; in a word, they were making me an aerostat, a model aerostat, enormous in its proportions—gigantic! I gave them the plan, directed the assembly, designed the safety-valves. I applied myself personally to the construction of my invention by supervising the manufacture of its various parts by the mechanic. In brief, I made preparations for my triumph, a triumph without precedent.

What were people going to say about me in Paris, in France, in the world? With what legitimate pride would my parents hear my glory proclaimed! That would be my noble vengeance against my father. It would be the recompense for my mother's devotion. Nothing was surer; the Académie des Sciences would throw open its doors to me. Take not that I was not seeking fame, however. The trumpets of publicity the cash-registers of advertisement and the bells of the charlatan were for others. Genius never lowers itself to such means; it soars, and like a sun, its rays fall equally on everyone; like an eagle, it attracts every gaze. I thus abandoned myself to the renown that, hitched to its lightning-fast chargers, would carry the marvels of my discovery and the power of my talent from the banks of the Seine to the ends of the Earth.

Would I not be seen to pass overhead, like a conqueror, dominating countries and the clouds, visiting the six continents of the world—Asia, Africa, Europe, America, Oceania and the Polar Lands—in turn, the Old World and the New, civilized countries and savage ones? What amazement there would be among the populations! A man in a balloon, steering to the right and the left, laughing at the seas, brushing the tree-tops, setting the snowy summits of mountains beneath my feet, descending and rising, floating at will: the king of the world, the master of the air, a spectator of tempests, a sovereign ruler!

Meanwhile, in all the windows on every floor of all the houses overlooking my courtyard, there was nothing but a mosaic of curious heads—white and brunette, blonde and red-haired, pale faces, sly faces, laughing faces, sad faces, wrinkled features, youthful physiognomies, ardent eyes, mocking eyes, incredulous eyes—examining my open-air workshop, wondering what was being done there, sending witty gibes more or less in my direction, and looking at me as if to say: "Has the poor young man gone off his head?"

To which I replied, privately: *Patience, patience! One more day, and I'll show you that it isn't Charenton that will claim me but the temple of Memory!*

Thus I laughed, covertly, and if I became serious again, it was because all the bells of Paris, London, St. Petersburg and Peking—of the whole world—were ringing in my ears, celebrating my conquest and singing my praises. Nevertheless, I could not help overhearing what some people were saying, prognosticating frightful misfortunes. Then, while some of my indiscreet neighbors, better instructed in the art of aerostatics, were starting to tell the story of that magnificent invention, I became calm and placid again, and set myself in opposition to everyone in conquering those infinite plains whose extent the eye is impotent to measure, through which I would travel as my own domain. The universe, in fact, had no more barriers for me, and I was proud of that—I made it my sin.

Let me repeat to you some of those ironic or savant conversations that were passing back and forth above my head.

"To begin with," said a worthy retired professor of the Collège de France to the children surrounding him, "you should know that it was the Englishman Henry Cavendish who discovered the extreme lightness of inflammable gas. Then, to test it, Dr. Joseph Black of Edinburgh suggested the idea of employing a bladder. But Tiberius Cavallo, finding that a bladder would be too heavy, also rejected paper as being too compact, and filled soap-bubbles with the gas, which suddenly flew up to burst against the ceiling."

"Tell them too, Monsieur," continued a merchant from Lyon, retired from business, "that there was a paper factory at Annonay owned by two very clever brothers, and that these two brothers, Joseph and Étienne Montgolfier—named after an estate they had near Ambert in the Auvergne—by virtue of contemplating the continual spectacle of the ascension of clouds over the ridges of the Alps, and having studied the causes of the suspension and equilibrium of those gigantic masses for a long time, conceived the project of imitating nature in one of its strangest caprices.

"They tried to enclose water vapor in a light but resistant envelope. Then they tried to enclose wood-smoke in a silken bag. Finally, having had the opportunity to make the acquaintance of other gases, they made a new one, produced from lightly-moistened straw and wool.

"Then, having filled a silken sheath with a volume of two cubic meters with that gas, they saw it suddenly rise to the top of the apartment. Immediately, they prepared a second balloon able to hold twenty cubic meters. Once filled with gas, the new envelope rose up so violently that it broke its ropes, rose up to three hundred meters, and fell upon a nearby hill.

"This time, they thought of a great experiment..."

"That of the fourth of June 1785, wasn't it?" said a magistrate from the imperial court, interrupting the Lyonnais. "It left great memories in Annonay. My father, who was a member of the Assemblée des États of the Vivarais, witnessed it along with all his colleagues. The aerostat was a dozen meters wide, and was only made of baling silk on which paper had been stuck. Ten pounds of damp straw and wool were burned in the heater placed beneath the orifice. When the machine was inflated, it was released, and within ten minutes it reached an altitude of five hundred meters."

"Five hundred meters!" said a naïve bourgeois, admiringly.

"So, at the request of Monsieur de Breteuil, a Minister of France, and that of the Académie, which appointed a committee headed by Antoine Lavoisier, Étienne Montgolfier came to Paris. The capital wanted to see his experiment. It was made possible by a professor at the Jardin des Plantes, who collected ten thousand francs by subscription and had the machine constructed by expert mechanics. A young scientist, Alexandre

Charles, supervised all the preparations. It was in the Place des Victoires that the balloon was inflated, and it took four days to complete that operation. Then, in order to satisfy public curiosity, it was transported by night to the middle of the Chap-de-Mars. More than three thousand spectators in gathered there, on the banks of the river or the heights of Passy. A cannon-shot announced its departure. In two minutes the aerostat rose up to a thousand meters; then it disappeared into a cloud, but climbed thereafter to an immense elevation..."

"And came down again near Écouen, five leagues from Paris," said a young painter, who also wanted to add his voice to the scientific concert, in a single breath.

"Add, too," the magistrate went on, that, notwithstanding the heavy rain that was falling, the amazed Parisian melted into tears of admiration, seemingly delirious. And to complete the story, know that the peasants of Gonesse, seized by terror when the balloon fell, thought that it was the moon falling out of the sky—to the extent that, seeing the object of their terror immobile, they tore it to pieces, attached it to the tail of a horse, and heaped every possible outrage upon it."

"Étienne Montgolfier only arrived as the balloon was departing," said the retired merchant in his turn; that was why Charles had taken so long to inflate the machine. But Montgolfier proposed to repeat the trial in a fire balloon—which is to say that, the one in the Champ-du-Mars having only been inflated by gas produced by iron filings, sulfuric acid and water, that of the other would be produced by burning straw and wool. On the fourteenth of September 1785, the new machine was tested, having been set up in the garden of Jean-Baptiste Réveillon, the famous wallpaper manufacturer of the Faubourg Saint-Antoine, who was later to perish in the first revolutionary riots of 1789. The new balloon had the form of a prism, twenty-five meters high and fifteen in diameter. It was inflated in nine minutes. It took off immediately, dragging a weight of five hundred pounds with it, but a tempest destroyed it."

"What did they do then?" asked the painter.

"They started again from scratch," said the magistrate, "but this time, Louis XVI was to witness the further trial at Versailles. It took place on the nineteenth of the month. When the aerostat had been inflated in the château's great courtyard, a sheep a cockerel and a duck were placed in a cage beneath the balloon, in order to become the first aeronauts. Paris came to Versailles that day. At noon, the king and the queen came down, with the lords and ladies of the court, walked around the aerostat, chatted with Montgolfier, and finally took their places on the platform that had been prepared for them. Artillery fire gave the signal for the departure. The aerostat rose magnificently into the air, described a great arc, driven as it was by a southerly wind, then remained motionless for some time, and finally came down to Vaucresson. It tore apart, but returned its guests safely to the ground, where they were collected by two gamekeepers. With them, however, was Jean-François Pilastre du Rozier, already passionate in the study of the new discovery."

"This Pilastre du Rozier was the director of the Musée Royale," the ex-professor continued, addressing himself specifically to his children. He thought of taking the place of the sheep, the cockerel and the duck. Aided by Montgolfier, he had soon constructed an aerostat, with which he attempted an ascent on only fifty feet. He also, by way of precaution, attached a rope-ladder to the balloon, in order to be able to descend at will. The experiment succeeded marvelously. Immediately, a great ascent was announced to the public, which gathered in a crowd every day at the gates of Réveillon's garden. But Louis XVI, on learning that a man was about to risk his life, demanded that the ascent be made by convicts condemned to death. Pilastre du Rozier resisted, and had a Languedocian gentleman, the Marquis d'Arlandes, speak to the king. In order to win the prince over and prove that there was no danger, the latter offered to accompany Pilastre.

"On the twenty-first of November, at one o'clock, the departure took place, ii the presence of the dauphin and his gentlemen, in the vast Jardins de la Muette. At a height of a hundred meters, the voyagers waved; then they were lost to sight, they rose so high. Nevertheless, the aerostat passed over the Île des Cygnes, went along the Seine, passed between Les Invalides and the École Militaire, floated over the Missions-Étrangères and approached Saint-Sulpice. Finally, crossing the city walls between the Barrières d'Enfer and d'Italie, the balloon came to rest on the hill at Cailles."

"It was after that fine trial," the magistrate continued, "that posters were put up in Paris opening a subscription for:

A SILKEN GLOBE
To transport two voyagers
who will rise up in the released balloon and attempt
to carry out observations and experiments in physics
from the air.

"The subscription was filled in a matter of days. Charles and Nicolas-Louis Robert were the two voyagers advertised—but the two men, distinguished for their love of science, prepared their expedition with wisdom and maturity. They designed the safety-valve, the gondola, the strings that would attach everything to the globe of the aerostat, the ballast, the rubber coating that made the silk impermeable, and finally the barometer that would serve to measure altitude.

"It was an immense progress in the art of aerostatics.

"The experiment took place in the garden of the Tuileries on the first of December. Scientists, the subscribers and courtiers occupied the garden. Outside, on the quais, in the streets, on the bridges and at windows, even on roofs, an immense, impatient and avid crowd was stationed. The advertised spectacle was all the more attractive for being seen from afar, swimming in the air, oscillating to the right and the left: a shiny dome striped with red and yellow, supporting a blue hull edged with gold. At one o'clock, to the noise of musket-fire, the balloon rose into the sky, in the midst of the crowd and among guardsmen presenting arms while their officers saluted with their swords. Four hundred thousand spectators clapped their hands.

"Having crossed the Seine between Asnières and Saint-Ouen, then crossed over again near Argenteuil, after having passed over Sannois, Francouville, Saint-Leu, l'Île-Adam and other villages, the aerostat came down at Nesles, nine leagues from Paris.

"That scientific excursion made an art of aerostatics. The people carried Charles in triumph. The Académie awarded the title of Associate to the two voyagers and to Pilastre du Rozier; finally, the king gave Charles a pension of two thousand livres."

"That's marvelous, Messieurs," said the professor, "but you've doubtless remarked that there are now two sorts of balloon in existence?"

"Of course," said the magistrate. "The Montgolfiers, which are merely silk inflated by the gas given off by damp straw and wool, and aerostats filled with hydrogen gas, like that of Charles—for it was the great basin situated in front of the Pavillon d'Horloge that had received the apparatus for the production of the gas."

"Now, Messieurs," said the worthy retired merchant, "it is for me, as a Lyonnais to tell you about the third aerial voyage, which took place in our city of Lyon.

"Monsieur Jacques de Flesselles, the superintendent of the province, and also opened a subscription, in order to give the kingdom's second city the spectacle of an aeronautical ascent. Joseph Montgolfier was given responsibility for the details. He made his balloon forty-three meters high and thirty-five in diameter. As soon as it became know in Paris what was happening in Lyon, enthusiasts began to arrive. As many as thirty people put their names down to take part in the voyage, but the cold and rain of winter delayed the departure considerably. They were also forced to modify the enormous machine, which offered no less volume than the cupola of the Halle-aux-Blés in Paris. The upper part was white and the rest different colors. On a shiny patch two words had been written:

Le Flesselles. Joseph Montgolfier, Pilastre du Rozier, the Comte de Laurencin, the Prince de Ligne, Monsieur de Dampierre and another man climbed into the gondola, but even before take-off, it was in a poor state. My father, one of the witnesses to the excursion, told me that it was riddled with holes, that there were broken cords, and that there was everything to fear for the lives of the voyagers. This prognosis became a reality, alas. When it reached an altitude of eight hundred meters the machine fell with an indescribable rapidity. Even so, the voyagers got out of it with nothing worse than a rude shock."

"Ah! The eventful chapter is beginning!" said an excellent dowager who was lending her ears to the gentlemen's stories.

"It was then that Jean-Pierre Blanchard appeared," the young painter said, timidly. On the second of March 1784 he made the first ascent from the Champ-de-Manoeuvres at the École Militaire. Just as his balloon lifted off, a young student at the École, who was claimed to be Napoléon Bonaparte but whom that noble exile revealed to us in his *Mémorial* to have been one of his friends, named Chambon, tried to get into the gondola with his sword in his hand. He was thrust back. Immediately, Blanchard rose up, remained in motion for an hour and a quarter, and came down in the plain of Billancourt.

"Blanchard claimed to have surpassed the ascents of his predecessors by four thousand meters; he even affirmed that he had directed his balloon against the wind by means of the oars and rudder with which he had equipped his apparatus, but one cannot rely on Blanchard, who was inclined to tell lies."

"That's the case with aeronauts, it seems," said the professor, laughing, "for André-Jacques Garnerin, another aeronaut of the same epoch, claimed that they had risen up, at Berlin, to a height of three thousand fathoms, thanks to the expansion of fluids—an altitude so great that his head swelled up and his hat fell off without his being able to put it on again."

"Mention also," said the magistrate, "that Étienne Robertson, another aeronaut contemporary with them, in order to reproach him for his exaggeration, maliciously replied that his own head, at high altitude, had shrunk to such an extent that his hat fell over his nose."

"It is certain, at least," the professor replied, "according to what Monsieur Margut tells me, "that in the upper regions of the atmosphere, an aeronaut feels his faces swell up and his veins stand out strongly. In a word, all the parts of the body tend to expand. That must be due to the diminution of the ambient air pressure."

You will understand, dear reader, why I shall let you off the accounts of the thousand other ascents about which my curious neighbors talked. What is the point, in fact, of telling you that on the fourth of June 1784 Madame Elizabeth Thible was the first woman who braved the perils of an aerial voyage in a Montgolfier , that she accomplished it in honor of the King of Sweden, who was then in Lyon, and that she was one of the lucky ones?

Why tell you, also, that Pilastre du Rozier, accompanied by the chemist Joseph Proust, had the honor of carrying out another voyage before Louis XVI and the King of Sweden; that, at a given moment, a screen that was hiding the machine was abruptly removed, and that, the four hundred workmen holding on to the balloon having suddenly released it, the immense Montgolfier rose with majestic slowness and came down at Chantilly?

Would you be glad to know that thereafter, Abbé Camus and Professor Louchet provided the spectacle of an aerial voyage at Rhodez? That Monsieur Guyton de Morveau made a number of trials scarcely worthy of mention at Dijon? That two businessmen at Nantes, another enthusiast at Aix, Coustard de Massy at Nantes, d'Arbalet des Granges and Chalfour at Bordeaux, went to visit the regions of the atmosphere? All cities had their aeronauts, those gentlemen repeated to me until I was weary, believe me—and allow me silence on the subject now.

I shall pass on to the matter of accidents, for that was the most terrible of all the chatter that rang in my ears. It was not only the women who, with their incisive words, wounded my heart with the excessively faithful memory of the deplorable events that overtook a large number of aeronauts.

This is how the funereal litany that I am going to repeat began, still according to my sinister neighbors:

"I don't have any appetite for such pleasure-trips myself," said the personal maid of a great lady to a chambermaid of lesser status. "For taking a stroll I prefer the Prés-Saint-Gervais; they're a little more solid."

"There's nothing but dust in your Prés-Saint-Gervais," the soubrette replied, "while in balloons, there's fresh air and bright sunlight."

"You'd be lucky to see sunlight, with all that fabric for an umbrella! You'd have to give me a fortune, my dear, to make me set foot in that shaving-bowl..."

"The gondola, you mean. It's quite pretty, though!"

"It would make your head spin just to open your eyes."

"The fact is that, on thinking about it...I feel sick."

"Oh, girls, one can't pay too much for the pleasure of seeing the earth at one's feet!" interjected an old woman who stuck her head out of a bull's-eye window.

"Hey, Mère Jouvence has youthful ideas now!" exclaimed the wittier of the maids. "Well, give yourself the pleasure—there's a gentleman who can offer you a place in his milk-pail. They've already loaded up the food supplies, and you like them, Mama Jouvence..."

"Zéphirine, Zéphirine, my wife, look," said an old man who was riffling through a book, "here's the thing I wanted to talk to you about. Listen, I'm going to tell you something. You listen too, young women..."

"You're always buried in your books, Papa Jouvence," said the mischievous maid. "Tell us what those machines are for that have been put in the balloon's gondola. I'd prefer that to listening to your story..."

"Firstly, Mademoiselle, that's a barometer, and the barometer serves to measure that altitude that the balloon reaches. Then there's a hygrometer, another instrument that aeronauts use to measure the quantity of water suspended in the atmospheric air. Then..."

"Shut up, Maximilien," said Madame Jouvence suddenly. "Listen to what the young painter on the third floor is saying. He's just said that Blanchard, after having his balloon inflated on a hill near Dover, set out for Calais with the aid of a favorable wind. The balloon began to come down over the sea, though, so steeply that he threw everything into the sea, and that he was about to cut the cords of his gondola, letting it fall into the water while he hung on to the rigging, when the balloon fortunately rose up again and deposited the lucky voyager, along with his companion, a certain John Jeffries, in an oak tree in our beautiful land of France. He added that they raised a column where the tree had stood, in honor of Blanchard, as the first person who dared to fly over the sea. Hold on, the painter's continuing—listen..."

"The laurels of Don Quixote de La Mancha—that was the nickname given to Blanchard after his expedition" my neighbor went on, "prevented Pilastre du Rozier from sleeping. Blanchard had come from England to France; Pilastre decided to go from France to England.. Having had the audacity to rise into the air first, he regretted only being the second to cross a strait. He therefore made his preparations in haste, aided by the Minister and encouraged by the King, who promised him a pension of six thousand livres. Finally, at seven o'clock in the morning on the fifth of June 1785, he rose up from the coast at Boulogne in company with an individual named Romain, a distinguished physicist from Boulogne.

It was close to the village of Vimelle, near the spot where Blanchard and Jefferies had landed, and where their honorific column had just been erected. Two machines, one a hydrogen gas aerostat, the other a Montgolfier, were bearing their gondola, and they immediately rose up to four hundred meters. Almost at the same moment, however, the aerostat tore, lost its gas, and fell on top of the Montgolfier—and both of them, dragged down by the weight, fell with a frightful rapidity.

"Pilastre was killed instantly; Romain died a few minutes later."

"A frightful fate!" said the women.

"A great and cruel misfortune!" said the men.

"To make you feel better," a medical student who had not yet said a word shouted, immediately, "let me tell you, beautiful ladies, that Pierre Testu-Brissay was, in his turn, the inventor of equestrian ascents. He mounted a horse, which, once placed on the platform of the gondola, remained motionless there, without any line, and was lifted into the air to a prodigious height. The horse bled from its ears and nostrils, but the man suffered no ill-effects."

"But what if the horse had taken a step?" asked Zéphirine.

"Well, my old dear, it would have galloped a little more quickly than usual!" the student riposted. "But Testu-Brissay kept a tight hold of the reins."

"Good for him," Monsieur Jouvence retorted. "But what if the beast had been headstrong and reared up?"

"It would have fallen, old chap, and, one carrying the other, the earth would have received them."

"I prefer Monsieur Poitevin's method myself," said the painter. "He attaches the horse to the tightrope by means of a suspension apparatus, which avoids any danger."

"Then a wooden horse would do just as well!" the student objected. "Monsieur *Testu* was a man with *balls!*[8] Imagine the peasants of Montmorency watching him come down one day in a balloon that had wings and oars. Furious, those poor fools grabbed the ropes, and, as some damage had been done, demanded money. Monsieur Testu-Brissay agreed to give them what they asked for, but on condition that the sum was fixed by the mayor. In order to go and find him, the aeronaut threw down a long rope, told the peasants to pull the bal-

---

[8] In the French version he is a man with *tête* [head], but the pun, awful as it is, actually works slightly better in English with the substitution I have made.

loon with it, and while they were carrying out the maneuver he threw off is ballast, cut the rope—which fell down on the peasants' heads, and flew off into the sky."

"That's one who got away—let's talk about another who fell," said the professor from the Collège de France. "You know that Jacques Garnerin surpassed Blanchard by making a parachute descent himself, whereas Blanchard only sent animals down. It was him who invented the parachute we still use now; he carried out a magnificent trial on the first of November 1797. First the wind carried his aerostat away from the crowd, but in order to make the spectators witnesses to his parachute the skillful aeronaut took his knife and cut the fatal rope above his head, which attached his parachute to the gondola. The balloon immediately exploded and the parachute deployed, oscillating wildly-which frightened the public a great deal. Piercing screams rang out from all directions, but the parachute descended nobly to earth, long after the burst balloon, and Garnerin was carried away in triumph by the crowd."

"Enough of all these trials!" said Monsieur Jouvence, making his voice tremble. "I'd only want to go up in a balloon as long as it was captive, retained by a rope that would only let it rise as high as a hundred feet."

"A hundred feet!" said Zéphirine. "Maximilien, I forbid you to commit any such imprudence. A hundred feet!"

"I've seen that at the battle of Fleurus,[9] for I was there," Maximilien Jouvence went on. "There was a man named Jean Coutelle who had the idea of disposing aerostats to rise above the battlefield and observe the enemy positions. It wasn't a bad idea—so pilots were created for service in war-balloons. The government gave Coutelle abundant resources at Meudon for the construction of balloons, but I think the invention was

---

[9] In 1794. The question of whether Coutelle's observation balloon, *L'Entreprenant*, made any significant difference to the outcome of the battle remains controversial; the French did win, but it was a very costly victory.

only used at Fleurus, where the smoke from the cannons was a great hindrance to the observers."

"So you've been a soldier, Papa Jouvence!" said the student. "Your civil and home-loving manners would have led me to assume that you were one of the members of the Congrès de la Paix..."[10]

"Precisely, Monsieur, because I've been all over Europe, I enjoy my repose all the more now. I spend my leisure time reading books and newspapers. Thus, I found in this almanac just now the following description of a parachute descent:

"An Englishman by the name of Cocking, having had the whim of constructing a parachute of his own design, another Englishman, Mr. Green, lent himself to the caprice. Cocking's parachute was not in the form of an open umbrella but that of an inverted umbrella blown out by the wind. It thus transpired that on the twenty-seventh of September 1836, Green embarked at Vauxhall in London took Cocking and his deplorable apparatus suspended from his gondola. They arrived at an altitude of twelve hundred meters, when Green cut the rope, delivering the unfortunate Cocking to eternity. In less than two minutes the aeronaut arrived on earth, flattened on the ground."[11]

---

[10] Le Congrès de la Paix, which had the optimistic aims of laying the foundations for a United States of Europe and putting an end to war, was held in post-Revolutionary Paris in August 1849 under the presidency of Victor Hugo. Hugo was exiled from France in 1851, after Louis-Napoléon's *coup-d'état*, as a dangerous radical, along with Eugène Sue, Alexandre Dumas and P.-J. Hetzel, the pioneering publisher for children, who subsequently made a significant contract with Jules Verne. It is of some relevance to Driou's career and the present text that Napoléon III's censors were still active and attentive in 1856.

[11] The unfortunate Robert Cocking was sixty-one when he made his fatal leap, and had no experience of parachuting.

"How horrible!" exclaimed the patrician maid. "Is it possible that the police permit all these abominations? Monsieur and Madame Poitevin, with their horses and oxen; Eugène Godard with his parachutes; Évariste Thevenin and his trapeze; and God knows what rascal mounted on a plank between two flying aerostats, ought to be put in Charenton until they renounce their desire to turn somersaults in the sky."

"And all the Parisians with them, then," put in the plebeian maid, "for the spectators are as guilty as the charlatans."

"Oh, don't see all that as charlatanry, Justine," said the merchant from Lyon, who had gone away momentarily. "It's the love of science that it's necessary to see in it, at least for the majority of aeronauts."

"Yes, in Madame Sophie Blanchard, for instance, who, having gone up at the Tivoli in 1819, wanted to set fire to a coronet of fireworks ornamenting the parachute of which she was about to make use. The torch she was using set fire, not to the fireworks, but to the gas in her balloon, which suddenly produced a column of fire, to the great alarm of the curiosity-seekers of Montmartre and Tivoli. Madame Blanchard came down to earth, for the silk of the balloon didn't burn, and might perhaps have escaped death if hr balloon had landed in the middle of a road—but it fell on the roof of a town house in the Rue de Provence. 'Help!' cried Madame Blanchard—but when her gondola caught on an iron spike, the unfortunate woman fell on to the pavement and fractured her skull."

"That was a pity," said the Lyonnais, "for Madame Blanchard was skillful. She was so used to those perilous exercises that it wasn't uncommon for her to go to sleep in her gondola while waiting for daylight to effect her descent."

"You interrupted me, Monsieur Metrum," said Madame Jouvence, who had just recounted the death of Madame Blanchard, "and you didn't let me ask you whether it was for love

---

Charles Green went on to become England's most famous and successful aeronaut.

of the art of love of money that she risked her life in that fashion."

"For love of money, I admit," said the merchant.

"Yes, but for certain scientists, like Messieurs Biot and Gay-Lussac, and Messieurs Banal and Biscio,[12] it's definitely for love of science!" the magistrate then replied. "Already, before them, Robertson had carried out a scientific ascent at Hamburg in 1803, in which he remained in the air for six hours, covering twenty-five leagues and rising up to seven thousand four hundred meters."

"On several occasions, people have gone further than twenty-five leagues," proclaimed the nasal voice of Monsieur Jouvence, "opening a newspaper triumphantly. Listen to me for a minute—I'll give you proof of it.

"*Le Constitutionnel*, 20 November 1853—number 324.

"Here is a new and striking example of the strange vicissitudes to which aerial navigators are subject. It will be remembered that more than two years ago, the Lyonnais aeronaut Arban, after an ascent carried out from Barcelona, disappeared completely, and since that time there has been no news of him. The general belief was that he had been forced down in the sea and had perished.

"Today, however, according to the *Gazette de Lyon*, the Spanish newspapers tell us that the unfortunate aeronaut has just reappeared, after an extremely romantic series of adventures. The following lines, written from Alicante, appear in Madrid's *Clamor Publico*:

"The misfortune that seems preferentially to pursue courageous men has not spared the intrepid aeronaut Arban. More than two years ago, in his magnificent balloon, in the burning

---

[12] Jean-Baptiste Biot and Joseph-Louis Gay-Lussac set a long-standing altitude record of 7,016 meters in 1804. I have left the names of the other, far more obscure, duo as Driou renders them, although the very scant references trackable through Google suggest that their names were probably Barral and Bisio.

sands of Africa, he was captured by a horde of savages, who took him to a market in a village in the interior and put him on sale there as a curious object. He was bought by an old cacique, of a dark and cruel character. His master, believing him to be a sorcerer, since he had been seen to descend from the sky, had him locked up in a dark dungeon, where he lived on bread and water for thirty days. Every morning, he was given twenty-five strokes of a lash by way of breakfast, and twenty-five more were administered every evening—in order, he was told, that he might find the putrid straw that served as his bed warmer.

"The unfortunate Arban had endured this torture for nearly six weeks when a caprice of the old savage allowed him to see the sun again and breathe pure air, but his sufferings were not over. Condemned with other slaves to work the land, he spend entire days exposed to a burning sun, not even having water to slake his thirst. When he stopped momentarily, exhausted by fatigue and covered in sweat, to catch his breath, and pray to God to return him to his fatherland and his family, his master's pitiless whip whistled down upon his shoulders, forcing him to continue his painful work.

"Later, to complete his misfortune, he was embarked on a slave-ship trading in black men. The service of slaves embarked like him was incessant and unrelenting; they never had a moment's rest. The punishments on board were even crueler than those on land; the overseer's whip, with iron-tipped thongs, was never idle, and the legs of unfortunate slaves were put between two planks, which were squeezed so as to break their bones. On many occasions Arban witnessed tortures that our pen refuses to describe.

"Finally, they day of liberty dawned for the poor exile; the slave was able to tread on free soil. He was received with a thousand demonstrations of sympathy..."[13]

---

[13] Although Driou is presumably quoting a real newspaper article, the story told therein is undoubtedly apocryphal; there

"Dear God, how he must have suffered!" exclaimed Zéphirine, wiping her eyes and blowing her nose, with a noise like the D of a trombone.

"Since you're talking about the distances a balloon can cover, I'll say something about the rapidity of that progress. Of what I shall say I've been the witness. You'll see how.

"Now, you know that Garnerin was summoned to Paris for the festival of the coronation of Emperor Napoléon I. He prepared an aerostat, but, you see, an aerostat compared to which the one being constructed down below would be a mere nutshell. He suspended an immense crown from his machine, lighted by three thousand pieces of colored glass, and, when the fireworks let off on the quais were coming to an end, the aerostat and its gondola, followed by the luminous crown, rose majestically from the parvis of Notre-Dame and climbed into the sky, to the cheers of the multitude and the sound—repeated by echoes from both banks of the Seine—of sixty thousand rifles firing into the air in every direction. The balloon made rapid progress, and, strangely enough, the next day—which is to say, from eleven o'clock at night to nine o'clock in the morning—the very next day, take note, the inhabitants of Rome saw a radiant globe poised on the horizon, advancing toward their city.

"I was in Rome myself that day, Messieurs, on business. I was one of the first to see that round and shiny machine, which seemed to the eye to be approaching slowly, but was in reality traveling rapidly. I was also one of the first to recognize that it was the imperial aerostat. Only I asked myself how, having departed the day before—the day of the coronation—it could have reached us already. But there was no mistake. Everyone could read the beautiful legend painted on a golden band around the aerostat, all the more easily because the aerostat came considerably lower, as if to be admired. That legend read:

---

is no reliable evidence that Francesco Alban di Lione ever returned from the flight in question.

PARIS, 25 FRIMAIRE, YEAR VIII
CORONATION OF EMPEROR NAPOLÉON
BY HIS HOLINESS PIUS VII

"When that magnificent machine had floated for a short while over the cupola of St. Peter's in the Vatican, it drew away; then, suddenly collapsing, it grazed the ground, marking its passage through the Roman countryside with its debris. Eventually, it encountered the angles of Nero's tomb on the Via Appia and was caught there, seemingly obliged to stop— but after a few minutes' pause it resumed its course, leaving the greater part of its crown on the tomb, and went on to fall into the waters of Lake Bracciano.[14]

"I had had the idea of mounting a horse in order to follow the balloon, which interested me. Thus, I presided over its salvage. They were able to pull it out of the lake, and it was transported to Rome; I know that until 1814 it remained suspended from the vault of the Vatican."

"The story of that balloon ended badly," said the magistrate, "but it had begun badly, as you were doubtless unaware. Thus, that same sixth of December 1804, at eleven o'clock in the evening, at the moment when the crown passed the tops of the towers of Notre-Dame, the wind extinguished some of the lamps illuminating its colored glass. People were expecting a magnificent spectacle, but the balloon produced no effect, at least by night..."

After a pause he went on: "In any case, the fate of your coronation balloon is that of almost all aeronauts. When com-

---

[14] The potential symbolism of Garnerin's accidental brush with Nero's tomb was not lost on the superstitious Napoléon, who sacked him from his position as the official supervisor of balloon ascents from Paris and appointed the ill-fated Sophie Blanchard in his place. Garnerin lived until 1823, but his views on the fate of the Empire do not seem to have been recorded.

merce replaces science, when people work for money, multiplying ascents in the hope of becoming a millionaire like Robertson, lined with guineas and roubles like Jacques Garnerin, embroidered with dollars like the Blanchards, how can one die other than how one has lived? Fifty ascents bring wealth, but it only takes one to bring ruination and death."

"You were told just now of the glory of a balloon in 1804," said the ex-professor. "Let me tell you about the misfortunes of another balloon in that same year. It's that of Count Francesco Zambeccari of Bologna, whom I shall make my hero. Zambeccari was a scientist, not a mountebank. He has carried out important studies and left behind writings on aerostatics. He is owed all possible respect.

"So, the government of Milan expected a great experiment from him, and had given him, by the gift of eight thousand écus, the means to accomplish it. His balloon was not ready until midnight, and a tempest was rumbling in the ar. Two friends climbed into the gondola with him. In spite of the hour and the bad weather, Zambeccari took off. Scarcely had it reached the lower regions of the atmosphere when his aerostat was carried into the upper regions with indescribable speed. The aeronaut and one of his companions were rendered unconscious. The other, with the aid of rum, was able to resist and did not fall asleep.

Suddenly, the young man who was awake thought he heard a strange murmur in the distance. At the same time, the balloon seemed to him to descend a long way. Unfortunately, the darkness was intense. Andreoli—that was the name of the poor student of aerostatics—shook his two companions in order to wake them up.

"Their terror was at its maximum; they were falling into the Adriatic Sea! At every instant the sound of the waves increased in a frightful manner. They were soon able to perceive their gleam. Alas, they plunged into the sea.

"The gondola was not completely immersed, however. At times, the waves covered it completely, but the balloon, still partly inflated, was floating on the summits of the swell, causing the gondola to remain on the surface. In that moment of supreme distress, they seemed to see a ship some distance away—but the ship did not perceive them and passed on. Then they prepared to die, recommending their souls to God.

"Providence did not abandon them, however. Dawn came, and by the daylight they saw land close by. Hope was already reviving in their hearts when a gust of wind drove them back out to sea. The sky and the sea formed their horizon for several hours. Ships appeared; the sailors saw their vessel but, frightened by its strange form, drew away in haste. Finally, a more learned captain sent a launch to rescue them. Relieved of their weight, the balloon immediately resumed its flight toward the empyrean. To describe their suffering in the course of that horrible drama would be impossible."

"I can believe it," said the honest bourgeois, who had so far only permitted himself one exclamation. "It's a true martyrdom that those poor men endured."

"Well, then," the magistrate interjected, "what about the martyrdom of Francis Olivari, seeing his Montgolfier catch fire on the twenty-fifth of November 1802, and falling from a height of an entire league."

"And that of the former lieutenant of the British Royal Navy, George Gale, who, full of alcohol, mounted a fine horse attached to an aerostat, made a brilliant ascent at Bordeaux on the ninth of September 1850, came down at Cestas, and, when his horse had been detached, poorly assisted in the operation by peasants who did not understand his language, was transported once again into the sky, with his head tangled in the rigging, seemingly strangled. What became of him? No one can say—except that, in the evening, a semi-deflated balloon was found on a heath and, a few days later, a cowherd saw his dog sniffing in a strange manner at something hidden in the heather. He ran to the spot; it was the unfortunate Englishman, broken, twisted and bloody, whose had and limbs had already been devoured by wild animals...

"That's my story, and I saw it," said the medical student, whose Gascon accent did indeed denote his origin.

"I'm shivering at the story you just told, Monsieur," said a young woman—doubtless the mistress of the mischievous chambermaid, for the latter disappeared on seeing the young woman arrive—"but permit me to dispel the emotion you have caused me by also reminding you of the sad story of poor Emma Verdier.

"It was last year, 1853, I believe. There was public rejoicing town of Mont-de-Marsan. Why? I can no longer remember—except that I know that, in order to entertain the inhabitants of the region, the Municipal Council had judged it appropriate to accept the services of an aeronaut. Alas, the man was nothing but a charlatan. Instead of going up in his Montgolfier himself and risking his own life, in return for a meager fee, he engaged the services of a poor abandoned girl, with no experience of aerial navigation. It seemed that Providence wanted to refuse to let that innocent victim sacrifice herself for so futile a cause. Dusk fell before the balloon was sufficiently charge with hot air to lift off; they were obliged to put off the ascent until the next day.

"Finally, at nine o'clock on the day in question, an immense crowd filled the streets and squares of the capital of Landes. Then, very pale and emotional, Emma Verdier appeared, crowned with flowers. She took her place in the gondola. The cowardly aeronaut gave the signal to release the balloon. The poor child disappeared, with lightning rapidity. For a long time her apparatus floated in the air like an eagle lost in the sky; for a long time, Basques and Gascons raised their eyes to satisfy an avid curiosity. Emma Verdier never came back! Two days later, naïve peasants perceived a body suspended from the highest branches of a centenarian oak, its face bruised, its eye-sockets empty, its hair sparse, life extinct...

"It was Emma Verdier."

Young readers, until then I had held firm, pretending not to listen to the tales of my pitiless neighbors, giving orders to my workmen, coming and going like the general of an army, trying to enclose my soul in a triple armor of bronze. On hearing that funereal voice relate in a sinister tone the deplorable death of the young female aeronaut, however, I remembered Émile Deschamps, who had also perished, quite recently—on the twenty-seventh of November 1851, at Nîmes—and whose cruel fate I might perhaps share the following day...

Thank God! Do you know who Prince Alexander Mentschikoff is? There has been much talk of him. One evening during the siege of Varna in 1829, when that proud and intractable captain was traversing the camp, he stopped, his legs apart, to take a pinch of snuff. Suddenly, a cannon-shot was heard, and the prince fell full-length. He was lifted up.

"Remove that bullet which has just passed through my legs," he said, "It's preventing me from getting back to my tent."

Well, the final adventure narrated, about Emma Verdier, had just produced the same effect on me as the bullet hat felled Mentschikoff. I was knocked down, but, like him, I wasn't dead. I recovered my self-composure immediately, and, stamping my foot on the ground, I set to work even harder.

I even said to the mechanic: "These people amuse me. If great misfortunes have happened before, it's because, unlike me, the aeronauts didn't have a sure mechanism allowing them to steer their balloons. People have been searching for that means for a long time. God has given it to me; I shall keep it, and make humankind party to it when I have reaped the glory I expect therefrom."

A sort of incredulity was imprinted on the workman's lips. He even dared to rely: "In spite of all your confidence, Monsieur, if you want my opinion, either you won't climb into that gondola or you ought to make your will before leaving the ground..."

"At least you have the merit of being honest, old chap," I retorted, "but your frankness is harsh and rings false. I shall study the science of navigation..."

"Excuse me," said the man, without letting me finish. "You say: *I shall study*...I'll stop you there. If you're going to study, it's because you don't yet know, right? How, then, can you think your success infallible? You see, with regard to systems for steering balloons, I've heard Monsieur Petin talk, for example, and also Monsieur Letur.[15] They were both, like you, very confident of success—but as you know, with their mechanisms, they weren't even able to get off the ground..."

"In matters of this sort, my friend, one can only appeal to proof," I replied, in a fit of pique. "Wait until tomorrow to judge, and you'll see…"

Finally, five days after the commencement of the work, the aerostat being completely finished, without loading myself down with iron filings, sulfuric acid, barrels and pipes, I simply opened one of the gas taps that opened into the courtyard—with the permission of the administration—and, introducing it into my aerostat, had the satisfaction of seeing it inflate visibly. It soon became a marvelous machine, gilded by the rays of the rising sun. I had to call upon twenty men to oppose its continual efforts to rise up.

The gondola was brought forth, and then hitched to the rigging and the mooring-rope. It was equipped with an anchor, barometers, thermometers, hygrometers, compasses, watches, pencils, paper and books. I also took care to place within it blankets, my reefer jacket, my cloak, a parachute and a cage in which I had various animals. Nor had food supplies been forgotten; by way of precaution a pâté from Chez Rollé,[16] a pullet, a ham, bread, a few bottles of Bordeaux, two bottles of rum, sugar, fruits and water were placed aboard. The cigars were top quality; they constitute the society of a man in solitude.

---

[15] Ernest Petin proposed building a "balloon train" in 1852 but was refused permission to test the device. Louis-Charles Letur built a "dirigible parachute" in 1853; he died experimenting with it in 1854 but is nowadays credited in consequence as a pioneer of heavier-than-air flight.

[16] The Lyonnais firm of Chez Rollé was famous for its pâtés throughout the 19th century.

It was the fifteenth of May 1854.

The clock on the nearby Mairie showed ten past nine.

Resolutely, I went into the gondola, with a telescope slung over my shoulder.

All the widows in the courtyard and the neighboring houses, the adjoining streets, the attics and the roofs, were overflowing with curiosity-seekers.

My twenty men were having great difficulty holding on to the rebellious aerostat.

I took a letter out of my portfolio, which I handed to my concierge; he was to deliver it after my departure. The letter was to my mother.

Then, gazing into the sky, I invoked God and made the sign of the cross, recommending my soul to the Lord.

Finally, raising my hat to all those faces that were looking at me sympathetically, I shouted: "Let go, everyone!"

The balloon suddenly bounded upwards, and launched into space like a shining meteor.

I

In the blink of an eye, as rapid as thought, faster than an arrow, my balloon had already risen so high that I was overlooking the whole of Paris, the least parts of which my gaze embraced, and the smallest details of which it followed.

My head was spinning slightly; my heart was beating with a kind of anxiety, and my temples were quivering under the friction of the air, but my energy and my will rendered me master of all my faculties. I leaned over to the right and to the left; everywhere, there were faces, eyes fixed on my carriage. I wanted to judge the merit of my invention right away, and I applied the brake. Immediately, like a docile horse, the balloon slowed down. I pressed harder on the mechanism, and the balloon stopped. I was then assured of the power of my discovery; I thanked God. At the same time, I got rid of a few pounds of ballast, and left the aerostat to its own devices. It launched toward the zenith again, like a wild thoroughbred mare.

There was no more propitious time for traveling thus.

The air was pure, the sky blue streaked with white, promising a splendid day. The spring sun, eager to complete the flourishing of nature revived, was shining with all its brilliance. The bells of Notre-Dame were ringing for some occasion or other, and the bells of several other churches replied merrily. The echoes of the Marne resounded in the distance to the formidable roar of the cannons of the Polygône de Vincennes. In the opposite direction, the Camp-de-Mars appeared as a large white sheet covered with a multitude of ants hurrying about their work; they were the regiments of the Armée de Paris, carrying out maneuvers. The sound of their fanfares rose and faded away, often extinguished by rapid gusts of wind. The Seine sparkled between its two granite banks, speckled by the boats at its quais. The obelisks of stone, bronze and lead, domes, towers, steeples, campaniles, columns, arches, triumphant gates, piers, minarets, cupolas and pyramids appeared to me in perfect clarity, with a thousand streets crawling around their bases like serpents.

The eye and the ear were not yet losing anything of what was happening in the seething crucible, the molten crater, that I had beneath me. I could make out all the squares, and the movement of the busy and noisy crowds within the squares. The murmur that those countless breasts exhaled, and the rumble of vehicles, combined with the rocking of human waves, growling dully like a continual bass-line. Around the palais, in the middle of the squares, on a hundred avenues within and outside the city, the trees, the lawns, the spinneys and the clumps of versant bushes were like emeralds framed by the golden tints of innumerable buildings. It was a truly unrivaled scene, an unparalleled agitation, an inimitable noise, a frightful harmony.

I saw and heard everything I have just described sharply and rapidly—as rapidly as you can think it, more rapidly than I can say it. In a situation like mine, sensation and observation are very swift.

My balloon rose up with ever-increasing rapidity. I soon measured an altitude of 900 meters.

For the benefit of those who do not know how the distance one is from the ground is accurately measured, I ought to say that it is done with the barometer. Given that a column of air, at sea level, weighs as much as twenty-eight inches of mercury, one can see that the shorter that column of air becomes, the lighter it is—which causes of mercury of a barometer to decrease as one rises into the sky, whether in an aerostat or climbing a high mountain. It is, therefore, child's play to count the degrees of one's ascent.

An immense horizon appeared to my gaze: Saint-Cloud and its palais, Versailles and its two towns, Meudon and the château that crowns it, Corbeil and the islets of its shores, the old tower of Montlhéry, the ruins of Etampes, the ancient church of Saint-Denis, the sunken bastions of Pierrefonds, and the straight lines of the railways with their gigantic leviathans, the golden ribbons of capricious fluvial navigation, the silver threads of a thousand steams, woods, towns, meadows, hills, villages, valleys, mountains. And the circle limiting my gaze was still increasing, to the extent that I recognized, by turns, Saint-Germain, where Louis XIV saw the light of day; Poissy, which saw Saint Louis baptized; Mantes, where William the Conqueror was wounded; Rambouillet, where François I died; Fontainebleau, which heard the sobs of the veterans of the old guard at the adieux of the immortal emperor; Compiegne, which received the first États-Généraux; Noyon, which saw kings crowned; and Beauvais, with its memories of Jeanne Hachette;[17] and Amiens, whose citadel was built by Henri IV; and Rouen, the old Norman capital, every street of which still retains some chiseled and sculpted jewel, marvelous work that causes archeologists to pale; and Blois, with its château full of illustrious shades and memorable dramas; and Tours, swimming in the waters of the Loire, which waters the garden of France; and Orléans, on whose ramparts my imagination still saw Jeanne d'Arc's plume and Fleur-de-Lys banner.

Paris was no longer anything but a miniature to my eyes; and the horizon, while still broadening, shrank in such a manner that after a quarter of an hour it was no more to my gaze than an immense painting charged with the most various colors. However, as the atmospheric layers that I was traversing produced the effect of a magnifying-glass, I discovered a new, charming and picturesque viewpoint with every passing moment, but reduced to proportions too delicate for me to be able to recognize or analyze its beauties. All sound had ceased; the rumors of the earth could no longer reach me. I looked down on Creation without being part of it.

---

[17] Jeanne Laisné earned her nickname (Jeanne the Axe) when she cut down a Burgundian flag raised on the ramparts of Beauvais during a 15th-century siege and allegedly turned the tide of the battle. Driou wrote a book about her, published in 1875 under the Valentin Fréville pseudonym.

It became easy to recognize the rotundity of the Earth from the point I had reached. At my nadir, which as the Earth's summit, the globe was subsiding, showing a gentle and graceful declivity that was becoming increasingly pronounced. It even seemed to me that I might see it rotating beneath my feet, and that countries and seas were offered to the investigations of my ardent curiosity—but no, as it rotated, it drew me along in its movement, and I still only saw the same aspects. My God, how beautiful they were, and how great and sublime your works seemed!

My balloon was so docile and its helm so effective that, as I have just said, it moved neither to the right nor the left as it rose above the Earth, but always followed the movement of the globe. As no breeze was blowing, I still found myself above Paris. I wanted to alter that monotonous progress then, and, having departed to study the unknown, I gave my machine such a thrust that the rapidity of my ascension became frightful.

In spite of the limpidity of the atmosphere, soon I could only see the Earth as an enormous green, gray and gilded mass. I could no longer make out anything of urban or rural locations. On the other hand, I began to sense various disagreeable impressions. I was cold—very cold, at first—and then the cold was succeeded by a sort of numbness; and when I tried to pass my hand over my cheeks, in order to warm them up, it seemed to me that my face was enormous in its volume. I looked at my hands; they seemed swollen; I took out my mirror and contemplated myself; my nose, eyes and entire head were swollen and puffed up. Blood was running from my nostrils. After a few minutes of rather pronounced malaise, like the commencement of asphyxia, however, I found myself returned to my normal state. Even so, I wrapped myself in my reefer jacket, and, my stomach feeling very desirous of food, I breakfasted with a hearty appetite.

I had just finished emptying a bottle of Graves when, darting a glance at the barometer, I saw that I had arrived at a height of three thousand meters. I brought my apparatus into play, for I was in a mood to brave any danger, and under the pressure of my machine the balloon bounded magnificently, and rose up rapidly to four thousand, to five thousand, to six thousand meters...

You would doubtless like to know what the blessed apparatus was that could make an aerostat leap in that manner, like a thoroughbred mare under the spur. I would certainly tell you, for I trust you, my young readers, in spite of the aspersions that people are pleased to cast upon the looseness of certain tongues; but, on the one hand, if I published my secret thus, it would lose its first and most essential quality, mystery; and on the other, although simple to manufacture, the mechanism can only be understood when seen, when it is working before one's eyes. I'm not refusing, however, to show it to you. Come to my house at any time when you're passing through my neighborhood; I'll be glad to have the opportunity to be agreeable to you by playing it in your hands and making it work in your presence.

The barometer soon marked seven and eight thousand meters—the same height as the Himalayas. There was therefore nothing very extraordinary as yet, you see, since there are mountains on our terrestrial globe that rise up to twenty-six thousand feet. So I used my invention and the balloon redoubled its speed. I reached ten thousand meters, then eleven, then twelve, etc.

I will spare you an account of the various impressions of temperature to which I was subjected. I will only say that the sun became much smaller to my eyes, but much redder, and infinitely less warm, by reason of the scant air that remained above me to bring me its rays. I will add that the blue of the sky faded away and that, the higher I climbed, leaving the greater mass of air beneath me, the more the blue that the atmosphere ordinarily gives to the firmament, being beneath my feet at the height where I was, faded away, giving way to a blackness that, in truth, did not delight either the gaze or the imagination.

It is not sufficient to expect a phenomenon to be un-moved by it. The finger of God and his power always make themselves felt when one is confronted with things with which one is not yet familiar. Thus, I knew the beautiful azure color of the firmament is due, not only to the mass of air, fifteen or sixteen leagues thick, that surrounds us, but also to the im-mense layers of water vapor that reflect the sun's rays con-jointly with the air. I felt that water vapor as cloud, for my balloon was dripping with it and I was drenched by its humidi-ty; I knew that, I tell you, from physics and from *Genesis*, which tell us that God, separating the waters from one another, placed some on high and made the oceans with others. I knew that, and I was moved.

I knew that the heavy and elastic fluid matter that is called air bears down on every square foot of surface with a weight of two thousand pounds, with the result that an ordi-nary man of average strength really bears an enormous weight on his head. If he is not crushed, it is because the air in his body, incessantly renewed, maintains an equilibrium with the frightful burden that weighs upon him. Thus, I had seen the air in the vast body of an elephant pumped out, and the poor beast was immediately flattened beneath the weight of the exterior air, and died. I had also seen, on the other hand, the air around a bull pumped away; then the air enclosed with its body ex-panded vastly, to the extent that the animal, having become monstrous, also fell down dead.[18] I knew all that, and I won-dered, with a certain emotion, what would happen if I was able

---

[18] The protagonist could not, of course, have seen any such things, any more than he could have risen above eight thou-sand meters without suffering severely from oxygen depriva-tion; Driou does not seem to intend him to be an unreliable narrator, and his account of the history of aeronautics has been as accurate as could possibly have been expected, but he does occasionally resort to bare-faced lies, which compromise his authority as a popularizer of science, history and geography.

to reach the limits of the atmosphere and no longer had anything above me.

Fortunately, as imagination extrapolated my ideas, less painful thoughts arrived to remind me of the poetic marvels of the air. I recalled that at the moment when the sun disappears over the horizon, without the presence of air, we would suddenly enter into the blackest night. How is it that that does not happen, and that, on the contrary, we enjoy daylight for some time yet? Why the twilight of dusk and the twilight of dawn? It is because, to prepare us for day and night, the delicate solidity with which the Creator has endowed that element causes it to bend and prolong the rays of light that escape the sun when they penetrate the atmosphere sideways.

I also told myself that air is the vehicle permanently disposed to transmit to us emanations gratifying the sense of smell; the messenger that brings us the sounds destined to inform us as to what is happening at a distance; a faithful monitor obligingly confiding to us what others are thinking; the zealous interpreter of harmony. Let a scream be uttered, a bell struck, a cannon fire, a trumpet sound, and suddenly, in one second, the air has transported the cry, the sound, the blast, the chord twenty four thousand feet, and the next second carries it an equal distance...

In the wake of that tirade I had begun another hymn in honor of breezes, winds, northerlies, southerlies, the sirocco, the simoom and the mistral, and varieties of air: calm, agitated, melancholy, sullen, furious, scorching or peevish, when, without my laying a hand on the apparatus, touching the brake or saying a word to my aerostat, it was gripped by a fit of ill-temper. Doubtless feeling damp, it performed a few pirouettes. Whether it was a desire to dry itself, to attract my attention, further water vapor or a current of air that had caused it t change course, I could not tell, but it took a few minutes to right itself.

It is said of Horace Saussure that during his ascent of Mont Blanc, when his guides, leaving the air beneath them, had reached the highest peak, the sky seemed so black to them that they recoiled in fear, thinking that an immense gulf had just opened up beneath their feet. Such was the impression that I suddenly had, on collecting myself in order to investigate the cause that had made my balloon behave turbulently.

The air was beginning to run out, and the aerostat had ceased climbing. It was rising slowly, ducking to the right and the left, swaying awkwardly.

I made my calculation; I must be thirteen leagues from the ground. That was too inauspicious a figure for me to stop. I activated the apparatus and the balloon resumed its progress, but like someone forced to advance without wanting to, reluctantly, under the lash of pressure...

If it had been endowed with sentiment, I would have thought that it was afraid.

That would not have been unreasonable; there were grounds to experience certain emotions.

Imagine that I was arriving at the final limits of the air, which was becoming increasing rarefied—and as it is the conductor of light, the daylight was disappearing. I was entering into a region of darkness—frightful darkness, I assure you! There, above me, was space—but what space! An immense, immeasurable, endless black abyss black enough to make one recoil in fear. In addition, a glacial cold, a thousand time sharper, more bitter and biting than what one experiences coming out of a warm room to brave a December evening in a broad and spacious street open to the north. I was wrapped in cloaks and blankets, but I was shivering. Besides that, a sort of terror griped me. Involuntarily, I closed my eyes...

In that state of mind, I raised my heart toward God, and invoked the Virgin, the guiding star; I thought about my mother, and then I thought about glory!

Well, I confess, God, the Holy Virgin and my mother found me very sensitive, but glory and its aureole did not render any heat, and left me cold.

In any case, I had little time to meditate upon its advantages and fortunate results. It was necessary to think about maneuvering. In the darkness, which was gradually overtaking me, I judged that the balloon was no longer steering itself sagely and I resolved to tack.

When I had arranged matters so that I was no longer rising sensibly, but remaining at the height I had reached, while navigating in the ultimate atmospheric layer, instead of raising my gaze I lowered it.

Heaven and Earth be silent! Lend an ear, children of men. Never had a spectacle similar to the one that was given to me struck human eyes, because no others had come, as I had, to seek the marvels of God above the confines of the world.

Above me, as I have said, extended a thick, black, frightful funereal veil. Beneath me, however, swayed the prodigious globe of the atmosphere, enclosing the Earth at its center like a nucleus—and that indescribable globe was luminous, flamboyant with daylight, gilded by the rays of the sun, silvered by softer reflections, tinted scarlet here, mingled with opal there, rutilant with ruby fire in certain places, violet-tinged by amethyst elsewhere: in brief, offering throughout its immense and marvelous sphere those charming and delicious prismatic colors that the dawn, and especially the sunset, sometimes show us. Except that, what we see on Earth, at those melancholy hours so beloved by artists, when nature is so rich, so beautiful and so fantastic, when the horizon hides the sun, and the moon rises at the opposite point of the compass like a shield emerging from a furnace, and the blue pavilion of the sky lights up with myriad fires, was only a corner of the magical tableau that was offered to me.

How I would liked to have someone beside me, then, capable of sensing those inappreciable splendors—but I was alone, alas. I became intoxicated nevertheless by the sublime contemplation into which I fell, and I adored, lovingly, the Creator, the Sovereign Being, eternal, immutable and infinite, the Being of Beings, the Author of Worlds.

What I saw was all the more admirable because, having risen further, attaining a distance of fifteen leagues, I was now only illuminated from below by the reflections of that magnificent globe, which was hanging heavily in that frightful black abyss, horribly black, against which I was swimming, towards which I was advancing. The summit of my aerostat was lost in obscurity, but the softest shades rendered its lower parts splendid, and the rigging seemed to be made of the purest gold, while the fabric had a purple gleam and certain stripes the richness of emerald green. Those colors, however, were weakening, and darkness soon became the queen and mistress of the region where I found myself.

This time, very evidently, the balloon was no longer rising at all.

A further surprise was reserved for me, however, and I entered into a long series of successive admirations, of which I ought to ender an account if my story is capable of interesting you.

In that obscure profundity—blacker, believe me, than the darkest night—I thought I saw a red dot. My eyes, fatigued by the cold and the various atmospheric impressions I had endured, were obliged to lose rather frequently, and not to remain open for long. That made observation of the fiery point difficult. Nevertheless, by dint of effort, I fixed my gaze and I recognized that the dot, as red as a mass of iron emerging from the forge, was nothing other than the sun.

But it was no longer the sun whose rays reach us magnified by the refraction of the air, the magnificent sun that spreads light and serenity, which inspires delight, which fecundates and disseminates light over our globe like a marvelous chandelier. No, it was a sun, a powerful jet of fire, an incandescent sphere, a gigantic creation of the Supreme Will, but in relation to me, a poor wandering curiosity-seeker, it was an orb without heat, as star without radiance.

That burning red mass, as sinister as a conflagration, rolling slowly across the black background, had something terrible about it, which gripped me.

"So that's it," I said to myself, "the globe thirteen hundred and thirty thousand times larger than the Earth, of which *Genesis* relates the sudden birth, at the word of God, and which has already been hanging, at the same point in space for six thousand years. For sixty centuries already, the Earth has been rotating around that pivot, that marvelous center of worlds, at a distance of thirty-five million leagues; and, obedient to the order of the divine Lawmaker, the monstrous giant distributes its light and its life without resting for a moment, without losing a second on the route it must follow. Moving at eight million leagues an hour, the terrestrial sphere receives its beneficial gaze endlessly. What is it, though?"

Alas, on that question, I remained mute. Where is the scientist who could resolve a problems of which God alone knows the mystery and the secret? Nevertheless, equipped as I was with a fairly powerful telescope, and blackened lenses, I set about studying that globe, from whose burning fires I had much less to fear.

The sun then appeared to me paler than to the naked eye, but, at the same time, I saw clouds of fire burning on its surface, which seemed to be melting together, drawing apart, drawing together, dissolving into one another and being reborn. Their tenuousness, however, did not prevent me from distinguishing the nucleus of the star. I thus perceived dark patches, irregular in shape, which seemed to be moving over its surface. Each patch, surrounded by a penumbra, had a luminous border, whose light was brighter than that of the rest of the sun. Extremely variable in their form, their number and their position, I was able to count up to fifty of them. A few months earlier, at the Paris Observatory, I had found seven at the most; that difference in number, already noted by Galileo, shows that the sun offers different faces, variously maculated, and that was how it was determined that it rotes on its axis in twenty-five days.

What struck me most forcibly during that serial study was the enormous size I recognized in the patches. According to the calculation that I was able to make, rapidly, some of them had four or five times the diameter of the Earth. But what seemed to me to be more positive in the sun's nature, and which I report here, is that the center of the sun had a light much more intense than the edges of its disk.

Does not all this indicate that there are at the surface of the enormous mass of fire lively effervescences of which volcanoes only offer a feeble suggestion? I could not say so for sure, but one is naturally led to conclude that the sun is a sea of fire from which the summits of various mountains emerge, which form the black patches in the midst of the flaming ocean, or a globe in combustion strewn with volcanoes, which, emitting a darker glare, create the impression of those patches, various in size and shape.

How, then, does it not consume itself? That is what people ask, with good reason, and a question I put to myself.

My response was this:

"It is probable that if the sun does not purge itself in the continual emission of its rays, it is because it enjoys, as chemistry has proved of certain substances, the faculty of warming its surroundings and spreading light around it, without ever diminishing itself. A grain of musk can perfume and apartment without losing any of its tiny mass, torrents of odorant matter incessantly escaping it for many years."

Monsieur Dominique-François Arago, whose recent loss France and the scientific world mourned, comes to mind; I recall that in a conversation I had with him, the famous astronomer explained to me that the sun is a dark body, but surrounded by two atmospheres, the inner one bright and blazing, the second dark but diaphanous, which allows us to see the other, illuminating us with the emission of its luminous rays. Then the patches on the disk would merely be glimpses of the nucleus, which reach us when it is affected by atmospheric currents powerful enough to traverse and momentarily part the luminous inner atmosphere.

Meanwhile, my balloon was floating at the surface of the ultimate limits of the atmosphere, and I had finished with the sun when my attention was drawn elsewhere. As the globe of fire that I had just been studying and admiring slowly descended and was about to disappear behind the horizon of the atmosphere that served me as a throne, I judged that night had already fallen. I looked at my watch, and could scarcely see what time it was, but on engaging the chimes, I counted four. It was difficult to hear the sounds, the air being so thin in the region where I was. I was also having difficulty breathing.

Suddenly, beneath my feet but at a great depth, there was a muffled noise, whose reverberations reached me nevertheless, arriving like the final echo of a tempest.

My balloon was subject to oscillations whose effects were communicated to my gondola; then calm returned. Shortly afterwards there was a further agitation, accompanied by dull explosions. At first I was able to count them, for at each blast I felt a strange tremor in my rib-cage, but almost immediately, a prolonged, powerful and terrible rumble, like the sound of a cataract or the roar on the sea, resounding in the inferior regions of the atmosphere.

It was, undoubtedly, a storm that had burst beneath me—at what distance or depth I truly did not know; but that slow, dull noise that extended as far as the surface of the atmosphere was nothing other than a violent tempest and its thunderclaps. I remembered that in the morning, before quitting Paris, when the sun had scarcely rise, there was already one of those stifling warmth that prognosticate a hot day and often, for the evening, a disorder of the elements. Since then, I had no doubt, a thunderstorm had passed over the terrestrial regions. It must be terrible, to judge by the violence with which even those much-enfeebled echoes reached me.

I confess that there was a certain charm in sensing myself being rocked in that manner by the tempest, at a distance at which its fury was not to be feared. The upper atmosphere, through whose layers I was drifting, was like a slumberous sea agitated by a bad dream, a kind of nightmare, stirring but with difficulty, leadenly, in spite of itself, under the effort of an interior pressure lifting it up, as a monstrous leviathan might before appearing at its surface. My balloon bobbed up and down, twirled and tossed, shaking the gondola and plunging its crest into the darkness, only receiving at its base a feeble reflection of atmospheric glimmers that were about to be extinguished.

Then, as I lowered my gaze to fathom the inferior air, which was getting dark, I saw serpentine streaks of fire running through its depths, at an immeasurable depth; the entire vaporous glove was tinted with a thousand exquisite, indescribable gleams; explosions reached my ears; then the somber, gray, discolored tone returned, soon losing its rosy, scarlet, luminous transparency to become dark again, to be furrowed again by lighting, running as worms of fire run over blackened paper completing its consumption by flame, and were extinguished once again.

Finally, the rumors of storm and tempest slackened, scarcely murmuring, and ceased entirely. Then a profound obscurity extended its funereal veil, even over those parts that a sort of twilight had colored mutedly.

I was hungry; I ate. Frankly, the pâté that I had bought in the Passage de l'Opéra tasted good. Monsieur Rollé undoubtedly did not suspect that the chicken and the ham with which I was equipped had flown toward the stars to be eaten beyond the clouds. I drank, likewise with a pleasure far superior to that which I would have experienced on the ground, a flask of rum, whose generous effect was to renew my vigor and curiosity, for which I was thankful.

My frugal dinner had come to an end when I rubbed my eyes, in order to assure myself that I was not the victim of an illusion.

During a part of the day, since I had reached the highest regions of the atmosphere, I had thought that I had seen tiny, almost imperceptible points of light scintillating in the black background of the firmament. I had imagined that, by dint of examining and observing the sun, my gaze was rediscovering its flames even in the darkness. But this time, the hour undoubtedly being more propitious, and the sun's fiery globe falling beyond the atmospheric horizon, there was no more doubt that I was distinguishing other luminous bodies, pale in color, the number and position of which I was soon able to determine. Almost at the same time, at distances that seemed to me to be fabulous, so minimal was their light, I recognized other stars, infinite in number, of the same redness as the sun, appearing as dots, but much smaller dots, in infinite space.

By their disposition, the figures they formed and the color of their fires, I recognized the fixed stars, those other suns which, strewn in space in their thousands, illuminate other worlds and proclaim the power of the Creator.

With the naked eye, as on Earth, I was only able to count twelve or thirteen hundred in our hemisphere, but with the aid of the telescope, it became easy for me to discover an infinite number of them, as had Herschel, who found more than fifty thousand of them in the space of a few degrees. And yet, the nearest one to our sphere is several millions of leagues away. That is Sirius, the beautiful star that shines on the horizon in the month of August.

I rediscovered all the constellations we know and love, the Zodiac constellations first: Aries, Taurus, Gemini, Cancer, Leo and Virgo, then visible, and Libra, Scorpio, Sagittarius, Capricorn, Aquarius and Pisces, hidden for the moment beyond the horizon. Then there were Ursa Major, Draco, Lyra, Cassiopeia, Coma Berenices, Corona Borealis, Delphinus, Antinous,[19] Andromeda, Orion, Triangulum—all our beautiful boreal constellations were displayed to me.

From my balloon, even more so than from the ground, that distribution of stars did not appear to me to be made at hazard. It seemed to me to be organized in such a way as to form systems, which we call constellations, of which God alone has the secret.

They all had the same fire; it was the fire of the sun, a reddish fire, which emitted a mobile flame producing a scintillation. But by reason of the brightness of some, I obtained a better explanation of why they are divided into stars of the first, second and third magnitude, and why others have been

---

[19] The constellation Antinous has been abolished since 1854, its stars now being considered part of Aquila.

given the name of nebulas; doubtless these differences originate from their greater or lesser distance.

The thought occurred to me that from Adam, the first human created, to us, those stars had faithfully maintained the same positions—but my astronomical studies then reminded me that, not only had they moved in such a way as to change the positions they occupied at the moment of creation, as the diagrams left to us by Hipparchus and other ancient astronomers assure us, but that modern observations attest that the relationships between several of them have been troubled in a visible manner. It is thus conclusively proven that these variations are sometimes sudden and sometimes periodic, and affect their color as well as their position.

In 1572, Tycho Brahé discovered one of that sort in Cassiopeia. Perfectly round, of a splendor equal to that of Venus, the star remained visible even by day. Its light then diminished by degrees, having excited admiration for more than fifteen months.

In 1604, in Cor Serpentis, another star that suddenly appeared offered astonishing variations, and disappeared again after several months.

I did not linger long in the study of these points of fire, in spite of all the pleasure I had had in rediscovering them—a pleasure similar to that one finds when one encounters an old friend in a foreign land.

What attracted my attention elsewhere was a spectacle for which our astronomers would give half their lives, if they did not have to do what I did—which is to say, to go and study cosmology above the observatory of the atmosphere.

In talking to you, my young readers, I fear that my language will not do justice to the great things I want to paint for you. To speak about the works of God, so great and so marvelous, would require a sublime language. Do not let my book slip from your hands in disgust, but be indulgent, and read on.

In the west, near the point abandoned by the sun, I discovered, white and luminous, a small star shining with all its glare. Higher up and closer to me, I distinguished a second, so pure and easy on the eye that I might have taken it for a meteor. I quickly recognized my error.

Thos two charming globes were none other than the two inferior planets—which is to say, those placed between the Sun and the Earth, Mercury and Venus, to call them by name. Much smaller than Venus, Mercury, although thirteen million leagues from the Sun, floats in a extremely dense atmosphere, and Newton has calculated that its heat must be more intense than that of boiling water. I looked at it with the aid of the telescope; I was then able to assure myself that the planet was offering one side of its truncated crescent. As I knew already that the truncation in question was only repeated after twenty-four hours, I concluded easily that its rotation had that duration. I could also make out perfectly the mountains with which Mercury is studded; the height of some, according to calculation, might attain thirty thousand feet.

Much more beautiful, however, both paler and brighter, Venus attracted my particular attention. It certainly merits the name it bears, or those of Lucifer and Vesper, which the ancients gave it, or even that of the Shepherd's Star, with which the people gratify it. The first star that shines in the vault of the heavens when evening comes, Venus might well have made frightened farmers say: "Woe betide your lambs, shepherd of the hamlet; if you don't enclose them in the fold, the wolf will come..."

I contemplated it for a long time; it too, truncated in a part of its disk, advertised a rotation of twenty-four hours. It was easy to see and appreciate the enormous mountains covering it. It passed before the sun just as that star quit our dark hemisphere, forming a round black patch on its disk, but with points of light. Those points were nothing but rocky mountains, so shiny in the sun's fires that one might think them covered in snow. Venus is almost as large as the Earth. It travels at eighty-five leagues a minute, while the Earth travels at scarcely eighty—but little Mercury travels at an even more rapid pace, orbiting at a speed of forty thousand leagues an hour.

The further the sun went beneath the horizon, the more the blackness of the firmament was covered with a fine dust of scintillating dark red dots, over which the superior planets lit up.

Among the fixed stars I could see Aldebaran marvelously, the eye of the constellation Taurus, whose volume is more than a thousand times greater than the Sun's. Then there was Virgo's ear, Hydra's heart, the Vendageuse,[20] and hot Sirius, the nearest star to the Earth—but I repeat, over the marvelous seed-bed of that fiery powder, the superior planets stood out, magnified by some mysterious prodigy of optics, but perfectly clear to the eye, trenchantly white in color, and establishing by virtue of that difference in color from the stars, the planetary system such as science delivers it to us.

I armed myself with my telescope, and immediately recognized Mars, the mot eccentric of planets, for it has a very irregular motion.

In that regard, I recalled what was said of Georg Rheticus, a disciple of Copernicus, who, unable to explain that original motions of Mars, invoked his familiar spirit. According to Kepler, that genius seized Rheticus by the hair, raised him up to the ceiling, let him fall back to Earth, and said to him: "That's the motion of Mars!"

I deduced that Mars had an atmosphere, for a star that was in close proximity to it seemed to be obscured. I also detected patches, and a fairly noticeable flattening.

From Mars I passed on to Jupiter. What struck me first were the dark bands striping the planet. Jean-Sylvain Bailly— the unfortunate Bailly, killed in the Revolution of '93, who said to his murderers as he went to his death in a fine cold rain, "I'm shivering, but it's with cold"—claimed that these bands are seas more extensive in length than breadth, for, according to physics, water absorbs part of the light it receives. What astonishes me, however, is that I had learned that these

---

[20] The Vendageuse is the name given by the French to the star interpreted by the ancients as Virgo's right hand.

bands were three in number, but I counted eight of them. At least there is one of them that is constant and very broad; it is a sort of threat river that traverses Jupiter in its torrid zone. I eventually distinguished, but with great difficulty, the four small moons that surround it.

A very special attraction drew me toward Saturn, whose enormous mass is to the Earth's mass what ten thousand sixty hundred and ninety is to one. My telescope was scarcely aimed in its direction when I saw clearly the ring that circles it like a sash and extends outwards to form two handles between which I could see the black sky again. Veritably, before the works of God, humans must bow down; but what can one say to express a sufficient admiration in the face of the strange mystery of a planet surrounded by a moon serving it as a belt, leaving an immense interval between itself and the central body? And when one thinks that the ring is double, and that besides that richness of satellites the planet has seven moons, one is obliged to fall silent, for what can science stammer before all that dazzling grandeur?

I kept that astonishing prodigy under my gaze for a long time, thinking that it had a diameter if twenty-eight thousand leagues, that it was four hundred and thirteen million, six hundred and four thousand, five hundred and four leagues from the Sun, and that it requires twenty-nine years to go around that star—after which I passed on to Uranus.

That planet is six hundred and fifty-six million leagues from the Sun; it requires eighty four years to complete its orbit, even though it travels are three thousand seven hundred leagues a minute.

What shall I say about Ceres, Pallas, Juno and Vesta?

I was dazzled, and my eyes were weary.

That fatigue did not result from the effort that I was making to distinguish the heavenly bodies more clearly, for, as I have said, by virtue of a strange optical effect, which probably resulted from parcels of air between the planets, the stars and myself that were doubtless still sufficient, the volume of the globes that I was looking at was magnified prodigiously when

I made use of my telescope. Or, if the parcels of air in question did not exist, I don't know what mysterious cause produced the effect of which I speak when I applied my eye to the telescope. What is certain is that I could see the stars with my lenses admirably well, and that our observations from the Earth's surface are infinitely less favorable. One might have thought that I had drawn several millions of leagues closer to the bodies I wanted to study. The fatigue, therefore, only came from the admiration I felt in the face of the marvels that had been unveiled to me.

I was only just beginning, however.

The Sun had finally been eclipsed by the Earth, which hid it, when my ear was struck by sounds so soft and harmonious that I thought a fresh breeze was getting up, which was causing an Aeolian harp to sing.

I remembered having been surprised in a vast and delightful garden in England, decorated with summer-houses and cottages, by a similar melody; I had hastened to run to the place from which the sweet chords were coming, but had only found, suspended from trees, square harmonic tablets over which two metal strings were extended with the aid of a bridge. Placed close together, these harps—called Aeolian because the wind alone causes them to vibrate—were responding to one another and producing the most delectable effect in that enchanting location. That harmony was perfectly explicable, for the strings, by virtue of the excitation of the air, especially when there was an abrupt variation in the atmospheric state, caused the notes to resonate in perfect harmony.

It was very evident, however, after rapid reflection, that there was no Aeolian harp in my vicinity or within range—for although Abbé Gattoni,[21] the inventor of these tablets, had once had the fantasy of extending from one bell-tower to another seven strings representing the notes of the diachronic scale, resulting in an aerial concert that had delighted the lei-

---

[21] Cesare Gattoni did not invent the Aeolian harp, but he did built a gigantic one near Milan in 1783.

sure of the inhabitants of Milan, his native city, he was now dead, and no one after him would have had the idea of establishing a giant harp at such an altitude.

I listened with pleasure, for the harmony increased gradually, penetrating, exquisite and ineffable, but as if muted by a mysterious distance, but simultaneously so powerful that one might have taken it for Jehovah's celestial orchestra signing the glory of God by the voice of magical choirs of angels, cherubim and heavenly virgins.

In the grandeur of God's works, you see, there are things so sublime and superior to the human mind that to want to express them and depict them with the aid off our feeble resources is truly to diminish and degrade them—so I shall not try to describe my impressions to you. Besides, the marvel was immediately followed by another, which was no less appropriate to excite my enthusiasm.

To my left, toward the east, the horizon of the Earth, long but soft pale golden rays launched into the nebulous void, drawing away from the center that projected them. That center was still invisible, but it was approaching, for the circle of the radiation was increasing, and its gleam, brighter in the middle parts, came to caress my aerostat and my gondola with its topaz and opal tints.

What could this singular surprise, this astonishing apparition, be?

I did not have to wait long for the key to the enigma. The center of the golden radiation was still hidden by the enormous block of the terrestrial atmosphere, which received it is soft translucency, but it could not be long in appearing. Indeed, a globe of gold and ruby, like a round metal plate emerging from a furnace, soon rose, dominating the Earth and its immense atmosphere, and I recognized...the Moon, our beautiful Moon, our satellite, our planet's night star.

Yes, it was the Moon; but it did not have the paltry appearance of a Basque tambourine that is familiar to us, and which prompts old village women to tell so many fantastic and far-fetched stories. The Moon displayed itself so immense and gigantic that my heart beat faster at the thought that my telescope would finally allow me to reckon with all the lunar mysteries.

That apparition, moreover, did not put a stop to the aerial chords of the celestial harmony by which my ears were still lulled. On the contrary, as the Moon drew nearer, the melody grew louder and found echoes in the prodigious depths of the celestial abyss.

It was sufficient to make me prostrate myself in adoration—but I was distracted then by further caprices of my aerostat. It was gripped by a new agitation, which frightened me. The influence of the Moon was making itself felt upon it, and with good reason. This is why.

It is generally alleged that the Moon has no atmosphere. On that point, astronomical scientists are in disagreement; some say yes, others no. What I can say is that the Moon's approach pushed a breeze before it—more than a breeze, a powerful breath that generated agitation. I was a long way away, it's true, but the Earth is at a even greater distance, and it feels that influence too, of which the tides are the result. Now, it was that breeze, that wind, which, extending as far as me, was unfurling its waves against my aerostat and producing the agitation I mentioned, as you will easily comprehend.

In very little time the splendid globe of the night star was above my head; so rapidly that, astounded, I had not yet made use of my telescope. I had surrendered my eyes to the admiration of the Moon and my ears to the charms of the celestial concert, when, all of a sudden...a few fathom as overhead, I saw a black dot appear, in the form of an aerostat, directly below the Moon—and what an aerostat! At the same time, a voice—but what a voice!—shouted to me:

"Good evening, Friend: come to me..."[22]

---

[22] This line appears in English in the original. The narrative undergoes the first of two marked changes of direction at this point, and it is not impossible that it is actually a portmanteau work, welded together from two or three once-distinct manu-

Astonishment did not permit me to rely. I recognized, however, that someone was speaking to me in English. Then the voice—my God, what a voice!—continued: "Usted no me entiende, Amigo? Mire usted por aca y vanga usted hacia mi!"

Good! I thought. *Now it's moved on from English to Spanish to hail me...*

Almost immediately, the voice—and what a voice!—added, switching to German: "Muss man dich denn so sehr bitten, zu mir zu komen? Lass es dir nicht mehr sagen, komm."

Is it going to try all the languages of Europe? I wondered. *It will certainly get to French eventually, then.*

"Non temere, amico mio, appressati. Non te lo far ripetere tante volte."

I interrupted suddenly, however, crying in my turn, as loudly as I could: "Come yourself—I'm French. A Frenchman never leaves his post."

"A man of the great nation!" said the voice. "I'm finally going to contemplate a Frenchman!"

And suddenly, I saw beside my terrestrial aerostat a lunar aerostat, beside my terrestrial gondola a lunar gondola, and beside an inhabitant of the Earth, an inhabitant of the Moon!

Alas, what a difference there was between the industrial products of each of the two globes!

---

scripts; it is certainly considerably longer than most of the books that Driou published in Limoges via Barbou or Ardant. This chapter was written some years before Camille Flammarion began his career as a popularizer of astronomical science in the early 1860s, and serves to highlight the rapid progress made in that brief interim, which allowed Flammarion and those who came after him to issue much more detailed descriptions of the planets based on telescopic appearances that were sometimes deceptive but nevertheless permitted far greater elaboration.

II

A burst of laughter, such as my poor ears had never heard—a Homeric burst of laughter, strident and sardonic, capable of shattering my eardrum in ordinary conditions—resounded beside me, at the same time as a powerful hand caused my aerostat to oscillate by placing itself on my gondola. I wanted to flee, and was already pressing the switch of my mechanism when a superior force halted my efforts, and someone said to me:

"For a Frenchman—and the French are the most famous of Terrans—you're not very curious, my dear chap. Come on, lift up that hood hiding your face and look at me frankly. It gives me great pleasure to look at you; let's get to know one another. For a long time I've wanted to meet a Terran, and if you've ever wanted to see a Lunian, the opportunity has come. Let's take advantage of it. So, my dear chap, as your Poquelin[23] said: *Pull yourself together, Monsieur, from such dire alarm!*"

You will understand, my young readers, how great my amazement was. I stood there, dumbstruck, before so strange a speech from a creature from the Moon. I rubbed my eyes to assure myself that I was not asleep, to be more certain that no hallucination was obsessing me with phantoms, and, finally turning toward the newcomer, I looked at him resolutely.

Truly, my poor talent as a narrator finds itself lacking with regard to giving you a worthy description of the Lunian.

What struck me first was that his head was giving off an almost imperceptible soft glow, but a veritable radiation, which became more sensible when his body moved in shade or darkness. I deduced that it was the emanation of the soul enclosed in the body, its prison, and that it emerged from the

---

[23] Jean-Baptiste Poquelin was (and is) better known by his stage name, Molière.

eyes and the head, the noblest part of the physical constitution. Now here is a sketch of my acolyte.

His head, marvelous in its beauty, seemed endowed with a superior intelligence. But his torso and shoulders, of the most irreproachable form, appeared to have the polish and firmness of Paros marble. A benign smile was designed on his lips, but one also encountered there something witty and sardonic, which tempered an exquisitely bountiful expression. His blond hair, very curly, was parted over a high, broad forehead to undulate over the shoulders and frame the most fortunate physiognomy.

He was tall, slender and yet robust.

His costume? Oh, have no fear; I can't forget it. And my task in describing it will not be difficult. He wore, with a charming negligence, a very ample white tunic, which surrounded him with its innumerable folds, from the breast, where it was fastened by a large emerald, to the waist, where to was secured by a golden girdle studded with fine stones, with a hem just above the knee. The leg was finely modeled in green leather buskins embroidered with pearls. His hand bore a singular kind of ring whose bezel formed a little diamond globe with a luminous gleam.

You see that nothing is simpler than such a costume, composed of a tunic of snow-white fabric, and buskins as green as meadow-grass in spring. And yet I have omitted nothing, save for the large silver circlet that gripped his temples and his hair.

While I was examining him attentively, he also carried out an examination of my person. Was I so eccentric, alas, in my paltry individuality as to call forth hilarity, to make the Lunian's lips quiver with suppressed laughter? I don't know. But I did not raise my eyes to meet my interlocutor's, lest I see the gaiety appearing in his features—but it exploded when, to give myself assurance and importance, my initial emotion having subsided, I coolly picked up the still-lit cigar that I had set down momentarily when the Lunian arrived, and drew long spirals of smoke therefrom. For I have forgotten to tell you, friend Reader, because it was not worth the trouble, that as the Moon drew nearer, in order to give more charm to my admiring thoughts, I had lit a first-rate Regalia.

"Aha!" he said. "So that's the great secret of Terrans! Often, when I look down on the Earth, in recent years, I see the faces of men almost constantly veiled by certain vapors, as if they were exhaling small clouds. From afar, they're reminiscent of little locomotives giving off steam. I understand now. It's that little stub of I don't know what that you carry in your mouth, in order to eat the smoke. Truly, it's curious..."

And my companion of the aerial highway started laughing, so wholeheartedly that my aerostat, whose gondola he was still holding on to, oscillated and pitched, receiving jerky shocks that would have frightened me if the Lunian had not restored order to my situation by recovering his seriousness.

"But what does the maneuver signify?" he asked me, interrogatively. "For what purpose do you take that smoke into your mouth, to expel it again. Is there perhaps a noble philosophy in the habit? Is it to remind you of the brevity of life and provide you with an image of it, in order to live better?"

"It's to charm leisure time, my dear Lunian," I replied. "A cigar bears within it reveries, inspirations and intellectual enjoyments..."

"You have a great deal of leisure time, then?" said the Lunian, without letting me finish. "Have you so few serious things to do that you waste time making smoke like that? Perhaps it gives you a longer life?"

"No, it doesn't," I said in my turn. "I even think that many maladies of the lungs, the larynx and the heart arise—especially among young people, who always tend to abuse everything—from the usage of the plant first imported to our country by Jean Nicot. In any case, we die regardless, some young, some old, as you probably do..."

Another, even more satirical, smile was the Lunian pilot's response. I was about to reproach him when he said: "On the Moon, my dear Parisian, no one dies!"

"To begin with, then," I objected, "there are inhabitants of the Moon? We have aimed our most powerful telescopes at that planet, invented by William Herschel and improved by Noel Paymal Lerebours, but have discovered nothing definite on our satellite. We are, however, very curious in that regard."

"I believe so, and with good reason" said the lunar aeronaut. "It interested the people of antiquity greatly. I've seen them all adoring it as a protective divinity, the poor fools."

"Pardon me, Lunian, allow me to interrupt you—you say that you've seen them?"

"In person, old chap. How old do you think I am? Don't flatter me!"

"Oh! You must be something like...forty years old?"

"Ha ha!" said the Lunian. "I am, old chap—remember the figure—five thousand eight hundred years old. I date from fifty years after the creation of the world. I've seen Adam and Eve in the terrestrial paradise; I've seen Cain kill his brother Abel; I've seen Noah; I've seen the Deluge. You can accept, therefore, what I told you about having known all the peoples of the ancient world."

"Then you've been witness to many curious things!"

"To whom are you talking? Yes, of course. But we were talking about the Moon—let's not leave the subject so quickly. So, you know that the Egyptians adored it under the name of Isis, the Phoenicians under that of Astarte; among the Greeks it received honors in the name of Selene, and among the Romans it was invoked under that of Diana, Hecate and so on. The Hebrews regarded it as the queen of the heavens.

"In order to observe it more closely in its progress the shepherds of Chaldea climbed their highest mountains, and as soon as the nascent Moon showed itself in the firmament, the brave people of that land laid out a sumptuous banquet."

"That wasn't a bad idea," I murmured. "It was a means of feasting every month."

"The magicians of Thessaly claimed to be in commerce with the Moon, and passed for terrible sorcerers by boasting, on the occasion of an eclipse, that they could recall the light by beating pans and cauldrons loudly."

"Another way to exploit the stupid! Unfortunately, the Earth is miserly with its shadow where the Moon is concerned," I said, with a certain pride, to make the Lunian see that I was not unacquainted with the elements of astronomical science.

"The Peruvians, even today, regard it as the sister and wife of the Sun. They call it the mother of their Incas. Muslims never fail to salute the Moon as soon as it appears, and present their open purses to it."

"Yes, but not so that it can take the smallest tip therefrom, I imagine?"

"No, my friend, the Mohammedans are more careful than that; it's simply in order that our lunar influence can multiply the cash therein as it increases in its course."

"All that's marvelous, my dear Lunian. We Terrans have infinitely less respect for your homeland. We often permit ourselves to make slightly profane jokes about it. In truth, that's excusable, since we didn't know that it harbored guests of such venerable antiquity.

"And to tell you right away what we think, I'll confess to you that we regard it as an inert and icy body, rounded in form, flattened at the poles and swollen at the equator, possessing a double movement of rotation and revolution, receiving all its light and its glare from the sun, distant from us by some eighty thousand leagues, and only being a forty-ninth of the size of our Earth.

"Our scientists affirm that you have no atmosphere, that no liquid accompanies you, that you have neither seas nor rivers. You are granted mountains, however; it is even said that they rise to a great height, and that they appear as brightly-shining points, accompanied by a dark lateral area whose position and extent varies with the progress of your phases. Some of our astronomers even claim to have perceived these mountains at the edges of the lunar disk, like jagged projections extending beyond the luminous line. The measurements they have made give us an elevation surpassing twenty-five thousand feet, five thousand feet higher than Davalaghiri in the Himalayas.

"As for volcanoes, the most *lunatic* of our scientists dare to say that you have them, and that our aeroliths come from your world, launched by violent eruptions. They cite, in particular, the enormous aerolith that smashed into a paved road with a frightful noise near Épinal in the Vosges in 1822, and displayed in the crater it had made an enormous block of black veined stone, reeking of fire and sulfur and still burning with volcanic heat. But there are a thousand of these bolides displayed as curiosities in our museums and scientific collections, the origin of which no one knows.

"For the inhabitants of the Moon, the difficulty is much greater. No one has discovered the slightest evidence with the aid of our telescopes, and none of you has yet considered making an aerolith to give us an idea of your existence up there. Except that we are convinced that there is no one there—not even polar bears, because of the absence of vegetation and the eternal presence of snow and ice, old extinct and frozen comet that you are...."

"Thank you. So, *Adhuc sub judice lis est?*"[24]

"What?"

"I said: *Adhuc sub judice lis est...*"

"The matter is not yet decided..."

"Precisely.

"So you know Latin?"

"Certainly! Having known all the peoples of antiquity, as I know all modern peoples, I know all their languages. Thus, Hebrew, Chaldean, Arabic, Assyrian, Median, Persian, Carthaginian, Greek, Latin and Egyptian have no secrets for me, and pose no difficulty."

"Perhaps, then, you can tell me which is the mother tongue of the other languages. It's said that a king of Egypt, seek-

---

[24] A line from Horace's *Ars poetica*, roughly equivalent to "The jury is still out."

ing to resolve that problem, had two children nursed by a she-goat, ordering everyone who went near them to maintain silence in their presence. After two years, the children distinctly articulated the two syllables *beccos*, the sound of which closely resembles the bleating of a goat. Now, *bek* signifies bread in Phrygian, and the judicious monarch concluded that the primitive language as that of the Phrygians."

"Yes, and I know too that your French Basques conducted a curious debate in the bosom of the Metropolitan chapter of Pampeluna, and that the decision transcribed in the register of the deliberations clearly states that the Basque language was the only one spoken in the terrestrial paradise by Adam and Eve.[25]

"Poor world! God has given it many subjects of dispute. I respect his views, my dear Terran, and I shall not satisfy your curiosity. I will only say to you that I give you the choice of conversing with me in English, Spanish, Italian, French, German, Chinese, Georgian, Sanskrit, Tamil, Malay, Annamite, Tartar, Kamchatkan, Russian, Madjar, Coptic, Nubian, Mandigno, Asanti, Bantu, Pécherais, Téhuelche, Mocobi-Abipon, Sioux, Oneida, Saki-Ottogami, Ojibway..."

"Please, leave it at that, my dear Lunian—you're hurting my ears. Be quiet, I beg you. You're a savant, a polyglot, I admit it; I kneel before you. Indeed, if you've had five thousand eight hundred years to relieve boredom, you've had time to learn all those languages."

"Learn" We don't learn anything, my friend. We know everything at birth..."

"Bah! Everything when you arrive in the world!"

"My God, yes. On your planet, the Earth, your first forefather Adam came into the world knowing everything. Unfor-

---

[25] The theory that the Basque language was the ancestral tongue spoken by Adam and Eve was first suggested by Dominique Lahetjuzan (1766-1818), based on extremely slender evidence, but it proved surprisingly popular, at least in the Basque country.

tunately, he sinned, sinned unworthily—and ignorance became his lot and that of all his descendants. On our planet, the Moon, we had the good fortune to resist temptation; we rejected the crime of pride and disobedience, so we are perfect, immortal, all-knowing, all-seeing, and nothing can be hidden from us... I'll give you proof, by waking my daughter, who is only fifteen years old."

"Your daughter?" I exclaimed, taking up the monocle suspended around my neck by a ribbon and screwing it into the cavity of the ocular orbit in order to see whether some sylphide was flying around our aerostats.

"What's that?" asked the Lunian.

"A lens that magnifies objects, or makes them seem closer," I replied.

"That trinket!" said my neighbor, who took possession of the monocle and put it to his eye...but he returned it to me just as quickly, laughing. "Another plaything of vanity...another human misery!" the Lunian murmured. "Another means of making oneself important, of posing, of creating an effect! Fashion, that's all... Baubles of pride, these so-called lenses impede sight rather than aiding it, and yet, wretched as they are, humans, even serious ones, play with monocles like stupid high-society dandies. If they knew how ridiculous it makes them look, and all the mockery of which they're the object...

"O primitive times, primordial nature, ancient naivety, what have you become? So, old chap, put down your monocle, of which you have no need; don't look for my daughter in the air; she's in my conch. Be careful that you don't seem too much of a fop. She would be pitiless, although she's only fifteen...

"Let's see...the Moon is in the middle of its course; it's midnight on Earth; it's the most favorable moment to enjoy the harmony of the spheres."

"It's the spheres, then, that are producing that harmonious concert?"

"Of course: the celestial globes—stars, the Sun, the planets, their satellites, comets, whether masses of fire or opaque spheres, sing to their creator and their God. It's the best moment for us to admire the work of creation. All our brothers on the Moon have attentive ears and eyes. It's appropriate that my daughter should also pay her tribute to the author of all being.

"Stella, my sweet Stella, reply to your father's voice my beloved daughter. Get up!"

"It's strange," I said. "Our fathers talk to our children in that fashion on Earth."

"Love, the veritable love of the heart, is the same everywhere," the Lunian replied. He added: "But tell me, my dear Parisian, whether your children resemble this little creature."

"I ought to tell you, for I have not yet described it, that my colleague's gondola was nothing but a long, profound and magnificent conch-shell, nacreous inside and colored externally with the most splendid crimson gleams, surmounted by a narrow circle of gold, to which silver cords were attached, passed through rich golden rings. These cords held the balloon captive with their shining network, and the balloon, whose fabric was a most beautiful shade of violet, unknown in our countries, was rounded in the form of a horizontal cone, connected at its widest and narrowed parts to the widest and narrowest parts of the conch. Its movements in the atmosphere were most graceful, and it was always the widest part of the cone that was the first to move forward.

"You're looking at my aerostat?" said the Lunian. "Yours suffers considerably by comparison, doesn't it? What do you expect? The Earth and its products are imperfect. Those that we Lunians have, on the other hand, bear the stamp of perfection, as marvelous as their author, and proof of infinity." He concluded: "Now behold Stella..."

Beneath the sheets of white fabric that hid the depths of the nacreous shell, I did indeed see a moving form that I could not yet define. Soon, however, the pale child stood up, chased away sleep, and became animated and lively—and I suddenly found myself facing the most beautiful child that one could possibly encounter.

"An Earthman!" her father told her.

Stella made no reply. She hastened to drape a chin-guard over her shoulders, fastening it around her neck in the Jewish fashion, which half-hid her face. Then, adjusting a kind of dazzling white chlamys with a red girdle, she lowered her eyes with a modesty full of reserve.

Soon too, however, timidly raising one of her eyes to begin with, and then the other, she directed them at my aerostat, my gondola and my person—and, plunging into her father's arms, she burst into laughter so naïve and engaging that, I confess, I started to laugh too...

Then, when she had yielded to that impulse of her jovial nature, she disengaged her face from the chin-guard, shook her head—whose long black hair floated loose, and displayed a face so cheerful, and so perfectly innocent, that I was glad to say to her father: "Your daughter lives up to her name. She's certainly the most beautiful star that I could ever see in our firmament. Thank you. The brilliant Stella merits my voyage on her own."

"Monsieur is French, I understand by his compliments," said Stella, in a voice as soft as the oboe's E. "But Lunians like simplicity of language, and purity of thought is the only way of pleasing them."

"My daughter will take her part in the conversation, my dear chap," said the man from the Moon. "I warn you to be on your guard. Let's agree how to proceed now. Would it please you to travel together, side by side, you in the Earth's atmosphere, we in the lunar atmosphere?—for out two atmospheres touch, and that of the Mon rotates around the Earth. Or would you prefer to leave us and remain in the solitude where we found you?"

"Dear Lunian," I exclaimed, "would you be so ungenerous as to abandon me suddenly, when I have scarcely raised to my lips the cup of happiness that your acquaintance gives me? That would be cruel!"

"Frenchman! No more fine words, my friend, or I'll break away suddenly, as you say. Listen: we are both human, both creatures of the same God, but the sin of your first forefather has rendered you mortal, and I am immortal. Besides, your homeland and that which belongs to it, is prey to disorder and tempests; our homeland is the image of Heaven, where peace and happiness reign. Can we really associate our existences, even for a few hours? I believe so, for nothing in my conscience tells me that it would be evil. If, therefore, we continue our fortuitous relationship, it will be to the advantage of your mind and the interest of your heart."

"Which is to say," Stella interjected, "that the works of God, which you can see at close range, and other than you ordinarily contemplate them, will lead you to love and adore him more..."

"How happy I am!" I cried. "Has any man ever been so fortunate as to encounter beings superior to him, who can reveal to him the magnificence of the Creator and enable him to penetrate their regions?"

"You are in error on that latter point, my dear Terran! Our abode is the abode of perfection, and thus of felicity. No profane individual can enter it. To live and breathe there you would need a constitution other than the one you have. You belong to the Earth; remain on the Earth."

"It would be violating the decree of God to let you set a mortal foot in the fortunate regions of immortality," said Stella. "What Mikaël, my father, can do is to instruct you verbally, to bring you closer to opaque, and even luminous, globes in order that you might contemplate and admire them..."

"But my aerostat, as you see, even making use of all its means with the aid of my mechanism—a mechanism of which I am the inventor—cannot surpass this limit, which is the last layer of the terrestrial atmosphere. I can go no further."

"Firstly," the Lunian went on, "you are much further—very much further—from the Earth than you think. Yes, you're at the ultimate limit, but that is already an immense distance from your planet. The scientists of your world believe the limits of their atmosphere to be very restricted; they suppose that our Moon lacks one—they are in error on both counts. Our two planets each have their own, almost infinite in their extent, and the point at which we find ourselves is that at which they come into contact and mingle their most tenuous and ethereal elements. That is why your aerostat is oscillating and assuming an oblique attitude, lying sideways, as if beneath a vault that opposes its progress, or like a winded horse. Fortunately, that oblique position allows you to see us, for our aerostat, arriving from the Moon, and yours, coming from the Earth, would ordinarily have interpose themselves between us, hiding us from one another, at the moment when we stopped. Mine is similarly inclined and immobile, because I have imposed that maneuver upon it—but, perfect in its manufacture, like all our works, it can travel in all atmospheres and from one globe to another, according to our will."

"But mine isn't like that, my dear Lunian, and I can't get it over the obstacle that has trapped it," I objected.

"Oh," said Stella—who, having picked up a flexible silver thong, both ends of which terminated in golden hooks, fixed one end to the rigging of my gondola—"by taking your aerostat in tow, linking it to ours like this"—she fixed the other hook to one of the rings of her conch—"your apparatus will be obliged to follow ours and, crossing that rebellious limit, will launch into our atmosphere. We shall even be able to give you a tour of the worlds."

"What shall I see, then?"

"Globes of fire, opaque bodies, planets, satellites, comets," Mikaël replied, whom I can call by his name, since I obtained it from Stella.

"Globes of fire!" I exclaimed. "In truth, I fear fire all the more since I do not have the nature of a salamander or asbestos. I'll let you off the globes of fire; to know them, a telescope is sufficient for me. But the planets, especially the Moon—our dear Moon, so beloved on Earth for the beautiful nights it gives us—oh, I'd like to see that, since it's possible."

"Well then, we'll take you to our satellite," Mikaël said, addressing me in the familiar form. "After which..."

"After which, what?" I said, hopefully.

"After which, we'll bring you back to your planet of origin, your dear fatherland, to wait there for the day when your soul will fly toward the great and true fatherland."

"Fatherland! Yes, that's a sacred word. The heart beats faster at the name. Now that I'm far away, I feel that I love it..." As I spoke those words, with feeling, a tear slid from my eyelid. I lowered my eyes toward the Earth.

At that moment, the Moon was shining its most beautiful light upon us. It was faintly silvering the terrestrial atmosphere, which, purged of all mist and cloud, allowed me to see the Earth as an enormous black mass, an elongated ball slightly compressed at the poles, floating heavily in space. It is thus that the Moon appears to us, gray and dull, in daylight, floating in the plains of the atmosphere—except that the Earth appeared to me a hundred or two hundred times greater in volume, and it was night on Earth.

"You can see clearly that your balloon has climbed higher than you thought," Mikaël told me, "and that you're a long way from your planet. But you seem sad, my dear chap. Are you afraid?"

"I'm not sad," I replied, "but I'm thinking..."

"In the interests of science, are you making some calculation at present?" the Lunian continued.

"No; I'm thinking about a tenderly cherished individual, perfectly beloved, who's asleep there, on the sphere I've quit...perhaps weeping, in thinking about me..."

"Father?" said Stella.

"What do you want, Daughter?" Mikaël replied.

"What if you lent him the sacred searchlight, which illuminates the worlds for our eyes?" the young woman said.

"What is this searchlight?" I asked, swiftly.

"This!" said Mikaël. And he showed me the strangely-shaped and shiny bezel of the ring that he had on his finger.

"What can I do with that?" I said, disappointed.

"What do you want to see?" the Lunian asked me.

"The Earth," I said.

"And on the Earth?"

"Paris."

"And in Paris?"

"The individual of who I spoke, my mother!"

"Although Terran, he has a good heart," Stella murmured.

"Look!" the Lunian said to me—and he put his ring on my finger, placing the bezel in front of my eyes, between the Earth and myself.

"Heavens!" I exclaimed.

"What is it?" Mikaël asked.

O dear readers, my heart beats faster again at that sweet memory. I saw my mother—yes, my mother! She appeared to me in her white nightgown, standing beside the bed that awaited her, bending over the night-light. The excellent woman was reading, and what she was reading was…my letter; the letter that I had sent at the moment of my departure. And while reading, her head was bowed, and while her head was bowed, she was weeping...

"It's an angel that God gives to us, poor lost children of Earth for a mother!" I exclaimed "Look, Mikaël! Look, Stella! That pale stature down there, which seems to be leaning over, like the genius of dolor, is a woman, and that woman is my tender mother! As virtuous as she is kind, according to the memory she has given me, you'll see her kneel down, I don't doubt. That will be to pray, and to pray for me. Mothers have so much to say to God on their children's behalf! Look—she's placing the letter under the muslin of her pillow. Now she's going to her crucifix, kneeling down and worshiping. A good mother, faith makes her present life and prepares her for the one beyond the grave. Goodnight, Mother, goodnight! I love you, and from the empyrean I send you this kiss, from a loving and submissive son. I'm sure that it will arrive on your forehead, for it is my heart, the most filial of hearts, that addresses it to you. She's shivering, you see..."

"I grant my esteem to the Terrans, Father," said Stella. "The sin has not degraded them to the point of removing sentiment from their hearts..."

"What!" said Mikaël. "You're already giving back the precious searchlight that you were so desirous of using, but which has not deceived your expectations?"

"Not at all—quite the contrary," I said, in a melancholy tone. "But after having seen my mother, I don't want to see anything else. I'm content with that good thought..."

"That's fine and noble, isn't it, Daughter?" the Lunian said to Stella.

"What of the Earth, though—your own world, Monsieur...?"

"Gerpré."

"Your own world, Monsieur Gerpré," Stella continued. "Paris, for example, certainly merits being examined with such an instrument. It's true that the Earth is sadder by night, but I no longer want to speak too harshly of it; you have rehabilitated it in my mind."

"I shall be doubly fortunate in my voyage, then," I replied, urbanely. "Your indulgence makes it evident that you are immortal and perfect creatures, so I beg you to continue."

"You're undoubtedly imperfect, my dear Frenchman, but in even in your degradation one finds proof of your past grandeur, which is ours still," said the Lunian, this time without combining his words with mocking laughter.

"Thank you for your kind words, my dear host; but since, on the one hand, you're accepting me as a traveling companion, and you have many things to show me, may we to depart right away? And on the other hand, as we have concluded the amenities, be kind enough to educate me and tell me, please, how it is that while inhabiting our satellite, which is a very small planet, you have not become too numerous for the space reserved for you?"

"I'll answer that in a little while," said Mikaël. "For the moment, I'll light up this tube that communicates with our aerostat, and, as you see, we're on our way..."

Immediately, a shock to my balloon made itself felt, so abrupt and rapid that I thought it was cleaving the air, and I opened my bewildered eyes wide while gripping my gondola with both hands for fear of falling. Dragged by the Lunian's, my aerostat went through the ultimate layer of the Earth's atmosphere with a kind of violence—but scarcely had it broken through the Moon's centrifugal force to fall into its sphere of centripetal attraction than I felt myself rising toward our satellite.

"Now, let's talk," the Lunian resumed. "My dear friend. I shall only tell you a little about our abode and ourselves. It is my duty not to reveal to humans what God has concealed from them. However, as our history has been yours, from certain viewpoints, I can tell you enough to satisfy you.

"In giving us justice, innocence and immortality, God has not permitted a numerous race to cover our globe. The Moon is perfect everywhere and offers us a veritable Eden. We're are divided into families and even the oldest among us retain eternal youth. Every family has its valley, its hills, its watershed and its dwelling. Our life, entirely patriarchal, is spent in light and pleasant labor. By day, the beauties of our nature occupy us; by night, the chords of the spheres, the melodies of the worlds, delight us. We sometimes surrender ourselves to peaceful slumbers, but without any rigorous need. Fruits, flowers, honey and milk form our nourishment. Our greatest distraction is to watch the progress of the spheres, their phases, their marvels, the spectacles they offer us, of which we miss nothing if the hand of God brings them close to us, and which we may follow with the aid of the searchlight of worlds, if the hand of God carries them into the infinity of the Heavens."

"Then you sometimes look at us?" I asked.

"No, I confess," the Lunian relied. "On the contrary, we turn our eyes away in…disgust; our only anguish is seeing the Terrans fallen into such profound abysses of evil.

"For our amusement, nevertheless, we borrow from you and recreate in ourselves and on our sphere, effortlessly, those of your lowly works that merit it. So we have, as you see, our aerostats, our railways, made of gold rather than iron, our palaces, our temples, our museums and our superb cities. We have no need of these things, however, either for our happiness or their utility. It is in that fashion that we await the end of time, a happy epoch that will finally put an end to the condemnation of the Earth, and bring all worldly beings together in a single abode, which is named Heaven."

"What about Hell? You're undoubtedly not unaware of it?"

"We're not unaware of it, my poor brother," Mikaël said. "On the contrary, we know from your example, alas, that God is terrible in his vengeance, and that he will punish those whom vice and pride have so brutalized that they are no longer worthy ever to take their seats at the banquets of eternity."

"Father," said Stella, while uttering a profound sigh, "everything that you have just said, which is nothing but the expression of the truth, shows by contrast how painful the situation of the poor Terrans is." With tears in her eyes she said to me: "I grieve for you with all my heart, brother, for, when I think that, scarcely come in the world by means of pain, you are incessantly subject to a succession of tribulations and sufferings that are only terminated by death, I cry: *How frightful sin is, since it draws such great misfortune in its wake!*

"So I do not hide from you that with our tenderness of heart, we creatures of a better world refrain from looking down upon your planet. What is to be seen there, in fact? You Terrans live only to die. Your life requires torture and suffering. You take the plumes from birds, the fleeces from sheep, the pelts from wild animals; you only have the clothes given to you by the death, the agony and the Gehenna of creatures who would have been glad to live. The fur that hides your hands, the leather that envelops your feet, death has given to you. Your simplest aliments, as to the delicacies of your table, are owed to death. Do you enjoy pleasure? One can be sure that it will be to the detriment of your fellows, by virtue of the danger, dolor, life and blood of creatures made to ornament the world.

"Would you like an example? Tell me whether there is an animal more noble and beautiful in all the worlds than the horse? You know what the Roman Virgil said in his admirable *Georgics*:[26]

Primus et ire viam, et fluvius tentare minaces
Audit, et ignoto sese committere ponti;
Nec vanos horret sttrepitus. Illi ardue cervix,
Argutumque caput, brevis alves, obesque terga.
...Tum si quae sonum arma dedere.
Stare loco neescit, micat auribus, et tremit artus;
Collectumque fremens voivit sub naribus ignem.

"And elsewhere, in the Aeneid:[27]

Quadrupetante putrem sonitu quatit ungula campum.

"Which means, Monsieur Gerpré—if I give a translation it's because I take pleasure in it, not to spare you a labor that ought to be agreeable to you:

"'The first that dares to go forward to attempt to pass over a menacing flood risks himself on an unknown bridge; no sound frightens him. He holds his neck high, his head outstretched, his belly meager, his rump round... A sound of weapons having resounded in the distance, the animal can no longer maintain his composure; his ears are pricked, his entire body trembles; the compressed fires of his breast flow in his nostrils...'

"And: 'The horse's hooves falling repeatedly together beat the powdery plain with their sonorous hooves...'"

"It's enough to mention the gallop of a horse," I exclaimed, "for me to appreciate singularly, at this moment, the joy of the charger running over the plain, through the meadows..."

"Why is that?" asked the Lunian.

"Because, being in my gondola since yesterday..."

---

[26] The author adds a reference to the *Georgics*, Book II, verse 77.

[27] The author adds a reference to the *Aeneid*, Bok VIII, verse 396.

"In your basket, rather!" said Mikaël.

"I feel a thousand ants in my legs, devouring them. I really need to stretch them, or to do some vigorous gymnastic exercises..."

"That's very difficult where we are."

"What are you talking about? Are you familiar with the infirmity of which I speak?"

"We know none, my dear chap."

"How fortunate you are! But I think that the circulation of the blood has been restored... Madame, you have just cited an author who once extended many traps for my young intelligence, and earned me more than one imposition. But I know another author, whom we count among our glories, who has spoken worthily about the horse, the ox, the dog, and animals in general—of their astonishing instinct, their fine intelligence, their aptitude for learning, and the precious qualities of which they give proof. What services do these admirable creatures of God not render to humans?"

"And how do humans reward them?" Mikaël put in. "All your Terran peasants ought to be familiar with the Monsieur Buffon of whom you speak. But I'd also like them, above all, to know what the Bible says about the horse. I love to talk about it, because it's the finest conquest of humankind. Do you know it yourself, Monsieur? I've noticed that the French have the common fault of being smitten by artificial beauties, and sometimes not even looking at real ones. Thus, for example, in the sacred book, *Job* makes the horse appear before your eyes full of strength, ardor and courage, striking the ground with its foot and launching itself boldly at armed men, scenting the approaching enemy at a distance; spreading terror with the breath from its nostrils; replying with its voice to the trumpet that sounds the charge; inaccessible to fear; pressing forward relentlessly against the blades of swords, devouring the ground when its rider guides it to combat.

"And yet, which is the animal you torture most on Earth? The horse. You impose burdens up on it its strength is impotent to bear; if it succumbs under the load, you brutalize the noble creature with blows! And often, in your stupid anger, you even break its limbs and deprive it of life! Is this odious spectacle not renewed every day?"

"Alas," Stella went on, "I never once lower my eyes to your planet, unfortunate Terran, without seeing blood, murder, pillage, war, rape, burning... Is there anything more odious than your wars, even the most just? It is, therefore, on their authors that the greatest blame must fall. Yes, I have a horror of your globe; it sweats blood; it reeks of agony; one hears nothing there but death-rattles. Everywhere, nothing but abattoirs, circuses, arenas, coliseums, victims, tortures, convulsions, sobbing, moaning, distress and death!"

"Finally, this is my daughter speaking," said the Lunian. "She is recovering her verve, and proving to you, my friend the Frenchman, how, even in our children, reason, judgment and wisdom are present from the outset."

"Unfortunately, she speaks very well, and what she says is only too true," I replied. "I bow my head in shame, but, even in our children, our innate degradation gives premature birth to a precocious perversity.

"You have given me proofs; here are mine: At Morsan, down there on a imperceptible point on our Île de France, I possess a charming small house surrounded by verdant hills, lush meadows, and lively springs jetting forth from every direction. But what I love best in that modest retreat, and which also charms my mother, is that we're not the only guests of that rural abode. In the immense frame of a Gothic window, imagine the vastest and best-organized colony of swallows. Yes, swallows, those first-rate architects, have constructed an entire city there, which reveals a prodigious architectural talent. I assured you that it is a magnificent work, in which the art of the mason and the knowledge of the plasterer are combined with the science of the architect.

"Now, in winter, that city, ordinarily so noisy, is merely a sarcophagus. Emptiness sleeps in its numerous cells. Scarcely has the breath of spring refreshed nature, however, and warm breezes promised beautiful days, than the chirping of a swallow greets us; then another, and a third, reply to it. It's like the trumpets of an entire troop greeting us with their fanfares. And make no mistake, they are indeed greeting us. They know us and love us, as we recognize and love them—for they really are the same little birds of previous years: here are the males, there are the females. By some sign we identify one, by means of another, we rediscover another. There's no room for deception; they are exactly the same tenants—and woe to any intruder who are idle enough or pretentious enough to take possession of their little domain. Each one recognizes its own nest and rapidly takes up residence in its own home.

"And do you know what we call these charming birds, in France? God's own birds. That's not without reason, as you shall see.

"There is no other animal species to which God has shown such partiality in lavishing his gifts and favors. The turtle-dove and the hedge-sparrow do not have its tenderness; the partridge cannot match its maternal devotion; the wagtail is far from its social charity; the flacon cannot compete with it for the forcefulness of its flight, the keenness of its sight and its agility. As for fidelity, Philemon and Baucis were no more by comparison than fickle children.

"The swallow is a friend to humans; it arrives with the first sunny days to liberate us from the insects that their heat produces. It is in our dwellings that they build their nests, in order to live with us and cheer up our leisure with their graceful flight and their innocent chirping. Following the spring through all latitudes, its life is but one long festival, and its song a joyful hymn to fine days and freedom.

"A swallow's household is indissoluble; death alone separates them; and then one sees the neighbors take responsibility for the children of the dead individuals and nourish them. What a lesson for bad mothers, who do not even care for their own! The spirit of maternity is manifest within them at the most tender age. So, when bad times arrive, it is not rare to see poor little swallows, scarcely emerged from the nest, pressing around their father and others and helping them in the concerns of a new education.

"You will understand now that I have made all these remarks about swallows, that I have a heartfelt affection, as well as for my mother, to my charming little boarders. In the morning I talked to them; my approach did not cause them to flee; on the contrary, they saved their sweetest concerts for me—but the enthusiasm of their joy reached its peak when my mother appeared.

"Don't believe that they were only thinking about their household joys and their own enjoyment. Not at all. They had a mission to fulfill, in the name of Providence, with respect to us, and they were faithful to it. I saw them protecting with their gaze and vigilance the chickens in our poultry-yard, the finches in our orchards, the linnets in our hedgerows and a thousand other birds that fluttered around the trees of our meadows. When they perceived an enemy, they would immediately give voice to a alarm call, and our delightful little neighbors would hide or flee as quickly as possible.

"How many times, too, on warm days when we were strolling around our estate, did I see our swallows soaring in hundreds above our vines, beneath our fruit-trees and our hemp-fields? Do you know how much good they do? They eat caterpillars and thousands of harmful insects, which often, undoubtedly, destroy crops worth hundreds of millions every years.

"O day, quite recently, I had to go to Rome. As we were at war then, my more trembled all the more because brigands were devastating the regions through which I had to travel. To reassure her I took with me one of our swallows, which I had tamed; I put a little piece of pink ribbon on its foot and took it away with me. I had arrived, after five days' journey, in good health and without incident, at six o'clock in the morning. I put a very brief note under the wing of my little captive, which read: *I am well. Rome, 18 June, 6 a.m.*

"At eight o'clock the same day, having been released at six—two hours later, in sum—my little voyager arrived, and my other had my news. It had traveled at nearly a hundred leagues an hour.

"Thus the ancient Quirites, who also had their bookmakers, made use of swallows in the guise of carrier-pigeons for the transmission of their bulletins of victories in the circus or the arena.

"My mother and I had great pleasure one evening, on my return from Rome, in seeing our swallows bathing and drinking on the wing, and, even better, feeding their little ones in flight. There is nothing more delightful, in fact, than that distribution of airborne beaks, so sagely divided as not to give rise to jealousy, nothing more charming than the zeal of parents directing the first wing-beats of their offspring in mid-air, and equipping them to hunt flies—and nothing, finally, more exciting and intoxicating than the joy of the latter at their first success. Then, the mother swallow generously brushes aside the prey she could have seized, in order to let it be taken by hr nurslings. We went back to the house calling them the queens of the air for their agility, their graceful capriciousness and the power of their flight.

"Imagine how alarmed I was when, scarcely having separated from my mother, I heard her utter a scream. I ran to her in haste; she was next to the swallow colony. My poor mother was as white as a statue made of Paros marble. She pointed at the colony, in ruins..."

"In ruins?" Stella exclaimed.

"In ruins," I replied. "Its debris littered the ground; feathers from the nests were being blown away by the wind; baby swallows, still almost featherless, dead and crushed, were scattered here and there. And what was saddest of all, the mothers and fathers, in hundreds, the young swallows, were arriving with a flicker of wings, uttering lugubrious cries, whirling around and around, chirping plaintively, and fleeing...

"What a night the poor innocent creatures must have had!

"Every morning, in the days that followed, we found the little corpses of poor swallows that had just died, near to their colony, beside our house, which they had rendered so happy."

"But how had that come about?"

"Alas," I relied, "a band of little vagabonds had come on to our property during our absence, under the pretext of permission that we had given them to collect dead wood in the forest, and the wretched children, badly brought-up, without sage notions about anything, having no thought for God or his works, almost without discernment, had found pleasure in demolishing the work of our swallows with sticks—and, what is frightful, were greatly amused by the torture they had inflicted with the aid of clubs and knives on the little victims of their stupid savagery."

"Such are the fruits of sin! Ignorance, concupiscence, imbecility, folly and blindness!" said Mikaël.

"Since that time, my mother has not wanted to see that place—which we left the following week—again," I continued. "and when we happen to encounter on the boulevards of Paris those odious creatures, unworthy of the name of women, who offer passers-by the swallows they have caged, for two *sous*, in order that they might be set free, my mother immediately empties her purse, as if to expiate, by means of the captives, the sack and pillage of our swallow colony at Morsan."

"For one thing," said Stella, "A swallow put in a cage does. The air of servitude is fatal to them. It is, above all, a bird of liberty, of the fields, of aerial life."

"In America," said Mikaël, "there is no farm, no country cottage, and no wretched Uncle Tom's cabin that does not have its swallow colony. That is because Americans, who know their own interests, love swallows, recognizing the immense serves they render, and look after them as best they can. In France, where people are often idiotic—pardon the expression—to the point of being unthinking, and where humans are the executioners of their own wellbeing, you destroy swallows stupidly. Your peasants, your beardless schoolboys and your ridiculous hunters are seen testing their skill on the poor creatures most useful to agriculture. Is it not just, then, that the Frenchman should expiate the fury of destruction by which he is devoured? Thus, you complain very year about the sickliness of the vines, of the cereals, of the potatoes…you have planted the cause; harvest the result!"

"Let us leave aside this unintelligent killing of certain animals we ought to admire, and, without mentioning the beautiful republic of the ants, the incomparable monarchy of the bees, the marvelous government of the beavers and, in sum, all the races of animals that the Creator has endowed with faculties that are indescribable, so great, various and prodigious are they, and allow me to grieve at belonging to a world so detestable, whose miseries desolate my heart…"

"But you're only a child, Stella; you haven't had the time yet to see and appreciate the calamities of the sublunar world," Mikaël said, bitterly, his face taking on a more serious expression. "What will you say when it's not only the surface of things that moves you? The Earth has only one resource for fining happiness, and that is religion. Outside of that, everything is disastrous. Cast your eyes upon it, as we are able to do now, with a wise and true reflection, what do you see?

"First, disease, whether it be cholera, yellow fever or plague under any other name—let me call it the plague. Is that not a homicidal giant, which seems to stride incessantly from north to south, from west to east? Can it not be said that it is reaping humankind?"

"Certainly," I replied, "One can say of it:

His furious breath, laden with black venom
Has sown the coasts of Benin with death.
Our world is red with the blood it had shed;
There is weeping from Colombia to China,
From the northern tropic to the southern
The great arms of his naked skeleton extend.
Devouring in turn the people of Germany,
Decimating the Turks, infecting Spain.

Cadavers please him, he laughs at death,
The more orphans he makes, the stronger he feels.
He needs Greece, he needs Russia,
By-passing Poland, he surprises Italy.
To the sobs and sighs that choke the bosom
He finds chords: dolor and hunger...

See, they fall, like the corn and the meadow-grass,
Beneath the scythe in summer,
Then in frightened tones the sinister swarm,
Last farewell kisses, shrouds overlaid,
Fits of terror, anger, and agony,
Punctuated sobs, sinister harmonies,
Rise up, rise endlessly, mingled with mourning
Church bells proclaim one more prayer
For all the dead thrown in haste into a coffin
In haste, too, confided to the ground!"[28]

"Are you giving us poetry, then, dear friend?" the Lunian continued. "I suspect you of being the author of those tragic verses."

"I shall say nothing more about plague," I replied, but I'll talk about famine:

First I saw hunger devouring humans
Of every era, gripped by her horrible hands,
Agitating wildly. Everywhere young women,
Mother, fathers and sons fell under the sickles
Of a nameless torture, an odious death.

---

[28] I have translated these verses, and the others in the text, straightforwardly, without attempting to reproduce their rhyme-scheme or their scansion. The patchwork quality of the narrative in this chapter suggests that fragments of unpublished poetry are not the only waifs and strays that the author is taking the opportunity to dump into a narrative that had evidently lost its initial impetus.

It was horrible to see; for her, neither
Beauty nor silver, neither name nor youth
Can protect lives from the strokes of her distress."

"Decidedly, that's an unpublished poem that you're letting us hear on the Moon, having found no readers on Earth,"
Mikaël resumed, with a melancholy smile. But I'll go on, and
I say that flood, fire, earthquakes, plague and famine are terrible evils, but that all those scourges put together are less disastrous than the wrath of kings of peoples, for it is from that
sinister anger that the most frightful scourge of all is born:
WAR. War, a cruel monster that always wants tears, screams,
blood, bone-heaps, ruins.

"If I were to pass over, merely as a bird flies, the disasters of the wars recorded by history, I would run out of breath.
If I were merely to touch with a finger the principal ruins
made by war, from Pharaoh to Napoléon III, from the Red Sea
to Alma, I would run out of strength. Yes, I would exhaust
myself showing you Tomyris, the queen of the Scythians,[29]
plunging the heard of Cyrus into a bucket of blood, and crying: *Drink of the blood for which thou hast ever been athirst!"*

"Soon, Father," Stella interjected, "may we not show the
Terran, on the Moon, the moving pictures?"

"Perhaps my daughter's idea is apt," the Lunian replied,
"and we can trace for you the reality of the things I say to you
in words. For the moment, I repeat that I would run out of
breath in showing you Europe in conflict with Asia in the
struggle begun by Achilles and ended by Alexander, which
dates from the taking of Troy and concludes with Bucephalus'
entry into Babylon. Yes, I would run out of breath following
the Roman legions to Alba, Cannes, Carthage, Numantia,

---

[29] Tomyris was the queen of the Messagetae. The story reproduced here is adapted from Herodotus, who frequently reported dubious anecdotes seemingly forged to emphasize mo-
ralistic judgments, but Driou seems to have no doubts as to his
reliability.

Pydna, and all over the world. What could I say about the overflow of the barbarians? There would be no strength left for me to cite Agincourt and Poitiers, Crécy and Moscow, Waterloo and Sinope, the greatest disasters that have ever fallen upon armies and peoples; all the evils at once, all the most frightful calamities at once: hunger and cold, water and fire; gunfire and treason, suffering and death."

"You are speaking there, my dear Master," I said in my turn, "of the great dolors of humankind, which have Heaven and Earth for their witnesses; but you're not saying a word about those other dolors of which apartments are the only theaters: those intimate dramas which happen in the secrecy of dwellings; those formidable miseries and unparalleled denouements that gather in unknown attics; nor of those silent martyrdoms that torturers inflict on victims beneath the sole gaze of God!"

"But, my God!" said Stella, "are more tears poured forth on the Earth than smiles are given birth there? Is it for that reason that whenever I listen by night, as I often do, all those sobs and moans strike my ears—and reveal to me that the sin of Adam was terrible and great, since his children are still lamenting, even in their beds, after six thousand years!"

"You're truly a good philosopher for a young woman," I said, trying to lighten the serious tone of our conversation. "I would have thought that, by reason of your age, you would have preferred to direct your ears and eyes to our festivals, games and pleasures, for there are, after all, sometimes scenes on Earth that attract and captivate the gaze."

"Of what interest are your serenades, concerts, Venetian lanterns, fairgrounds, walks beside lagoons, chariot races and joys to me?"

"You're difficult to please, Mademoiselle. Perhaps there's some enjoyment in seeing people make golden flower-baskets of themselves, in which lace undulates over silk and velvet, in which diamonds and pearls sparkle with lustrous fire, in which perfumes..."

"Oh! Oh! Mercy! Stop, my poor Terran, and don't go to such expense in description. I've looked at the society of which you speak, that famous hypnotic serpent; I've asked it to deploy its marvels and enchantments for me; I've even been obliging enough to study its caprices, intended as artistic, its fantasies and its prodigies, which your fashion admires to the point of rapture, in the caravanserai that is called Paris. I've contemplated your arts and works, gather into dazzling sheaves, forming an aureole for the banquet of life, and…you won't be annoyed?"

"No, speak, finish…"

"I was unable to suppress the laughter that is bursting out now…" As she spoke these words, Stella emitted a sardonic burst of laughter so mischievous, so hilarious, so mocking and so joyful that, carried away by the contagion of the example, I laughed in my turn.

"I haven't finished," Stella suddenly added, becoming serious again. "Would you care to listen to me a little longer? Thus, I've seen the lions and lionesses of that bizarre Ark. Well, I did not allow myself to be deceived by the veils of make-up of the clouds of white ceruse, but, digging beneath the vanities of these heroes and heroines of the Gentry, I set my eye to the little window of the heart and the bull's-eye of the soul, and what did see? A void, a frightful void! Monstrous egotism! An ant-hill of trivia, of wretchedness. Oh, no, no, none of that seduced me. And…become serious again in saying it, but that society moved me to such pity that I wept for it…"

"There's some truth in that, I admit," I replied.

"Happy, then are those who have faith, hope and charity," said Mikaël, slapping me on the shoulder.

"But unhappiness," said Stella, "thrice over to those who make an idol of their pride, and neglect their sole resource on Earth, the love of God and humans!"

"So, you know," I exclaimed, "I'm very confused to find myself with you, Lord Lunian? My talents are among the most problematic, my knowledge scarcely extends above zero; in matters of philosophy I have only that of the heart, which is to say that I'm a Christian, I believe in my Catholic religion, and I do good to my fellows when the opportunity arises."

"But that's the best philosophy of all, my dear Terran," Mikaël exclaimed. "Now you're showing me self-love in disguise."

"No, not so. I simply wanted to say that I'm far from knowing causes and effects, premises and conclusions, facts and their consequences, as you do."

"You represent imperfection, my friend; we, on the contrary, are archetypal specimens of perfection. There is, in consequence, a world of difference between us. If, on the one hand, we ought not to conceive any pride in our grandeur, you ought not to be discouraged by your abasement. We owe what we are to God; you, by the expiation of Adam's sin, are repaying God, and you are close enough to us that, one day, we shall find ourselves mingled together in the delights of Heaven."

"In the meantime, I'm ignorant and you know. At least, my dear Lunian, since you have the key to the mysteries of nature, allow me to profit from your lessons. Better still, to satisfy my curiosity somewhat, tell me how it is that you know what our various authors have said, whether they be Greek, Latin, Chinese, Jewish or Berber?"

"It's the simplest thing in the world, my dear Terran. We have our libraries, and it's sufficient for us to read the books comprising them once, and only once, and rapidly."

"You have your own authors, then?"

"The Moon does not produce any authors, and has no need of them, my dear chap, but no book is published on your Earth that we do not immediately have. Does that astonish you?"

"I confess that it does, for how do you procure them?"

"In a perfectly natural fashion. A little while ago you saw the letter you wrote to your mother yesterday being read, did you not?"

"Yes."

"You knew what was on the page at which your mother was gazing, and you did not even think of reading it yourself? But what if you had not known what the letter contained and were desirous of finding out?"

"Could I have done that?"

"Of course. Try it on a few books..."

"Your searchlight seems to me to be somewhat indiscreet, then."

"Not at all. We only want to know things that are good and just, as we are."

"That's true."

"You understand, then, how we know the works that are published, and even those, good in themselves, that publishers reject and which remain in manuscript."

"What! Are the published on the Moon?"

"Undoubtedly, from the moment they merit it."

"*O fortunatos nimium sua si bona norint!*"[30]

"As soon as a work appears, our apparatus functions."

"You have printing-presses, then?"

"We each have at our disposal a sequence of letters, nothing more, which position themselves so as to print on large white satined sheet that we appropriate from a magnificent tree, as rapidly as we can read, no matter what people or language the works belong."

"But isn't that plagiarism?"

"No, it's counterfeiting at most. I deem that in acting thus we do honor to the geniuses of Earth."

"After all, if the authors were dissatisfied, I imagine you'd give them the right to sue you?"

"Yes, certainly."

---

[30] The author does not bother to credit this line of Virgil's *Georgics* (II, 458-459), the original of which adds the word *Agricolas* [field-workers]. Roughly translated, it means "[Field-workers] would be too happy if they were aware of their happiness!"

"Your libraries must be enormously voluminous, though?"

"From the famous library on the fronton of which the Pharaoh Ozymandias wrote: *Treasure of remedies for the soul*, to that of Alexandria which was burned by Julius Caesar; from the minimal library of Charles V, comprised of only nine hundred and fifty volumes, assembled with difficulty and pompously placed in a tower in the Louvre, to that which is flaunted in the Rue Richelieu in your Paris, there has not been a single book published in China, Holland, Europe, the world, by Elzévir or Barbou, Étienne or Didot,[31] that we have not placed in our lunar libraries."

"In fact, there's no nobler way of banishing boredom than reading!"

"Firstly, Monsieur Frenchman, we don't get bored," Stella interjected, in a piqued tone. "We don't have time for that. It's all right for you mortals, who have too much of it. Secondly, it's rare for us to read those books, very imperfect as their writers are. The books that we prefer are those of Heaven. Those always tell us new things and entertain us constantly with marvels."

"But, as well as your libraries enclosing the treasures of the human mind..."

"The human mind!" said Stella, accompanying the words with her strident mocking laughter.

"Besides which," Mikaël went on, "we have the museums that my daughter mentioned to you. Those museums bear no resemblance to yours. They reproduce..."

"Not the treasures of the human mind," said Stella, "but the follies, the anger, the turpitude and the shame of human history..."

---

[31] Abraham Elzévir, Jean Barnou, Henri Étienne and Firmin Didot were among the most important pioneers of the printed book.

"We'll talk about that when the time comes," Mikaël concluded. "At present, we're approaching the Moon, and it's as well to initiate our host in the things he will see."

"And fortify him with the aid of liquor drawn from the spring that flows beneath the aloes and liquidambars of our meadows," Stella added.

At the same time, the young Lunian presented to me, in a golden cup decorated with magnificent pearls, a beverage as white as frost and more odorous than a rose.

"You're trying to prove to me," I said, accepting the cup, "that in all regions on all worlds, at all latitudes and all longitudes, woman is always the most charitable of beings and the most compassionate and most tender of creatures."

I drank some of the liqueur...

Dear readers, no Constance, no Madeira, Tokay, Malaga, Xeres, Lachryma-Christi, Johannesburg, Porto or Rum of the highest quality ever produced the generous and beneficial effect that I felt. I drained the rich substance to the last drop, I confess.

After which I felt warm and courageous; I felt transformed.

"It's very sober refreshment that we've given you, my dear Terran," said Stella, "and perhaps it seems unworthy of you, for, permit me to say, you people from down below only draw enjoyment of life from the alimentation of the stomach. Truly, it's enough to make one laugh in pity and wonder whether you make a god of your belly, for you only find a dinner sumptuous if it's like those I have seen served in Paris.

"For soup, you require turtles in the English style, the queen of soups, clear turtle.

"As an intermediate course one sees you savoring pullets à la Toulouse, ham braised in Madeira wine, turkey with chipolatas or in Bechamel sauce, or fillet steak à la Napolitaine.

"Then come the entrées: salmi of woodcock; chicken supreme with truffles; lamb cutlets with asparagus tips; timbale of macaroni à la Milanaise; warm pâtés of *mauviettes à la financière.*[32]

"And for roasts, there are ducklings, pheasants and teal.

"All the desserts are mixed together: orange jelly, apple charlottes, coffee-favored Bavarian pastries, meringues, butter sauce, Viennese maraschino cherry gateaux, fruit salad, pineapples, shrimps on pedestals, mayonnaises, chestnut puddings with apricot, Polish rum babas."

"In truth, Mademoiselle Stella, you're making my mouth water, and I confess that if, at this moment, I had at my disposal the thirtieth part of the delicious things that…"

"Shut up, old chap," said Mikaël, sharply. "With your cuisine, you're running more rapidly to your death—that's your history. Listen to my advice for a moment, and take note of it.

"You often have grand dinners, but you rarely have good ones. Your repasts generally lead you to gall-stones, gout, obesity and apoplexy. At first glance, nothing in more tolerant that that vast pocket called a stomach, of which you make a gulf where food is piled up—but in reality, there's nothing less obliging.

"Your most skillful chefs are mere food-spoilers, so indigestible do they make the frightful salmagundis of aliments that they poor into your esophagus like corrosive molten lead. Only the stomach of an ostrich could cope with the infernal amalgam that you swallow.

"Believe me, my dear Terran, if you sometimes pose as an Amphitryon, if you value the health of your guests, and your own, if you want the reputation of a man of good taste, firstly, and above all, don't pile everything up, don't pack people like sardines into a room that is too small, which might

---

[32] André Viand's classic work *Le Cuisinier royal* [The Royal Cookbook] (1822) includes recipes for *cailles à la financière* (quail with minced cockscombs and mushrooms, including truffles, in a Madeira sauce) and *mauviettes en croutarde* (skylarks in pastry); Driou appears to have hybridized the two.

routinely accommodate a dozen but can never expand its capacity to twenty. Prepare comfortable heating and refrain from scorching the air with the fire of lamps that absorb all the oxygen in the room by themselves. Illuminate it with elegant candelabras crowned with constellations of candles; and group flowers and fruits, delicate confectionary and dainty cakes, on the finest Saxe linen. Have servants perfectly dressed, after which: *Doors open!* and, my noble cavaliers, introduce your ladies.

"Away with glutinous tapioca, and the intolerable *julienne*. Present the most fragrant soup, and let it show, floating on its surface, a few grains of sago tinted with a furtive aroma of Constantinople saffron.

"Then, tuck into a fine salmon trout, sleeping on a bed of carp roe, half-steeped in an exquisitely-flavored *coulis*. Then, have a fillet of roe deer cooked in pastry, reposing on a hash of truffles and morel, sprinkled with an unparalleled *jus*. Surround these principal dishes with a few salmis, fresh sorbets, with an abundant flow of sherry, an old bottle of vintage Pommard, and sparkling champagne.

"Finally, bring on a Mans pullet, richly truffled; and as truffle can have no rival, and everything seems insipid thereafter, let a delicate Châteaubriand serve on its own as the transition between the truffle and dessert. Let a Bordeaux finish off the work of art, and after a glass of Constance, let the Mocha make its entrance—and then you'll have a dinner."

"Your eloquence is persuasive, my dear Lunian, and the logic of your language places me among your adepts. Truly, Carême[33] and Chevet are mere dabblers compared with you."

---

[33] Marie-Antoine Carême was known as "the king of chefs and the chef of kings." The modern reader might well have difficulty making the clear distinction between the supposedly over-fancy menus credited to such celebrities and the allegedly simple dinner outlined by Mikaël that the author evidently expects; we can only speculate as to what kind of fare Driou

"Say poisoners—for, admit, when you emerge from your ostentatious repast, does not the food on which you have gorged howl in protest at being confused in the same recipient, your stomach? So, sated like a boa constrictor, do you not long for sleep—a heavy and perfidious sleep—and, the next day, on waking up, do you not feel your mind obtuse, your heart sad and your soul peevish?"

"Lord Mikaël, I swear that I shall no longer live to eat, but I shall eat to live. Except, let's cease our culinary dialogue, for here's the Moon."

---

had become accustomed to while in holy orders, or what his opinion might have been of modern "junk food."

III

I remember that as a child—and who does not have that sweet memory?—I spent entire hours contemplating the Moon. I saw a human face therein, and then the image of Ocean and land, as if by reflection in a mirror. Then, my old governess told me boring stories, which nevertheless kept my young imagination awake, and soon sent me running to my mother as to a sacred refuge.

When I grew up, I studied astronomy; I observed the stars; I lingered for preference on the Moon. My sympathy for it caused me to examine it with sustained attention. I read everything related to it. Satellite of Earth and, after the Sun, the most remarkable of all the heavenly bodies, I knew that it described an ellipse in space of which our planet occupied one of the foci. My professor explained that the extremity of the long axis of that ellipse closest to the Earth was called the perigee, the opposite extremity the apogee, also designated by the name apsides.

In addition to its diurnal movement, I recognized that it had a proper movement that tended in the opposite direction, the former being from east to west and the latter from west to east. That second movement being thirteen degrees per day, it was demonstrated to me that it completes its revolution around the sky in twenty-seven days, seven hours and a few minutes, and in relation to the Sun, in twenty-nine and a half days. I had learned very rapidly that the various appearances of its light, during that time span, were called phases.

Thus, after having disappeared for a few days in the Sun's rays, when it passed in front of that star, the Moon begins to show itself in the evening to the west, shortly after sunset, in the form of a thread of light shaped like a bow, which is called a crescent, the points of which are opposite the star. After five or six days, that crescent assumes the form of a semicircle, and the luminous part is then terminated by a straight line; that is the first quarter. At that time the Moon is said to be in quadrature.

As it draws away from the Sun, its light becomes increasingly circular, and after seven or eight days its entire disk shines all night long; that is the time of the full moon—or opposition, because it is facing the Sun relative to our Earth, which is between the two spheres. Then comes the decrease, which repeats the same phases, so that when the moon reappears in the form of a semicircle, it is in its final quarter. Then it diminishes further, its crescent becoming narrower every day, its horns being, in the inverse direction to its first appearance, still opposite the Sun. Finally, it is lost in the rays of that globe of fire—which is known as the new moon, or conjunction, because it is conjoined with the Sun.

Eclipses of the Sun revealed to me, in their turn, that the Moon is an opaque body, which has no light of its own. In fact, when the Moon is directly between the Earth and the Sun, one sees that, after having intercepted the light of the sun in broad daylight, it seems absolutely black.

I noticed quite distinctly, after the new moon, that the crescent that forms the most luminous part is accompanied by a feeble light, spread over the rest of the disk, that enables me to glimpse the roundness of the Moon. I knew that scientists called that appearance "ashen light." It was explained to me that the secondary light came from sunlight reflected by the Earth. Moreover, on positioning myself in such a fashion that a roof hid the luminous part of the moon, I found the ashen light much brighter. I was struck by another phenomenon: I mean the apparent dilatation of the luminous crescent, which seems greater in diameter than the obscure disk of the Moon. My professor gave me to understand that this came about because the intensity of a bright light placed beside a dim one effaces the lesser.

As for the heat of the satellite, it was proved to me that it had one; I even read in one scientific work that its light was three hundred thousand times less than that of the Sun, comparing both with the light of a candle placed in darkness.

It was also calculated for me that the mean distance between the Moon and the Earth is eighty thousand leagues, that it is only a fourth of size the Earth, that it always presents the same face to us, while sometimes allowing a little of its other face to show, as if it were swaying, its mass being heavier and rounder on the side facing us, while the other is flatter; that swaying is called libration.

With the aid of a telescope, I convinced myself that it had the form of a spheroid flattened toward the poles, and that it was comparable to an egg with flattened sides. I observed irregularities that seemed to me to be composed of luminous points growing as the sun reaches them, behind which dense shadows are projected. They are undoubtedly high mountains, whose summits receive the solar rays before the less elevated parts, and the dark points valleys, craters and fissures that the sun does not reach directly.

Finally, it was often repeated to me that the Moon has no detectable atmosphere, that it is deprived of seasons, given that, its axis being almost perpendicular to its ecliptic, the Sun does not depart from its equator; that one of its halves is illuminated by the Earth during the absence of the Sun, and has no night, while the other has one that lasts three hundred and sixty hours; that if one imagines lunar inhabitants, our planet would see, thirteen times larger than the Moon appears to us; that the Earth is only constantly visible for half the satellite; that the satellite has a burned appearance, presenting manifest traces of ancient volcanic upheavals; and, lastly, that it exercises a considerable influence on our seas, whose tides it causes, when the Earth is placed between it and the Sun.

Then again, as a dedicated lover of the phenomena of nature, I had already seen a few eclipses and studied them. Thus, that was no longer any mystery for me, since I knew that, the Earth and the Moon being opaque bodies, every time one of the two planets places itself in front of the other with the sun behind, the latter will be covered by a more or less profound obscurity, and will experience an eclipse—for, whenever the Earth occupies a point of the interval that separates the Moon from the Sun, when it is in opposition, if the former penetrates the shadow that the Earth projects, it cease to be illuminated and is, in consequence, in eclipse. If, on the other hand, it is the Moon that assumes the position we have just described relative to the Earth, we shall cease to see the Sun; it will be eclipsed. It is easy to understand, however, that such a phenomenon can only occur when the Moon is new.

It should not be concluded, however, that when the Moon is in opposition or conjunction, the points of its orbits known as syzygies, there will necessarily be a lunar or solar eclipse. In that case, the Moon completing its revolution around its orbit in twenty-nine and a half days, we would have one kind of eclipse or the other every fortnight. That is not the case. Because the lunar orbit cuts the ecliptic at two points of intersection, the Moon assumes variable inclinations to that plane. Thus, if, in consequence of its various movements, it is far one of these intersections while it is in opposition to the sun, it will merely brush the terrestrial shadow without penetrating it; but if the line joining the centers of the Sun, the Earth and the Moon is the same for each body, which happens when the Moon is at the intersection or very close to it, there is a lunar eclipse. It is partial if it only penetrates the terrestrial shadow in part, total if it plunges into it entirely, and central if its center coincides exactly with that of the terrestrial shadow.

I do not regard it as necessary to say that an astronomical intersection means either of two opposite points where the ecliptic is cut by the orbit of a celestial body.

Now, the phenomena of which I speak are reproduced exactly when the Moon is interposed between the Sun and the Earth, and the various partial and total eclipses result.

A word about appulses, or close approaches. When the shadow of the Moon only brushes the edges of the shadow lightly, or by-passes it entirely, there are appulses. When the Sun, hidden by the Moon, overlaps in all directions in the form of a luminous ring, the eclipse is annular. Finally, an eclipse is called central when the observer is placed on the prolongation of a line that traverses the centers of the Moon and the Sun.

I have said that eclipses were no longer a mystery to me. I made allusion hereby to the strange beliefs of many peoples regarding the eclipsed Moon. As early as 640 B.C., Thales, among the Greeks, had already calculated the periodicity of eclipses, which show that astronomy was already surrendering its secrets; nevertheless the Hellenes attributed eclipses of the Moon to the visits rendered by Diana to Endymion in the mountains of Caria. They also believed that witches, especially those of Thessaly, could attract the Moon toward the Earth by their enchantments, and made a great racket with pots and pans in order to make it return to its place.

The Romans modified this custom slightly. When an eclipse of the Moon occurred, they lit a great many torches, raised toward the Heavens in order to recall the light of the eclipsed star. The Egyptians had a similar custom, honoring the goddess Isis, considered as the symbol of the Moon, with a similar charivari.

Furthermore, eclipses were often a considerable resource for learned men. Thus, Drusus, according to Tacitus, made use of an eclipse to calm sedition in his army. When Cyaxares, the king of Persia, attacked the Lydians the two armies were about to engage in hand-to-hand combat when day suddenly changed to night and the frightened soldiers stopped; Cyaxares reassured his men and won the victory. The Thessalians, oppressed by Alexander of Pherae, implored Thebes for help, which sent Pelopidas with an army. At the moment of departure, however, an eclipse of the Sun frightened the soldiers so badly that the majority refused to leave. Pelopidas explained the phenomenon, and the expedition set out. Christopher Columbus, among the savage peoples, took advantage of the terror of the indigenes to the benefit of his fleet. I shall pass over other and better examples.

It is, in fact, appropriate that eclipses should generate fear, as profound darkness abruptly covers all the points on the Earth attained by the Mon's shadow. The stars reveal themselves as during the night. Animals immediately become terrified and seek shelter. Dogs howl, bulls bellow, elephants trumpet on the savannah, tigers roar in the desert, wild boar grunt in our woods, eagles screech on mountain summits. Then silence falls; a great silence succeeds these cries, the winds that blow, the agitation of the trees, the plaints of nature. Then one sees around the Moon a kind of pale light that is believed to be the Sun's atmosphere. The name penumbra is given to that intermediate state between light and pure shadow. Then the eclipse begins to decrease and the first ray of sunlight, launched like an arrow, dissipates the gloom. That is a solar eclipse.

For eclipses of the Moon, produced by the shadow of the Earth placed between the Sun and its disk, when it begins to show a curved line imprinted in black on its surface, that first movement is called immersion. Then the eclipse becomes more of less pronounced. When it is total, it lasts little more than five minutes. When the end of the eclipse approaches, that is emersion.

Eclipses of the Moon are visible from all points of the hemisphere that have the Moon above the horizon when they occur. Civilized people admire them but barbaric peoples, like those of antiquity, still fear them. The Mexicans fast during eclipses, and their women maltreat one another, in the belief that the Moon has been wounded by the Sun in a quarrel. It's probable that in this, the Mexicans are reasoning somewhat by analogy. The Indians believe that a malevolent dragon is trying to devour the Moon, and while some make as much noise as possible with all kinds of instruments, others, immersing themselves in water, humbly beg the dragon not to devour entirely the beautiful and melancholy planet that does our little Earth the honor of serving as its satellite. Who can ever reproduce the terrible images, the frightful stories, and the incredible terrors the Redskins experience under their wigwams during eclipses?

That is what books, the scientists and my studies told me about the Moon. Shall I tell you now what comets are? Yes. As our balloon, or rather our two balloons, rose higher, with a fearful rapidity, I soon saw a long streak of fire against the black of the sky, preceded by an enormous dot blazing with all the gleams of a conflagration.

"That's a comet you see there, my dear Terran," Mikaël told me. "I would be insulting your astronomical science if I were to tell you that comets are not what vain people think. For, as Georges de Brébeuf has said:

From a lugubrious ascendant the secret influence
Made of luminous fire a sinister comet.

"Although the movements of comets are well known to you, however, it is not the same for their physical nature. Are their nuclei opaque or transparent? Is the light of such bodies their own, or do they reflect that of the sun? What is the nature of the matter making up their tails? Why are those tails sometimes turned in one direction, sometimes another? Are comets with one tail similar in nature to those that have several? So many questions, my friend, the answers to which you could easily take back to Earth, in order to pass for a scientist of the first rank and to have the doors of the Académie opened to you. But my conscience obliges me to keep silent with respect to the secrets that God has reserved for himself."

"Or that he has abandoned to the profound studies of our mathematicians, for we have some famous ones!" I exclaimed, with cool self-assurance. "Do you know that Monsieur Le Verrier, for example, having deduced from the perturbations of the movement of Uranus that there was some heavenly body interfering with it, simply by means of calculation, without using any telescope, discovered the presence of an unknown celestial body in the vicinity of Uranus. 'Aim your telescopes at that point in the sky,' he said, 'and you'll find a planet there.' And the planet was found, and now bears the name Neptune. It's glorious, you know, for human genius to accomplish such a powerful operation and such a fine result."

"That's true, I acknowledge with pleasure, and it's for that reason that I find in humans, in spite of the degradation inflicted on them by their sin, the image of God, our creator.

What would you have been, my dear chap, if you had not been struck by the curse for your revolt against the Master of us all?"

"Alas, thrice alas!" I replied. "We would be, like you, the possessors of worlds, instead of being in exile on our poor planet, whose abode makes so many dolors felt. We would be able to follow the comets describing their closed curves around the sun, which we call ellipses, and we would know how they differ from planets, whether it is true that their globes are solid, why, sometimes more and sometimes less bright, they are always enveloped by vapors, part of which form luminous trails that we call their tresses or tails."

"And you would believe in the innocence of comets and the Moon, wouldn't you?" said Stella, "So that you would write, with Ponce Lebrun:

These disheveled comets
Which cleave the air in burning flight
Display their winged spheres
To the eyes of trembling peasants
Who dread that their fatal course
Might set fire to the celestial vault,
And destroy the universe.
But to the pensive eye of Urania
Their disorder is a harmony
Which repopulates the desert sky."

"I shall return, my poor Terran, to the grandeur of fallen humankind," said Mikaël. "I have told you that we reproduce, purely for pleasure, the great and beautiful inventions of the Earth, especially those marked with a touch of genius. Now, I confess, it's not only for our pleasure that we copy your works, but by virtue of admiration for God, who inspires you to them, and who sometimes permits humans to receive the splendid reflections of his intelligence and divine science."

"Notwithstanding their misfortune, humans are, in fact, great and sublime," asserted the young Lunian woman, standing up and raising herself to her full height. "On the day after the original curse, they received from God the arid Earth, covered with thorns and brambles, but hiding treasures and riches in its entrails. After the Deluge, they found it bare and desolate again, covered with buried rubble, sparse ruins, turned upside down by the breath of celestial wrath, hiding its mines and wealth better than ever.

"Far from being discouraged, humans raised themselves up full of ardor, intoxicated by audacity, sensing their intelligence, and ready for work. They fathomed the abysses of the Ocean, the depths of the Earth, and commenced a long series of admirable discoveries.

"Firstly, they took possession of the fleeces of sheep, striped the fur from ferocious beasts, took the silken thread from crawling worms, and utilized the blades of grass where insects moved. Then they produced dye, silk and the thousand elegant and sumptuous textiles in which the delicacy of the fabrics disputes with the grace of the design and the variety of the colors. Descending into the deepest gulfs of the Earth and valleys of the sea, they brought forth dazzling crystals, sparkling diamonds and precious metals. They found marble there and animated it. The found bronze there and gave it life. They made iron breathe; they made canvas breathe. They invented art, one of the beauties of human effort.

"Matching God, their energetic will tamed the elements and enslaved them. They combined water and fire, enemies until then, and it is marvelous to see how those formidable workers, captive in their hands, work with ardor, precision and naïve docility. Moved by them, the most ingenious machines take their power to the ultimate limit. Thus steam, has become the magical lever with which humans, a veritable Archimedes, will someday lift the world on its axis if they wish.

"Is it not the case at present that the conquered atmosphere in opening its plains to vast winged fleets? To complete their work and ensure their triumph, perhaps humans will then tame the soul of the world. Masters of electricity, they will replace our precarious subsidies with that indestructible agent.

They will doubtless apply it to everything. In infinite proportions of simplicity as of well-being, we shall see it become the light, the heat, the vehicle and the steed of its conquerors, throughout their immense domain."

"Bravo! Bravissimo!" said the Lunian in his turn. "Yes, humans will impose their yoke on the seas, using the winds for the flight of their balloons, which they will be able to steer, as our illustrious guest has proved by his recent discovery, playing with the fire that gives us steam, applying electricity to other uses, as it has provided the telegraph that follows the railways of the two worlds, they will truly become the kings, the superb kings of creation."

"I'm confused now, by the panegyric you have just made in envy of our poor humanity," I said, timidly.

"Not so," said Mikaël. "We're attributing these great things to God, their author, who inspires them in humans. Thus, from the simplest discovery to the most savant, humans have only been the instrument of the Creator, the mirror in which he reflects his power. When, in the 130th year of the world, a beautiful young woman, Noëma, the daughter of Lamech and Zillah, took from the bushes the wool that white sheep had left there in passing, and began to spin it, and invented the fabrics that clothe humans, it was God who inspired her in her work.[34]

"When Enoch, the eldest son of Cain, became the inventor of carpentry, founded the first city and gave it his name, it was God he had within him."

"It is of that city," I said, interrupting my hosts, "that it is said in a French work, *Le Monde antédiluvien*, written by a sage, Ludovic de Cailleux:[35]

---

[34] Noëma's name is sometimes rendered Naamah; the legend linking he to the first spinning of yarn comes from the Talmud.

[35] Ludovic de Cailleux's *Le Monde antédiluvien, poème biblique en prose* was published in 1845. The author had published

"'In that time, the stormy waves of giants beat the black battlements of ancient Hénochia, the daughter of the homicide.

"'The walls of the city, the color of rust, where scarred by the fires of Heaven, like towers burnished by the Inferno.

"'At the top of the ramparts, twenty-four brazen bulls turned toward the north wind.

"'In the west, the tombs of the Colossians extended beneath cedar-wood, a Golgotha of giants.

"'Before the eastern gates grew two sterile palms, with fig-trees, on a desolate lawn.

"'The desert, scorched mountains, forests, torrents, surrounded the city of Cain.'"

"That's in the Biblical style, what you just said, my dear Terran, and it's a pleasure to hear it. But I'll go on and say: in the time when Tubalcain, in 3100 B.C., discovered the use of iron and applied it to the work of humans or his pleasure in hunting, and then, on the day when, in 1500 B.C., Isis, the wife of Osiris, king of Egypt, imagined making use of it to construct a plow in order to furrow the Earth and confide seeds to it, it was God—always God, who, out of pity for humans, gave them ideas by means of which to facilitate their onerous labor."

"But wasn't it the same Isis," I stammered, "who first had the idea of navigation and had ships built?"

"Yes," the Lunian replied. "and under Necho, one of the successors of Sesostris, some of the new Egyptian ships departed from Arsinoë, doubled the Cape of Storms—now the Cape of Good Hope—came up the coast as far as the Pillars of Hercules, now Gibraltar, and returned, via the Mediterranean, to anchor in Egypt, at the mouths of the Nile.

"Then there were Phoenician navigators who went as far as Thule, the Iceland of today, in the north, and the Canary Islands in the south-west.

---

one previous book a decade before, but the signature vanished thereafter.

"Finally, the compass and the astrolabe were introduced into marine affairs, and brought about a complete revolution. It was no longer simple flat boats like the Egyptians, nor galleys with two or three banks of oars, like those of the Carthaginians and Romans, nor crude canoes like those of savages, nor light gondolas, nor coarse catamarans, as in India, nor even merchant vessels like those of the peoples of the North, but elegant and vigorous three-masters, which, under the reign of Ferdinand and Isabella, in 1492, took Spaniards to the beaches of the New World—which ought to have trembled and moaned, for the arrival of that new people in the regions of gold was the signal for the massacre of more than twelve million Peruvians, Incas and unfortunate Mexicans.

"Then, almost at the same time, under João II, King of Portugal, Bartolomeu Dias and Pêro de Alenquer doubled the Cape of Good Hope, and Vasco da Gama, the son of Emmanuel, went to conquer the Indies for his master.

"It was not enough that Christopher Columbus, via Amerigo Vespucci, his lieutenant, had discovered the new continent of America, after having found the Antilles himself; after him, Vincent Pinçon discovered Brazil.

"The Magellan's squadron, departed under Charles V in 1519, circumnavigated the world.

"Under the following reign, Spain discovered various rich and famous islands.

"In her turn, England took possession of Newfoundland, Virginia, Guiana, etc. By means of Arthur Barlow, Henry Hudson, Parry, John Davis she made every effort to find a passage into the Pacific Ocean. George Anson, Byron, Samuel Wallis, James Cook and George Vancouver continued the discoveries of those skillful navigators.[36]

---

[36] I cannot identify a sixteenth century explorer by the name of Byron; if the name Parry is a reference to Sir William Parry it is anachronistic.

"After England came Holland, which, via Olivier Van Noort, Pieter Nuyts and Abel Tasman discovered Van Diemen's Land.

"Finally, Russia, too, sent Adam von Krusenstern and Otto von Kotzebue into unexplored regions."

"Have you nothing to say about France then?" I hazarded.

"It's to give you greater pleasure, my Terran friend, that I've left the French for last, because in this, as in so many other things, they have been the most ardent and the most devoted. Thus, between Jacques Cartier, who went up the Saint Lawrence river in 1554 and thus opened the way to the beautiful colony of Canada, and modern times, one can count Louis-Antoine de Bougainville, Louis-Thomas Chabert, the Comte de Fleurieu, Jean-Charles Borda, the inventor of the circle of that name,[37] and then La Pérouse, Antoine Bruni d'Entrecasteaux, Paul de Rossel, Charles-François Beautemps-Beaupré, Charles Baudin, Jacques Hamelin, Milluis,[38] Louis and Charles de Saulces de Freycinet, Marie-Jules Dupré, Louis Legoarant de Tromelin and Dumont d'Urville, so deplorably killed by fire on the Versailles railway in 1844."

"You see," Stella put in, "when Horace said, in talking about the navigator of his time: *Illi robur et oes triplex, Circa pecus erat,*[39] etc. he was certainly far from rendering all that was audacious and great in his view, or, rather, in the contemplation of one of your vessels under sail, that enormous mass floating like a plaything, and the will of a human being, and carrying the abridgement of the world as far as the world's limits. But it's in storms most of all that all the genius and

---

[37] This subsidiary reference is unclear, but probably refers to the fact that Borda measured the meridian that helped establish the length of the meter.

[38] I cannot identify a French navigator of this name.

[39] "There was oak and a triple layer of bronze around the heart [of the man whom first launched a frail craft upon the wild open sea]."

power of the mariner reaches its finest development. It seems then that the vessel, impatient to use the movement and life given to it, is ready to share with humans the efforts of the struggle that they must sustain against all the elements. How it stirs, how it shivers beneath the first blasts of the wind and the sea! How proudly it rears up under the first squalls that attempt to defeat it! And when the tempest is at full force, how rapidly it obeys the slightest impulsions communicated to it by the tiller, or the smallest shred of sail! One might think that it understands that it is on the promptness and docility of its movements that its salvation depends, and that of the humans who have confided their destiny to it."

"In addition," I replied, "one cannot conceive of the sympathetic and mysterious relationship established at sea between the mariner and his ship. The former is often prouder of the elegance and bearing of the latter than of his own. They are united by a solidarity of interests; they call one another by the same name; they are like two parts of the same whole. It is, in sum, a kind of double life, which continual hazards, the picturesque quality of navigation and the majesty of the sea often fill, for the mariner, with a poetry of which someone who has never sailed cannot have any idea."

"After serious things," Mikaël went on, "humans, by way of relaxation, apply the faculties of the mind to matters of pleasure, but which nevertheless display all the talents they have. In 1420 B.C. a famous artist by the names of Daedalus, who was Greek, imagined the saw and set about making automata, statues with springs, which walked, talked and sang as well as being endowed with intelligence and life."

"From automata to clocks was a short step," said Stella. "Nevertheless, a long time went by between the first invention and the second. It was under the reign of Charlemagne, one of your great kings, that the astonishing marvel of a clock was seen in France. It was sent to that prince by the famous Caliph of Bagdad, Haroun al-Rashid. It was made of brass, and marked the hours by means of twelve little horsemen who opened and closed twelve doors, and throwing little brass balls at a bell, which thus sounded the hours."

"That reminds me," I said, daring to interrupt Stella, "that in Sweden, at Lunden, I saw a clock so singularly designed that to divide up the time, two knights came together and gave one another as many blows as there were hours to chime. As soon as they had finished, a door opened and one saw an enthroned Virgin Mary appear, holding the infant Jesus in her arms. Then the Mage Kings came to adore him and offer hi their presents. Two trumpets sounded at the same time. Then the entire apparatus was concealed, to reappear an hour later."

"You must be less surprised by that work of art than that of the astronomical clock of Strasbourg?" the Lunian asked. "As a Frenchman, you must be familiar with it. Nothing is as curious as Death sounding the hours, the cockerel crowing that it is always necessary to be awake, and the thousand relative indications of the movements of the spheres, with golden numbers, epacts, etc."

"I have, indeed, admitted it greatly," I replied, "for I've had the pleasure of seeing and hearing it, as well as the magnificent clock in Louis XIV's apartment in the Château of Versailles, the Jacquemarts[40] of Dijon and the very ingenious clocks of Belgium."

"Enough on that topic," said Stella. "Let's not engender monotony, and pass on to the organ.

"The bell, the first harmony of your churches, was invented in the time of Clovis, who made a gift to Paris of the first bell that city had possessed. It was about 500 A.D.

"Since then, all the churches in the world have been provided with them, and that's fortunate, for, as Vicomte Joseph Walsh said, in a sublime book that is a hymn to Christianity: 'The rope that hangs down beneath the porch is the conductor

---

[40] Jacquemarts are bell-striking automata simulating human form; the couple on the bell of Dijon cathedral are among the oldest.

with which the indifferent hand of the ringer spreads joy or sadness through the countryside; with it he will awaken, in the heights of the tower or the steeple, the silently sleeping bell.

"'Immediately, it raises its sonorous voice: sometime slow and vibrant, three times, in the midst of the nascent light of dawn, it sounds the Angelus, and that first voice of the Earth, that first sigh after the repose of the night, says to those who are sleeping beneath silken sheets, and to those who lie on hard beds: *The day is beginning; lift your souls to God!*

'And, when the light dies, when the shadows descend from the sky, it says again: *Here comes the hour of rest; here comes the night with all its stars; weary humans, rejoice, and bless thee one to whom you prayed this morning!*'"

"Those words are holy, Mademoiselle," I said to the Lunian woman. "Since you like sacred poetry, especially when you think about religious matters, let me remind you of these beautiful verses by Augustin Devoille:

Bell that is swinging
At the top of the tower,
Voice of Heaven launched forth
With the voices of day,
To my soul that prays,
Speak of the homeland.
Of hope and of love!"

"My dear child," said Mikaël to his daughter, "you spoke too lightly just now in attributing the invention of the bell to the time of Clovis. The bell became known to the Gauls of that era, yes, but it had been invented long before by the Egyptians."

"That's true," said Stella, who wanted to redeem her error. "The Egyptians even claimed to have possessed a bell that Noah himself had founded, on the orders of God. The Athenians made use of bells to summon people to the festivals of Proserpine and Cybele. The Romans used the sound of bells to indicate the hour in baths and markets. Among the Hebrews, the robe of the high priest was garnished with a fringe of golden bells."

"Nevertheless," Mikaël went on, "it was in Italy that the invention of the church bell, such as we know it today, took place. In the year 400 A.D., the first church bell with a batten and funnel, crowned with a drop-hammer, was founded at Nole in Campania, from which comes the word 'campanile,' which means bell-tower.

"In 659, when Clotaire besieged Orléans, Saint Loup, the bishop of that town, had the bells of the Église Saint-Étienne rung. The Frankish soldiers were so frightened that they fled, and Clotaire was obliged to lift the siege."

"Our largest bells of the seventeenth century," I added, "were the Emmanuel, in Paris, weighing thirty-one thousand, and Georges d'Amboise in Rouen, which counted thirty-three.[41] The Kremlin, the palace of the tsars in Moscow, lost one in the fire of 1814 that weighted two hundred and forty thousand kilograms."

"Anne de Bretagne," said Stella, "passing through Chartres one day, heard a child in the choir whose voice and song surprised her. She asked the canons to let her take him away with her. 'Gentlemen,' the queen said to them, 'I don't want you to lose by it. Instead of a little silvery and piping voice, I promise you one that will make itself heard for five leagues around.' The wife of Louis XII kept her word, and Chartres Cathedral was glorified by having the most sonorous and beautiful bell of all the cities in the region."

"I believe you wanted to talk to us about organs, my dear daughter," said Mikaël, ironically, "but I see we're far from that topic."

"Not at all," Stella replied. "Are not bells and organs sisters?"

---

[41] This reference, from which some words appear to have been accidentally omitted, probably refers to the bell in the Butter Tower of Rouen Cathedral, the building of which Cardinal Georges d'Amboise financed.

"That's true," I hastened to say, "and it's to organs, even more than to bells, that we owe the beauty, the solemnity and the pomp of our religious solemnities. I've heard it said that the first organ we had in France was sent to Pépin the Short in 757 by the Emperor Constantine Copronymus. Since then, music has been cultivated—which, however, made little progress until Louis XIV..."

"I must interrupt you, my dear Terran, to tell you that the organ does not go back to the seventh century, as you imply. In the most remote centuries there was an analogous instrument to the organum: the syrinx, or the Panpipes, the mythological origin of which testifies to its great antiquity.

"Pindar, in his twelfth Pythian Ode, attributed to Minerva the invention of an instrument with which she attempted to reproduce the lugubrious screams of the Gorgon at the moment that Perseus exterminated her, and the hissing of the serpents that surrounded her head. The ode is addressed to Midas of Agrigente, skillful on that instrument and a victor in his art at the Pythian games. Pindar's commentary adds that an accident occurred while Midas of Agrigente was playing the instrument, obliging him to invert it and play it with the pipes alone in the manner of the syrinx. Now, an inverted syrinx is nothing but an organ.

"A few centuries after Pindar, Ctesibius of Alexandria applied discoveries made in hydrodynamics to the organ. The organ then, instead of remaining a wind instrument, took the name of *hydraulus*. In that epoch, it had the form of a small altar. The power and beauty of its sounds, as well as the complication of its mechanism, made an object of study for famous mathematicians. Those organs—I have seen them—were constructed in such a way that the pressure of the air in the pipes was replaced by the impulsion of water.

"It was in the fifth century that the pneumatic organ was invented. The Emperor Julian, the stigmatized Apostate, said in one of his epigrams: 'I see here an entirely new kind of pipe; they have taken root in a soil of bronze. Their loud sounds are not produced by our breath, but he wind, launched by an antrum formed of bull-skin, penetrates into all its conduits, while a skillful artist parades his agile fingers over the corresponding keys and immediately produces the most melodious sounds.'"

"Cornelius Severus," Stella interjected, "wrote a poem on Etna, before the era of Augustus, and compared the effect of the water that drives the air in the cavities of the earth to that of the hydraulic organ, the powerful sounds of which filled the vast arenas of theaters, according to my father, who has heard them."

"Yes," Mikaël replied, "for the gladiators and athletes competed to the sounds of the hydraulus. Nero, the terrible Nero, vowed to make himself heard on that instrument, if he escaped a danger that was threatening him.

"Then, in the fourth, fifth and sixth centuries, the organ was known and cultivated on the banks of the Jordan, in the north of Italy, in the heart of Gaul—everywhere, in fact, where Rome had brought its luxury and its festivals. Theodoretus, Cassiodorus, Saint Augustine and Saint Isidore were all familiar with the pneumatic organ.

In Jerusalem, in the time of Saint Jerome, I saw an organ that counted no less than twelve sets of bellows, and could be heard at a distance of a thousand paces. It was with the aid of my golden cornet that I was able to collect its sounds. They were admirable."

"You have a cornet, then, for hearing things on the Earth and in other worlds, as you have a searchlight for seeing?" I asked.

"Absolutely," Mikaël replied. "and it's this same ring, the bezel of which serves as a telescope and the funnel of the cornet. If necessary, I'll let you try it out. But let's get back to the organ. In the time of Ammien Marcellin so much time was devoted to the study of the instrument that the illustrious man made bitter complaints in his works about the abandonment of the sciences. In the same vein, Sidoine Apollinaire praised Theodoric for not admitting one into his palace."

"In what epoch, then, was the organ introduced into our churches?" I asked Mikaël.

"The entirely profane usage made of the organ until the seventh century had prevented Christians from admitting it into heir temples, but once the festivals and spectacles of paganism had disappeared, along with its divinities, organs were transported into Christian basilicas."

"So Venantius Fortunatus, in his verses to the clergy of Paris," said Stella, "listed the organ among the number of instruments of which use was made to accompany the voice—but its employment in churches was not solemnly consecrated until 660, n a decree by Pope Vitalian. The first celebrated organist was Francisco Landino, nicknamed Cicco, because he was blind. He was organist in Venice in 1340.

"Squarcia Lupo, in Florence in 1430; Antonio Degli Organi; Alessandro Milleville, a French organist who followed Duchesse Renée de France, the daughter of Louis XII, to Italy; Francisco de Correa d'Aranxo of Seville; Bernard Schmitt, also in Venice; and finally John Bull, Queen Elizabeth's organist, were the most celebrated artists whose names remain to us."

"But I've read somewhere," I said in my turn, "that in the seventeenth century, a certain Girolamo Frescobaldi flourished in Rome as organist at Saint Peter's. According to Giuseppe Baini, thirty thousand listeners assembled in that basilica when Frescobaldi played there."

"He was indeed a maestro of the first order," Mikaël replied. "We possess fugues and toccatas by him that are regarded as masterpieces of science. Along with Bach, Handel, Mozart, Haydn, Nicolas Isouard, alias Nicolo, Étienne Mehul, André Grétry and François Boïeldieu, who were illustrious organists, one might add Adolphe Adam, Louis Niedermayer, François Monpou, Sigismund Neukomm, Féris[42] and Charles-Alexandre Fessy, who produced marvels on that admirable instrument.

---

[42] I cannot identify an organist of this name.

"I will add, to conclude, that the greatest known organs are those of Saint Sulpice in Paris, Saint Paul's in London, Beauvais, Caen, Friburg and Harlem."

"Now, as a woman, I shall take the floor to praise the admirable discovery of silk. The worms that produce it, so charmless to the eye and so precious for their gilded cocoons, were introduced to Europe in about 552. Two Persian monks, after a long sojourn in China, stole the eggs of the worms, which they transported in a hollow staff. Having arrived in the climate of Europe they were made to hatch with the aid of the warmth of a dung-heap. Then, Comte Roger, the first king of Sicily, having sacked several villages in Greece that were already celebrated for their silk factories, brought a great many workers to Palermo. Soon, the art of silk-making spread throughout Italy, Venice, Milan and Florence. Lucques became abruptly famous for the new discovery. It was in the thirteenth century that the magnificent art was brought to Avignon. Finally, in 1480, under Louis XI, Greeks, Venetians and Genoese established considerable factories at Tours, in exchange for great privileges."

"So it's to monks," I exclaimed, "and I congratulate them, that a good half of the human race owes the splendid fabrics of which they are so fond and which they seek so keenly! Our ladies of France, Mademoiselle, are less modest than you; they are not content with white fabrics; they require a mixture of colors, and, on that point, unfortunately, luxury is overly prodigious; for, in order to dress a mortal body, quite frankly, at present, people go to mad and ridiculous expense..."

"Then there is definitely good in Terrans," said Mikaël. "I hope that our fortuitous meeting will bring further advantage to the honor of life and the wisdom of the soul."

"This voyage will be very useful to me," I exclaimed. "I shall obtain an immense profit from it. The good inspiration that I shall have drawn from you, will be my compass."

"Compass!" the young Lunian woman put in. "Do you know, Monsieur Terran, that that is another one of your beautiful inventions?"

"It doesn't belong to the French," Mikaël interjected. "It was the crusaders who made that precious instrument know in Europe. The Chinese had revealed the discovery to the Arabs, and the Arabs gave it to you. The ancients had a few vague notions about the property by which magnets attracted iron, but polarity was unknown to them. Tell me, is it not marvelous that a magnetized needle possessed of the faculty of always turning toward the poles guides ships from one hemisphere to the other, and indicates to mariners a certain route over the liquid plain?"

"It was Flavio Gioja," said Stella, "who, in 1303, created the veritable compass, such as you have it now. Gioja was from Naples, but Portugal made a contribution to that great achievement. A Portuguese divided the compass rose into thirty-two sectors, collectively forming the three hundred and sixty degrees of the horizon, and thus the compass was perfected."

"You are reforming my ideas on many subjects, my dear Masters," I said, addressing myself preferentially to Mikaël, "that, the question being the discoveries of human genius, I shall ask you for the truth regarding the history of gunpowder.

"So many ridiculous tales are told in France, and doubtless elsewhere also, about the origins of gunpowder—among historians, some attribute the discovery to Roger Bacon, others to the monk Berthold Schwartz—that your account of this matter will be singularly precious and profitable to me."

"If you ask me, my dear chap, who was the inventor of gunpowder, I will reply to you with the question, who invented chimneys?" Mikaël replied. "No one discovered gunpowder, my poor Terran, or, if you wish, it was you...and everyone else...

"At all times, has it not, war has had recourse to fire as one of the most terrible means of attack? Thus, there has been Greek fire, which the besiegers and the besieged launched with the aid of long tubes or attached to arrows or darts. Every epoch and every people, seeking to perfect their incendiary mixtures, slow but successive improvements were revealed, and the explosive properties of these mixtures and their force of projection were discovered. Thus, after several centuries of effort and experiment, that terrible agent was eventually created which, by displacing brutal force within armies, completely changed the art of war.

"After the taking of Constantinople by the crusaders in 1204, Greek fire passed from the Greeks to the Arabs. Besides, the Arabs had learned from the Chinese to mix saltpeter with sulfur and carbon. That resulted in a powder, but the powder fused and did not detonate, because of the impurity of the saltpeter. Soon, in the fourteenth century, having purified the raw material better, not only did the powder cause an explosion, but one could use it to launch projectiles."

"Then it's to the Arabs that we owe the discovery that changed military tactics completely?" I asked.

"As you say," Mikaël added. "And what proves it is that in an Arabic manuscript taken from the library at Saint Petersburg, a description of firearms can be found. So much for Terran authors. For us, however, as witnesses of events, I will say that the Arabs reduced their fighting compound of carbon and sulfur to a fine powder, with which they filled a third of an iron tube named a madfaa. To compress the powder, which you call tamping, they had another madfaa of wood connected to the iron madfaa. After that, adding to the charge either a bondoc or an arrow, they set fire to the primer, and woe to the enemy!"[43]

"And since then, farewell to helmets, breastplates, coats of mail, am-bands, thigh-bands, etc.," I said.

---

[43] The esoteric terms permit the determination that this passage is copied, almost word for word, from Louis Figuier's *Histoire des principales découvertes scientifiques modernes* (1851), from which many other data in this chapter also seem to be borrowed. A bondoc is a primitive cannonball.

"As bastions also fell and were replaced by ramparts," Mikaël continued. "For soon, Arabic madfaas developed into bombards, which hurled large stones that smashed buildings as they fell and ruined exterior defenses. At Robecque, at Crécy, at Calais in 1347 you French had artillery. In 1348 Brive-la-Gaillarde was defended by five cannons. Then, after Crécy, where there were one a few firepots, they began to appear in hundreds. Thus, Olivier de Clisson and Bertrand Du Guesclin were able to repel the English at Saint-Malo, aided by four hundred cannon. The army of the Duc d'Orléans, under Charles VI, had no less than four thousand cannon or culverins. Ten thousand culverins were in the service of the Swiss army when, in 1746, it won the bloody victory of Morat against Charles the Bold."

"Who was Berthold Schwartz, then?" I asked, impatiently.

"Berthold Schwartz was a Franciscan resident in Friburg. In 1378, having gone to Venice, he talked about improvements that he had thought of making to firepots. In fact, the year 1380 saw his artillery employed at the siege of Chiozza. To reward him, the Venetians put Schwartz in prison. It is even claimed that Emperor Wenceslas, to punish him for his talent for making firearms more terrible, made him sit on a barrel of powder that was ignited..."

"But you must know whether that is true, my dear Lunian?" I objected, impulsively.

"Mark my words, old chap, "Mikaël replied. "When cannon of all kinds are talking and smashing things up, one sees nothing but fire!"

"Well, let's leave gunpowder in its arsenals, my dear Lunian," I went on, "and let's talk momentarily about another invention that has made as much noise as that of powder."

"You're talking about the printing-press, aren't you?" said Mikaël. "You had said goodbye a long time ago to the wax tablets that the ancients used, and the fine papyrus of the Nile, so usefully employed for several centuries, for which vellum was initially substituted and then hemp paper, devised at Nuremburg in 1319, when there was talk, around 1440, of a mysterious, astonishing, sublime invention that was going to change the world. That was in Mayence. A man by the name of Gutenberg, after many fruitless trials, had succeeded in putting movable characters to work, each of which, employed thousands of times, reproduced human thought in such a manner as to make it known to all."

"The printing-press had been invented!" I murmured.

"Yes," said the worthy Lunian, with a sigh. "It was to render marvelous service to science, letters, arts, society, the world!"

"And sow tempests," Stella added, "and spread calamities without number, and offer itself as an alembic for the poison of evil doctrines."

"Oh, the more civilized nations become, the more enlightenment spring from contact with other enlightenments," I added. "Thus we progressed toward the great discovery of steam."

"First, my friend you're mistaken; people already had notions regarding steam a hundred and twenty years before Christ. A Greek in Alexandria, Heron, after having written a little treatise called *Spiritalia*, had invented and constructed the first steam engine. The one Heron made was no more than a toy, it's true—but in the final analysis, the invention was made and the idea found.

"Then again, you Frenchmen are convinced that only your own time has value, and you cast disdain on the times preceding it. You're wrong, Monsieur; know that in France, in Paris, in 1605 or thereabouts, one of Henri IV's gentlemen, Florence Rivaut, who was Louis XIII's tutor, used steam in applying it to bombs filled with hot water.

"Learn too, Monseigneur Terran, that a revolution was brought about in the sciences under the great knowledge of Francis Bacon, in England, René Descartes, in France, and Galileo, in Italy. All minds were extended toward new things. Luther had broken the religious brake, the political brake was shaken. Then those three heroes of intelligence surged on to the world's stage, who revealed the secrets of wisdom and of celestial mechanics.

"Then Salomon de Caus wrote about motive forces, among the number of which he placed heated water; then Père Leurechon, a Jesuit from Lorraine, invented aeolipiles: windmills turned by the motive power of steam; then Giovanni Branca, Bishop John Wilkins, and Père Athanasius Kircher wrote about steam and its properties.

"Finally, after the discovery of the barometer by Evangelista Torricelli, and of the weight of the air by Blaise Pascal, came Denis Papin, born at Blois in 1647. That hard-working man first wrote about vacuum and the machines that produced it; then he invent the machine known as Papin's pressure-cooker, which he soon furnished with a safety-valve. From there to steam engines was only a short step, and Denis Papin, aided by the machines of Thomas Savery and Thomas Newcomen, took the step that would lead to such great consequences in the world.[44]

"Then the Marquis de Jouffroy d'Abbans carried out the first trials of navigation by steam power. At the same time, experiments were made on the river Doubs with a web-footed apparatus; then came the paddle-wheeled boats, tested at Lyon under the guidance on the same Marquis de Jouffroy. This Jouffroy was a young gentleman from Franche-Comté, who went from Provence to Paris, where he launched his career in science. Exile from Provence, forced on him by an affair of honor with the colonel of his regiment, had been profitable for

---

[44] What Driou, as a good Catholic, fails to mention here is that Papin, as a Huguenot, was exiled from his homeland. While taking temporary refuge in England, the presentations he made to the Royal Society, in the presence of James Watt, effectively handed the invention, and the lion's share of the early wealth it was to generate, to the English, while Papin went to die in abject poverty in the Netherlands. Thus France threw away the chance of technological and economic hegemony, for the sake of religious bigotry.

him, because he prepared for his work on steamboats by is studies of galleys.

"But the trials of John Fitch and James Rumsey in America, then those of the Irishman Robert Fulton—who, born in America, came to France in 1796 and navigated a boat on the Seine in the presence of the Académie and the whole population of the great city—considerably advanced the progress of the noble discovery, but the indifference of the government of the time held it back.

"Better supported in the United States, Fulton finally produced navigation by steam power. New York and Albany are two cities situated on the banks of the Hudson, sixty leagues apart. Fulton's steamboat, the *Clermont*, made the journey in thirty-two hours, and returned in thirty."

"That was a veritable triumph!" I said.

"What was an even greater one, my dear Terran," Mikaël continued, "after the emission of the first ideas about steam locomotion, thrown into the scientific world by Denis Papin; after the consecration of the steam-pump by Savery and Newcomen to the expulsion of water from coal mines; after the accomplishment of a revolution in the mechanism of steam engines by James Watt, was the adaptation of steam to vehicles, under the inspiration of William Robertson of Glasgow; then the terrestrial locomotive of the Frenchman Joseph Cugnot; then that of Oliver Evans; and finally Richard Trevithick's steam-carriage."

"To make that kind of apparatus maneuver more easily," I hazarded, "didn't they think of using artificial grooves, then wooden rails, and finally iron rails?"

"Yes, my dear Terran; it was thus that the magnificent discovery was completed, of which you are doubtless proud on your planet, but which your unfortunate condemnation allows to be accompanied by more serious dangers."

"Alas, events prove that only too well!" said Stella, who had been silent for some time. "It's understandable, moreover. To obtain the steam in such a way as to be in continuous usage, it's necessary to heat the water that serves to produce it in closed vessels, against the walls of which the elastic force acts continuously, with increasing energy as the water is raised to a higher temperature. Now, it sometimes happens that the substance forming the receptacle proves too weak to resist the pressure on its walls, and is forced to give way; an explosion takes place, and the debris of the vessel, violently propelled by the elastic force of the steam, knocking down and destroying everything in its passage as it disperses."

"Fortunately," I objected, "the invention of the safety-valve prevents these terrible accidents. These valves, which are obliged to open when the steam has acquired sufficient force to cause an explosion, allow the vapor to escape—which, reducing the pressure on the interior wall of the boiler, relieves the danger of explosion, at least for the moment."

"And in spite of these precautions, and many others, my poor Terran," Mikaël exclaimed, "you know how many sinister pages the chapter of accidents already contains. All your lines to Bordeaux, Nantes, Lyon, Rouen and Versailles have already donned mourning many time over—and that's just France. If we count the misfortunes that have occurred in England, in America, and everywhere else, what lugubrious tales we would have to tell!"

"So let's leave the tears of Earth," said Stella, "and, while still occupying ourselves with that planet, let's talk about its progress in the sciences..." The beautiful Lunian continued: "Would you believe that rumor has reached us regarding troublesome prejudices on the part of certain inhabitants of a few French provinces. The Champenois are notorious for their lack of intelligence and imagination—but one of your beautiful discoveries has given the lie to your popular prejudices, Messire le Parisien. Philippe Lebon was Champenois, for he was born at Brachet near Joinville in the Haut-Marne in 1765. But Philippe Lebon was not only Champenois, he was an engineer of bridges and highways.

"This naïve provincial had sometimes seen emerging from the bosom of the earth certain elastic fluids susceptible of combustion. These fires were not extraordinary; they exist at Pietra-Mala and Barigazzo in Italy; in Dauphiné there is an ardent fountain; on the banks of the Caspian Sea and in many places in America one sees these phenomena reproduced frequently. On the surface of a vein of coal, in 1664, an English savant had noticed the same fantasy of nature. Since then, learned men, including James Clayton, Stephen Hales and Richard Watson, Bishop of Llandaff have found the means of extracting an inflammable gas from these substances.

"Then, Philippe Lebon conceived the idea of making use of gas produced by the combustion of wood for the public lighting of cities. His first success was at Versailles. Shortly thereafter, however, at daybreak one morning, Philippe Lebon was found dead with multiple stab-wounds in your capital's Champs-Élysées.[45]

"You know the rest. Paris, London, France and Europe were endowed from then on with splendid and inexpensive lighting."

"If only they were as brightly lit by the illumination of a healthy and just intelligence!" said Mikaël. "If only they could see where their true interests lie! If, instead of being constantly bent over the earth to extract gold therefrom and increase their perishable fortune, they were to lift their eyes to Heaven more often to think and to cry: *That is where we came from; it is there to which we must return!* Then there would be a veritable Age of Enlightenment, whereas...I believe that it is only the Age of Darkness, the Age of Egotism, the reign of gold, and the loss of true happiness!"

"Now that my father has launched an attack on the vice of your era, my dear Terran, and has said things to you so just as true—from which you will profit, I hope—it's scarcely the moment to talk about photography. As that discovery also belongs to fire and light, however, I'll permit myself to say a few quick words about it.

---

[45] Lebon's murderer was never identified, nor any motive for the crime discovered.

"Two or three centuries ago. Jean-Baptiste Porta, a physicist from Naples, devised the *camera obscura*. Thus, by placing a convergent lens in the orifice of a sealed box, one reproduced on a screen within the box an entire view of the surrounding locations and individuals.

"One man had enough talent and genius to fix these fleeting images; that man was Louis Daguerre. The *camera obscura* thus gave rise to the daguerreotype."

"Oh!" I exclaimed. "I remember the concert of enthusiastic acclamations that the announcement of that marvelous innovation excited."

"God, but I haven't finished," Stella went on. "The discovery was not thought to be susceptible to improvements, but it required them and obtained them. The photographic imprint of a landscape or of a face, at first so fugitive that a child's breath or the slightest breeze sufficed to remove it, was soon fixed in an unalterable manner.

"Photography on metal plates, on which images formed by exposing them to vapors spontaneously given off by iodine, was replaced by photography on paper. It was to the Englishman Fox Talbot, on the one hand, and to Louis Blanquart-Evrard on the other, that that improvement was owed. To obtain on paper the result obtained on the metal, it was necessary to receive the image on paper impregnated with silver iodide mixed with a small quantity of nitric acid.

"Another improvement was that of collodion. That substance, unfortunately, cannot be applied to paper, but it coats glass marvelously, and then receives the luminous impression so perfectly that it can even reproduce bodies in rapid movement: the waves of the sea in fury, for example; carriages rapidly drawn along a road; a horse galloping; or a steamship making headway, with its smoke and its wake of white foam.

"Judge the consequences of these discoveries for the arts and the sciences. They are due to Frederick Archer, an exceedingly skilled English photographer."

"I confess to you that I'm beginning to be very distracted," I said to my Lunian hosts, "for your satellite is now very close, enabling me to see such curious things, that I beg you to quite the things of the Earth in order to allow me to see those of the Moon. Meanwhile, if you please, tell who was the true inventor of telegraphy?"

"Abbé Claude Chappe," Mikaël replied. It was in 1793—a fateful date if ever there was one! Put in prison, with so many poor priests to whom only one reproach could be addressed—that of doing too much good—Chappe, who was from Angers, and who had been preoccupied with the idea of rapid communication since youth, ruminated his plans and finally devised the aerial telegraph. I have no need to tell you anything about the signals adopted to transmit news.

"His invention, which rendered great service, has now been dethroned by the electric telegraph. The discovery of electromagnetism gave many scientists—in particular, an American, Samuel Morse—the idea of extending iron wires from one placed to another and connecting the extremities of apparatus keys which, set in motion by electricity, caused the corresponding keys to move at the far extremity. As you're impatient, I shall only say that magnets play a role in that astonishing mechanism. You only have to see an apparatus to understand it and judge how fine and advantageous the discovery is."

"Finally, my dear Lunian, by way of conclusion, please tell me to whom we owe the new procedure of etherization, which I have heard mentioned triumphantly by some and fearfully by others. But hurry..."

"Etherization, friend, touches the very sources of life," Mikaël replied. "Let us be discreet in its regard. It is another of the gifts that the grandeur of Providence has revealed, but it is also a powerful weapon that might injure humankind.

"First, it's essential that you know that the ancient also had their anesthetic methods—which is to say, means of rendering our organs insensitive to pain. In modern times, you have improved them, and it was a certain Humphry Davy who identified the ability of laughing gas to abolish pain. But it was Charles Jackson who, inspired by Horace Wells,[46] communicated to the dentist William Morton in America his reflections, the results of his trials and his ideas about the inhalation of ether as a method of anesthesis so perfect that it was immediately tested on poor sufferers. Teeth extracted, amputations made, and the most painful operations executed with difficulty, left no trace of the atrocious suffering that patients would have endured in their normal state.

"These experiments, carried out in the New World, have been repeated in Europe, in France, in Paris, with the most marked success—except that infallibility has not always been obtained; there have been terrifying cases..."

"As for all human inventions, the Earth is the theater of calamities and imperfection," said Stella. "The most admirable things bear within them their accidents, their weaknesses and their miseries." Then, immediately, she added: "Futile effort and wasted reflections! The Terran is no longer with us..."

"The Moon!" I cried. "The Moon! Look!"

---

[46] Wells was the first dentist to use laughing gas as an anesthetic, but his inspirational value was somewhat compromised by the fact that he became addicted to chloroform and went to the bad before committing suicide. Driou misspells his name "Horace Wels," although he could not have known that the error in question would one day become wikipedia's type-specimen of a mistyped search entry, connecting to a version of the entry on "Horace Wells" in which almost every word is misspelled.

IV

If I were a poet, a painter, or even a historian, what a hymn of admiration I could intone, what marvelous colors I could employ, what sublime things I could say in order to make you understand by what shining splendors I found myself surrounded, my young friends!

Beneath me, in depths already infinite, hung the Earth, the appearance of which was nothing but a gigantic moon shining with all the gleams of silver on the side on which the sun was ready to rise, but whose orb hid and extinguished its fires.

Above me, floating in the immensity of the skies, was the enormous globe of the Moon, no longer white with reflected sunlight as we see it at a distance from Earth, but admirable with beauties so diverse that to describe them, individually or collectively, would require the pen of an artist and entire volumes.

Now, it was not in an atmosphere different from that of the Earth that our satellite was displaying itself. Before drawing so close to its mass, we had still seen the black sky, and thousand of reddish fires—fixed stars and the milky globes of planets—still shining, dotting and scintillating its funereal crêpe. As we came nearer, however, the layers of air, increasing in density, had rendered to our eyes that beautiful blue appearance that is the charm of the firmament.

Jets of gilded light, then fiery streaks overflowed from one edge of the ponderous and grandiose terrestrial sphere; then an orb, reminiscent of a shield reddened in a furnace, showed one of its segments, and finally, the entire Sun reappeared, emerging into the open—illuminating the Earth, whose silvery tints weakened—resplendent in space, striking the Moon with its rays, which received the most marvelous appearance therefrom.

At the same time, the sublime concert of the aerial globes, which I had never ceased hearing, murmuring in the obscurity, resumed as if in a *rinforzando*, and it was an ineffable harmony, and inexpressible union of indescribable cantatas, that the spheres and the worlds were singing.

We maintained silence for a few seconds, for I was in ecstasy, enjoying the sublime spectacle, aspiring those delightful chords, of which human symphonies cannot give any idea.

Mikaël was kneeling down on the edge of his gondola; Stella, leaning profoundly over the other side, was contemplating infinity. They were both worshiping and praying. How, indeed, was it possible not to worship, not to pray? Oh, if, like me, the unbelievers—I won't say atheists; there is no such thing, but unbelievers—were able to contemplate the Creator's works, sown in infinity, as numerous as the sands of the ocean, rubies and pearls here, topazes and diamonds there, amethysts, emeralds and opals further away, everywhere, they would suddenly become ardent neophytes, and their souls, with their affections, faculties and desires, would suddenly take flight, borne on the wings of love, toward the author of that eternal wealth.

I bowed down like the Lunians; I prayed, like them. It is so sweet to pray for those one loves, so sweet to worship, when the gaze gives the mind the idea of the grandeur of the sovereign! One speaks so well, one asks for so many things, one loves with such warmth, when one knows that the Master is there, among his works, that he is listening to us, that the imploring voice will not be lost, that he is there, that one can almost see him!

Mikaël and Stella began to speak in an unknown language, of an ineffable softness; I heard them as one hears vague noises while half-asleep.

How astonished I was when, in the regions of the Moon over which we were traveling, I saw, seemingly coming to meet us, and soon scattering around us, an innumerable multitude of balloons, coming and going, rising and descending, increasing in every direction, apparently intent on forming an escort for us! Many of these lunar aerostats were made of white fabric, many were decorated with gold or silver; there were red ones, green ones, gray ones, yellow ones, violet ones and bronze-colored ones. All of them bore their networks of cords, of a shade that harmonized with the color of the balloon. The rigging of some held a charming shell of agate, others a sanguine pear, this one made of a gigantic onyx, that one of marvelous aventurine glass. At the summit of each aerostat floated a banderole of a color contrasting with that of the balloon. In consequence, there was a veritable rain, a bizarre avalanche of twenty thousand balloons hanging in space, all around the Moon, and nothing could be as picturesque and graceful as that innumerable aerial flotilla.

In each of the gondolas of those aerial voyagers I soon saw male and female Lunians, the Adams and Eves of our satellite. As I saw, though, I was seen myself. My poor aerostat, Parisian as it was, made of superb Neapolitan fabric, make no mistake, perfectly rubberized and as well stitched together as possible, was, alas, a blot on all those light and graceful vehicles. My paltry Terran vessel was seen, and immediately I was identified, surrounded and studied. In brief, I was the focus of attention, the object of general curiosity of the inhabitants of the Moon.

I owe it to the truth to say without delay that their amiability, their courtesy and their wisdom did not make me regret for an instant having dared to introduce myself among them. To do them justice, they showed themselves more affable than can be imagined. It is true that I was under the patronage of Mikaël, who seemed to me to be very highly-regarded among the Lunians, and Stella, whose wisdom doubtless gave rise to frequent smiles and a thousand charming greetings.

It was doubtless deduced that I was a Terran—or perhaps Mikaël's daughter was indiscreet. What is certain is that our vessels were soon encircled, that our ascension was retarded, and hat a hundred gondolas were bumping into ours. I was not displeased by that, for if the Lunians wanted to see a Terran at close range, the Terran was no less delighted to see the male and female Lunians. It is my duty once again to recognize immediately the superiority of their nature over ours, and to proclaim that, if humans displayed in their attitude and the dignity of their expressions a boundless generosity and the external reflection of the perfection of the soul, the women had the perfume of modesty and the pose of innocence that revealed their justice and sublime grandeur. All those noble heads of Lunian men and women eclipsed the beauties of the Earth, as the rose and the camellia hold sway over brambles and thistles.

Suddenly, as the daylight brightened a little around us and the most obstinate aerostats finally moved aside, I saw the Moon at close range—at very close range, close enough to touch the treetops and the monuments, but without being able to set foot on the ground.

O Earth, you too, what are you in comparison with the Moon?

Men, women, the Earth, we all bear the stigmata of the sin of Adam, but you, Moon, male and female Lunians, you are rich in all the gifts of the Creator, who has remained your friend!

The Moon, my friends, is entirely an Eden, with its delights, its joys, its voluptuousness, its richness—but an Eden without the terrible serpent that tempted Eve.

Imagine it if you can, for I would need a hundred mouths to tell you, and they would become weary in telling you everything; I had before my eyes immense regions strewn with hills, cut by valleys, variegated by verdure, enameled by flowers, planted with fig-trees, myrtles, aloes, splendid palm-trees and magnificent terebinths.

No vapor hid the blue ether, and the Sun projected its most hectic rays on the fortunate orb that appeared to my eyes. On the slopes of mountains lost in the distant mists, volcanoes ejected their sparkling fire. Here, the red streaks of their molten lava spread the colors of fireworks over the shady valleys; there, the silvery blades of rivers embroidered vast and sinuous meadows, veiled by high and luxuriant forests. Everywhere there were scenes that charmed, whose harmony was untroubled by excessive contrasts.

From flocks of birds, coots with blue plumage, savias with yellow throats, ouaras with red wings edged in black, white seagulls, incarnadine bee-eaters, green curlews, heathland grouse, mangrove doves, albatrosses, petrels, cormorants, woodland birds, littoral birds, lake birds, island birds, all first-borns of Creation, were fluttering in thousands over the lines of the immense horizon.[47]

Large goats with floppy ears could be seen coming and going, leaping and prancing, along with long-necked camels, black buffaloes, lions with golden manes, mares and stallions of every hue, whiskered panthers, brunette and blonde gazelles, onagers with velvet hides, quadrupeds of the deserts, the mountains, the prairies and the rocks, all first-borns of creation, ruminating, playing under the cedars, in the shade and under the blaze of that marvelous country.

And on the lakes, among the madrepores on the banks and under the waves, violet sea-urchins were moving over

---

[47] I cannot find any reference to the use of "savia" as the name of a bird; "ouara" is used in different ways in early French works on ornithology but the intended reference is probably to the scarlet ibis. The reference to all lunar creatures as "first-borns of creation" is intriguing, in that it helps to highlight a question scrupulously unaddressed by the author: does the fact that Lunians live in families imply that they indulge in sexual intercourse? Given that there are mares and stallions on the Moon, being "first-borns of creation" obviously does not imply the absence of secondary sexual characteristics, but presumably does imply either abstinence from intercourse or sterility, else the flocks of birds would not consist entirely of such "first-borns." Alas, the author does not specify any details of Stella's origin, so we are left to wonder whether the humans of the Moon arrive in the world direct from the Creator's hand with ready-determined family relationships.

banks of coral; red seaweeds, scarlet bivalves, harp-sells tinted like tulips, deep-sea fishes, reptiles of the thickets, grass-snakes, tree-snakes, marine cetaceans, fresh-water mollusks, all first-borns of creation, were wandering among the gladioli, bathing in the waters, enjoying a life that involved neither dangers nor vicissitudes.

On a whim, I tried to see whether the movement of the Moon would be visible to me; but we were carried along by that movement, in such a way that we could not detect it. I even dared to express my desire to Mikaël, who smiled at me, and by means of pressure that he put on his aerostat's brake, immediately rendered it stationary.

Then the rotation of the Moon became evident. We ceased to see the same objects, confused and mixed up, but they appeared to us grouped with an exquisite harmony, distinct to the eye, incessantly renewed. It was a prodigious thing to see that mass, delightful in its appearances, animated, picturesque and populated here, solitary there, turning on its axis, incessantly bringing us new locations—gorges, plains, peaks, valleys, bluffs, hills—that were ever more enchanting.

It was then, at intervals, that volcanoes appeared: the volcanoes that sometimes send us lumps of their lava, which we call aeroliths when they arrive on our planet. One of those volcanoes—the largest, I think—was close to a circumvallation so immense that it can be seen from Earth without the aid of a telescope. It has the form of a crater, and twice a year, the Lunians all go there in order to hold festivals preceded by a great religious ceremony. That festival is none other than the anniversary of Creation.

That volcano was expelling flames, scoria and lava—was, in brief, in eruption—when I saw it. Its crater was directly underneath us at that moment, so it was easy for us to measure its depth and see the waves of fire seething within. We were momentarily enveloped by its fumes, but there is nothing to fear from the fire and fumes of volcanoes on the Moon. Among the Lunians, a volcano is a caprice, a fantasy of nature intended to break the monotony and reveal all the prodigies of creation. In fact, a few of the other volcanoes I saw, produced from afar the effect of gigantic broad-based candelabras, some crowned with violet flames, others green ones, yellow ones here and blue there—all projecting their gleams over the neighboring mountains and valleys.

And in the atmosphere surrounding the Moon, in the quivering of its trees, in the meadows and the spinneys, there were warm and teasing breezes flowing and gliding, evoking nameless and seemingly limitless felicities.

Strangely enough, I found that I knew the names of all the things I saw, and, without having any need to interrogate my two companions, who were enjoying my surprise, I immediately applied names to the things I saw of my own accord.

There was one moment when I distinguished, beneath a clump of tamarinds, groups of young women with necklaces of scarlet grenadines tumbling over their breasts, and diadems of topazes in their hair. Their paleness equaled that of the milk of gazelles at dawn, and the veins in their limbs had the color of blue sea-waves. In order to spare their feet, which were treading on mosses and flowering broom, they had put on moccasins made from the fabric of lantanas.

Several of them were holding cinnors[48] and accompanying their sisters, who were singing, while others were lifting the sheaves of dazzling flowers with which their arms were laden to the heavens, as if to bless them and thank them. The youngest, sitting on urns, were braiding pale anemones collected from damp fissures in the rocks, and crowning their companions, uttering joyful bursts of laughter.

Then, on seeing me with Mikaël, they fled like a flock of doves frightened by a mountain eagle, and hid in the coverts of a verdant valley.

"They return to their mothers as their best shelter," Mikaël told me, "for the soul of the world is here, as it is everywhere—except that it is very miserable on Earth, stifled as it is

---

[48] A cinnor is an obsolete Hebrew instrument resembling a lyre.

by a thousand passions, whereas here it still remains sublime and pure."

"What do you mean by the soul of the world?" I asked the Lunian.

"Love!" he said. "The love that flows from God and carries everything back to God. The love that warms our hearts with gratitude, which inspires perpetual submission in us, which causes us to cherish the author of our being and appreciate the wealth of creation. The love that reveals to us the perfection of God, and tells us that nothing is more worthy to be loved. The love that causes us all to cherish one another, and which even shows us a human of Earth as a friend, as a brother for whom we ought to pray, for whom we should mourn. The love, in sum, that ensures that our life is an action of perpetual thanks, like our happiness, and that we have no greater felicity then praising God, blessing him, seeking to avoid that which might makes him weep and never yielding to that which might offend his gaze."

I was immersed in the profound reflection that Mikaël's words suggested to me, and I thought of our Earthly tenderness, so often lost and never recovered, and always so fragile, when the Moon, turning without pause, showed me a spectacle that demanded all my attention and caused Mikaël to fall silent.

To begin with, files of agile and vigorous dromedaries were skirting the slopes of a hill, whose successive slopes advertised mountainous country. In fact, jagged peaks were rising up on the horizon to gigantic heights, their blue summits producing a magnificent frame for the entire region. The caravans were composed of old men and women, young Lunians and maidens in the flower of youth. Seated on their mounts, they were singing as they moved. The hill, climbed by a sandy path, was bordered by marvelous flowering sassafras, whose sweet odor the wind spread far and wide. In the depths of the valley a broad, deep river ran, whose calm and limpid waters reflected the luxury of its banks. To the right, under the shelter of a wood of enormous lemon-trees, was a dormant lake with blue waters. To the left, on the slope of a bare bluff whose base was formed by rocks, the red and white flames of a volcano sprang forth, the dull detonations of which imitated the sound of musketry, which mingled with the murmur of the waters and the songs of the travelers.

Lower down, winding around the flanks of the mountains, a noisy railway locomotive was smoking; the track was made of silver and the carriages of a black wood crowned with awnings of a fabric as white as the purest muslin. A large number of Lunians, with their families, packed these agile and graceful carriages—and notwithstanding the different means of transport that I saw with pleasure on our satellite, we still encountered numerous aerostats of every hue at a height a few meters above the ground, crossing one another's paths as they moved in every direction.

"This landscape is enchanting," I said to Mikaël and Stella. "Assuredly, we have nothing on Earth to compare to it. But tell me, why do we see many more inhabitants hereabouts than elsewhere?"

"For a very simple reason," Mikaël said. "We're approaching the place that Stella mentioned to you, which offers the gazes of Lunians a series of pictures as old as the world..."

"Do you practice painting, then?" I said, quite surprised. "I wouldn't be at all surprised—you have your libraries, you might very well possess museums and enrich them with your works."

"Our museum, here, is nature," Mikaël replied, "but a nature apart, a mysterious nature, a nature that I ought not to define for you, my dear Terran, for your mortal ears cannot grasp it, nor your limited intelligence comprehend it. Let it suffice or you to know that, just as you have metal plates that, in the dark chamber we were talking about before, reproduce and fix the objects placed before their lenses, so we have a special place disposed by the hand of nature to receive the impression—but magnified, in a natural fashion, and in all its verity, save for the life it lacks—of the sequence of events accomplished on Earth since Eve, your mother, presented the forbidden fruit to Adam, your father, until those of your present day—the war in the East, for example..."

"But that's a truly curious thing," I exclaimed, "and one that I am most desirous to see. I beg you, my good Lunian, take me to this strange museum."

"All the more willingly, my dear Terran, because my daughter, who has finally stopped smiling at all her companions whom we meet, will doubtless be glad to be the cicerone of whom you will have need in that circumstance."

Dear reader, I have seen that mysterious pandemonium of all the great dramas of the Earth. I have spent many hours there; I could say days and nights...for days and nights were passing, passing quickly without my perceiving them, so many attractions did the curiosities of the Moon have for me...but how can I tell you about the astonishing marvels that passed in turn before my eyes? It would be necessary to stop recounting the story of my aeronautical voyage—and yet, I would like to satisfy your curiosity. Permit me, therefore, in order to achieve the double objective at which I ought to aim, to continue my story on the one hand and, on the other, to reveal to you the prodigies of the lunar museum, begging you to accept a work in which I shall offer to your gaze the scenes that moved me so much. I shall give it the following title, which will help you to recognize it:

THE MARVELOUS ALBUM
PROOFS OF AN AERIAL DAGUERREOTYPE

If the book interests you, read it; if it bores you, throw it in the fire. But be sure that it includes nothing but the truth, and that, in writing it, I shall have had no other desire but to increase your knowledge.

Forgive me for the interruption; I shall resume my story.

It was evening on the Moon. It was the hour when the hills and valleys were crowned with the last splendors of the sun, as radiant as the bdellium[49] of lands burned by its fires. It was the moment when the young Lunian women climbed into the baskets of their aerostats in order to admire the works of the Creator at their ease, to sing his glory and mingle their voices with the hymns of the spheres.

Mikaël made a sign to Stella.

Without saying a word, but with a smile of commiseration, Stella took from a cedar-wood box locked with a golden key a pâté as transparent as a topaz and as tremulous as a flower stirred by the breeze, and offered it to me, gazing at me as she did so.

Then, in order to embolden me, Mikaël ate first.

The flesh of pineapples and citrons are not as fresh or exquisite as the delicious foodstuff I had in my mouth. It gave me a sweeter enjoyment than Turkish delight. After having savored it, I found myself strong and robust, healthy and intelligent, as on waking up after a long night's sleep.

Then I drank an entire glass full of a roseate juice, which could not be matched, either for taste or bouquet, by our finest wines.

Meanwhile, the Lunians' aerostat, charged with the finest elements of a subtle gas, remained fixed, so expertly steered by Mikaël and so docile in his hands that it defied the movement of the Moon, rotating slowly on its axis and producing a soft and harmonious sound. It was in that harmony most of all, which could not be analyzed, and to the indescribably picturesque locations—the villas and other dwellings, the splendid costumes and physiognomies of the crowd, the curious aerostats coming and going in the warm dusk, the strange gleams of faraway volcanoes sending us their luminous reflections—and, finally, to the joy with which everyone seemed to respire with the breezes, that I recognized the preeminence of the Moon over the Earth.

---

[49] Bdellium is a mysterious shiny substance mentioned twice in the Old Testament. Nobody knows what it was.

I said as much to Mikaël, who replied: "Sin is rooted down there and reigns there; here, innocence is enthroned. There, malediction weighs with all its mass; here, the springs of paternal benediction flow incessantly. There, you bear the weight of all calamities; here, the torrent of a nameless felicity inundates us."

"Yes," Stella went on in her turn, "while you groan under tempests, storms, torments, plagues, cholera, sterilities, famines, wars, maladies, tortures, agony and death on your Earth; we here, as in all the spheres, have serenity, calm, peace, health, perpetual springtime and immortality."

"Because our Eve did not sin!" said Mikaël.

"And our Adam did not succumb!" Stella added.

"While on our poor Earth..." I did not finish, for my poor Terran balloon, as if to put in a word of its own about the terrestrial miseries of which it bore its share, began to oscillate and twist, as if it were in a current or some injury had been done to its fabric. Fortunately, Mikaël came to my aid, by imparting a movement to his aerostat that, while drawing mine, to which it was linked, along, restored its equilibrium and velocity.

Night had succeeded dusk—a gentle and pure night. The Lunians had retired to their homes. In spite of the shadows that covered the Lunian zones that our balloons, now set at liberty, were traversing, however, I extended my every-curious gaze, sometimes toward the Moon and sometimes toward the sky, which offered me the spectacle of fiery spheres as red as a bead of blood and as numerous as the sands of the sea, and the much rarer planets, whose larger white orbs drew my interested attention, and a few comets passing through the depths of the void at infinite distances, leaving long trails of luminous threads that astronomers estimate to be several millions of leagues in length.

When Mikaël had returned impulsion to our balloons, they rose up high above the Moon, which as rotating beneath our feet. From that elevation I saw the globe of our satellite tinted by a pale twilight, which did not prevent the distinction of the various accidents of the ground: valleys, jagged mountains of a prodigious height, bare slopes and the peaks bristling on its surface; its luxuriant plains, its solitudes where white elephants and gracious giraffes were wandering, with animals of forms unknown to me—and all living in peace, browsing flowers, eating large leaves, and animating the lands abandoned to them by the Lunians. A few inhabitants of the Moon were traveling in their aerostats beneath ours, and for the decoration of those vehicles they had attached to them, by means of golden cords, pale luminous searchlights, whose gleam—red, green, yellow or violet—gave fantastic appearances to their aerial progress.

We also passed over another railway, whose rails were made of gold. It connected two of the cities—for, as I have said, the Moon has its cities, which are constructed not for the needs of society, but simply for the charm of aggregation, like shade in a painting, as a contrast, in order to break the monotony. From afar, as at close range, I saw several of these cities, their walls, their palaces, their concentric streets, their squares, and a thousand monuments in marble, jasper, porphyry, malachite and other precious materials appropriate to their decoration.

One of those cities bears the name of Lunos. It occupies the center of the Moon, on its equator. It is constructed in a circle, and I have some reason to suspect that Earthly astronomers, having discovered it with good telescopes and placed it on their maps, have called it a crater.

A second city bears the name of Trinos. All its plazas, its dwellings, its edifices and its pavilions, even its boundary wall, are triangular.

A third, by the names of Jésos, in its disposition, its intersecting streets, the wings of its houses, its squares and its monuments, recalls a Greek cross, a worshipful and sacred symbol of salvation.

A fourth, which I also saw, named Virgo, is located at the antipodes of Lunos, similarly on the lunar equator but in the part of the Moon that always faces the Earth, like Trinos and Jésos.[50] In Virgo, which means virginal, everything is snow white, and young women live with their mothers and their families in dazzling white summer-houses.

We stopped briefly above the last-named city; there, in each of its squares, planted with aromatic trees whose branches seem to be laden with the sparkling frosts of winter, and flowerbeds spangled with white flowers as dazzling as diamonds, rose up not a temple or a church but bell-towers, obelisks, pyramids and open, hollow spiral columns. The latter are delightfully formed, some with external staircases and some with internal ones, gently inclined, with bronze balustrades and broad foundations of the most beautiful flawless marble, leading to a height superior to that of the steeple of Strasbourg Cathedral or the tallest of the pyramids of Egypt, that of Cheops. From these towers the most harmonious symphonies escape, produced by thousands of little bells, organ-pipes, golden and silver gongs, which it is sufficient for the breeze to stir to set off the light batten suspended over their funnels.

But I was soon to contemplate other marvels, which summoned my gaze, every-ready to study and become familiar with such strange and curious things.

I saw purple and gold bands on the horizon described around the globe of the Moon, and the planet offered us the most vivid colors of the rainbow at its extreme borders. It was daylight.

My paintbrush is insufficient to render the beauty of that rebirth of light; my palette does not possess colors rich enough to depict its splendors. I shall limit myself to telling you that the points of fire soon faded away in the black sky, and the sun appeared. I greeted it with love, like a true friend. At the same time, my heart began to beat violently.

---

[50] This makes no sense, as Earthly astronomers could not have discovered Lunos if it were on the opposite face. It is probably a mistake, the author having meant to place Virgo on the side of the Moon perpetually hidden from the Earth.

The day before, after having studied, examined and admired the Lunians' magical museum for such a long time, constantly instructed regarding events on our planet by the facts reproduced there, Mikaël had announced that he would take me to see his dwelling—but he had not told me that we were approaching it

Suddenly, turning toward me, he put his hand on my shoulder, and made a gesture, with a kind of self-regard, that I translated as: *Behold my residence, my palace, my property!*

Are the property-owners of the Moon, then, like those of Earth, enamored of their wealth? I wondered.

Listen, my dear friends; what I am saying is the truth: no artist's palette and brush, no poet's pen, no tourist's travelogue, no imagination of enchantment, could ever express the ravishing scene that I had before my eyes. The *Thousand-and-One Nights* describes for us incredible splendors that do not exist; the most glorious legends display to us the most prodigious riches of art, nature, superfluities, palaces and basilicas. Well, all that is nothing but a hovel, a ruin, an assemblage of bad taste compared with what I contemplated, my eyes bulging from my head, my mouth open and my hair standing on end.

The Escurial in Spain; the Alcazar in Castille; the Golden Palace in ancient Rome; the famous palace of Psammetichus in Egypt; Schoenbrünn in Austria; Potsdam in Berlin; Versailles or the Trianon in France; Westminster and Windsor in the United Kingdom; the Kremlin in Moscow—in brief, the most beautiful palaces in the six continents of the world—were mere huts compared to the one that I was looking at.

It was not the grandeur but the exquisite simplicity of Mikaël's dwelling that struck me.

The city was some distance away, grouped within walls of illuminated silver, lying and standing amid mounds of verdure, charming beneath the yellow rays of light coming from some unknown fire—for I could not see the sun. But I paid little heed to the city. In a valley speckled with clumps of aloes, terebinths, nopals and a thousand unknown trees, among clearings covered with moss that was easier on the eye and softer to the touch than any other, stood a principal building in the form of a vast rotunda lade with three stories of successively diminishing circumference, of which a broad marble staircase formed the base, along with a smaller edifice: a bizarre fantasy in the Moorish style, the thousand details of whose sculptures fascinated the gaze. Further away were superimposed basins, from which a silvery flood escaped, falling back like rain into immense bowls rutilant with gold and rubies. Elsewhere, there were hollow pyramids that might have provided shelter, for opening allowed the interior to be seen, and capriciously formed constructions so strange that I could not divine their precise usage. From the principal dwelling to the simplest stable, there were no thick walls hiding the secrets within, but pilasters of every dimension, protruding caryatids, twisted columns, pyramidions—all entities that, while sustaining an edifice, were separate from one another, according to the rules of lunar architecture, permitting the indiscreet eye to look in and see everything. There were many rich and magnificent draperies between these supports, but as they were open during the warm hours, the Lunians concealed nothing from one another. Thus, as it was one of those fortunate times, I could see everything.

First, I ought to say that the external columns were not marble, jasper or malachite, but of the blackest ebony, with plinths, capitals and filaments of the purest silver. The substructure was made of bronze, like that of Corinth, and the entablature was gold. The architrave was crowned with silver and bronze, studded with enormous diamonds in the guise of modillions, rubies as large as ostrich eggs, topazes forming billets and emerald in which the play of the light produced delightful effects. In addition, charming statues of raw ivory stood on the acroterium, at the corners and along the ridge. In the bays, the richest stained-glass windows imaginable were sparkling.

Shall I tell you about the bronze caryatids with their pedestals of polished iron, the pilasters of gold and silver, the figurines of which were decorated with flowers and mottoes inscribed in precious tones? What would be the point?

"What can I say that would be more eloquent than my silence?" I said to Mikaël. "I congratulate you, not on your taste, since perfection is your lot, but on the supreme felicity that you have been able to conserve by your virtue. This palace—or, rather, this sequence of palaces—far outshine the Terran Alhambra, and your abode is a thousand times preferable to our Eldorado. Young Lunian woman, you are the pearl of this rich jewel-box; allow me to compliment you on being the beloved daughter of a God whom you serve with love, and who rewards you handsomely for it. But it requires no less than this admirable vegetation and this brilliant dwelling to frame a jewel s splendid as yourself..."

"Why, friend," said Mikaël, "what do you believe on Earth, to employ such language? Look at this, and tell me what you think."

I looked in the direction indicated to me by Mikaël. This is what I saw:

I saw a tree that had the tall strong stem of a palm, but of what substance was the stem formed? It had the color of bronze, and the frequently-repeated nodes bore the warm tint typical of nuggets protruding from a matrix. From that tall and slender trunk, such a large quantity of palms protruded in every direction, disposing their leaves in such large fans, that they formed an indescribable dome—for the leaves produced gleams that the prism, the rays of our sun, the rainbow and the clouds at dawn and the most beautiful of our evenings, even in Mexico, could not imitate.

It was, therefore, like a magical parasol planted there by the hand of nature. I admired it with such enthusiasm that I did not see in the penumbra of its trunk, so bold, so vigorous and so rich, that an entire society was moving around a...divan, of the most beautiful white velvet.

Yes, it really was a divan; and on that divan, in a relaxed abandonment, clad in a simple purple chlamys hemmed with gold, slept—yes slept—a female Lunian.

I immediately recognized Stella's mother in the woman's face. Her daughter resembled her so strongly that no doubt was possible. There was the same beauty, the same freshness, and also the same finesse—and, although sleep ought to have altered that expression, the same delicate but mocking smile.

She was asleep, as I have said, and her sleep was that of innocence and justice. Mikaël smiled at that scene, and gestured with his hand to the young Lunian women who were coming and going along pathways powdered with gold, silver or a fine dust of precious stones of the richest colors, communicating his thoughts to them. They disappeared immediately, not without darting curious glances at me and smiling at Stella.

They immediately reappeared, however, in even greater numbers. They now carried zithers, cinnors, psalteries, viols and other instruments that bore some resemblance to the flutes, tabors and horns of our artistes, except that they were made of gold and much smaller.

Then, ranged around the sleeper, they commenced the chords of a music so perfect that the Earth has never heard its like. My God, what must that of Heaven's angels and cherubim be? There were instruments, but there were also voices. What voices! Melody, sweetness, charm, sighs, allegretto, stretta, andante, elevations of the soul, prayers, cantilenas, melopoeias, inexpressible flourishes; everything was there...

To the sounds of the music, which soon filled the air, not only did Mikaël's wife awake, perceive him and smile, but from all the points of the horizon came, as if by enchantment, thousands of aerostats of every color, with their floating flags teased by the breeze, laden with curiosity-seekers, friends, young Lunian men with long hair and bronze-colored tunics, Lunian woman wearing peplums of every hue, crowned with flowers, musicians singing about the bounty and grandeurs of God, and the felicities with which he inundates those he loves.

Then Mikaël and Stella spoke to them.

What did they say? I don't know; they were speaking in an unknown language. But it was so soft, so sweet, that it was another harmony. They were talking about me; I was in no doubt about that, for all eyes were fixed upon me at that moment—and any doubt I might have had was dispelled when Naïs came to stand beside Mikaël and to hug Stella to her heart. She greeted me with a smile. To take her into his conch Michaël had taken his aerostat down on to the lawn. All the other Lunian balloons formed an escort for it.

I understood that it was not permitted for me to set foot on the Moon, and that it was a matter of accompanying me in order to take me back to my unfortunate planet. Tears came to my eyes, but I accepted my lot.

Mikaël came to take his place next to my aerostat again. Then, as the entire flotilla of lunar balloons got ready to sail with it toward the terrestrial atmosphere, he was about to give the signal to depart when my aerostat, instead of holding its own in the contest and behaving with self-respect, began to falter, lurching to the right and the left, becoming flaccid, and threatening to collapse on to the lunar surface.

My anxiety was increasing, and a smile was already showing on the lips of the Lunians, when Mikaël took pity on my embarrassment, passed from his gondola into mine, and said to me: "Courage friend! The Lunians will not allow such a beautiful Terran balloon to enrich their museum."

And he added: "Look..."

V

I looked, as Mikaël told me to do.

With one hand he opened the valve of my aerostat, and the gas immediately began to escape.

"I'm doomed," I told him. "This way, my balloon, already low on gas—for it's been several days since it was charged—will fall abruptly..."

"You're saved!" he replied.

At the same time, with his other hand, he placed beneath the orifice of the open valve a kind of ball as large as a coconut; then, striking this ball with a golden hammer, he caused an explosion and it caught fire—but the fire produced so much smoke engulfing the balloon, that the creases in the envelope were soon stretched, and my aerostat resumed the round and spherical form that it had give me so much pleasure to see on Earth.

Then Mikaël blew on the globule, which was extinguished.

"That's how we make gas here!" he said. "Now we're going to undertake a circumnavigation of the world. Your aerostat will return you safe and sound to Paris, old chap! Close the valve again, though."

"Thank you, Lunian," I said.

"Now," he said, "let's salute the Moon, friends. To you who are remaining, love and happiness!" Then, immediately, like an admiral addressing his fleet, he added: "Go!"

At that cry, all the aerostats launched forward and leapt into the air. I ought to say that my balloon, doubtless refreshed and keen to reestablish its reputation, then took the lead, followed closely by Mikaël. It was a charming spectacle to see that multitude of machines, in a hundred varied colors, set off into the ether like spirited chargers, displaying their oriflammes on all sides, fluttering in the breeze.

Our progress was so rapid that after a few hours we reached the limits of the lunar atmosphere. I was the first to perceive that, for my balloon suddenly stopped in its tracks, oscillated, and finally, entering the terrestrial atmosphere, turned upside down so rapidly that I lost my balance and nearly fell out.

Mikaël followed my maneuver and came to place himself at my side.

Then, like a general facing his regiments, he took up a position facing the flying army, stopped s balloon, signaled to me to fix mine, and finally gave me the floor in order to make a speech to the Lunians, who were about to quit my company.

Readers, don't expect me to deliver to our curiosity that morel of eloquence. There are fortunate improvisations, as you know; they are the ones that have been given mature reflection and composed in the silence of a study. Mine was not one of them. It had its merits, however. Besides, you know the axiom:

Si vis me flere flendum est primus ipse tibi.[51]

A tear slid down my cheek in the guise of a peroration; my triumph was complete.

Prolonged acclamations on the part of the Lunians, who remained in their atmosphere, followed us for a long time while we penetrated that of the Earth.

The Earth! It already seemed to me that I was breathing its beloved emanations already. I thought about my other. I recited these verses by Ernest Fouinet:

To the mother who weeps and whose only hope you are,
To the spouse who weeps and makes you a long confession,

---

[51] The saying, improvised from two lines of Horace, is usually rendered *Si vis me flere, dolendum est primus ipse tibi*, but the difference in meaning is slight: "If you want to see me weep, you must weep/become sad first."

To the poor child who weeps and addresses his prayer to you,

Return the son, the spouse and the father, O my Lord!

Naïs and Stella, and Mikaël too, reading my thoughts, respected my silence.

Our descent was very rapid. I saw the Sun floating in the sky; after that, like a leviathan swimming in the azure waves, I discovered a mass that weighed beneath our feet.

"The Earth! The Earth!" said Mikaël, comprehending my uncertainty.

"I thought so," I said, "but I have so many new things crowding my brain that my ideas are somewhat confused. So, my dear Mikaël, can you tell me exactly what point in my existence I have reached?"

"It's the month of May 1854, my dear Terran."

"Yes, I know that—but how many times since my departure, which took place on the fifteenth at nine o'clock in the morning, has night succeeded day?"

"Seven nights have replaced seven days," the Lunian replied, "during which you have contemplated the Heavens, studied your planetary system, admired our Moon, collected the beauties of our museum to compose your *Marvelous Album*, and..."

"Seven days!" I cried.

"Yes, seven days. It's the twenty-first of May,[52] and it's nine o'clock in the morning in Paris..."

"Listen, dear Lunian, I believe you, for you are infallibly precise, but at least explain to me how seven days and nights

---

[52] For a being possessed of perfect knowledge, Mikaël seems a trifle weak in matters of arithmetic. The French conventionally reckon a week as *huit jours* [eight days] rather than seven, counting from one Sunday (say) to the next, but Mikael has explicitly said that seven nights have elapsed since the departure, so that it must now be the morning of twenty-second in Paris, not the twenty-first.

could have passed without my perceiving them, without the time seeming long, and without darkness..."

"Firstly," said Mikaël, "we have always been in that part of the Moon that never has sufficient night for it to get dark; secondly, our alimentation, which you have sometimes shared, has not permitted you to feel the appetite that terrestrial humanity produces; finally, we are good enough people for all that we have shown you not to have wearied you."

"Perfectly clear...and the result is that, after the time elapsed, we have set a course for Earth, sand now we're approaching it. Indeed, I can see, shining like an immense mirror reflecting the sun..."

"That's the Indian Ocean that you can see beneath us," Mikaël explained. "It's bathing Arabia to the left, Hindustan and Indo-China to the east."

"To enter the lands on one side under the name of the Red Sea, and to moisten China on the other under the name of the Blue Sea," I continued. "So we're going to see the lands and countries that were once the domain of the Assyrians, the Medes, the Persians and a hundred other peoples?"

"Precisely," said Mikaël. "Except that for you, the Earth is at this moment as it was on the day when it emerged from the Creator's hands—so, while waiting for it to be within closer range of your gaze, tell me why certain seas have names that evoke the idea of colors, like the White Sea, the Black Sea, the Yellow Sea, the Blue Sea and the Red Sea?"

"Doubtless because their waters are thus tinted."

"Of course. But why are those waters red, blue, yellow, black and white? That's the nub of the question. You don't know? Listen to me:

"Quintus Curtius claims that the Red Sea was thus named in memory of King Erythros, who lived in Arabia, and the name Erythros means red—but Quintus Curtius is mistaken. The waters of the Red Sea really are red at certain times, as the waters of the Yellow Sea become yellow, and these names were given to them by the nature of their waves.

"Now, this coloration reveals the presence of microscopic zoophytes, of a species of *Oscillatoria* that the botanist Candole once found in Lake Morat, whose waters became bloody in 1825.[53]

"In 1835, a former consul-general of France in Havana, Monsieur Mollien, found the same microscopic zoophytes, but yellow, in the Yellow Sea.

"That is how scientists were convinced that the cause I'm giving you was real and true. They extracted a certain quantity of theses colored waters and let them settle. The sediment the liquid deposited was examined under a microscope, it and was observed that it did not contain soil particles, but was formed by the agglomeration of tiny algae, some of them *Oscillatoria* and others *Trichodesmium eythreum*, which is found more commonly in the southern seas."

"I accept your explanation," I said, "all the more so because I've read the reports made to the Académie des Sciences, and I believe that you are confirming them fully. For the moment, allow me to greet the Earth; it's my homeland."

Mikaël's only response was a smile.

We were, in fact, getting closer, and I was already recognizing objects. It was not Europe that I could see, alas, and yet, by virtue of the nostalgia that took possession of me, it was toward that continent and my Paris that my desires reached out. I understood them very quickly, by virtue of the sudden reflection that I was an exceedingly privileged mortal, since, without fatigue, perfectly comfortable in my gondola, I had seen the Moon, and I could make a circumnavigation of our globe. Scientific curiosity returned to me in full force, and

---

[53] *Oscillatoria*, like the *Trichodesmium* species mentioned in the following passage, are filamentous cyanobacteria, the latter sometimes known as "sea sawdust." They do occasionally form colored "blooms" on water, but this explanation of the nomenclature of various seas is highly dubious. The two Candoles who reported on the micro-organisms in question signed themselves "P. and A. Candole."

I had not eyes enough to see Asia, great and beautiful Asia, which displayed itself to me in all its luxury.

I recognized its rich countries, its mountains, its rivers and its cities. In particular, I recognized the Indian Ocean, above which we were floating, and which I had only ever seen on maps. The sea was beginning to rise, for the tide was coming in, and its waves, in coming to break upon its rocks and banks, sent forth flecks of foam tinted pink by the sun's rays.

Its immense surface was streaked by ships of every shape and size, from rapid steamboats to majestic three-masters—but I was more desirous of paying attention to once-celebrated countries that I had seen on the Moon in their former state. So, when we arrived above land, I asked Mikaël to give our balloons an immobility that would not be contradicted by the movement of the Earth, in order that it might rotate beneath our eyes and offer us the successive sight of all the continents of the world—which Mikaël hastened to do, for our edification.

Naïs and Stella were as content as I was, for the Lunians had never been so close to the Earth, and their eyes, like mine, remained avidly fixed on Asia, which was displayed to us first.

"Let's see, Daughter," Naïs said to Stella. "Do you know your terrestrial geography? Speak, I shall simply enjoy it; I feel an invincible disposition to idleness."

"Be satisfied, Mother. I shall speak as a veritable pedagogue, and shall not spare you the slightest valley."

And while Stella's soft voice provided the most harmonious accompaniment to that grandiose spectacle, I saw passing beneath me the great continent that was the cradle of humankind, the seat of the first and greatest empires of antiquity, of the richest and most populous cities, witness to God's prodigies in favor of his people, to the birth and death of Jesus Christ—and with its vast countries passed the ancient rivers under new names, the ancient mountains under modern names, and the renewed nations founded on the ruins of extinct nations.

Thus, with their frame of contours cut by the innumerable inroads of the sea, I saw appearing, first Siberia with its immense Steppes and its three rivers, the Ob, the Yenisei and the Lena; Lake Baikal and its seals; the Ural, Altai and Yablounai Mountains, its copper and iron mines; its sables and black foxes; its serfs and exiles; its populations, known by be animals of which they make use in their migrations, reindeer Tunguses, dog Tunguses, horse Tunguses, Yakuts and Yaukahires, Koriaks, Kamchatkans, Voguls, Samoyeds and Ostiaks. There was nothing more curious than seeing an entire family of the first-named people grouped around a sled harnessed to dogs, launching those ardent animals forth at a gallop, sliding over the snow with the rapidity of a rock detached from a glacier.

Then came Turkestan, with its Aral Sea, its desert plains, its rivers with fertile banks, and its rubies. We saw galloping hordes of Cossacks, Bukharas and Kirghiz, drinking mares' milk delightedly. We also discovered troops of Kalmuks, but the distance did not permit us to judge their ugliness.

Then Persia advanced, displaying very few rivers and even fewer forests. In the delightful valleys of Shiraz, Ispahan and Yezd, however, we saw magnificent vines, tobacco plants and quantities of mulberry-bushes. On the coast of the Persian Gulf people were fishing for beautiful pearls, and there were camel-trains everywhere, transporting opium, nut-galls, wheat and rice. In the cities, such as Tehran, Herat and Ispahan, women appeared dressed in magnificent silk robes embroidered with gold and spangled with silver; the men, wearing turbans, wore glistening damascened steel armor. The attitudes of the city-dwellers, however, showed the traces of an effeminate life to which the tyranny of the Shah had accustomed them. As for the nomadic tribes, we found them lying in ambush behind the thickets and the smallest bushes, to hold up and rob travelers. Finally, in the middle of certain villages and city temples we distinguished Persians prostrating themselves before flamboyant weapons: they were the Zoroastrians or Parsees, worshipers of fire.

Then came that immense part of Asia once known as Asia Minor, which had now become Turkish Asia or Anatolia, enclosing—within limits formed by the Caspian Sea, the Black Sea, the Sea of Marmora, the Mediterranean, the Persian Gulf and the Sea of Oman—Syria, Phoenicia, Palestine, Mesopotamia, Babylon, Assyria and Chaldea.

So, imagine the enthusiasm that gripped me and went to my head when I found myself face to face with the land that was once the terrestrial paradise.

Stella put her hand on my arm and said to me, pointing with her finger at various points that she indicated to me:

"The terrestrial paradise that you have seen depicted on our Moon, and about which you will talk in your Marvelous Album."

But that enthusiasm quickly drained away, alas—for what was that once-blessed now? My God! The prey of brambles and brushwood, through the middle of which flowed one, two rivers with muddy waters...

Sin, the angel's avenging sword, and the curse had passed this way...

And I contemplated the land profaned by Eve and Adam, reddened by the blood of Abel, slain by Cain...

I searched with my gaze for Mount Ararat, on which, after the Deluge, Noah's Ark had come to rest. I divined, in a mound of bricks covered with mosses, lichens and briars, the place where rebellious humans had built their tower of Babel—and then the plains occupied by the tents, the pastures and the flocks of Abraham, Isaac and Joseph, and those of Laban, Rachel and Leah.

"Behold," said Stela, "the classical land that saw the exploits of Nimrod, the first hunter and great founder of empires; of Ninus, Semiramis, Sesostris, Cyrus, Alexander, Pompey, Marius, Sulla, Antony, Caesar, Titus, of a great number of Christian heroes under the leadership of Godefroy de Bouillon and, more recently, those of the immortal conqueror Bonaparte.

170

"It belonged successively to the Assyrians, the Babylonians, the Medes, the Persians, the Greeks, the Jews, the Parthians and the Romans.

"It is the cradle of all civilization; it is the country that is always beautiful in spite of its ruins; it is the most ancient theater in which the principal faults of history and nature materialized. All of ancient history is merely the history of the various races and different empires of Asia. Languages, sciences, arts, commerce—in a word, al the means of hastening civilization have been given birth in this part of the world, which passes for the most beautiful, the richest and the most interesting of all.

"The most famous cities were there:

"Troy, the city of Priam, Hector, Anchises, Aeneas and Hecuba, the tomb of so many illustrious warriors;

"Smyrna, the city of Tantalus, destroyed by the Lydians and rebuilt by Alexander the Great, the fatherland of Bion and the most disciplined as well as the most opulent of Asia Minor;

"Ephesus, founded by the Amazons, famous for its temple of Diana, burned by the stupid Erostratus on the very day of Alexander's birth, the fatherland of the illustrious painters Apelles and Parrhasius, and the philosopher Hercalitus;

"Antioch, the city of Seleucus Nicanor, with its five-league encircling wall, its temples, its sumptuous palaces, its vast theaters and its suburb of Daphne, planted with the laurier-roses that gave it its name;

"Damascus, contemporary with Abraham, the most ancient city in the world, the workshop famous for making the Emperor Diocletian's swords and daggers, the place where Saul became Paul and the apostle of the Gentiles instead of the persecutor of Christians he had been;

"Tyre, the colony of the Sidonians, the Mediterranean port, the conquest of Nebuchannezzar, Alexander's stopover for seven months, the city of Omar I;

"Sidon, the work of Sidon, son of Canaan, the worshiper of Baal and Ashtoreth, the victim of Cyrus, the fatherland of Zeno, the city of commerce and industry;

"Palmyre, the desert oasis, the pride of Odenat and Zenobia, the prey of Aurelian;

"Babylon, the masterpiece of Semiramis, the observatory of the Chaldean astronomers, the conquest of Cyrus over Balthazar, the residence of Alexander;

"Nineveh, the creation of Nimrod, the preferred dwelling of Ninus, the theater of Jonah's complaints, the receptacle of the orgies of Sardanapalus, the prison of Tobias;

"Ecbatana, the colored plaything of Dejoces, the treasure stolen by Alexander, Antoichus and Seleucus Nicanor.

"Susa, the splendid winter residence of the Persian monarchs, witness to the vision of Daniel of the four kingdoms of Babylon, Persia, Greece and Rome, the location of the touching story of Esther and Mordecai, the place from which Nehemiah was able to go to Jerusalem to rebuild it walls, and, finally the tomb of Daniel.

"Bactria, of which Ninus rendered himself master thanks to the skill of a woman, Semiramis.

"Persepolis, the most magnificent city of the Persians, the rival of Babylon, Susa and Ecbatana, the victory of Alexander, who burned it in spite of its splendors;

"Heliopolis, whose temple of the Sun was its glory;

"Libyssa, famous for the death of that same Hannibal.[54]

"Zile, the temple of which was consecrated to Venus-Anaisis, in the vicinity of which Mithridates fought the Romans and where, twenty years later, Caesar fought Pharnacius, the son of that same Mithridates;

"Timbrea, famous for the battle that Cyrus won over Croesus,[55] and which put an end to the Lydian Empire;

---

[54] The form of this line suggests that a city has been omitted from the list, presumably Bithynia, where Hannibal first took refuge while fleeing the Romans

"Ipsus, a location even more famous for the bloody battle that Alexander's successors fought here, and in which Antigone was killed;

"Gordium, which conserved the chariot of King Gordius, the knot of whose helm was so complex that Alexander, knowing the oracle that promised the empire of Asia to the man who could untie it, cut it with a sweep of his sword;

"Sebaste,[56] which made Pompey great, and where forty soldiers who were part of the fulminating legion were decapitated;

"Melina, which Trajan founded, and where Polyeuctus, the hero of your poet Corneille,[57] was martyrized;

"Halicarnassus, the capital of king Mausolus, for whom his wife Artemisia, inconsolable at his loss, built a tomb that as one of the seven wonders of the world, from which the word mausoleum comes;

"Gnide, of the temple of Venus-Gnidian, which hid the marvelous statue of the goddess by Praxiteles;[58]

---

[55] The battle of Timbrea (Timbrée In French) was, indeed, where Cyrus defeated Croesus, but it is odd to see the location named as a city; it was near the city of Sardis, whose omission from the list similarly seems odd. Driou presumably obtained the name Timbrée from Charles Rollin's massive account of ancient history, from which several other names on the list seem to be extracted.

[56] There were several cities in Asia Minor bearing this name (the Greek equivalent of the Latin *Augusta*); the one to which Driou is referring is the one now known as Sivas.

[57] The reference is to Pierre Corneille's *Polyeucte martyr* (1643).

[58] The name of the city in question is usually rendered as Cnidus, but Driou would have been familiar with it by virtue of the Baron de Montesquieu's extended poem in prose *Le Temple de Gnide* (1725), so I have allowed his version to stand.

"Tarsus, on the Cydnus, in which Alexander, having imprudently bathed therein, nearly lost his life because of the extreme coldness of its waters;

"Mopsus, famous for the death of Seleucus VI, king of Syria, whom the inhabitants burned alive in his palace;

"Isus, where Darius was vanquished by Alexander;

"Ur, the abode and fatherland of Abraham;

"Edessa, which played an important role in your crusades;

"Tigranocerta, founded by Tigranes, King of Armenia and son-in-law of Mithridates;

"Rages, work of Ninus and abode of Gabelus, to whom Tobias had lent ten talent that his son went to reclaim;[59]

"Arbela, made famous by the battle the Alexander won against Darius Codomannus, which put an end to the Persian Empire;

"Cunaxa, which saw Cyrus the Younger loose his life fighting with ten thousand Greeks against his brother Artaxerxes Mnemon, 401 years before Christ;

"Pasagardae, the work of Cyrus the Great, which saw the kings of Persia crowned, and possessed the tomb of that same Cyrus."

"I admire your memory, charming Lunian," I exclaimed, when Stella finally brought that long geographical list to an end.

"You have many other things to admire, Monsieur Terran," the young woman immediately went on. "We talk a great deal about that famous Asia, as you can see from what we have just said, but we have not yet said anything about the part most interesting to you, young Catholic. That is Palestine, the Holy Land, the promised land of the Hebrews, the people of God."

---

[59] The reference is one of several to the Biblical book of *Tobias* or *Tobit*, which is included in the Catholic Bible but is omitted from Protestant Bibles or consigned to the Apocrypha.

Stella was standing, leaning idly on her elbow, in the Oriental mode, striking a solemn pose. "Now, Monsieur," she continued, "whatever the homeland of the modern man might be, there are three cities of which education and study makes him a citizen, to wit, Athens, Rome and Jerusalem.

"Behold Jerusalem, one of your fatherlands—take off your hat and bow to it! Behold Jerusalem, I say, founded by Melchisedech, the contemporary of Abraham, on the Mounts Moria and Acra. It was once called Salem—which is to say, Peace, Taken be the Jesbusites, descendants of Jebus, son of Canaan, it received the named Jebus-Salem, vision of pace.

"I shall not repeat its history to you; you know it. You know, above all, the terrible drama that Heaven demanded of the earth on the bloody mount. There died a God! Yes, a God died for humankind on that bare and sterile rock...

"Worship and pray...!

"But after we have prostrated ourselves before Jerusalem, look at the land of Canaan, which became the promised land of Israel, which became Judea, which became the Holy Land, which became Palestine.

"To the north, first greet the Lebanon, which separates it from Syria. That chain of Taurus took the name Lebanon, which means white, because of the snows that, in several places, cover its summits constantly.

"Those mountains, rising atop on another, offer four distinct zones to the eye. Cereals cover the first, with a great number of fruit trees. The second is nothing but a belt of bare and sterile rocks. In spite of its elevation, the third offers the aspect of evergreen trees; the mildness of its temperature, its gardens, its orchards laden with the most beautiful fruits of Syria, the streams that irrigate them, have made it a place of delights. The fourth is lost in the clouds. The eternal snows with which it is covered, and the rigor of the cold, render it uninhabitable and almost inaccessible, especially at certain times of the year.

"The famous cedars of which Scripture speaks, which are almost as ancient as the world, are found, as you can see, on one of those summits."

"In 1833," said Naïs, who had remained silent for a long time, "those famous cedars, which form a veritable forest, received the visit of one of your most renowned poets, Monsieur de Lamartine. "The ice on the mountain did not permit him to walk beneath their branches, but he contemplated them for a long time, and penciled this notes in their regard, which I read, very indiscreetly:

"'These trees are the most celebrated natural monuments in the world. Religion, poetry and history have all consecrated them. Holy Scripture celebrates them in several places. They are one of the images that poets employ with predilection. Solomon wanted to consecrate them as the ornament of the temple that he first raised to the unique God, doubtless because of the renown of the magnificence and sanctity that these prodigies of vegetation had in that epoch.

"'Arabs of all sects have a traditional veneration for these trees. They attribute to them not only a vegetative force that enables them to live eternally, but also a soul that gives them signs of wisdom and foresight similar to those of instinct in animals and intelligence in humans. They know the seasons in advance; they move their vast boughs in anticipation, like limbs; they extend or bend their elbows; they raise their branches toward the sky or lower them toward the earth, according to whether the snow is preparing to fall or to melt. They are beings in the form of trees. They only grow in this group of locations in Lebanon; they take secure root above the region where all large-scale vegetation expires. All of that strikes the ardent imagination of the peoples of the Orient with astonishment.

"'These trees are diminishing every century. Travelers one counted thirty or forty of them, later seventeen, later still, a dozen. There are now only seven of them, whose mass allows the presumption that they are contemporary with Biblical times. Around these old witnesses to times gone by, there still remains a little forest of younger cedars, which appear to me to form a group of four or five hundred trees or saplings.

"'Every year, in the month of June, the populations of Beschierai, Eden and Kanobin, and all the villages in the neighboring valleys, climb up to the cedars and celebrate a mass at their feet. What prayers must have resonated under those branches! And what temple is more beautiful, what altar nearer to Heaven? What dais is more majestic and holier than the ultimate plateau of Lebanon, the trunks of the cedars and the tome of those scared branches, which have shadowed over and over again so many human generations, pronouncing the name of God differently, but recognizing him everywhere in his works and worshiping him in his natural manifestations.'"[60]

Naïs fell silent after this quotation, and Mikaël spoke in his turn, to guide me in the examination I was making.

"See how Palestine is divided by a large number of mountains," he said. "What steep crags! How their fissures allow the perception of long valleys and profound ravines! This slope, which faces the desert, present nothing but asperities and abrupt peaks; the opposite slope, by contrast, of an entirely picturesque character, reveals itself watered by cool springs and azure lakes, and brings together various populations, as much because of the fertility of its soil as the mildness of its climate. Its plains are fecund with beautiful crops and its mountains laden with rich vegetation. Lilies, tuberoses and laurier-roses grow along the hedges and streams, and embalm the air with their sweet odors. An innumerable multitude of wild bees collects perfumed honey from the flowers, which they deposit in the hollows of rocks and old trees."

"This was the land flowing with milk and honey that the Lord had promised his people," I said to the Lunian, "and how different it is from the sterility and malediction with which he

---

[60] The quotation is from Alphonse de Lamartine's *Souvenirs, impressions, pensées et paysages, pendant un voyage en orient* (1835; tr. as *A Pilgrimage to the Holy Land*).

struck Jerusalem! But again now, in spite of the sloth and negligence of the Turks and the Arabs. I see it proud of its riches; it grows green beneath its orange-trees, lemon-trees, figs, olives and date-palms, which are laden with flowers and fruits everywhere."

Stella signaled to her father that she was about to show me the important points of that land of promise, and I fell silent in order to listen.

"There, to the north," she said, "in the tribal lands of Aser, is Akko, which became Ptolemais, then St. John of Acre, at the mouth of the little river Belus. The Israelites left that town to the Phoenicians. It was on the banks of that river that the latter discovered the art of glass-making, a thousand years before Christ.

In the tribal lands of Nephtali, to the east, you will notice Lake Gennesaret, on that lake, Bethsaida, homeland of St. Peter, John the Evangelist, James the Elder, their brother, and Philip.

"Then Capurnaum, in the most charming spot, as indicated by its name, which mans *field of beauty.*

"Then Dan, where Jeroboam was foolish enough to erect one of two golden calves, which he stupidly exposed for the people to worship.

"In the tribal lands of Zabulon, below Aser, similarly on the lake, is Tiberiad, build in 17 A.D. by Herod Agrippa, tetrarch of the province called Galilee on the side of Nazareth.

"Further to the west, behold Nazareth, the abode of Mary, Joseph and Jesus, where he spent thirty years of his life.

"Even further to the west, remark Cana, where Jesus performed his first miracle of changing water into wine for the two spouses.

"In the tribal lands of Issachar, not far from Mount Gelboa, there is Shulam, the homeland of Abishag, David's last wife, where Elisha resuscitated the son of a Shulamite;[61] then Naïm, where a widow persuaded Jesus to recall her son to life;

---

[61] cf 2 *Kings* 4:8-37.

and Bethulia, which saw the terrible Judith cut off the head of Holofernes, who was besieging the town.

"In the part of the tribal lands of Manasseh near the land of the Ammonites, far to the east, I'm showing you Jabesh-Gilead, which was sacked by the Israelites.

"In the other part of the tribal lands of Manasseh, on the shore of the sea, there is Caesaria, enlarged by Herod, who gave it that name to flatter Augustus, the first Emperor of Rome. Its wall, its harbor and its monument are almost whole, but do not have a single inhabitant.

"In the center of the tribal lands, behold Samaria, built on Mount Gerizim by Omri, King of Israel, who made it the capital of his kingdom. There, close by, are the ruins of the famous temple of Baal.

"In the tribal lands of Gad, do you see ruins under those bushes and rocks? That's Rabbath-Ammon, the capital of the Ammonites, very important in the time of Moses, taken by David. On that side, look, the ruins have a veritable splendor. That's because Ptolemy Philadelphia decorated it, after having given it is name, when Judea became a Roman province.

"There, to the east, are the wood of Ephraim, the village of Phanuel and, a little further away on the frontier of Iturea, the village of Ramath-Gilead, on the torrent of Jabbok. It was a Levite city and refuge. It is famous for the defense of Ahab, King of Israel, 897 years before Christ, and for the coronation of Jehu.

"In the tribal lands of Ephraim, to the south-west, on the shore of the sea, there is Shiloh, situated on a mountain, celebrated as the abode of the Ark for more than three hundred years, from Joshua until the high-priest Eli, in 1116 B.C. It was there that the Israelites came to consult the Lord, and at Shiloh too that Eli lived, and where Hannah consecrated her son Samuel to the god of the Jews.

"There also is Shechem, the capital of Israel before the founding of Samaria. It existed in the time of Abraham. Beside it is Jacob's well, named Sichar. It's there that Jesus conversed with the Samaritan woman.

"Near the mountains, there, in the direction of Gaza, is Thamnathsare, where Joshua died..."

"I'm looking, but I can't see anything," I said, nonplussed.

"That's true; your mortal eyes can't discover the traces that no longer exist, but for us, who have seen it before, it's there that Thamnathsare was."

"But I can see, for example, from Caesaria to...?"

"Joppa."

"Joppa, on the sea-shore, magnificent meadows."

"They're the meadows of Sharon, which were once covered by roses, narcissi, anemones, terebinths, wallflowers, odorous immortelles, and white and yellow lilies."

"At least the plain is still fertile with cereals."

"You're looking directly at the Jordan," Stella continued. "It's the only watercourse in Palestine, except for torrents that only flow in winter. Its sources are on Mount Hermon, one of the glaciers of the Lebanon. It traverses Lake Gennesaret, as you can see, and empties into the Dead Sea, or Lake Asphaltite. During the winter, it's subject to periodic flooding. It's there, not far from Jericho, that Joshua brought the Hebrews over the river, and it's here that Jesus was baptized in its waters by John the Baptist.

"Lake Asphaltite, as you doubtless know, was thus named by the Greeks because of the bitumen extracted therefrom. It was on the Dead Sea that Sodom, Gomorrah, Admah, Zeboiim and Zoar were located, which God caused to perish by means of fire from the sky in the time of Abraham and Lot. These waters occupied the ancient valley of Siddim or woods once rich in pastureland, but here was death under the flowers, for the soul, so brilliantly adorned, only owed its fertility to the fire that underlay it, and whose furnaces the Lord opened to punish the wicked inhabitants of the five cities. Under that beautiful ground, sulfur, bitumen and other volcanic substances were seething, awaiting the moment to plunge into eternal oblivion that creatures who had dared to defy the Creator's laws. So, one day, the fire from the sky ignited the fires in the earth, and all the igniferous substances began to flow in blazing torrents. Then the waters of the Jordan, which had previously run into the Gulf of Arabia, stopped, engulfed by the immense void that a horrible crack had just opened, and nothing could any longer be seen but a long sheet of water, as heavy as liquid metal, though which the shadows of the impious cities could sometimes be detected."

"So these banks seem desolate," I exclaimed. "There is nothing to be seen but sadness and desolation. The mountain slopes are arid and bare; there is nothing but frail bushes struggling against a rebellious nature. The ground sweats salt; the springs in the vicinity must be bitter."

"They are saltier than any other known water," said Mikaël. "It is doubtful that their water, like that of the lake, can support living creatures; that is why the lake has been given the name of the Dead Sea."

"But it's said," I objected, "that for a long time, thick columns of smoke rose up from the lake, testifying to the continued burning of the cities. It's also said that the vapors emerging therefrom still kill birds flying over it."

"No," said the Lunian.

"Finally, it's claimed that the oranges that ripen on its shores contain nothing but ashes, a horrible surprise for the thirsty traveler."

"Yes," replied my guide. "That results from the nature of the soil. Except that, rather than ashes, it ought to be said that the fruits only contain dry flesh, detestable to taste."

"Is it true that when one tries to bathe in it, the weight of the water refuses to allow the immersion of the body?"

"In that regard, Monsieur Terran, I can tell you that the Emperor Vespasian, wanting to try the experiment, had poor wretches who could not swim and whose hands were tied thrown into the lake. The unfortunates sank to the bottom, to rediscover Sodom and Gomorrah in the depths of the abyss."

"I'll conclude now," Stella resumed, "if you care to look beyond the Dead Sea, my dear Terran."

"Speak, charming child."

"In the tribal lands of Reuben, to the east, near the land of the Moabites, there is Machaerus, a fortress situated on that rock bathing its feet in the Dead Sea. You can see that the rock is enclosed by profound valleys. It's there that the beheading of John the Baptist took place, on the orders of Herod Antipas.

"In the tribal lands of Benjamin, in the center, I have no need to point Jerusalem out to you—but there is Bethany, a town situated on the Mount of Olives, where Jesus resurrected Lazarus, and the house of Simon the Leper is to be found;

"Jericho, in a plain planted with date-palms, of which Joshua took possession with the sound of trumpets;

"Gibeon, on a hill. It was near that city, in that plain, that five kings of the desert, having formed an alliance against the Gibeonites, were vanquished by Joshua, who prayed to God to stop the sun in order to have the time necessary to defeat his enemies;

"Bethel, similarly on a mountain, where Jacob had his celebrated vision of the mysterious ladder. Jeroboam placed the other golden calf that he had the Israelites worship there;

"Rama, whose valley must have resounded with the cries of the dead when Herod massacred the sons of the Jews after the birth of Jesus, in order to encompass the new king within the massacre;

"Emmaus, where Jesus revealed himself to two of his disciples on the day after his resurrection.

"In the tribal lands of Dan, separated from the Mediterranean Sea by the Philistines, behold Joppa, formerly Japho, which was witness to the embarkation of Jonah, escaping to Tarsus instead of carrying out God's order to deliver threats to Nineveh.

"In the tribal lands of Simeon, I can only show you Beersheba—the ancient dwelling of Abraham and Isaac, from which the patriarch took his son to Mount Moriah, then desert, to sacrifice him, in the very spot where the savior of humankind expired in torment, when Jerusalem had been built on that mountain—and Siceleg, a little town given to David by the King of Gath.

"Finally, in the tribal lands of Judah, there is Hebron, the tomb of Abraham, situated at the entrance to the valley of Mamre, where Isaac and Jacob dwelt in Abraham's tents. Sarah was also buried there. It was the birthplace of John the Baptist.

"There also are Engedde, on the Dead Sea, and Bethlehem, formerly Ephrata, which means fruitful, made famous by the death of Rachel, buried under the road to Bethel, by the birth of David, and above all by the coming into the world of Jesus Christ, the sun of all justice."

"But today it's no more than a simple town," I said to Stella. "Except, what is that superb church?"

"The temple that the Empress Helena, mother of Constantine, had raised on the location of the cave, the stable that saw the savior of humankind born to the Virgin Mary."

"And what are those villages, in the midst of the ruins that border the Mediterranean Sea?"

"The former lands of the Philistines:

"Acheron, the capital of one of the Philistines' five kings, where Beelzebub was worshiped, who had an oracle there;

"Gath, the birthplace of the giant Goliath;

"Ashdod, famous for the worship that was rendered there to Dagon, and where a temple disturbed by Samson crushed him as it fell, Psammetichus, King of Egypt, having besieged that city in 170 B.C. could only take it after twenty nine years."

"That is, without doubt, the longest siege in history," I said.

"Gaza," my Lunian cicerone continued, "which was taken successively by the Chaldeans, the Persians and Alexander the Great. It was at Gaza that, for the two wounds the conqueror received, he had the inhabitants massacred and sold. There's no longer anything there but ruins, as you can see, my dear Terran."

"And the last city, which you seemed to have forgotten?"

"That's Ashkelon, in a fertile valley, which was the birthplace of Semiramis, whose education by doves you have seen in our lunar daguerreotype, and about whom you ought to speak in your *Marvelous Album*. Herod the Great was also born there.

"Finally, there's Gerar, near the torrent of Bezor, the capital of King Abimelech, a contemporary of Abraham..."

"Thank you, a thousand thanks, my dear Lunian," I said to Stella, who resumed her Oriental pose on the cushions of her gondola.

While she had been speaking, pointing out to me one by one the cities just cited. I saw them in all reality, no longer as in the days of their opulence, their richness and their splendor, no longer as in the days of their glory and the noble deeds or crimes to which they had been witness, no longer as I shall describe them in the *Marvelous Album* in question, but as they are today, in 1854; which is to say, some barely preserved, mutilated, but with beautiful debris, others—the greater number, alas—covered in mossy ruins, scattered amid the brushwood and brambles of the desert.

Then, in Anatolia, or Asia Minor, which slid slowly and ponderously beneath our motionless aerostats, there was the ancient Troad, with the village of Bunarbachi, formerly Ilion, formerly Troy, of which no vestige any longer remains except, on a nearby rock, the debris of constructions shaped as irregular polygons, a cistern hollowed in the rock and three tombs—which, Mikaël told me, belonged to the ancient citadel of Pergamum. Then, at the foot of Cape Sigeum, there were the other tombs of Achilles and his friend Patroclus, and, near the other cape, Rhetea, the sepulcher of Ajax.

After that passed immense collapsed subterranean vaults, around which the wind sighed in a thousand heaps of rubble—and Mikaël said, his voice becoming lugubrious: "The temple of Ephesus!"

Then came a modern city, very busy, with beautiful aspects, but with nothing ancient or grandiose about it.

"Smyrna," said Mikaël, in a melancholy tone.

Then, as we turned our gazes eastwards, there were vast ruins and a colossal tumulus, affecting the form of a cone of earth.

"Sardis and the sepulcher of Alyattes, the father of Croesus," said Mikaël.

Next appeared a fortress whose walls had sculptures built into their cement, representing funeral processions and battles between naked and dressed figurines.

"Halicarnssus and the tomb of Mausolus, now Boudroun..." said Mikaël.

After that, more heaped up rubble, then a fairly large town. "The Temple of Gnide and Tarsus," murmured the Lunian.

"But what is that city situated on an arm of the river, in a vast plain at the foot of high mountains?" I asked my guide.

"Erzerum is the town, the river is the Euphrates, the plain is Armenia and the mountain the Taurus," he replied.

Then came an immense space covered in vast ruins, between two rivers, connected by numerous dried-up canals, strewn with fragments of bricks and tiles, with a high hill formed by rubble at the center. Fragments of walls seemed to have served for the foundations of aerial gardens, for one of the piles bore a tree grafted on to an old trunk. There were long corridors and rooms in which we saw a lioness nursing her cubs and a female panther playing on the moss with one of her offspring, and a thousand items of debris that could not be described.

"Babylon!" sighed Mikaël.

"Babylon!" I repeated, like an echo.

"Babylon!" he said, again. "That hill was the Temple of Belus, and that prodigious heap of bricks forming its base was the foundations of the Tower of Babel. That hill of bricks, of the finest type, baked in fire and perfectly molded, has o less than twenty thousand feet on each side of the square it forms. Those ruins of gardens are the remains of the work of Semiramis—and those rooms and corridors belonged to the palace of Nebuchadnezzar, in which Alexander the Great yielded his last sigh...

"That's all that remains of Babylon the Great! Now desolation inhabits these ruins; ferocious beasts make their lairs therein, as you can see, and the word of the prophets is perfectly accomplished."

Tears streaked my cheeks, I confess. My soul was profoundly moved, for everything that I saw, which had been so great in times past, was lost in immense deserts, where thieves robbed pilgrims and rare caravanserai scarcely offered a miserable pittance to travelers.

And Syria passed in its turn; and then I saw the desolate place where Tyre was, now Çur. Then came Sidon, which offered only the debris of tombs carved into the rock. Then came Caesarea, almost intact but devoid of inhabitants.

But an expanse of uncultivated steppes suddenly appeared between two chains of mountains. That narrow gorge soon broadened out and, at its extremity, I saw immense and magnificent ruins in an ocean of sand. The eye became lost in the midst of immense files of columns, unable to distinguish anything in the distance but forests of pillars, destroyed tombs, mutilated stocks and capitals scattered on the ground. In the center was the debris of a temple whose door faced westwards—a strange thing, for in these regions, temples always faced the orient.

"Palmyra, Tadmor, or the Oasis of Palms!" Mikaël murmured, in his hollow voice.

It was a place of surprises, assuredly, for suddenly, on the horizon, the globe of the Earth led us, on the last slopes of the black mountains of the Anti-Lebanon, to a marvelous assembly of ruins gilded by the sun's rays, which outlined the shadows of the mountains admirably. What splendor, even in those ruins! Gigantic walls; dazzling colossal columns that appeared to extend, to grow, to elongate as they drew closer to us; blocks of marble that time or the vicissitudes of nature had expelled from monuments; an Acropolis or artificial hill allowing glimpses of superb constructions between the branches and above the heads of tall trees; red granites; sanguine porphyries; carved capitals, architraves, volutes, corniches, entablements, pedestals, scattered limbs, recumbent statues, the profiles of monuments standing out in golden colors against blue of the firmament, seemingly intact, as if they had emerged from the workman's hand only yesterday... No pen, no brush, could describe the impression that scene gave to me eyes and my soul.

"Heliopolis, now Baalbec," said Mikaël. "And notice," he added, "the hill of Baalbec, a platform a thousand paces long, seven hundred feet broad, all built by the hand of man, in carved stones, some of which are fifty or sixty feet long and twenty or twenty-two deep."

"Superb monuments to human pride...
By the insult of time you are abolished,
And your cheerful aspects are now destroyed;
There is no cement that time cannot dissolve!"[62]

I said to Mikaël, while plunging my gaze into those Pelasgic works.

It is quite impossible to forget such spectacles once one has seen them. At that moment the golden rays of the sun struck the great temple consecrated to it, and in the distance, as far as the gaze could reach, there was nothing to be seen but a sea of marble debris and broken stones, like beach covered by their white dust and their foam.

Meanwhile, Palestine passed by.[63]

---

[62] These are the first four lines of a famous sonnet by Paul Scarron (1610-1660)

[63] There is an apparent error in continuity here, which initially gives the appearance that a stray page from an earlier draft was somehow incorporated into the final manuscript— although the author, seemingly confused, then makes hasty corrective adjustments to the course of the narrative, after the double line of dots presumably signifying a time-lapse. It

After beautiful broad plains, and far from the desert, there was first a labyrinth of mountains of conical form. And in the valleys troops of camels with drooping ears, ewes with long tails, the onagers of the holy books were coming and going with their herdsmen. Young Arab girls could be seen exposing grapes in the open air to dry them; women were coming back from a spring with large urns on their heads; the smoke of hamlets rose in white vapor above the trees; she-camels trotted over the pebbles of dry stream-beds with their riders in red burnooses; and the songs of confused voices could be heard rising from the ground.

Suddenly, the ridge of a plateau that appeared to us became a long line of Gothic walls, flanked by square towers dominated by the spires, cupolas and pyramids of edifices. And all around one profound valley, a torrent, tombs, ruins, bare hills, olive groves, bare and devastated slopes, broken rocks, a lugubrious scene of desolation and death.

"Get up and worship, said Stella then; you have before you Jerusalem, one of your fatherlands!

......

......

"Now," she had resumed, "let us lend impulsion to our balloons and go on, getting ahead of the rotation of the Earth, in order to go back toward the east and go to see other ruins.

And when we had disposed our aerostats for the flight, we had passed, leaving Egypt behind us, over vast Arabia and the tip of the Persian Gulf.

Already we had lost to sight the valley of Jehosophat, the torrent of Kedron, the Garden of Olives, the Field of Blood, Mount Tabor, Mount Sinai, which I had perceived from afar, and, turning our backs to the sea, to Palestine, and to the

---

ought to be noted that anyone trying to figure out the trajectory followed by the two aerostats as the Earth supposedly rotates beneath them will have been confused for some time, even making allowances for the fact that they are obviously tracking northwards as well as westwards.

desert, we had arrived over the Persian Gulf when I distinguished a vast plateau in a plain fertilized by the Araxes of the ancients, now Bend-Enier,[64] near a village at the foot of a mountain of grey marble. The whole of that platform, at which my guides were aiming, presented the form of an amphitheater with several terraces raised upon one another. One could climb from one terrace to the next by stairways so spacious that then horsemen could have ridden abreast there. At the end of each terrace were the remains of porticos and the debris of buildings, with ruined apartments. Finally, at the back, against the rock of the mountain, I distinguished two tombs hollowed in the rock. The chambers, porticos and stairways were made of the purest marble, so neatly fitted in all its sections that I could not distinguish and juncture.

"Persepolis," Mikaël stammered, in his funereal tone. The ruins of the palace that Alexander burned when, led astray by drunkenness, he wanted to advertise forever the fall of Cyrus' Empire. It has been impossible thus far to discover the entrance to those tombs. A few miles to the north, you can see four other similar tombs—and in the plain, there, look at that small square edifice with and enormous pedestal of white marble. That's Cyrus' sepulcher, and that plain is none other than Pasagarde in Latin and Persepolis in Greek."

I noticed columns that did not belong to any known genre; cuneiform inscriptions that I had seen nowhere else; allegories and figures covering the walls that astonished me, and which I admired...

"Persepolite architecture, unique, as devoid of models as of imitations," Mikaël told me.

A moment later we passed over a large sterile space, abandoned to snakes and wild beasts. I would never have supposed that a city had ever set its foundations there, but in his doleful voice, Mikaël droned, sadly: "Susa! Esther and Mordecai, Haman and Ahasuerus!"

---

[64] The river once known as the Araxes is now the Aras, but I cannot identify the location to which Driou is referring.

Of that city, once measuring a hundred and twenty stadia in circumference, little remains but a few vestiges of a terrace a mile or two round, and nail-head inscriptions. Susa is nothing but a vast solitude, in which I can hear nothing but the roaring of ferocious beasts. I'm mistaken; I perceive a tomb, and near the tumulus, Jewish and other pilgrims...

"The tomb of the prophet Daniel!" said Stella.

"Ruins and tombs!" I exclaimed. "*Vanitas vanitatum!*[65] Seek your happiness in glory, then!"

Then passed a river, which I did not recognize at first. Mikaël was obliged to tell me its name, and that of the ruins...

"The Tigris, and Nineveh," he said.

"Tobias and Jonah," I replied, saying along the thought that had come to me as a whisper in memory.

Alas, even fewer ruins than at Babylon! A miserable village by the name of Nounia, and, to one side, inequalities of terrain, clefts, thickets, caverns, snakes in the grass, lizards on the mosses, and lions, tigers and leopards in the depths of their lairs...

"An Italian archaeologist, Paul Botta, excavated these ruins in 1845," Mikaël told me, "and he discovered Assyrian bas-reliefs representing kings and priests, and very evident traces of fine colors still remaining on the sculptures. Those figurines had Oriental costumes, imposing miters, long-sleeved robes decorated with braid and cut away on both sides at the front in such a fashion as to allow a glimpse of fringed tunics, ornate footwear, necklaces, weapons, hair and frizzy beards, arranged in stages curled symmetrically."

"All that brought back to life a distant epoch, evoking the effeminate races of Sardanapalus and his worthy rivals who reigned over the ancient world!" I said in my turn.

"And all of it is in Paris, at present..."

"I know, my dear Lunian; I've seen it at the Assyrian Museum in our imperial Louvre. There, too, I've visited the

---

[65] "Vanity of vanities"—the first words of the book of *Ecclesiastes*.

double colossus of granite extracted from these ruins, which represents a winged bull with a human face."

"Yes," said Mikaël, "the symbol of the monarch, which combines power, agile vigilance, strength and majesty. But let's go on! In this disemboweled ruin, already excavated by a French commission and soon exposed by a new team of scientists, it is believed that the palace of Khorsabad has been recognized, which is connected with Sargum, the Shalmaneser of the Bible."

"I have also seen, my dear Lunian, bas-relief that depict Sennacherib's invasion of Judea, when he took Samaria." But I fell silent, for our aerostats were moving with frightening rapidity.

Indeed, having passed Bagdad—the ancient residence of the Caliph Haroun-al-Raschid, the contemporary and friend of Charlemagne, the city of the Abassids, the Garden of the King, according to the etymology of its name; a round city flanked by towers, with a marvelous mosque whose cupola was sustained by columns sixty cubits high, its unparalleled castle and its two million inhabitants, the commercial center of Persia—we completed the tour of western Asia that we had seen partly by virtue of the rotation of the Earth and partly by maneuvering our balloons. Having shirted Nineveh, heading northwards again, we arrived at more ruins.

They were situated on a conical mountain, admirably disposed in a beautiful plain, not far from a lake that was terminated by a large plateau, strewn with rocks and mossy rubble—but there was no sign of any monument.

"Ecbatana," Mikaël murmured, dully.

"What!" I exclaimed. "That's all that remains of the famous fortress of Deioces, and the palaces, and the seven circling walls, gold, red, blue, silver, green, yellow and violet, which must, indeed, have been very visible from the plain?"

"Nothing other than the rock of the citadel and, on that rock, the holes in which the pivots of the great gates forming its entrance rotated. Nothing, except for a stump and a column with its lotus-leaf capital, in the Persepolite style with which you're familiar."

"It's a very slight smoke to recall so much vanished glory!" I said, with a sigh that emerged from the depths of my abdomen.

We had finished with the present-day ruins of Asia, and the grandiose phantoms that they evoked in my imagination: Semiramis, Ninus, Deioces, Cyrus, Croesus, Alexander, Caesar, Pompey, Sulla, Marius, Mithridates, Augustus, Antony, Cleopatra, David, Solomon and so many others. So Mikaël steered our aerostats toward eastern Asia, and sent them speeding toward that rich part of the world, in order to show me its beauties and grandeurs.

We flew over delightful countries, irrigated by the most beautiful rivers in the world. Emerging from the flanks of the mountains with which it bristles, they formed beds over innumerable shelves of rock, through gulfs and ravines, bearing richness and abundance into immense plains, and following all directions in going to empty themselves into the seas.

Soon, the king of mountains showed us its menacing points. It was the Himalayas, with its Davalaghiri, twenty-six thousand eighty hundred and sixty-two feet high. The valleys surrounding it where shaded by cedars and firs. The Ganges, the sacred river of India, appeared to our eyes after having hidden by snows and masses of ricks which gave the country an appearance of religious terror.

Thus, in the vicinity, precisely because those terrible sites inspired a religious dread, we perceived the gigantic throne of Mahadeo, placed, like the altars of Hindu gods, at the foot of Davalaghiri. We were now in Hindustan, in fact, and, unable to recall exactly what the country's religion was, I asked Stella to refresh my memory.

"Rest, Daughter," said Naïs, "and let me satisfy our friend the Terran; you've said enough, about western Asia."

She continued, with a charming smile: "down there, among the plantations whose powerful vegetation astonishes you, under the trees whose long braches fall back as lianas that fix themselves in the ground in order to climb up toward the sky again and produce another tree, beside those elephants digesting their fodder, can you see a narrow and paltry temple whose top is rounded into a cupola? That's a pagoda. Don't worry about those enormous reptiles, frightful serpents crawling through the undergrowth and stirring those plains of enormous reeds or leaping over the rocks; they're so common in these torrid countries, like the tiger and the lion, that the indigenes scarcely notice them, or avoid them with great skill.

"Now, in that pagoda they honor a god, Buddha, born of a virgin, Maya, also known as Suchi, or *the pure*. No other religion in the world is closer to Catholicism. Even their ceremonies are so similar to yours that the first Christian missionaries to arrive in Tibet were so struck by the flagrant imitation that they thought they were rediscovering their own religion. Do they not have bells, the rosary, relics? They even have bishops, in their Lamas, who were miters and carry crosiers.[66] The supreme chief of the religion is called the High Lama. He is similar to a god. He is splendidly nourished in that city over there, Lhasa, in a splendid palace. The worthy man is held to be so holy that..."

"Finish, Naïs," said Mikaël. "Have no fear of wounding modesty. The High Lama is held to be so holy that everything of his is preciously preserved, including...the residues of his meals. You understand which residues, Terran? Dried, they are placed in rich sachets..."

---

[66] From this point on, the narrative becomes wildly inaccurate and nakedly slanderous in its account of exotic populations, their beliefs and mores, probably because, like this particular passage, it is derived more from the account of Catholic missionaries than from reporters who were at least attempting accuracy. The thought that this section of the novel might have been intended as instruction for the young is likely to make the modern reader shudder, but it is interesting as a record of ideologically-based misconceptions.

"And all the worshipers of the Buddha," Naïs continued, "the lords, warriors, merchants, artisans and common people that you see emerging from the pagoda after the rites of the religion, fight over the simplest of these sachets, in order to wear them around their necks like a talisman..."

"That's an amulet of a new kind, and very odorous!" I said. "But what are those men in turbans as large as monstrous candle-snuffers or hennins, with long beards and long robes, and those nun-like individuals marching in procession?"

"Lamas of the second order," Naïs replied. "They're doubtless going to collect the High Lama's relics. After them, there are the bonzes who turn around as they pray like living tops, for hours on end. Finally, the Buddhists, those with rounded helmets, are priest distinguished from the others by the fact that they can marry. And those supposed nuns are *bonzies* or *biconis*, sacred daughters that populate the thirty thousand monasteries of the single city of Lhasa and its region.

"Let's not pass on, "said Stella, nonchalantly interrupting her mother, like a beloved child, "without naming admiring the celebrated valley of Kashmir, there to the north, long known as the paradise of India."

Indeed, a veritable nest of verdure and flowers, that valley displayed itself to us, hollowed out by the waters, in the very bosom of the summits of the Himalaya, surrounded by mountains, only communicating with other regions by three difficult passes, enjoying the most delightful temperature and the most fertile soil, combining the productions of Europe and those of Asia, irrigated by cascades and springs, with scattered lakes, on which floated islands of plants, fruits and flowers.

Kashmir itself, the city once named Srinagar—which means the station of happiness—appeared to us in magnificent basin, dotted with little villages and cheerful habitations, framed by orchards embroidered with fruits, quilted with clumps of trees, and drowned beneath festoons and clusters of vines and roses. There were terraced roofs everywhere, covered with earth, reproducing the hanging gardens of ancient

Babylon, and the most beautiful flowers were blooming there, seemingly awaiting the passing of the cool mountain breezes.

"What do you think of these admirable locations?" the Lunian asked me, catching me in an admiring pose. Then, pointing to city charming to behold, he said: "But don't let Kashmir cause you to disdain Golconda, there. You know that Golconda is the relay station of all the precious stones brought there to be polished. Apart from that, though, look at the center of the city. You see there a pagoda in the niche of which—where people pray as in a chapel—is a monolith so voluminous that it took five years to extract it from its quarry."

Meanwhile, to Golconda, Bombay, Surat and Pondicherry, the luxurious locations, marvelous factories and prodigious movement and agitation of which I admired;

To Lahore, the capital of Punjab, where I knew that Ranjit Singh, the zealous king, had handed over part of his authority to the Frenchman Jean-François Allard, to direct his people toward European civilization;

To Benares, the city so dear to the Hindus, the richest city in the world, which has houses of five or six stories, narrow and tortuous streets, numerous mosques and temples, palaces with brilliant galleries, variegated balconies and inclined roofs;

To the mountains of Gathes, the elevation of which produced two opposed seasons simultaneously, in Malabar and Coromandel, eternal spring in Kashmir and Nepal, winter in Mahé;

To the coasts of Ceylon, where we could see pearl-fishers, diamond-mines and precious stones being excavated from ravines;

To immense and magical plains, all populated, in their valleys and their slopes, by antelopes, rhinoceroses, lions, leopards, elephants, tigers and serpents, and birds with fiery plumes;

Hindus speaking Sanskrit; Radjiputs of the second caste; Marhasts of the third; Sikhs of the warrior tribe; Pariahs, the disinherited on the world; and finally, the Anglo-Asian city of

Calcutta, the French city of Chandigar; Benares, the cupola of whose observatory turns on a pivot.

To Jagganath, which displays, in one of its great pagodas, an idol whose eyes are enormous diamonds;

To Goa, Calicut, Madras, Seringapatan, where the famous Tippoo Sahib, the enemy of the English, perished.

To Baluchistan and Afghanistan, with their hyenas and dromedaries;

Finally passing on to China, Indo-China and Japan.

But in arriving there, from the Caucasus to Tiflis, where the Georgians certainly merited a glance; from Taman, the city of the indolent Circassians to the celebrated Adam's Peak, which the Hindus honor with their pilgrimage; and from Urghan-Dagha to Tibet and from Tibet to China, our eyes had encountered in the north of Asia plains eight hundred leagues in length, entirely covered with stones, salt-water lakes, with no other vegetation than rare desiccated bushes and stunted trees. At considerable distances, we found no other indications of life but animal bones and human skeletons. After casting an eye over the mountains of Kamchatka, however, whose numerous volcanoes, extinct or active, interested us, we finally found ourselves in China and Japan.

Who has not dreamed about China and Japan? Who is unaware that the unhandsome Chinese are the most ancient people of the world, that they worship the god Fo, whose temples are full of images, that Confucius, their legislator *par excellence*, was and still is their philosopher of predilection, that their land is rich and fertile, and that nothing is as fantastic as their constructions?

In fact, when we saw from afar the cities of Peking, Canton and Nanking emerge over the horizon, for Naïs and Stella, as for myself, there was but one sentiment—that of admiration.

The walls of Peking, remarkable for their elevation, half-brick and half-stone, their nine gates of the most astonishing architecture, the houses painted in various colors, the shops with eccentric fronts, the sandy streets that would make the

196

housewives of Flanders despair, the triumphal arches erected at crossroads, in parks and the emperor' pleasure-gardens, on the one hand; on the other, Canton and the charming river that bathes it, the affluence of the buyers, the street of porcelain, the monstrous vases, the splendid cornets, the marvelous ewers, the thousand curiosities in the form of vases, urns, cups, drinking-vessels and bowls, the variegated junks going back and forth on the canal, the velvet and silk fabrics extended between the houses, the most picturesque costumes; and, finally, the famous nine-story tower of Nanking, covered in varnished faience, the plantations of canes, those of tea, the vigorous camphor-trees, and also the colossal idols of Japan, especially the statue of the great Buddha twenty-four meters high, all excited my surprise, and the laughter of my friends, in their turn.

"Truly, what is said about the eyes of the Chinese men and women is much mistaken," I said to Naïs. "I think that to find something beautiful in them, it's necessary to look at the feet of their young women."

"Yes," Naïs replied, "but when one thinks that the advantage in question is only due to the suffering that is imposed on them by heavy bandaging, it's a little sad, not to say ridiculous."

"At least these worthy people have great knowledge to compensate for their ugliness, for it's said that their mandarins..."

"Are merely ignorant," Mikaël put in, "as well as being infamous despots. Under the pretext of having a superior knowledge and power—for some are generals and others treasurers, inspector and commissars—they conduct themselves as infamous tyrants. Thus, we sometimes see one of them, carried in a litter through the streets of Canton, suddenly have a Chinaman, seized, and order that he be whipped, without anyone saying a word in his favor. A hundred lictors announce his presence with a frightful howling, and if anyone is not quick enough to flatten himself against the wall of the street, which is generally narrow, he is immediately stunned with blows of chains or bamboo rods-which does not prevent the mandarin in question receiving a cruel beating, a few streets further on, from receiving in his turn, for a superior mandarin, or the slightest prevarication."

"My Terran friend," Naïs said to me, seizing my arm, which was dangling over the side of my gondola, "say farewell to Asia, for we are now going to lose sight of its palmtrees and lentisks, cajuputs and balsams, myrtles and buckthorns, fan-palms and arecas, and the *Ficus benghalensis*,[67] so beloved by these peoples because its vast branches incline toward the earth describing a right-angle and rise again by growing a new trunk, to the extent that a single tree can become an entire forest.

"Bid farewell to the copper-tinted races with regular features, high foreheads, large but slanting eyes, long but slightly-curved noses, and black hair shaved off shaven for a long tress at the top of the head; and those with yellow skin, flat noses and protruding mouths, woolly hair and prominent cheekbones.

Bid them farewell...for here are the islands, here is the Ocean!"

---

[67] The banyan tree

VI

The sea—a sea without limits—was indeed approaching.

And in its rotatory movement, the terrestrial globe made a frightful noise heard—that of waves rolling and breaking, rising up and falling back, only to rise again.

Nothing caught the gaze over that immense orb, frightful to see—except at intervals, islands and more islands, always islands, like picturesque flower-baskets amid the golden or silver waves of the Ocean, showing in every direction.

My guides pointed out Malaya to me, of which Borneo is the center and the nucleus;

Micronesia, of which Yap is the only populated place.

Polynesia, with its archipelago of the Carolines; Melanesia, of which New Holland forms a continent, exclusively inhabited by black Papuans and Andamans, very ugly and thin.

All these islands male up Oceania, or the Pacific isles, and that fifth part of the world appeared to me to be the one whose surface is bristling with the greatest inequalities. I saw a large number of volcanoes shining there. I counted as many as a hundred and sixty-three. Some of the islands were dominated by long-cooled craters. Others were ravaged by torrents of lava that prevented the growth of any vegetation.

In Java, blue mountains elevated their granite summit to a height of twelve thousand feet. Mikaël remarked to me that their flanks hid gold and emeralds, and the alluvial terrains rubies and diamonds.

The majority of the islands seemed to be mountains raised from the bosom of the Ocean by the action of volcanic forces. Some of them had coral reefs, formed by the polyps inhabiting them. It is difficult to imagine the labor of these tiny animal constructors, whose calcareous edifice rise up like fans, or ramify into trees, or are rounded into balls, reflecting the most beautiful shades of red, violet and blue.

In a thousand places, however, nothing can equal the luxury of the vegetation of Oceania. From the viewpoint of flowers, plants and verdure, valleys, peaks and bluffs, it is a veritable Eden.

Except that the Eden in question is very thinly inhabited.

I saw copper races, black races, yellow races, scarcely mingled, watching one another with grim eyes.

Here there were Zealanders, horribly tattooed, who eat their prisoners of war, roasting the palpitating flesh that they devour half-raw. There, the ferocious savages of Ombay break the skulls of their captives with hammer-blows in order to such the raw brains and imbibe the most delicate parts.

At Hawaii, where Captain Cook was killed in 1779, I noticed a mountain that was a good eight hundred feet higher than Mont Blanc, at the foot of which the islanders were holding a cannibal feast, eating the children captured from their enemies. Further on, the ferocious negroes of Fiji were drinking the blood of their victims, delicately opening a vein in the neck, which allowed the frightful liquor to spurt out like a fountain. Elsewhere, the ferocious tribesmen of Nuku Hiva, naked and painted a terrible red, were picking their enemies hearts with sharp fish-bones, in order to make them die slowly. Finally, the peoples of Vaigou were trading their fathers, mothers, wives and sisters, and violating all the laws of nature in God's bright sunlight.[68]

---

[68] This account of the habits and customs of Pacific islanders is not merely grotesquely false, but—and this cannot be a coincidence—stands in stark contrast to the accounts of the lives of such peoples brought back to France by travelers such as Bougainville, which represented Tahiti, in particular, as a paradisal place, and lent considerable inspiration to Jean-Jacques Rousseau's notion of the essential benignity of tribes uncorrupted by civilization. Although he never mentions Rousseau, Driou seems to be consciously writing in opposition to that supposed enemy of Catholicism, in an excessive man-

"Nowhere," Mikaël told me, "is anthropophagy as widely practiced as in these islands. Thus, in Nuku Hiva, not only do the savages devour their prisoners, but in addition, in times of famine, they devour their children, their wives and their parents.

As we passed over Vanikoro, Mikaël pointed out to me the place where La Pérouse perished in 1787, and where Dumont-d'Urville collected the debris of his ships, now exhibited in our maritime museum.

While Mikaël talked to distract me from my violent emotions. I admired the savages' pirogues, constructed not only with skill but with extreme elegance. They were authentic small ships, able to travel long distances, and capable of containing abundant food supplies. The hull of each canoe was skillfully caulked.

As I became more attentive, in order to observe the nuances of these pirogues laden with men and women, one of the women, raising her eyes, perceived our balloons, which were floating ponderously. She pointed at us, uttering a horrible scream. Immediately, a savage clamor went up from all the pirogues. Many of the men seized their bows, armed them with poisoned arrows and fired at us, for they could see us quite clearly. The arrows passed close by, whistling, but none of them was able to reach us. Mikaël, Naïs and Stella did not even seem anxious about them.

Even so, Mikaël steered out vessels in another direction—not to flee the danger but to show the savages, who were astounded by our aerial navigation, that we were untroubled, and also to show me, in the approaching Marquesas islands the famous Queen Pomaré and the illustrious King Soulouque.[69]

---

ner that seems distinctly suspicious in its lascivious emphasis on cannibalism and cruelty.

[69] This reference seems to be confused. Pomare IV was, indeed, queen of Tahiti in 1854, but Faustin Soulouque, the for-

I could wrote volumes solely about the palaces, the pomp of the court and the entourage of those sovereigns, but that will be for another time—but I took great joy from seeing a French ship and a good number of our soldiers on that foreign ground. My heart beat faster and I had tears in m eyes, in discovering something of our civilization there, after the horrors to which I had just been witness in the Australian islands.

We soon passed over other lands where such execrable crimes of savage and bloodthirsty cannibals were carried out that fury rose into my head. Naïs and Stella dolorously turned away, while these infamous abominations were accomplished—but I said to them, in a mild voice: "Let us hope for the transformation of these peoples by the cross. I can already see the black robes of priests and the violet robes of apostolic missionaries in the islands. God is watching, and the blood of the Savior will not be wasted for these poor savages, who have remained in darkness until now, only worshiping their fetishes."

Already, the New World was approaching, and beyond its hills and the isthmus of Panama, as on the sea over which we were flying, we could see ships, which like halcyons, were furrowing the waves and announcing civilization and industry.

Three-masters and frigates, corvettes and brigs, ferryboats and yachts, dispatch-boats and sloops, lighters and pinnaces, luggers and launches, schooners and steamboats, dinghies and yawls of all shapes, sizes and nations were represented in these dispersed fleets that were sailing, anchoring, appearing and disappearing. Their funnels vomited flame, their sails paled; long wakes labored the humid surface; it was an admirable spectacle. In their rapid, majestic, impetuous progress they all attested to the prodigious movement of nations, the thirst for gold that was devouring them and the need for international trade and enterprise that agitated them.

I became ecstatic in contemplating them.

---

mer slave who was briefly Emperor of Haiti, had no connection with her.

"On the subject of the sea, Monsieur Terran," Naïs said to me curiously, "it's for you, who belong to a maritime country, to explain to us the different uses of these ships, whose names are as different as their forms and their rigging. I'd like to receive a lesson from a man who belongs to the world's leading people."

"Naïs, Naïs, don't be so flattering!" said Mikaël, mischievously.

"Have no fear," I replied. "I'm proof against pride. My knowledge seems to me so limited, since I'm with you, that it will be difficult for me to try to answer you."

"That's the king of ships, I imagine?" said the Lunian, pointing to a ship of the line that was leaving the Marquesas and heading for the coast of California.

"Oh, certainly!" I replied. "It's a vessel of the first grade; it has a hundred and twenty cannon, three decks and four batteries. In France, our ships are classified into ranks. Those of the first grade have the number of cannon I've just cited. Those of the second grade have two decks, three batteries and a hundred cannon. Vessels of the third and fourth grades also have two decks and three batteries but the former only carry ninety cannon, the latter eighty

"All these ships have three masts, and nothing is as terrible as the maneuver they carry out to vomit, in turn, from each of their flanks, a murderous fire that hurls death without respite, especially as each ship is equipped with a propeller that accelerates its already-rapid movements.

"Now, that vessel with a slender mast, which carries its vanes and pennants so high in the air, is a frigate. Its light pose on the water, like that of a swan enjoying itself on a pond, its graceful appearance its rapid progress and proud allure cause seamen to love it. It has but one row of cannon, for the two lines of carronades you see on its deck do not constitute a second battery, but they shoot well when required. Moreover, it's not only a floating citadel designed to figure in a battle line, it's also an officer of the general staff, which must transmit the admiral's orders, repeat signals and go anywhere as needed, while playing the pretty copper toys shining in the sunlight.

"And what name do you give that other sailing ship, which is heading straight toward us, as if it perceived us?" asked Naïs.

"I call it a corvette," I replied. "It's intermediate between a frigate and a brig. It carries between twenty and twenty-six guns. It's difficult to see anything more elegant. The brig, one of which you a see bobbing in the wind there to our left, its rigging set against a background of golden, appearing to us as a vast spider-web, is only provided with two masts. They're perpendicular, but a third can be added, an inclined mast called a bowsprit. One might almost say that it's a three-master when its mizzen-mast is taken out.

The same privilege is given to the schooner, which you see there, close to that island. It has only two masts. Aboard brigs, each low mast is surmounted by a top; on schooners, the low masts only have bars.

"One of the principal sails of a brig is named a brigantine, which was once the name of a ship of a similar sort.

"Just now, I compared a frigate to an officer of the general staff who carried the admiral's orders; look now at the dispatch-boat, a very light aide-de-camp, very rapid in its progress, running left and right and back and forth with information and dispatches.

"Often, in difficult circumstances, little luggers are substituted for them, which sail close to the wind and, when there is a ship in sight, have only to lower everything, including their masts, to remain unperceived—or, even they are seen, they can sail into the wind and brave the enemy.

"The pinnace, the launch and the dinghy are, as you can see, only to provide services provide around the ships at anchor in harbor, being very light and maneuverable vessels, carrying at least half a dozen crewmen and four oarsmen. These *trincadores*, as the Spaniards call them, are armed with swivel-guns, sometimes cannon and rigged like a lugger.

"As for the lighter and the ferry-boat, the former is simply a cargo-boat and the latter a transporter. Commerce employs them for freighting merchandise, and all those funnels crowned with black plumes that darken the sky reveal the latter, whereas the truncated masts reveal the former."

"Bravo, dear Terran!" said Mikaël. "The lesson is complete, and Naïs can take ship on one of those transatlantic liners which carry their flags to all points and all shores.

"At present, reserve your attention for the world discovered in 1492 by Christopher Columbus, so ungratefully rewarded by the Spanish court, and stolen by Amerigo Vespucci, who gave his name to the country—an honor that ought to have belonged to poor Columbus."

Indeed, the first coasts of America had appeared on the horizon, and as we were placed between the sun and the ground, its brightest rays lit the scene that we had beneath our eyes; until nightfall, we would not lose the slightest detail of the things displayed to us.

I had scarcely ceased watching the numerous savage canoes that were following a ship leaving a wooded isle, whose shore was stained with blood in the vicinity of wigwams occupied by barely-clad women in bark loincloths, when I finally decided to contemplate the fourth part of the world.

First I divined the isthmus of Panama, forming the link between the two Americas. It was a chain of high rocks, reminiscent of an immense dyke; it loomed over the two oceans like the gigantic remains of a destroyed world. On the other side of the gulf I could see the Antilles, as green as oases in the idle of a desert. To the north, the soil of America extended to lose itself under the ice; to the south it terminated in Tierra del Fuego, from with it was one separated by the Magellan Strait, named after the second Columbus of America.

On one side I immediately recognized Hudson Bay, Newfoundland, Labrador, Canada, Georgia, Virginia, Louisiana, Kentucky, the Rocky Mountains, Lakes Ontario and Michigan, Illinois, Indiana, Delaware, the Floridas, Mexico, California, with its *placers* and San Francisco; on the other, the Guianas, Brazil, Colombia, Peru, Chile and the Argentine Republic. But to the magnificent aspects of the north, its peaks, its ridges, its rivers and its prairies, I preferred the riches of the three realms of the southern part. I could not take my eyes off the mountain chains, losing their summits in the clouds, the virgin forests full of gigantic trees, populated by monkeys, parrots, and hummingbirds, and the immense savannahs, the pampas extending as far as the eye could see. There, all of nature seemed to me to bear the seal of grandeur, invested with a character of majesty that one would seek in vain elsewhere.

I remained ecstatic before the fertile plateau of the Llano del Pinal, raised eight thousand seven hundred feet above sea level, and so rich in ipecacuana and quinine; facing it, the Cordilleras, perpetually covered in snow, appearing to me with their ground so frequently disturbed by terrible earthquakes. Mikaël told me that the earthquake of 1797 had been one of the worst. He told me that Alexandre de Humboldt, who was on the summits of Pinchincha at the time, at an altitude of four thousand six hundred and sixty-five meters, counted eighteen shocks in thirty minutes, but he added that, in reality, there must have been many more.

Indeed, the land at the base of the Andes, seemed to me to be fissured everywhere by irruptions of the internal fire that they cover. Burning plains were visible there, which exhaled sulfur, whose odor rose up as far as us, and the hills of which emitted plumes of smoke. I was even able to contemplate immense volcanoes, of which the principal ones numbered twenty-six, launching from that perpetual hearth of combustion, except that, instead of vomiting lava and pumice-stone, like our Hecla in Iceland, Vesuvius, near Naples, Etna in Sicily and Stromboli in the Liparian isles, these were only throwing out hydrogen sulfide, aluminum carbonate, and sometimes considerable masses of fish.

Naïs told me, in her turn, that these immense mountains, which form the dorsal spine of the two Americas, receive the name Andes from the Peruvian word *antis,* copper, and that of the Cordilleras from the Spanish *cordel*, which means elbow. I saw, moreover, that the extended from Cape Froward and Point St. Isidore, which advances into the Magellan Strait, as far as the isthmus of Panama, where they suddenly decrease.

But what occupied me more, as you can certainly imagine, my young friends, was the land of California, which, as a magnet attracts iron, now attracts to it from all parts of the world those blind maniacs agitated and tormented by the thirst for gold. So I exclaimed: *"Auri sacra fames quid non mortalia cogis pectora!"*[70]

"Ah!" said Mikaël. "Our Terran philosopher is casting his eyes on that little corner of the world called California, and deploring the crazed intoxication and stupid cupidity of brothers quitting their pleasant hearths, the peace of their households and the cultivation of their fields to come, under an inexorable sun, in the midst of murders, blazes, agonies, yellow fever and privations of every sort, to seek a little of that metal, that powder, that trifle called gold!"

"Yes," I said to my guide, gold—that's the magic word that dooms the world! The passion for wealth has claimed many victims already, and yet people never want to profit from the lessons given by their predecessors. They dream of possession, and lose sight of their nudity. Having come into the world in dolor and suffering, they forget that they must quit it in poverty and death. What can they take with them into the tomb, that they must amass so much in life? My God! Is not the real treasure that of virtue, that of doing good to one's fellows, that of a conscience ready to appear before the supreme judge, whom one ought to render indulgent and good by serving him lovingly?

"Oh, my dear Lunian, that your fate..."

"I was about to continue my soliloquy, when a cry that suddenly emerged from Stella's throat caused me to look at

---

[70] The quote is from Virgil's *Aeneid*: "Execrable thirst for gold, what do you not compel mortals to do?"

the young Lunian woman anxiously. What could have caused her terror—a terror so keenly felt by an immortal?

I had only to follow Stella's finger to discover the cause of her fear. The young woman's fearful gaze and extended index finger showed us an unexpected spectacle.

Far away, on the edge of an immense prairie, on the horizon of which the rumps of a few hills undulated and which was interrupted by parcels of forest, very far from the cabins of the white men and the Indians' wigwams, bison, elk and wild horses were wandering. The uneven ground revealed skulls, skeletons and desiccated limbs. Either a battle had once taken place there, or a cannibal orgy had exercised its fury. Some distance away shone the Red River and its tributaries, the long curves of which over the vast prairie refreshed the gaze.

Suddenly, on the apex of a rock, a savage appeared on horseback, tattooed crimson, green and white, who uttered a cry so horrible that the grazing animals fled as if carried away by a simoom. It was that Indian, so frightful to behold in warpaint, that had frightened Stella.

"You've seen these savages twenty times over from the Moon," Mikaël said to his daughter.

"Never at such close range," Stella replied, still pale, "and they certainly don't gain anything from being seen at such a short distance."

Stella was right. The savage was not handsome. He wore no clothing save for the moccasins on his feet. In his hand he clutched a terrible tomahawk, and around his waist, attached to a thong, we could see at least ten scalps hanging.

He must have been a great warrior, and I'm sure that in his tribe he might have been called Desert Flame.

His cry had been heard. From the slightest cranny in the ground, from the bottom of dark ravines, the depths of the woods, clumps of bushes and the mists of the horizon emerged, stood up, came forward and surged such a quantity of savages of every color, every size and shape, that I felt a fever of terror myself.

They were ugly and repulsive enough to freeze the blood in one's veins.

Some, with gray and oily skin, had blue stripes circling their bodies like serpents; others, copper-red, had white eyes that floated, wide and furious in yellow plaques that they had applied to their cheeks, while on their breasts, arms, backs and thighs they had painted eagles, parrots and vultures. Others, as black as ebony but whose skin shone as if varnished, with florid red eyes, were laden with white tattoos that rendered the hideous. Some, tinted green, had copper rings around their limbs, others were painted with a thousand violet and gray fantasies—and all of them were holding assegais, hatchets and clubs, some of them carbines. They were howling so frightfully as they came together in a principal group, shaking their weapons, that Naïs and Stella shivered.

I think that I would have been able to count five hundred, so many were arriving from all directions.

Many of them had their hair drawn up to the top of the head and fastened with a red crest. Several also wore feathery head-dresses, long-tailed bonnets that rendered them even uglier. Most of them were mounted on small horses full of ardor and fire, but a considerable number were on foot. I had assumed the total number to be five hundred, estimating the number of tribes that were there at less than a hundred each, but I soon had to more than double that number, for they were arriving incessantly. There were Sioux, Pawnees, Hurons, Iroquois, Osages, Ojibways, Iowas, Navahos Oricks, Mohicans, Redskins, Chesapeakes, Anakotas, Delawares and Penobscots.

Undoubtedly, the most handsome in form were the Osages. They had bare heads and short-cropped hair, with the exception of a strip at the top of the head, which produced a sort of crest, and a long pigtail hanging down at the back. They had a sort of woolen blanket over their loins, which, leaving their arms and torsos bare, caused them to resemble beautiful bronze statues.

There were also some, already near to the civilization that was taking hold of them, who had pale blue hunting-shirts with scarlet fringes. Brightly colored kerchiefs were wound around their temples, one of the ends of which hung down from the ear, giving the impression that they were wearing turbans.

The chief—the one that I had baptized Desert Flame because of the crimson illuminating him—repeated his cry, and all the tribal groups immediately became more distinct, and settled into immobility. Desert Flame, as attentive until then as an Arab lying in ambush, galloped his little horse to the center of the army, and all the tribal chiefs gathered around him.

They then began to hold a discussion, utterly incomprehensible to my ears—but the knowledgeable Mikaël was able to give me the gist of it.

It was the approach of the Europeans, felling the forests, clearing the ground, invading the prairies, threatening all these savages with death, that had united all these tribes, previously enemies. They were taking up arms in order to meet force with force. The Great Spirit was with them, so what could the white men do?

An indescribable enthusiasm followed these words.

"Now," said Mikaël, "look in that direction."

Mechanically, we followed the direction given to us, and in the center of a clearing in a vast virgin forest, we saw an army of Europeans—English, French, Spanish and Dutch—encamped, preparing a meal in which freshly-killed bison were to provide the principal fare. Their flesh was sizzling over the charcoal of a barbecue, and advance scouts were protecting the rustic joys of these new filibusters.

Suddenly, news reached the camp that the savages were close by. The number of savages was still increasing.

To describe the frightful tumult that followed would be impossible. In the blink of an eye, the army was on its feet, and advanced in battle order to meet the Indians.

"Let's get away, quickly!" cried Naïs and Stela.

"You wanted to see the Earth at close range," Mikaël replied. "Like Eve's, your curiosity will be punished."

The Lunian had scarcely finished than the battle began. It was a frightful spectacle. For a while, the savages had the upper hand, so much had they frightened the Europeans with their terrible war cries. It was necessary to see what marvels the tomahawk accomplished in their hands; they broke limbs, cleaved the breasts and skulls of their enemies with a single blow of that redoubtable instrument. Then, when a stricken European fell, they seized him by the hair, detaching a sharp knife from their belt, made a body stripe around the victim's head, and tore away the skin and hair, denuding he head, which no longer displayed anything but a red cranium streaming blood. Truly, nothing was as horrible as that operation, which the Indians completed in a second. In their turn, the Europeans immolated entire masses of those miserable creatures under the fire of their battalions.

An unexpected incident put an end to the butchery, however, changing the arena of carnage into a zone of human blood and mud, A muffled sound, a murmur like that of a distant sea, a vague agitation, suddenly covered the combat. Naïs seized me by the arm. Stella pointed at the horizon.

The sky was veiled by a thick dust rising room the prairie, and it seemed to me that I saw an army of negroes in retreat, arriving at a run. It was a resounding tread as rapid as thunder. We soon found out what we were looking at. From that cloud of dust I saw an enormous bison emerge, and realized that it was followed by perhaps ten thousand of those animals, frightened by some unknown cause but fleeing, as often happens, under the guidance of their leaders, to go in search of pasture elsewhere, without paying any heed to the Europeans, the savages and the battle. They passed like a hurricane or a whirlwind over the scene of combat, without the victors of vanquished having time to think of seeking shelter, other than by throwing themselves flat on the ground—but the hard hooves of the herd, which arrived from the plain like a living avalanche, making the earth tremble in its furious course, crushed, broke and pulverized the greater number of the combatants.

It was a horrible, indescribable sight: a frightful, hideous expanse of blood, pulped flesh, reddened earth, like a river, traced on the ground by a long trail of human blood and stripped bones.

The savages, following the instinct of their nature, set off in pursuit of the bison, and must have killed a few, as they were drawn into the distant desert. As for the Europeans who escaped the massacre, they returned to their banquet in the clearing.

Then, seeing the battlefield now devoid of fighters, we were about to draw away when we saw in the distance, on the edge of the horizon, something like a shiny moving star appear. One glance was sufficient for us to recognize a helmet reflecting the rays of the sun, following the movements of a galloping horse.

It was one of the savage chiefs, who, having dressed himself in the headgear of a French cavalryman he had killed, was returning at top sped to the location of the combat. He was followed by another Redskin chief who, for his part, after having killed some superior chief, had stripped him of his clothing and, previously nude, had dressed himself in it proudly, giving him a most grotesque appearance.

"Wah! Wah!" they cried.

They found no more Europeans on the plain, but enemies of another kind; white wolves and coyotes, attracted by the odor of blood, were arriving in great numbers to feed on the shreds of flesh and gnaw the bones of the cadavers.

The two horsemen, an Osage and a Navaho, astride their magnificent fast-galloping mustangs, were as black as coal, with ardent eyes and red flared nostrils. It was as if they were coming to issue a challenge to the Europeans. No longer finding the there, they uttered a terrible war cry to advertise their presence, bringing their horses to an abrupt halt—which, under the unexpected shock, suddenly spread their hind legs, their tails spread on the ground, their manes bristling, their nostrils fuming and white flecks of foam marbling their breasts and shoulders.

The savages themselves, with their shiny helmet with the floating crest, their bronze skin and their tall stature, were reminiscent of living statues. It was impossible for us not to admire those men of the desert. After retaining that attitude for a few minutes, having gazed at the woods and listened to the last vibrations of their war cry fade away in the air, seeing nothing appear, they spoke briefly to their horses—which, turning around, departed like arrows in the direction followed by the majority of the savages.

"But how do these Indians tattoo themselves like that?" I asked Mikaël, while our aerostats drew away from the scene of the carnage.

"With the aid of plants," Mikaël replied. "With the point of a fish-bone they prick their skins in a thousand bizarre designs, which they rub with the juice of certain poisonous herbs, which then imprint them with indelible colors. The designs may be spiral lines, oval figures, squares, arabesques, checkerboards, animals, snakes circling the torsos, the image of the moon on the shoulder, that of the sun on the breast—the most fantastic and heterogeneous objects. All the designs are executed with the greatest regularity, those on one cheek, arm or leg corresponding exactly to those on the other, and that diversity presents a frightening appearance.

"Moreover, we have only seen naked and tattooed savages. In my opinion, the most frightful are not those, but those who have mantles, trousers and tunics made of the debris of various fabrics, so strangely fitted to their bodies and so grotesquely attached, that one cannot take account of the eccentric vestment. And in addition, these girdles of scalps, hairpieces taken from their enemies, and their long sharp spears, and their tomahawks, and their sharpened arrows...that enough to make one shudder. I can't look without terror at their chiefs, whose heads are coiffed in gigantic bonnets of black feathers, beneath which glisten odious red and crimson faces, or blue—the magnificent blue that cobalt yields. I shiver merely to think of it."

Our aerostats were passing over the countries of the north-west, to which the savages had been pushed back by the European invaders of the east. The virgin forests were soon revealed to us, and, as Mikaël was steering our vessels around the globe in such a fashion as to avoid darkness and always to have the sun rising over each country we saw,[71] the spectacle we had before our eyes gained hereby in freshness and poetry.

Nothing is as beautiful as the vast woodlands we call Virgin Forests. The first days of the sunlight, springing forth over their domes and penetrating their thick foliage, were doubtless awakening the guests of those immense solitudes, or an infernal racket was bursting forth there. There was something like the screeching of monkeys, the mewling of tigers, the roaring of lions, the groaning of leopards, the hissing of serpents, and bellowings such that I could not identify the animals that might be producing them. The echoes of the woods and the bluffs surrounding them or rising up in their depths returned these discordant sounds, and one might have thought that bands of demons were summoning one another to a grandiose Sabbat in those strange savannahs.

It was evident that no roads divided these forests. Vegetable debris, tall grass, inextricable tangles of lianas, the enormous carcasses of trees felled by lightning or high winds, rotting trunks and dense undergrowth cluttered the ground. Palm-trees, oaks, date-palms, coconut-palms, banana-trees, tamarinds, carobs, acacias, aloes, sesame, ground-nuts and

---

[71] Not easy when one's general direction of travel is eastwards, in the opposite direction to the sun's trajectory across the sky—but if it were not obvious already, the subsequent description of the virgin forest makes it very plain indeed that the protagonist is not really in the north-western USA, or in any part of the Earth familiar to us. This image seems to have been formed by reference to René de Chateaubriand's famous but fanciful "romance of the virgin forest" *Atala* (1801).

twenty other species of tall trees were so dense there that daylight and the sun's rays had difficulty penetrating the vaults of verdure. From the humus covering the earth, the enervating perfumes of tropical flowers that saturated the stifling air rose up to our height. Sometimes the sparkling plumage of macaws, hummingbirds and paraques appeared to us on the branches, catching golden-winged insects; sometimes, the fawn coats of guenons or oustitis could be glimpsed, chewing the aromatic berries of the carobs.

We sailed for a long time over the domes of those admirable woodlands that had not yet been subject to human axes, and which seemed to have emerged from the hand of God as on the day of creation. Finally, we came to the extremity, which was signaled to us by a faint column of blue smoke rising into the sky, escaping from a delightful clearing at the entrance to the great forest.

"The cabins and wigwams of savages!" Mikaël told me.

Indeed, we found ourselves at that moment above a tribe of Anakotas, whose village was composed of huts made of wood and earth, covered with layers of reeds and large leaves, placed in the form of a roof. The huts formed a large square, with a much larger cabin in the center, dominating all the rest. In front of the low doors of the huts of these children of nature, women clad in little more than loincloths were feeding their babies. Some of them had all the graces of youth; others, withered by time, were repulsive to behold. A large number of little savages were playing on the grass around the large wigwam, which was the meeting-place of the elders, chiefs and principal members of the tribe. At the entrance, we perceived a few old men squatting on the sand, smoking their calumets.

Other, younger Anakotas were working in a kind of garden where I saw leguminous plants accumulated and the most beautiful fruit imaginable. A troop of tribal warriors was returning from the hunt when we passed over the cabins. They were on horseback, with their hunting weapons. Quarters of bison hung down bloodily from their saddle-bows. We heard the clink of their tomahawks on the iron of their spears. We could easily make out the paint with which their faces and breasts were adorned.

When they arrived in the village, before going into their wigwams, we saw them plant stakes in the ground, place bark cords between them, and hang up pieces of bison-meat to dry them in the sun and preserve them. Other portions were given to the women, who lit fires outside and roasted the most delicate parts of the animal. The bloody meat crackled in the flame on wooden spits; the Indians laced pine-nuts in the ashes, and, while the hunters left their mustangs to graze in the clearing and smoked their clay pipes, the meal was prepared.

Our aerostats did not allow us to perceive any more, and drew away.

"The Anakotas are now at war with the Apaches," Mikaël told me. "I just heard the old savage leading the hunting-party say so."

"So much the worse!" I exclaimed. "I don't want to see any more of their battles; I had enough of that a little while ago."

"At least see what skillful spies they are, while keeping watch on their enemies," Mikaël said.

In fact, the hunters, doubtless having been attacked by the Apaches, having talked about the necessity of defending themselves while going back to their wigwams, the entire tribe got busy. The old men held council; the younger ones raced off toward neighboring tribes to raise the alarm. At the same time, though, the lightest among them, naked save for moccasins on their feet, drew away at a rapid stride in the direction of the enemy. Once they thought they were in the vicinity of the camp of the savages who were doubtless disputing their hunting-grounds, they wormed their way into the thickets like serpents to observe the plain as vigilant scouts and take account of their adversaries' slightest movement.

We soon lost sight of them.

Mikaël then drew my attention to Mexico, the ancient empire of Montezuma, the former theater of the bloody rapacity of the Spaniards of the sixteenth century—in sum, the land of gold.

A country of bleak, arid mountains, poorly irrigated by a stream, was passing beneath us at that moment. The current of the arroyo had hollowed out deep ravines in its course through the mountains, and its waters were flowing over an almost-inaccessible bed.

"Is that one of the streams that yields gold?" I asked Mikaël.

"It's a good opportunity, my dear chap" he replied. "If you want to enrich yourself, descend—except that we won't have the patience to wait for you to make a fortune. Should we leave you there?"

"Don't you dare!" I exclaimed.

Soon, other mountains loomed up on either side of the horizon, rising up sheerly from the plain and affecting fantastic forms, which delighted me. We were overlooking enormous steeps ricks forming frightful abysses, and discovering silent and desiccated plateaux.

Suddenly, far to the north—as far as my mortal vision could extend, a shining mass whose rock had the gleam and color of gold reflected the sunlight. The reverberation of its fires on that mountain dazzled me, and I was seized by vertigo.

"Gold! Gold!" I cried.

"They're only sheets of mica and translucent selenite," Stella told me. "That's typical of humans! They always allow themselves to be fooled by deceptive appearances."

"This will cheer you up," said Naïs, extending an indicative finger toward a plain and lakes, in the middle of which I saw a city.

A magnificent panorama was, indeed, unfolding before me. An immense surface of verdure, whose plane was punctuated neither by bushes nor hedges nor hills, extended into the infinite distance. At different points on that sheet of emeralds the silver leaves of dormant lakes scintillated; and between the emeralds and the silver, an unrivaled city loomed up in the center. Around it, in the distance—the far distance—a border of magnificent mountains was designed, with a jagged outline. There were enormous ridges of granite dominated by strangely-formed peaks.

My eyes settled on the city with keen curiosity. I made out the profiles of houses, still far away. They had terraced roofs. In certain places, high temples loomed over them. Canals cross-hatched the ground. Groups of wild swans, herons and blue cranes were swimming on the lakes that surrounded it or diving in their waters. The domes reflected amber tints, and the beauty of the blazing ether rendered the magical and grandiose spectacle imposing.

"Mexico," Mikaël eventually told me. I had forgotten to interrogate him, so deeply plunged in ecstasy was I.

"Mexico," I stammered, without taking my eyes off it.

Soon we were passing over the city, and I contemplated at my ease its buildings, all constructed of carved stone, two or three stories high, painted white, red or green, ornamented with verses from the Bible or porcelain tiles forming Moorish designs. The flat roofs were tiled with bricks and decorated with bushes and flowers.

"There's the Plaza-Mayor," Naïs told me. "In sequence, there's the palace, the bank, the main barracks, various ministries and chambers, the President's residence and, finally, the Cathedral.

"Toward the northern suburbs, don't neglect the promenade of the Alameda. You don't have one like that in Paris, my dear Terran. See how those eight pathways form a star, the center of which is decorated with a superb fountain."

"My God!" said Mikaël. It's easy to see that we're among a people of Spanish origin. Look at the multitude gathered in that great open space near the Alameda for a great spectacle—there must be bullfights...exactly! Mexico shares the tastes of Madrid, its motherland. We're arriving just in time. Except for you, Frenchman; that battle a little while ago has upset you..."

"Silence, Messieurs; the spectacle's beginning," said Stella. "Fortunately, the Mexicans' eyes are all directed toward the ground at present, not raised to the skies."

"Just let me tell our Parisian," Mikaël continued, "that the arrival of the bulls took place yesterday, and what is called the *encierro* has already been a festival for the people, so avid for these combats that the smallest village in Spain has its *Plaza-Mayor* for that purpose. When they arrive thus, the bulls are preceded by *cabestros*, themselves guided by *picadors* armed with lances known as *garoches*. Brilliantly-mounted amateurs escort the procession; the windows are garnished with spectators, the air resounds with hearty cheers. Then they are put into niches established in the circus, and those niches closed by means of a swing-door."

"But what is that little cell," I asked, "in which there is a prie-dieu beside a bed, where I see a priest and a..."

"Physician? Well, there are dangers, you see, for the men to run in this contest, and its sometimes necessary to make provision for their souls..."

"And their bodies. I understand."

"There are only common people in the arena, but they've already released a bull?" said Stella.

"Yes," Mikaël replied. "It's the *valde* bull—the favor, if you like. It's the preface to the drama; a gallantry offered to the people who cannot pay.

"Indeed—the bull has been killed and now the wretched crowd is leaving," I said. "But here come the rich people, the grandees, the aristocrats, the people of the court, the President—God forgive me!—who are entering in their turn and filling the splendid platforms."

"The orchestra's playing—pay attention!" said Naïs.

In fact, a city official armed with a baton, followed by a few *alguazils,* entered the arena and came to bow to the President. Then, following the orders of a master of ceremonies, who threw him the key to the niches, garnished with ribbons, a runner picked it up. Immediately, four picadors appeared, mounted on horses of little value, for they were doomed to

219

certain death. The poor beasts were blindfolded. The picadors, wearing chamois-leather trousers lined with sheet-metal, waistcoats of glen cloth, small jackets of lustrous silk, covered with fringes and frills, saluted in their turn. Vast white hats, around each of which a ribbon as flying, covered their heads. Their flexible *garoches*, each eighteen feet long, were tipped with copper balls from the centers of which six prongs extended.

Fanfares sounded as they entered, but they sounded even more loudly when the *chulos*, clad in rich and elegant Figaro costumes, appeared in the arena. They were holding long silk scarves in the most striking colors—red, yellow or sky blue. Having bowed briskly, they withdrew through the openings in the *barauda*, or wooden fence.

It was then that the matadors came in, clad no less elegantly in silk stockings, with naked swords in one hand and a *muleta* in the other: a sort of small crutch, thirty inches long, which bore a little flag. They also bowed and withdrew.

Only the picadors remained in the arena.

Suddenly, the trumpets sounded, and a bull was released, bellowing.

Then, frightened by the sight of the multitude, who saluted its entrance with cries of joy, the animal hurled itself at the first picador it encountered. The latter received it with his garoche, whose point struck the shoulder-blade, according to the rules. Excited by this prick, the bull immediately launched itself at the other picadors. Every new wound stimulated its rage. Woe to any inexperienced horseman! Woe to any whose garoche breaks! His mount is immediately overturned, pierced by thrusts of the horns. Horror! I see two of them, thus perforated, still galloping, in spite of the atrocious wounds, trampling the debris of their intestines.

One of the picadors was about to fall victim to the bull himself. Already, the animal, with its tail stiff and its eyes on fire, was rushing at him like a thunderbolt when a chulos suddenly appeared, who threw the little pieces of silk rolled up in his hand at the bull's head. Immediately, the animal turned its fury against those new enemies, but as soon as the unhorsed picador was out of danger the chulos ran away, and the beast charged the picadors again.

The bull killed eight or ten horses in that fashion. The arena was bloody. Quivering, disemboweled cadavers whinnying their death-rattles dishonored the arena. Chulos then arrived to fight in their turn, by launching their *banderillas*, little sticks two feet long armed with a sharpened nail curved into a barb. One of the chulos, still according to the rule, planted them in the victim's withers by facing it head on and reaching around the horns. If he had missed his thrust, his belly would have been opened and he would have been tossed twenty feet in the air—an accident that usually delights those excellent people, the spectators.

Rendered furious by the pain caused by the banderillas, surmounted with little flags and garnished with petards that burst into flames, the bull found itself face to face with the matador. The latter had to put an end to the contest. Assisted by a quartet of chulos, sword in one hand, the muleta deployed in the other, he went straight toward the animal. Believing its enemy within reach, the bull anxiously observed every movement of the muleta, then launched itself at the fabric—but the muleta disappeared; the animal passed under the matador's left arm. The latter, with his right arm, plunged his blade into its withers, in such a way as to cut the spinal cord by insinuating itself between two vertebrae, still according to the rule.

The bull fell, motionless, like an inert mass.

The victor did not abandon the blade, which he drew out of the wound, and saluted the assembly with the bloody weapon.

Immediately, acclamations rose up on all sides. The ladies threw flowers and candy to the happy matador, and the rich joined in with a rain of gold.

Needless to say, the frightful spectacle was repeated seven times; forty-two horses perished, that one chulos and two picadors were horribly mutilated. One matador, because he had wounded the bull without killing it, was heaped with insults and nearly maltreated by the muttering crowd. The slain bulls were removed by means of a team of mules as richly-caparisoned as the poor horses, while nothing was heard but cries of "Bravo toro!" and "Viva flor de las espadas!" Oh, yes, long live the flower of swords—but when the life of God's creatures is exposed for better reasons than the pleasure it gives to grim and cruel generations!

"Please, let's get out of this place!" I said to Mikaël. "My heart hurts too much at the sight of all that blood."

"Besides, we have other things to see," Mikaël replied, "and I ought to tell you, who seem knowledgeable in archeology and seems to me to be a meritorious antiquarian, that this rich capital is built on the ruins of ancient Tenochtitlan.

"The place where the Cathedral stands, the balustrade of which, surrounding the altar, is solid silver, of which the lamp, also silver, is so large that three men can go inside to clean it, the numerous statues of which are made of gold and studded with precious stones, was once the sanctuary of Tezcatlipoca, the first of the Aztec gods after Theotl, the Supreme Being. Five thousand people were attached to the service of the temple, and there were thirty other temples around it. The heads of all the human beings immolated in honor of the Mexican divinities decorated its walls. In addition, Montezuma had a palace with more than a thousand rooms, the largest of which could accommodate three thousand people.

"The Spaniard Cortés destroyed all that."

"And thus it is," added Stella, "that the Earth is the abode of mutation, disorder, hatred, war and dolor."

Meanwhile, our aerostats were still sailing, carrying us toward horizons as infinite as the heavens.

They were the prairies.

But what sights those prairies offered! Firstly, as far as the eyes could see, one saw flowers, nothing but flowers. It was like an uninterrupted flower-bed; no tree, no hillock and no hill broke its surface. The gentle breezes of those warm climes caressed them with their perfumed breath. Humming-birds fluttered over them, more living flowers, as bright as the rays of the setting sun, making a banquet of their pure corollas, hovering next to their pistils, going to sleep in the depths of their calices.

Then the flowers were succeeded by grasses, immeasurable lawns, meadows as green as emerald, surfaces shaven by the wind of the plain, undulating like silk, all dappled by shadows and light, in accordance with the movement of the clouds in the firmament. There was nothing to arrest the eye in its hectic flight, nothing to wound the foot on that soft carpet, which extended over an area two or three hundred leagues from one region to the next, nothing to oppose the progress of a human but a vicuna or an antelope—unless that grass should catch fire when the sun has dried it out and an imprudent hand touches a torch to it somewhere, as sometimes happens when the local savages pursue a European trying to escape their vengeance, or when a European wants to drive the savages away from the farms and houses that represent civilization toward the east.

But the scene changes again. Now the ground is no longer uniform; on the contrary, it undulates like the last waves of the retreating tide; and this crumpled terrain recalls the waves of the Ocean after a tempest.

Then comes the verdure of spinneys; then thickets; then forests appear. The foliage is varied; its tints are bright and its contours smooth and charming. Anyone might think that he were arriving in an inhabited savannah, the colonists' pampas; it is nothing of the sort. Solitude still reigns in the distance: no farms, no haciendas, no villages, no towns, but only the huts and wigwams of savages. The desert wind blows through these trees, and if any harmony comes to disturb the monotonous accord, it is the songs of the green woodpecker, the cooing of doves, the squeals of squirrels, the laughter of the mockingbird and the raucous cries of parrots.

In the nascent mountains that are approaching, however there are lakes, rivers, cataracts. Heavens, how admirable it is!

"Yes, it's admirable, isn't it?" Stella says to me, divining my thought from the expression of my physiognomy. From

Lake Erie, from which it escapes to flow into Lake Ontario, the bed of the St. Lawrence suddenly descends over a rocky bed. The leap it makes is no less than forty-four feet; it's called Niagara Falls."

"So this is the famous Niagara!" I cried.

"It's less a river than a sea," Stella continued, "and a sea whose torrents present the gaping mouth of a gulf. An enormous block of rock divides the cataract into two branches as it falls. Between the two currents is an island hollowed out below, and that island, with its two trees, overhangs the chaos of the waves. The mass of the water that is precipitated is rounded out in the form of a gigantic cylinder, flowing in a white sheet, and sparkles I the sunlight which all the colors of the prism. The other mass descends in frightful shadow. A thousand gleams curve and hollow out over the abyss, striking the quivering rock. The water rebounds in swirls of foam, which rise above the woods like the smoke of a vast conflagration. Pines, wild trees and enormous ricks decorate the grandiose scene. Birds with a marvelous wingspan, drawn by the agitation of the air, circle above the gulf, and monkeys, accustomed to the magical scene, hang by their flexible tails from the branches that overhang the terrible and astounding cataract."

"I was nonplussed by what I saw; I would have liked to stay there and contemplate it, but our balloons were already dragging us toward Newfoundland, where England has established its domination, the United States, the Natchez, the Floridas and all the lands from which rise up, for me, the stifled cries of a horrible dolor—that of slavery!

To be sure, the cleared ground offered a curious mixture of the state of nature and that of civilization, for, in a corner of woodland that had only ever resounded to the cries of savages and the howling of wild beasts, I saw lands under nascent cultivation, farms almost side by side with wigwams; I perceived Indian huts alongside the planters' farmhouses. Beside the desert I admired the richness of the soil in its sugar-cane plantations, true treasures of their owners—but I also quivered with muted indignation, when my eyes fell upon those black troops of negroes, stolen from their homeland by the sanguinary cupidity of white men, in order to force them to enrich them with their sweat, beneath the whip of an inflexible overseers.

"By what right do white men make negroes slaves?" I cried, in my interior soliloquy.

"God will judge!" said Naïs, raising her beautiful eyes to the heavens, while Stella covered her face.

The horrible scenes of tyranny, misery and cruelty to which I was then witness, I shall not describe to you. But how much mute chagrin and ineffable suffering there was on the part of those poor slaves I had beneath my gaze in Canada, Kentucky and elsewhere. Oh yes, the necessity of another life, which will render to each according to is works, is demonstrated solely by the fact that the Earth is witness to the monstrosity that is named NEGRO SLAVERY!

Fortunately, the horizon brought us large and beautiful rivers in the east, their cities, cut into a checkerboard by the straight parallel streets that firmed them, their industrious plains, their active factories, and all the movement and life of young cities full of hope and expectation.

Soon, the United States and the Antilles appeared to us in turn, then the unhealthy Guianas, the basin of the beautiful River Amazon, twelve hundred leagues in length, where pyramids are found similar to those in Egypt, which gives rise to the supposition that the purpose of pyramids was merely to have fires by night on their platforms to light the way for travelers. Then came Brazil and Paraguay, and finally Peru, with its capital Lima.

It appeared to me set in a magnificent Andean valley, surrounded by sumptuous country houses, gardens and orchards. A great city, though narrower than Mexico, it offered the image of a triangle surrounded by a brick wall, flanked by thirty-four bastions and pierced by seven gates.

But nothing was as beautiful, above all, as its edge on the sea coast: a vast district, delightful promenades, a cathedral with high towers, a magnificent bronze fountain with a re-nowned elephant expelling water from his trunk and eighteen lions expelling it through their mouths, churches even richer than those of Mexico, silver cages full of birds suspended from their ceilings—a strange habit, Everything there was large, beautiful, bizarre and magnificent—and what a climate and what a sky!

"Lima is only the modern capital," Mikaël said to me. "Cuzco, the ancient abode of Atahualpa and the rich Incas of the Peruvians, the city of a high civilization, attested by the Temple of the Sun, the quipos that served as their writing, the Peruvian calendar, the roads and highways five hundred lea-gues long, which traversed the mountains and the valleys, and a thousand other things.

"Where was the Temple of the Sun, then?" I asked my guides. "I've seen it in your marvelous album, but refresh my memory."

"It was there," said Naïs, hastening to reply, while we were arriving over Cuzco, "in a splendid location, sparkling with the fires of the sun, where you can see a Dominican mo-nastery, that the marvelous temple was located. Its four walls were covered with tablets of the purest gold. On a great altar one saw, radiating from one wall to the other, an enormous Sun, also made of gold, in a single sheet, with an infinity of flames, all gold.

"Surrounding the temple was a cloister with four faces, on which were festooned enormous golden astragals more than a meter in breadth. Pavilions with pyramidal roofs were backed up to that attic at intervals. The Moon, wife of the Sun, had one of those pavilions, the doors and walls of which were clad in silver sheets. The Moon, in silver, had a woman's face.

"The other pavilions belonged to the stars, the daughters of the Sun and Moon. One of them served as the abode of the priests, who were all from the family of the Incas. The virgins consecrated to the cult were enclosed in a monastery some distance from the temple. I confess to you that horrible sacri-fices took place under those vaults to the Sun and the Moon.

But then, the good Peruvian people, having no vestments but a short cloth skirt sewn with gold and silver on blue and red, coiffed with those elegant bonnets formed like broad circles of gold surmounted by long straight plumes of every color, were very free in their actions and their enjoyments.

"Now, the infamous Spaniards, under the leadership of Pizarro and Cortés, disembarked in the vicinity of Cuzco shortly after the discovery of America. Imagine their avidity on seeing all that gold: the gold of the palaces, the gold of the houses, the gold of the city. They attacked Cuzco; they killed the inhabitants; they killed the virgins; they killed the priests; they killed the Incas. They took possession of the vast empire of Atahualpa, and went to Caxamarca, where his residence was at that time—where our aerostats are taking us—and there murdered the entire family of the unfortunate Incas. Except that hey imprisoned Atahualpa in a vast room, where they made him endure the most cruel tortures, to force him to tell them where his treasure was. Look, there's the chamber in the ruins. Can you see a scratch on that wall made with a knife? That mark was made by Atahualpa himself, promising to heap up the gold and silver of his ransom at that spot..."

"Well?" I said. "They were billions that he was offering!"

"The rapacity of the Spaniards was unsated. They cut his throat on that stone, there, in the center of that chapel."

"Horror!" said Stella.

"Further away, there are the ruins of another Peruvian city. The remains of some houses are still standing on that mound—but there are other ruins still. That was what became of the empire of Peru, and Spain ruled over its rubble..."

"One of the hundred thousand dramas of the Earth!" said Mikaël.

To help us recover from these emotions, the Earth showed us the cities of other countries, glittering with gold and precious stones, and their florid bluffs and cheerful solitudes;

The forty-nine mouths of the Orinoco;

The Plata and its river with a silvery bed;
Rio de Janeiro, with its incomparable bay;
Campeche and its woods...

And I said to myself: "How great God is! And how terrible the sin was, since it covered the Earth, his masterpiece, with so many miseries, vicissitudes and dolors!

VII

Finally, here comes the sea that bathes the shores of France!

Oh, how it bounds with such an impetuous surge
Toward cherished ricks, toward my sweet homeland,
Where my mother awaits me, and while waiting, prays.[72]

But I shall not see it again yet. Does not Africa, one of the unknown worlds, remain for me to travel? So we are crossing the Atlantic.

There also, there more than anywhere else, we find scattered fleets coming and going, at all latitudes and longitudes, crossing one another's paths, cutting across one another, hailing one another, saluting one another with the voices of cannon.

Yes, God is great on Earth, but he is even greater on the sea! The ocean, calm and green-tinted, agitates its waves with a gentle cadence. At daybreak, a light wind dissipates the mantle of mist covering the horizon; then, as if to salute the star announcing it triumphal march, the waves begin to stand up proud and foamy. They beat the flanks of the ship with curt, dull blows, and when the star appears, its fires are reflected by a thousand facets of waves, whose crests and plumes they gild.

In the evening, however, there is a very different spectacle! How beautiful nightfall is at sea, when the last gleams of the day salute the vessel and silhouette all the parts of the ship—masts, rigging, down to the smallest rope—against the red curtain of the occident, like a gigantic spider-web. How beautiful nightfall is when, on that limitless and boundless sea,

---

[72] This uncredited fragment of verse is presumably another of Driou's own.

one sees the beautiful constellations of the heavens rise, one by one, reflected in the mirror of the waters. How beautiful the darkness is at dusk, when, while the torch of day is extinguished, until the moment when the stars shine through, one sees the wake of the hull resplendent with phosphorescent sparks, and thousands of luminous fish silver the distant waves, as if covering them with dazzling steel armor and throwing off reflected fires!

And again, how manifest the power of God is when he covers the sea with his irritated breath! The ocean roars then like a tiger struck by an arrow; it rears up like the Titans desirous of storming the heavens. At the commanding voice of the master, however, it lies down like a meek slave. Under the blows of the tempest, it weeps and moans; its sighs and plaints mingle with the thunder; it pursues the lighting with its waves, and tries to extinguish its naked flamboyance in their flanks. Yes, the Lord presides over the storm, and it is his hand that steers the tempest, as one does with a spirited horse. If he speaks, the ocean will suddenly become calm again, stifling its cries, wiping away it foam, and soon, like the iron of a polished shield under the breath of the wind, it will reflect in its waters the starry splendors of the firmament.

"Yes, the Lord is great on Earth," said Mikaël, as if replying to my thoughts, "but he is sublime and terrible over the ocean depths—and I expect the tempest that is forming to be further proof of it." He added: "And there's the infallible precursor: look at that tornado over there to our right. It consists of a vertical column of air, reaching the sea at its lower extremity and a dark cloud up above. It sometimes moves slowly, sometimes with hurricane speed; it is rotating with prodigious rapidity, drawing up sea-water. Marine tornadoes, more terrible than those on land, caused by contrary winds and electric currents, can cause ships to capsize and sink."

"Oh my God!" I said, without reflection. "What is the significance of those little flames I can see playing in the rigging of that enormous vessel passing beneath us?"

"Those flickers are called St. Elmo's Fire," the Lunian relied. "They're produced by the abundance of electricity in the atmosphere when the sky is stormy, as it is now. Look—the blue of the firmament is hidden by large red-tinted black clouds, and the thunder is already rumbling."

"And what is thunder?" asked Naïs.

"Whenever it is not pure," Mikaël said, "the evaporation of water produces electricity. The combination of gases also produces it. It is necessary that the atmosphere makes restitution of all the electrical fluid with which it is charged, and that restitution takes place via lightning and thunder. The clouds, once electrified, more or less isolated by the interposition of the air, manifest the effects of attraction and repulsion, discharging themselves by means of explosions, sometimes to neighboring clouds, sometimes—but more rarely—to the ground. The electrical spark, the flame that accompanies the explosion, is the lightning; the explosion itself is the thunder."

"But the fires that flutter over marshes in the evening, and which engage in crazy dances, as if they were being pursued and want to escape, or which have the appearance of signals leading a traveler astray, are they not also the effect of gas?" Stella asked—and added, as if to excuse herself:. "We have nothing similar on the Moon, which is why I'm uncertain."

"They're fire-follets," said Mikaël, laughing. "Hydrogen gas[73] gives rise to them. Those little flames, light and capricious, almost always skim the surface of the ground. They play on ancient battlefields, in cemeteries, at the feet of gibbets and in bogs. They like sinister places, because those plac-

---

[73] As Stella has no innate knowledge of the phenomenon, Mikaël is presumably not echoing the judgment of the Lord in this instance but merely reporting an mistaken hypothesis (the gas responsible is actually methane) with excessive self-confidence. His subsequent mistaken explanation of the aurora borealis probably arises in the same fashion, his own explanation of his own lack of lucidity notwithstanding.

es are generally damp. Their preferred retreats are marshes, whose perfidious vegetation, at dusk, simulates a meadow in the eyes of the late travelers. It's in summer and autumn that they appear more often. When you pursue them, they flee before you; when you flee them, they follow you. Those fires often roll in the fashion of waves; they often flare up and scatter like sparks, but they're inoffensive and never burn anything."

"In fact," I replied, "I've read in *L'Histoire de Daniel*[74] that when King Charles IX was hunting in the forest of Lions in Normandy, a fiery specter suddenly appeared, which frightened his followers so much that they left him alone. The king threw himself upon the flame, sword in hand, and it fled—the chronicle does not say that the king was burned."

"Do you know what the English call a fire-follet?" Mikaël went on. "It's a delightful romanticism. They call it a Jack-o'Lantern."

"A Jack with a lantern?" I queried.

"Exactly. So fire-follets frighten villagers, women and children."

"Four leagues from Grenoble," I continued, "there is a narrow patch of ground six feet long by four wide, over which a light flame can be seen running, like that on punch. Hydrogen gas and phosphorus are the sole cause of those fires, as you say, my dear Mikaël. That is what explains the sinister fires exhaled by tombs, places of execution and battlefields. But I'm more curious to know how you explain the aurora borealis?"

"How beautiful it is, the aurora borealis!" said Stella, enthusiastically. "Especially for us, who see it in its entirety on the Moon! First it announces itself by a luminous mist; then comes a bright glare that takes of delightful tints of red, violet and blue. It is striped by darker bands, and emits jets of light

---

[74] This slightly gnomic reference is presumably to Joseph Avenel's *Histoire de la vie et des ouvrages de Daniel Huet* (1853)

so bright and swift that the polar aureole seems to be moving. Finally, the phenomenon appease in all its magnificence; at the zenith it is manifest as a flaming crown, which appears to be the center toward which al the movements of the fire are directed. Then it diminishes gradually; the jets of light and vibrations become rarer; the colors fade; the mist vanishes in its turn. It's over."

"Oh, certainly—the aurora borealis is one of the splendors of the northern climate!" I said.

"Which is to say, my dear chap," Mikaël interjected, "that the other pole also has the same grandiose spectacle— make no mistake, my friend, for it's necessary for you to know that the Earth's two poles are merely the two ends of a huge rod of magnetized iron. The Earth encloses an enormous quantity of iron; now, iron being endowed with magnetic properties, its properties are added thereto—combined with it, if you prefer—and the result is that the terrestrial globe acts like an attractive magnet. With regard to certain dispositions of gaseous emanations of the terrestrial mass that rotate around the pole as on a pivot, the movement produces an inflammation of these gases and..."

"I accept your explanation, Lunian, although it's not the most...lucid..."

"Oh, that's because the supreme Creator does not make the secret of his works known to anyone."

"That's fair enough...but while we were talking about the aurora, it's become dark. The storm is very violent beneath us—a ship has just fired its alarm cannon."

"I should think so!" said Naïs, with a pained expression. "A thunderbolt has just struck its mainmast; its hull is on fire. Poor fellows, they're in an awkward situation. Look how agitated they are. They're using the pumps, but the fire's taking hold. Sad Earth, you always have heart-rending spectacles to show us!"

"It's a warship too," Mikaël went on. "If they don't put out the fire and it reaches the powder-magazine, you'll soon have a terrible spectacle—the ship will blow up!"

"Alas," Stella continued, "the fire's gaining; from port to starboard everything has caught. The sails are going up like fireworks. Lord, what dazzling sprays! The vessel is surely doomed..."

"See how the sea reflects the flames," I aid in my turn. "If so many people were not victims of the disaster, one would say that it's a magnificent sight."

"Good! In spite of the bursts of thunder, the alarm cannon has been heard—here come yawls and dinghies, trying to reach the burning ship by means of oars. Unfortunately, the sea is rough, and I fear..."

Mikaël did not have time to finish his sentence. The noble vessel, that sublime invention of humankind, gave voice to a terrible explosion. Flaming debris was hurled into the air, red and black: torn bodies, bloody limbs, a thousand fantastic objects without discernible form. Then, in the blink of an eye, the fire was extinguished—by the waves, which opened up to allow the immense hull of the shattered vessel to pass; after which the abyss closed up again, and it was all over. Only a few cadavers, items of clothing and pieces of wreckage floated momentarily...

I knelt down to pray. How many souls were accounting to the tribunal of God at that moment, which had taken them by surprise, for the days of their lives: the uncertain life that had been entrusted to them in order that they might employ it well!

Naïs, Stella and Mikaël prayed too; then they shook me by the hand, saying: "Earth, Earth! What anguish and dolor sin has given you! God have mercy on it!"

Mikaël went on: "I saw a shipwreck that moved me cruelly the other day. It was in the region of the trade winds. The only people who escaped the abyss, thanks to a lifeboat that someone succeeded in detaching from the ship that was going down, were a young girl and four passengers with no experience at sea. The poor child fainted in despair; she had just seen her mother perish. Her mother, her only support! Oh,

I owe her the justice that she did not regret her own fate; she only wept for her mother, her worthy mother!"

"The trade winds my dear Mikaël. I'd like to have an explanation of them from your mouth."

"Air expanded by the heat of the sun near the equator is elevated and replaced by two currents of cold air coming from the poles; these two currents, forced to curve by the eastward movement of the Earth's rotation, combine and blow westwards," Mikaël replied.

"That's quite clear this time, my dear Lunian," I hazarded. "So I beg you to define as clearly the winds known as monsoons."

"Monsoons originate from the situation of the continent of Asia, north of the equator," said the Lunian. "Heat, accumulating on land in greater quantity than over the sea, is manifest alternatively, because of the seasons, to either side of the equator, giving rise to contrary winds. Thus, between the months of April and October, it always blows from the southwest, and between October and April, it blows from the southeast."

"While you're being so precise in your definitions, my generous friend," I continued, "I'll ask you to say a few words about mirages."

"Mirages, my dear chap, are another of the beauties of terrestrial nature. The rarefaction of inferior layers of air by intense heat, and the refraction of light rays, give rise to the phenomenon, which sometimes produces on plains the appearance of a vast lake in which villages, trees and so on are depicted, albeit inverted—but the image seems to draw away as one approaches it."

"The storm is dying down, finally," exclaimed Naïs. "So much the better; I was suffering frightfully. There's the Lord's rainbow showing itself."

"Well, as for the rainbow you're pointing out to us, Naïs," Mikaël said, "I will say that when aqueous globules come together in such a way as to form water drops, the light rays passing through them are divided by refraction and go on to strike a point posterior to the drop; then, reflected once or several times in the interior, they emerge divided into their primitive colors—which is to say, into seven colors."

We had stopped talking for a few moments, and the sea was continuing to glide, relative to our immobile aerostats, with its familiar hoarse murmur, when Stella's pure voice pronounced an exclamation that stirred the depths of my entrails:

"Africa!"

Oh, the name of that land vibrated in my breast and echoed in my heart, like a sonorous bell awakening and charming the plain at dusk. Indeed, in the distance, the cost of Africa was emerging from the sea-mist.

That land so fertile in prodigies, celebrated for so many centuries, whose burning lands have served as the tomb of so many glorious victims of the love of science, had captured the desires of my curiosity a long time ago. Precisely because a thick veil still covers the interior of the vast region, and so few travelers, save for Mungo Park, Richard and John Lander, and a few others, have tried to lift it, I was desirous of seeing it, especially in the company of Mikaël and with the safeguard of an aerostat to avert the dangers—for savages are numerous there.

I directed all my attention, therefore, to that coast.

I was looking forward to the ruins of Carthage the Great, whose Roman debris Apuleius, Arnobius, St. Cyprian and the great Augustine saw, which heard Tertullian declaim his beautiful apologies for the Christian religion—Carthage, whose enclosing isthmus the sea has now invaded, whose harbor is no more than a desiccated plain, and where ferocious animals have made their lairs again in the woods emerging from its ruins. Its rivers would not seem to be very numerous; after having examined numerous rocky gorges, however, which appeared here and there as immense gulfs, there would be the much-vaunted oases—hardly worthy of the name, for there would be nothing there but shadows and muddy pools—and then the Sahara and its brethren, so numerous in the center.

We arrived at the tip of Cape Cantin, not far from the straits of Gibraltar. Then our aerostats, steered in that direction, went along the western coast of the vast near-island, carried by the air current, away from Carthage.

The ruins of that illustrious city passed beneath our balloons, sparse on the sand: the arches of aqueducts made of enormous carved stone bocks, so polished and exactly fitted that the cement binding the together was scarcely visible; subterranean so-called elephant-stables; immense ruins occupying a considerable area, covered with fig-trees, olive-trees, carobs, angelicas and acanthias, strewn with marble debris of every color.

Then I evoked the great names of Asdrubal, Hannibal and all the heroes, male and female, who had sustained the most desperate struggle, so energetically, against the unjust and infamous cupidity of the Romans. I conjured up the great shades of Arnobius, Apuleius, St. Cyprian and St. Augustine, who had lived on that devouring ground; I saluted the hillock that bore the Byrsa of the unfortunate Dido, and heard her moans as she expired on the fatal pyre that she had lit with her own hands, while repeating the name of Aeneas. From the summit of those ruins I paraded my gaze over the isthmus, the sea, the distant islands, over a pleasant countryside, blue-tinted lakes, azure-tinted mountains. I discovered forests, ships, Moorish villages, Mohammedan hermitages, minarets, the modern abode of new peoples—and I noticed, dolorously, that the sea had invaded the isthmus of that ancient Byrsa, that opulent Carthage, whose harbor was nothing but a desiccated plain, and whose ruins served as lairs for ferocious animals hidden in the rubble and the brushwood.

Then there was the battlefield of Zama, which saw the glory of Hannibal extinguished; then the plain that witnessed the defeat of Juba by Caesar; then the river Bagrada, whose dragon devoured the army of Regulus; then the countries of Masinissa and the regions of Numidia passed in their turn, recalling a thousand memories to my mind and making the chords of my memory vibrate.

There were also Hippo, Utica, where Cato killed himself, and Juba's Caesarea, which also passed before our eyes.

Finally, the Atlas, displaying its enormous mass, its inaccessible slopes and its frightful precipices in the midst of sandy regions, and plunging its summits into the clouds—which caused the ancient to say that its head reached the skies. Then the Barbary states: Fez, Morocco, Tunis, Tripoli, all the way to Biledulgerid in the kingdom of Darah also pass within our range.

Then comes the Sahara, the great desert with its sands scorched by the tropical fires, extending from the Atlas to the banks of the Niger, offering us an oceans of moving dunes, strewn with rocky hills and a few valleys where the collected water scarcely nourishes a few spiny genistas, ferns and grasses.

"Three great human races make up the populations of the globe," Mikael told me. "The Semitic race, or that of Shem, in Asia; the race of Japhet, in Europe; and that of Ham, in Africa. The peoples of America are formed from the race of the sons of Japhet, who must have arrived in that country via the Bering strait. But each of these races has changed its color and its constitution under the influence of the different zones it has inhabited. The equator has rendered the negroes black; the neighboring zones have produced yellow complexions; the other zones have causes the coppery complexions or Redskins; the temperate zones have conserved the white or primitive race, and the glacial zones have caused the pale complexions of their rare inhabitants.

"But here, in Africa, the population is divided into two colors: the yellow, or Caucasian, race in the north; the black, or Ethiopian, in the center and the south.

"The Kabyles, the Berbers, the Copts, the Negroes, the Kaffirs and the Hottentots are the primitive inhabitants of this part of the world. The Arabs, the Turks, the Moors, the issue of barbarians who arrived in the great invasion, are only colonists."

Mikaël added many other observations on this subject, but I was only lending him half my attention, for in that famous Sahara, which summoned my gaze, I could not weary of contemplating the immense depths of the solitude. I saw, scattered on the land, as if forming the landmarks of a road continually erased by the desert wind, the skeletons of camels, horses, mules—beasts of burden—and even travelers who, unable to endure the thirst, must have perished in the burning sands, and, before dying, had doubtless pronounced the names of their mothers, their sisters and their homelands. It was like an immense ossuary that represented to me the image of life.

Elsewhere, prowling around the caravans that I saw traversing the sands, I heard the terrible lions of the Sahara roaring, tigers growling, panthers howling, hyenas whistling, jackals yapping, rhinoceroses bellowing, antelope muttering, elephants trumpeting, giraffes snuffling, and I saw gazelles leaping from oasis to oasis, so timid and graceful. On the Niger, as in the waters of Senegal and the banks of the Zaire, I also found hippopotamuses and cunning crocodiles, but especially hippopotamuses, whose numerous herds uttered cries so shrill that one could hear them at a great distance.

In the woodlands beyond the desert, were true virgin forests like those of America; there was, to begin with, an unprecedented variety of birds, but also monkeys and intelligent chimpanzees. I confess that in the presence of these numerous families of animals, I was very glad to be in the balloon, for I still shiver in thinking about the enormous boa constructors and all the reptiles we saw undulating through the dry grass, and becoming the spectator of their combats when they happened to encounter some poor animal, weaker and frozen by terror.

But above all, in the sandy zone that stripes Africa over vast distances, as the Milky Way stripes the heavens, I studied all the peoples, all the yellow and black tribes, all the savage indigenous populations who slipped by beneath the slow navigation of our aerial skiffs, some indifferent, others astir, some perfidious, some hospitable, simple or sly, meek or cruel: no-

madic sons of solitude, wandering in the desert on their marvelous horses, scarcely panting in spite of the excessive heat;
or asleep in the shadow of their dromedaries, one foot of
which was hobbled to keep them in place; or hunting in vigorous forests of baobabs, the largest trees known; or colleting
the fruits from their palm-trees; or carving bows out of syca-
more; or feeling coconut-palms to obtain the fruit; or harvesting their bananas; or zealously caring for the tamarinds, the
lychees, the cassia and the sandalwood from which they made
perfumed boxes; or harvesting pepper, indigo, cotton, hemp
and sugar.

Beyond the Sahara there were the rich plains of the Su-
dan, which passed by, their countryside dotted with tall millet-
mills, their herds of cattle, goats, camels and horses grazing
the spontaneously-grown herbage. There, villages succeeded
the caravan routes; the population became dense, distinguished by its sedentary habits. The people no longer had the
pale physiognomy and covetous gaze that testified to the empty stomachs and purses of the inhabitants of the desert. They
displayed the ugliness, laxity and indolence of satisfied appetites.

Here we have, for example, in the Damerghou, at Zinder,
the great Sultan of Borno, who reigns over hundreds of thousands of souls; now, there I saw nonchalant men and languor-
ous women shuffling along, accessible only to the passion of
doing nothing. Some, lying on the sand, gathered in groups,
were chatting without vivacity, others applying themselves
absent-mindedly to the details of their costume.

Well, who would believe that those benevolent, squat
faces reflecting the impressions of child-like ideas, could pass
suddenly from that expression to one of cold and refined fe-
rocity? That is, however, the case.

"In England," Mikaël told me, "the courts condemn
criminals to hang by the neck until death ensues—and it's a
frightful effect, I assure you.

"In France, they are guillotined—and, by virtue of the
rapidity with which the hundred-pound blade, which slices off

the head immediately, it's said that the body retains life and pain for a further thirty minutes...

"In Span, they are garroted—which is to say that you catch the neck of the patient, seated against a gibbet, in a circle of iron closed by a screw, which tightens, tightens, tightens around the neck until it's reduced to the sate of a quill. You will understand that no breath or life any longer remains.

"In Switzerland and Prussia, they are decapitated with a two-handed sword, and the head, suddenly separated from the kneeling body by the blade, leaps and flies away, rolling and rolling...

"In Turkey, they are impaled, and it is frightful to see a poor unfortunate sitting on the iron lance, which perforates his intestines and eventually emerges through his side or shoulder.

"In China they are put in cangues...

"Here, one is burned alive, there buried alive; elsewhere they drown you; in other places they poison you...

"But in Damerghou, criminals are neither condemned to be hanged, nor guillotined. One has the breast of the victim opened up, cutting through the living flesh, and tears out the heart. Or else they suspend you by the feet and let the blood out slowly through little cuts."

I saw the horrible executions that Mikaël described to me carried out; there was a tree of death, a solitary tree, which, growing on a rock, was forty or fifty feet high. Skeletons lay at its foot; it was frightful to behold.

I repeat that I was witness to it, that barbarism is so commonplace that the greatest amusement of a child in those countries is to cut the throat of an animal, to listen to its screams and see its flesh palpitating under the knife. At certain times, it is customary to sacrifice poor animals. They are given to passers-by in the street, to whomever will kill them with the greatest enthusiasm. This disgusting slaughter is carried out amid crises of joy, and there is no young woman who does not have bloodstained hands. By the time these animals fall to the ground, there is not a scrap of flesh left intact on their quivering bodies.

Gentler scenes, fortunately, come to restore serenity to my curiosity. There is the dance of young women who emerge from all the huts in the village to the sound of a tambourine. A few men take turns to strike the skin of the instrument with their arms, while hopping on one leg in a circle. The dancers imitate this movement with a timid gait, and bow to their partners when the dance was finished.

Now it is Senegambia that we reach, with its Fullahs, its ebony-black Joloffs and its Mandingos. Its climate is torrid and unhealthy, and the Senegal, the greatest river of Africa, irrigates it. I discover our French possessions there and the counters of our trade. A fort and a few barracks, such is the abode of our soldiers and representatives of France. Fortunately, the unaggressive negroes gladly devote themselves to agriculture.

Here is Nigeria and its deserts, which is something else entirely. Beautiful in their ugliness, strong and vigorous by utterly devoid of energy, these children of burning Africa, hidden in their warm valleys, brutalized by indolence in their filthy huts, drink at and sleep like vile livestock. Almost without any notion of god, they scarcely worship miserable sculpted sticks, abominable fetishes that they believe to be gods. Abandoned to all the disorders of gross and sensual appetites, they pullulate in numerous hordes, disobedient to their leaders, incapable of defense, deprived of the sentiment that makes humans sublime. Also watching our approach, hidden by clumps of alicondas, bamboos and lataniers, are bands of European filibusters. Alas, they are lying in wait for the black livestock, of which they make an object of trade. It is necessary for us to be subjected to that scene of horrible violence, a revolting monstrosity known the world over, to which one never gets accustomed and bears the name of the Slave Trade.

And what difference is there between these children of Africa and those of Europe and other worlds? None, except color.

But there is nothing more astonishing about the color black than the color white, brown, yellow or reed. It is neither the blood, nor the brain, nor any other substantial element that is black. That skin color depends uniquely on the external causes that produce it—the sun and its heat. What else is it that renders the Portuguese, after a few centuries in Africa, so similar in color to negroes? And besides, what is it that distinguishes by so many nuances the negro races in Africa itself, if not the climate? The blackest negroes live in the lands where he wind blows from the east, having traversed the full extent of the land, bringing the fiercest heat.

By what right do other humans, because they are white, treat the negroes like wild animals because they are black?

And when I say that the mores of these people are hospitable, and much gentler than those of other peoples; when I repeat that a traveler can advance with confidence into their villages, that he will find a good welcome there, and often a respect that extends to adoration, how can one justify the turpitude of white men going to hunt black men?

Now, in the empire of the Ashanti, near the Congo, we see a slave-ship approach the shore to take on a load of "ebony wood"—the name given to a cargo of negroes. There, the chief of Ajouan, a harsh negro, immediately sells and delivers three hundred of his subjects. And it is not as if the matter is limited to giving these unfortunates in exchange for the bagatelles brought by the ship—no, is it not necessary to *prepare the merchandise?* Thus, it is prepared—which is to say that every negro is submitted to the ordeal of a pitiless hand that subjects him to a thousand dolors to force him to a suitable state of agility and flexibility. After which, his marked with a red hot iron on the shoulder the calf or the hip. Then he is chained to a companion in captivity.

The unfortunates are heaped up pell-mell in the hold, men, women and children alike. The can scarcely breathe in the fetid air, corrupted by themselves. That is of no importance. However, in order not to allow their limbs to become numb, the sellers take them on to the deck every day and force them to dance and, without and distinction of age or sex, with blows of the cat'o'-nine-tails, the lash and the whip. If nostalgia—homesickness—takes possession of them to the point of making them ill, they are thrown into the sea. If the ship runs short of food, five or ten of them are killed per day to nourish the others. If the slave-ship is threatened by a cruiser, the unfortunates are attached to one another in pairs and thrown into the water like contraband merchandise. Finally, if they are able reach a port in America where slaves are sold, they are disembarked, taken to market, tied to a stake and fetch one thousand five hundred or two thousand francs, according to their beauty, appearance or strength.

By contrast, during the crossing, if the seller and his men suffer, whether from cold feet or boredom, the warm body of a negress is placed beneath their feet to warm His Honor, or a negro or negress is forced to sing, to amuse His Grace.

Poor victims! Once having become the property of some planter or other, the negroes must labor without respite in the harshest terrain, on the most ingrate soil, in the blazing sun. And there, far from their homeland, their families, their huts, how many mute dolors, tears, sighs and suicides!

Go see the Congo, on the one hand, and Kentucky, on the other. What an account will one day be rendered to the master of worlds!

Our aerostats subsequently pass over the lands of Loango, Angola and Benguela. Here we witness the burial of a chief whose death calls forth gaiety rather than grief. There is drinking and dancing on the grave; a piece of cloth is placed in his hand on which his gods are painted. There, before a fetish of parrot-feathers, an accused man is made to drink poison. If he is innocent, the poison will do him no harm; if guilty, he will die on the spot. I leave you to imagine how many more guilty individuals there are than innocent ones.

We then sail over arid desert coasts, scenes devoid of poetry—except that we discover the island of St. Helena, which I salute for the bitter memories it brings to mind.

Finally, come the lands of the Hottentots and Kaffirs.

"Here, I'm in familiar territory," I tell Mikaël.

"What do you mean, my friend?" he asks.

"I mean that in Paris, at the Salle Bonne-Nouvelle and the old Cirque, I've had the honor of being greeted by a troop of Kaffirs, brought at great expense to France, for me to see and touch them with my hands. Those savages gave a brilliant performance of their manners and customs, awakenings, meals, marriages, combats, festivals, dances, war-cries! Oh, how war-cries are still resounding in my ears. Moreover, they were a truly magnificent ash-gray color, of a stature of which a Frenchman would have been more than proud, and possessed of a kill in juggling that more than one circus performer would have liked to have."

"Then I have nothing to tell you about Kaffirs, except that they're not all cannibals, but they like to eat the morsels of flesh offered to them raw. Now let's pass on to Hottentots. They're less pleasant."

"Yes, for they're hideous," Naïs interjected. "Look, their faces have a hideous animality. Those gross features, soft and insidious, those lips elongated in the form of a snout and that flattened nose; everything about them advertises stupidity. Their shaven hair, which extends down their backs, is more reminiscent of animal fur than human tresses."

"And their women, Great God!" exclaimed Stella, covering her face.

"Strangers to any idea of family, they don't build villages," Mikaël concluded. "Clad only in a sheepskin during winter, armed with a bow and a quiver full of poisoned arrows, they roam the mountains and deserts alone. As cruel as they are stupid, their greatest enjoyment is to drink the blood that flows from their enemies' wounds. They take indecency to the ultimate degree. Thus, do they not regard the entrails of defeated adversaries as an ornament without equal?"

"Oh, Father, what are you saying?" said Stella.

"Mikaël, my friend!" said Naïs.

"Covered in a grease that they mix with black pigment," Mikaël continued, imperturbably, wearing the intestines of their enemies as a luxurious belt, they provoke horror!"

"Enough, my dear Lunian!" I said in my turn.

"Poor Earth!" said Mikaël again. "What abysms of mystery you enclose! Humans would do well to raise their gaze toward God, their terrible master, when they lend themselves to evil!"

"Well, dear Lunian, in the words of the poet: *Os homini sublime dedit coelumque tueri/Jussit et erectos as sidera toelere vultus...*"[75]

"Let us look elsewhere, are you going to say?" said Mikaël. "As you wish, my illustrious Parisian. We're here for your instruction; we shall do as you wish."

Soon Cape Town comes to set itself beneath our aerostats, but not without our balloons receiving the terrible shocks of a violent wind, blowing furiously. The cape, once knows as *Cap Tormentoso*, the Cape of Storms, fully merited its name, but Philip of Spain—I don't know which one—with the aim of reassuring his navigators, substituted the name of Cape of Good Hope for the ominous name that the southern tip of Africa bore.

So, Cape Town appears, situated on the slopes of Table Mountain and Lion Mountain. It forms and amphitheater extended to the shore of the sea. The streets, although broad, do not appear to be comfortable, for they are very poorly paved. The houses, almost all uniform in style, are beautiful and spacious; they are covered with reeds to prevent the accidents that heavier covers might cause when the big winds make themselves felt.

The entrance to the city, via the castle square, offers a superb view, but what attracted my gaze most of all, was Table Mountain, which initially seemed perfectly flat at its summit, but in reality has considerable inequalities. I could see immense pools on its plateau, formed by rainwater. Strangely enough, on top of the mountain it was winter, while at its foot, summer appeared to be in full flower. From the depths of the

---

[75] The lines are from Ovid's *Metamorphoses*. "Humans were given an upturned visage in order to gaze at Heaven/while other creatures incline toward the Earth."

valleys of its slopes, other less elevated hills emerged, rounded or oblong, all covered in verdure, but leopards and hyenas could be seen swarming in their bushes. And yet, here and there lay groups of well-kept farms, whose houses were white beneath black roofs, while the backcloth, evenly divided between vines and orchards, presented rich masses of vegetation.

Meanwhile, we began to turn around the cape to go along the eastern shore of Africa and overlook, between the kingdoms of Sablo and Sofala, the states of Monotapa and the isle of Madagascar, separated from us by the Mozambique Channel.

I shall not tell you anything about those countries, except that they were infinitely more populous, and in delightful locations, which explained the number of towns and villages I saw set on the banks of rivers. I will add that Madagascar is the largest island in the world; we were able to judge that by the grandiose appearance that it offered us. The olive-colored race is dominant there, but the maladies of its climate are terrible, especially when wintering.

Soon I discovered another island funded on a near-circular rock rising up in the form of a cone with a summit that was truncated, or lost in the clouds. It was like a volcano with an arid base. Indeed, a volcano soon let us see its smoke, and the lava-flows covering enormous areas of ground, which are called "*Brûlé*." It was none other than the Île de Bourbon, where the French established themselves in 1657. The Île de France, the theater of the imaginary but sublime scenes of the beautiful drama of *Paul et Virginie*, passed in its turn.[76]

Then we discovered the Lupata Mountains and the Mountains of the Moon, on the edge of the unknown lands of Central Africa. It is there that the famous Niger, the location of whose sources was so avidly sought by explorers, emerges

---

[76] *Paul et Virginie* (1787) is a feverish tragic romance by Bernardin de Saint-Pierre, which was immensely successful. The Île de France is nowadays known as Mauritius; the real tragedy enacted there was, of course, the extinction of the dodo.

from the bosom of the earth. It is there too, in the foothills of the Mountains of the Moon that the ancients placed the origin of the Nile. For us, from the height of our aerostats, which overlooked immense, infinite horizons, all that was truly marvelous: mountains and deserts, the cruel nations of the Mossegayes and the coasts of Zanzibar, nomadic populations and cities in a primitive state, Muzimba cannibals and the races of Ethiopia, Abyssinia and the kingdoms of Adel, Nubia and Dongola, wild nature, astonishing curiosities of a still-mysterious and always little-known Africa.

We skirted the ancient Red Sea, and eventually, Stella, who had become very pensive and was leaning nonchalantly on her mother, said: "Egypt!"

I emerged from my own mute contemplation, and prepared to plunge my gaze into that classic land of the Bible and the first ages of the world.

It was not modern Egypt that would interest me most; it was the ancient Egypt that we were going to rediscover in all its scattered ruins. Thus, I was truly glad to see that Stella was preparing to become my cicerone once again in the inspection of what was already attracting everyone's attention.

First, I ought to say that, apart from its magnificent debris, which makes it an enchanted abode, the general appearance of Egypt had not changed from the one I had seen in the marvelous album of the Moon. Agriculture possesses the same lands, bordered by the same quantity of fallow land, as it did in ancient times. There is the same flat, arid soil with burning sands on the one hand; on the other, the cultivated part is a more or less narrow valley and a line of vegetation that furrows the desert, as it is furrowed itself by the Nile, which gives it its fecundity in descending from the mountains of Abyssinia—which give it birth, not the Mountains of the Moon as was mistakenly believed for a long time.[77]

---

[77] When *Les Aventures d'un aeronaute parisien* was published, Richard Francis Burton and John Hanning Speke were only just setting out in search of the source of the Nile, which

"We're entering Upper Egypt," said Stella, and there, first of all, is the famous Elephantine, and Philé, no less famous. Both cities possessed beautiful temples, but as you can see, my dear Terran, civilization in these deserts is as deadly as barbarism, for those superb ruins were removed to construct buildings in Syene. The plain is level now, and if it were not for the asperities of the ground at the site of Elephantine, no one would know that it had once been there.

"As for Syene, it enriched itself with their remains; in addition, it took the treasure from their catacombs, excavated in order to steal the superb monoliths that decorated Egypt, and the beautiful stones of the great cities. Except that Syene now calls itself Aswan.

"There, Silsila shows you its vast quarries, which are no less than six kilometers long, and from which the principal monuments of Egypt were excavated, block by block, dispatched in series along the Nile.

"Here, further along, nearer and directly below, you will discover the rubble of cities named Edfu, Esneh, Hermon and Abydos. But only that rubble you can admire the grandiose ruins of marvelous temples. It was there, at Abydos, that one of your savants found the chronological table of the ancient Pharaohs on an enormous stone.

"Here's Dendera. What a sublime construction the ruins of that temple ought to be! You know that a zodiac was found inscribed on the vault of one of its upper rooms, which is now in your Louvre—and you doubtless also recall that attempts were, by means of that zodiac, to demonstrate the falsity of the Holy Books with regard to the date of the creation of the world. A scientific study of the famous granite recently

---

they eventually tracked to Lake Victoria. The source supposedly identified in antiquity by one Diogenes (not the Cynic) was probably imaginary; it was not until 1889 that the source of the White Nile was discovered in the Rwenzori Mountains, which were then tentatively identified as Diogenes' "Mountains of the Moon."

proved, however, on the contrary, the truth of the accounts of Moses. Poor demi-savants! They always want to be able to deny God, but God speaks through the mouth of true science, and they are confounded!

"God in Heaven!" I exclaimed, interrupting Stella, in spite of her caustic verve. "I can see ruins whose splendor effaces that of the most beautiful ruins I've seen!"

"You cry out in enthusiasm, my dear Terran," said Mikaël, exactly as the French army did, on arriving on those hills and discovering these ruins for the first time, during the celebrated Egyptian expedition of your famous General Bonaparte."

"It's because these ruins fully merit that one stands before them in ecstasy," Naïs said in her turn.

"How beautiful they are, Lord, how beautiful!" I replied.

"It's the queen of ancient cities, the great Thebes of the Hundred Gates, the illustrious Diospolis of the Greeks, which has today become the miserable village of Meynet-Abou!" Stella went on. "Menes was its founder, and its greatest splendor dates from Sesostris. It was then thirty miles in circumference, and its temples and palaces had the unprecedented wealth that Cambyses pillaged, having destroyed everything."

"And even though everything was destroyed, what beauty!" I repeated, in a state of exaltation.

"Look first at the gates, twenty-five feet high, covered with hieroglyphs, that preceded the temples," Stella continued. "The desert winds heap up sand in vain. Those courtyards surrounded by porticos and those thousands of sculpted columns defy them. They sustain stones of an inconceivable grandeur, laden with signs of the religion that raised them. Forests of obelisks snake around the outlines of immense edifices.

"Here is the temple of Luxor, built on an embankment of the Nile, which serves as its base. There, on the left bank, are the tombs of the ancient kings, carved into the rock, in the bosom of an arid valley. The walls of their vast chambers are covered in sculptures and paintings.

"Further away, but similarly on the left bank, is the necropolis or cemetery of Thebes, hollowed out in the flank of the mountain. Some of those sepulchers have enclosures of an astonishing grandeur."

"You call them tombs," I said to Stella, "but I see Arabs and Bedouins everywhere, at their entrances, as desiccated as the mummies they sell to travelers. Look, there, near to that avenue of sphinxes, horses and buffaloes are grazing a few meager tufts of grass..."

"These sinister retreats are home to those poor tatterdemalions," she told me. "Their families are lodged in the tombs. The mutilated stumps of statues serve their wives as hearths. Thus, an entire village has been constructed in a corner of the great temple of Luxor, which sent you one of its obelisks; another village is in that necropolis; another here and another there.

"On the right bank is Karnak, a temple perhaps without equal, preceded by an avenue of monolithic columns seventy feet high, unfortunately fallen. In that temple is a room more than three hundred feet long by fifty broad, the vault of which is supported by more than three hundred columns, still standing. The circumference of their capitals is sixty feet."

"A capital sixty feet around!" I exclaimed.

"Sixty feet," Stella repeated. "A hundred men could stand comfortably on the platform of each of them...and in the courtyard is the largest obelisk, measuring ninety-one feet."

"It was on the friezes and murals of that edifice, in fact, that your savant Jean-François Champollion recognized the portraits of the ancient Pharaohs, and the face of a King of Judah, captive of one of the Pharaohs," said Mikaël, pointing at the palace.

"Now," said Stella, look this way at the celebrated memnomium of Ozymandias and the colossus of Memnon, sixty feet high..."

"The one that made harmonious sounds hard when it was struck by the fires of the rising sun?" I asked.

"The very same. In addition, that colossal statue of Ramses the Great is fifty-three feet high, although seated, not counting its base.

"These ruins are beautiful," I said. "Yes, beautiful, admirable, marvelous. But what are they beside that rich Thebes, the city *whose rival the sun never saw*, the capital of Sesostris, the city that I have seen so brilliant and glorious in your Moon?"

"And which you will resuscitate in your *Marvelous Album*!" Naïs murmured, mischievously.

Meanwhile, our balloons were drawing us away from Thebes, carrying us toward Middle Egypt, and the further we went, the more I realized that the Egypt in question was merely a vast graveyard, an immense ruin, so strewn was it with funereal pyramids, hypogeas, the catacombs of humans, cemeteries of animal mummies, sphinxes and pylons: all the mortuary attributes that ought to have preserved memories but have only given birth to oblivion!

"There's the Memphis of your, now Menf," Stella soon proclaimed. "It was there that the Pharaohs dwelt, and you can see the ruins of their palaces, which extended along the left bank of the Nile from one extremity of the city to the other."

Indeed, we were arriving over a lain enclosed by mountains, Arabic on the right bank, Libyan on the left, which became narrower a little further on, all covered with magnificent debris extending as far as the eye could see.

"Here was the temple of Vulcan,[78] whose colossus was seventy-five feet long," said Stella, pointing things out to me. "Facing its southern portico was the palace in which the bull Apis was nurtured. All these canals communicated with Lake

---

[78] Just as Driou routinely replaces the names of Greek deities with their Roman equivalents, so he substitutes the names of Roman gods for the Egyptian gods that the Greeks considered to be equivalents of their own. Thus, the Egyptian god Ptah, worshiped at Memphis, and identified by the Greeks with Hephaestus, is named by him as the Roman Vulcan.

Moeris, which you can see shining in the distance. And as the Egyptians did not know the art of building arches, they have no bridges. That's why Memphis is only situated on the left bank of the river.

"But the marvel of Memphis was the Serapeum over there. Four years ago, I would not have been able to show it to you, but thanks to a Frenchman, Auguste Mariette, who undertook a bold excavation, there gradually emerged from the sands, without any other clue than his divinatory genius, first a roadway of sphinxes, advancing in a straight line in the midst of the nearby monuments, and comprising a hundred and forty-one of those symbols, not counting those of which only the bases were found. One day, after long labor, your compatriot saw emerging from the earth a statue of Pindar, bearing his name in Greek. Then came other statues, of Lycurgus, Solon, Euripides, Pythagoras, Plato, Aeschylus, Homer and Aristotle, all recognizable by their names and their attributes. Finally, between the hemicycle formed by the statues and the two final sphinxes of the avenue, a transversal dromos appeared, the left branch of which led to a temple constructed by Amenardis in honor of Apis, and the right branch directly to the Serapeum, or the temple of Serapis.

"In brief, on the night of 12 November 1851, the door of a immense subterranean passage was discovered.

"It was an entire hidden city, the sepulchral cave of Apis. Arranged in order there were the Apises that had died under the eighteenth dynasty and the first kings of the nineteenth. Each of them had its sepulchral chamber hollowed out in the living rock...but they had been violated even in antiquity! Only one had escaped the profaners. What an excitement for Monsieur Mariette when he penetrated that secret! Inside, to the right and left of the door, stood two monuments in black-painted wood, each in the form of a sarcophagus. On the floor of the chamber stood two immense alabaster vases, similar to those your antiquarians call canoptic jars. Little niches, carved into the rear wall, contained stone statues, and the entire floor of the chamber was strewn with other funerary statuettes made of enameled faience.

"I need not tell you that he found pieces of gold and precious objects in the bitumen mixture, including a large golden hawk with a ram's head, with its wings deployed, formed of partitioned enamels simulating feathers, of which not one of your skilled sculptors would have been loath to glory in being the author. Nor need I tell you that he soon found himself confronted by the skeletons of oxen and humans, but I shall tell you—and look over there—that the intrepid archeologist gradually cleared colossi, that of Osiris among others, and the entire vast temple know as the Serapeum."

"There's a Frenchman well worthy of science and his fatherland," I exclaimed, "for this is admirable!"

"Pyramids! Pyramids!" said Naïs, while my eyes were searching for the famous Labyrinth without being able to discover it.

I looked. Indeed, our aerostats had placed us above the eternal Pyramids. My pen would never be able to render the impression I experienced. My soul was gripped by a combination of surprise, stupor and enthusiasm that emerged with difficulty, so great was its paroxysm. Eventually, I collected myself. The angles of the gigantic, Pelasgic, cyclopean monuments formed long staircases. Some English people were making the ascent at that very moment. A platform that might have contained more than thirty people received them, and when they had gone down again, after staying there for some time, more than fifty Arabs fought to serve as their guides. Torches were lit and, bent almost double, I saw them enter a narrow corridor about three feet high.

When they came out, I heard one of them say: "It's frightful to have one's face assaulted like bats in that manner, in order to get to the king's burial-chamber!"

"And not to see anything but a granite sarcophagus!" added an aristocratic lady, thin and wrinkled. "Personally, I was choking in the smoke of the torches."

For me, in the air, high above the Pyramids, I thought I was seeing the world entire unfold before me. The Nile seemed to be parading its immutable and silence beneficence at the feet of the monuments.

"The oasis of Siwa," Stella said, showing me a desert scorched by the sun to the left, and clumps of trees in the middle of it. "The ancient temple of Jupiter-Amon[79] was there. Look, you can see the vestiges of the monument, its triple enclosure and the fountain of the Sun."

"You'll remember, old chap," said Mikaël, "that the statue of Jupiter was made of emeralds and other precious stones. It had the form of a ram from the head to the waist."

I did not reply.

I had beneath my eyes the armies of the Macedonians and the Persians, swallowed up by the sands, and I saw, floating in the air once again, the great phantoms of Alexander, Cambyses, Sesostris, Ozymandias, Moeris, Ramses and Cleopatra, and the gentler images of Joseph and Jacob. And I searched with my gaze fir the land of Goshen...

My meditation undoubtedly lasted for a long time, for, when I returned to myself we had passed over Cairo and Mansoura and I was about to mention the holy shade of our Louis IX, the conqueror of these regions, when Naïs said to me: "Behold Alexandria!"

"Alexandria, that?" I said. "But it's the saddest and most desolate place on Earth..."

Indeed, I could see nothing but a bare sea whose waves were breaking on an even barer shore, harbors that were almost empty, and the Libyan desert fading away to the midday horizon. As for the city that had counted three million inhabitants, which had been the sanctuary of the Muses, witness to the glories and miseries of Cleopatra, the beloved masterpiece of Alexander the Great, it was no more than an inanimate shell, an empty, silent sepulcher and an enclosing wall ruined by despotism and brutalization.

---

[79] i.e. Amon-Ra, or Amun-Re.

"*Vanitas vanitatum*, always and everywhere, on your Earth, isn't it, my dear Frenchman?" the Lunian said to me, with a certain irony.

I maintained silence, like the sleeping city—but I darted a long last glance on that Egypt, so famous in times past; on the coasts of Palestine, still radiant with gory in spite of its accursed ruins; on the Asia that we had visited previously—and, sailing through the air in convoy with my beloved Mikaël, we began to float over the Mediterranean Sea.

"One can sail over these waves without encountering a more grandiose memory," Naïs said to me.

"Those African coasts echo the moans of Dido," said Stella, "and, better still, the masculine tones of the Bishop of Hippo, Augustine, the tenderly cherished son of Monica."

"There, the Son of Man saved the world," Mikaël added.

"There, Alexander destroyed Tyre."

"And in Salamis there, Xerxes was defeated by Themistocles, in the presence of Artemisia, Queen of Halicarnassus."

"And further on, Actium, which saw Augustus defeat all his rivals and become master of the world..."

"Then we're going to reach the European shore in Greece?" I said, enthusiastically. "If that's the case, my dear Lunian, let me catch my breath for a moment, and since, in visiting the modern world, we have so frequently fund traces of the ancient world, permit me not to return to my Paris without having seen the debris of Sparta, Athens and Rome. In that manner, having admired in your Marvelous Album what the great cities were, I shall be able to judge what has become of them after their fall, among our new races..."

"Let it be as you desire, my dear friend," said Mikaël, "All the more so as, bathed as you are in the love of antiquity by the authors of your studies, it would be cruel not to give you the enjoyment of contemplating once, in reality, that of which you have undoubtedly dreamed so many times beneath the white sky of your student bed."

"And it's then, most of all, that you will be able to judge: *Sic transit gloria mundi*,"[80] Naïs added. "We shall scarcely be able to see where Lacedaemon and Corinth were. Beautiful Athens will only be able to offer us the meager debris of its splendid Parthenon."

"Finally, I shall be able to see my unknown worlds!" I said, with a deep sigh of satisfaction.

---

[80] "So passes the glory of this world." The quotation is taken from *The Imitation of Christ* by Thomas à Kempis.

VIII

At the words "unknown worlds" Mikaël gave voice to his familiar burst of laughter.

"Oh! You think you have all the unknown worlds in your game-bag now, old chap?" he said. "Not at all, my poor friend—and I'll prove it to you when I've recovered from my...emotion in the face of your...knowledge!"

"First, what do you mean by *unknown worlds*?" Stella asked, maliciously, sharing in her father's caustic humor.

"Well, naturally, they're the worlds situated in spaces that are...out of our reach," I stammered.

"Good! My man is floundering even over the matter of giving me a definition. Know, then, my dear chap, that there is an infinity of unknown worlds that you will never know, and which you do not even suspect. It is over them that you walk, treading them underfoot, in which you wade, carelessly."

"*Ignoti nulla cupido!*"[81] said the savant Stella.

"Give me an example of what you're talking about," I said to Mikaël, getting straight to the point.

"This sea here! That Ocean there!" he replied. "For the sea is a world, a whole world, a world that has not yet had its Christopher Columbus or its Vasco da Gama, a world that encloses marvels that would made you swoon; a world with indescribable curiosities, antiquities as worthy of capturing your gaze as the beautiful treasures of Assyria, Persia or Egypt; its peoples, its cities, its forests, its animals, its thousand most prodigious fantasies..."

"There is all that at the bottom of the sea?"

"All that and many other things."

"And you have seen them?"

"What! But I see them—we see them—every day."

---

[81] "One does not desire that of which one knows nothing." The aphorism is from Ovid's *Art of Love*.

"Have you ever descended into the depths of the abyss?"

"Never in reality; by the power of sight, a hundred thousand times."

"You must have a very piercing gaze, for the sea has an average depth of nine thousand seven hundred and twenty-three meters, which is almost ten kilometers..."

"You're forgetting the famous spy-glass," said Mikaël, triumphantly, showing me the tip of the half-hidden lens shining in his pocket.

"Oh, dear Master," I said to the Lunian, putting my hands together. "Lend me your spy-glass, please, just for an hour!"

"Only an hour? The Terran is modest! Go on! As we shall only meet once, I ought to do everything possible to please you..."

I leapt for joy, and my aerostat performed an alarming somersault with me. I had the lens, the revelatory lens. Without losing a minute, I looked...

"God in Heaven!" I cried, immediately. "Yes, there are magnificent horizons, illuminated by the reverberation of the waters; splendid valleys, mountains, hills, woods, forests, meadows. But it's wonderful! And in the midst of that beautiful subterranean nature, an entire hearth of life; life at the bottom of the sea, like in various environments; life in all the upper and lower layers. Only the forms of the creatures are different.

"What movement! Movement in the plains, movement in the woods. For all the seaweed that one encounters on the surface of the waters is merely the detritus of these submarine forests. Was I right to be so curious? Just look at all the different species of inhabitants: animals of the surface, animals of the middle regions, animals of the depths, warm-blooded animals, cold-blooded animals. And then, as you said, my dear Mikaël, the sea-bed is not merely sand and pebbles, plants and woods; there really are cities and towns, very different populated than our sublunar cities. What a host of madrepores!

What masses of polyps! What groups of corals! And madre-pores polyps and corals, all of that is moving, all busy...

"Life without parallel, which shows that God has not left anywhere without inhabitants. And infusoria, and monadines! And billons of little phosphorescent creatures! But in truth, this unknown world presents a thousand marvels, which I can only see in aggregation for wanting to discover too much too quickly...oh, what's that monstrous animal! Heavens! It's not an animal lying there on its side, it's a ship...which has sunk to the bottom, alas! I can see a number of unfortunates on the deck, still kneeling, as they were at the moment when death surprised them. But they're French! Yes. French soldiers. Where are we? Not far from Cape Bonifacio. Indeed, it was there that one of the ships carrying our troops to the Crimea, in that frightful war begun by the Russian invaders, perished. I remember...it was a terrible episode!

"But the entire sea-bed is strewn with such debris! Here are galleys with several banks of oars...Roman galleys scarcely sketched out, Carthaginian galley infinitely more perfect. Some naval conflict of the Punic Wars took place here. Then too, so much jetsam thrown overboard by ships in distress! Here are cannons, a thousand marine instruments...what violent tempest made itself felt in this place?"

Etc...

I could have talked in that fashion for six hours, while the power of the Lunians' lens permitted me to see an infinity of things—but in order not to bore my traveling companions, who would have learned to dread Terran verbosity, I put a stop to the flow of my language and plunged myself into a mute contemplation, from which nothing would have been able to snatch me back had Mikaël had not said to me, tapping me on the shoulder: "Friend, we've passed the island of Cyprus to our right; here's the island of Rhodes, and Crete. Look at the illustrious Cyclades and Sporades of the Aegean Sea, and salute Cape Trinacrium. We're flying over Morea, once the Peloponnese."

"Dear Master," I said to Mikaël, "do you think that one day, the genus of humankind will realize a means of visiting the bottom of the sea? It's an inexhaustible mine of curiosities..."

"Yes, that will happen," Mikaël replied, with a blissful smile, "but come back to the land."

We were, indeed, entering the countries that Scripture calls the Isles of Nations; among these peoples, whose glory effaced that of the Assyrians, Persians and Egyptians, as it was effaced in its turn by that of the Romans and that of the Romans was terminated by disorder and ruination. We were passing over Cape Matapan, formerly Trinacrium.

There I saw a chain of mountains cutting the near-isle in two, its summits laden with snow, forming a striking contrast with its base, darkened by black fir-trees. The northern part was a vast fertile plain, only interrupted by a few Cyllenian mountains. On the southern slope, a river whose banks were covered in laurier-roses, undulated through charming valleys on its way to the sea. Then another river, equally beautiful, for it irrigated the most poetic locations, displayed the paleness of its sash, with a radiance quite different from that of the first.

"Taygeta is the name of the mountain chain."

"Eurotas is that of the first river."

"Alpheus is the name of the second watercourse."

My traveling companions all spoke at the same time.

"Where, then, are Sparta, Lacedaemon and Mistra?" I asked, impatiently, excited by those great names.

"There!" Mikaël pointed with his finger.

I looked in the designated direction, which was nothing but a hill covered with protuberances, and I saw sunburnt Greeks hastened their oxen to work, cattle-prods in hand. I saw vines interlaced with mulberry bushes, and then, on the hillside, a little debris, of stones still disposed in a semicircle. It was all on the verdant slopes at the western edge of Taygeta, the feet of which were bathed by the calm Eurotas, whose waves were undisturbed by any white swans, as in times past.

"Lycurgus! Leonidas!" I cried, three times.

Nothing, not even the echo of the eminence, replied to my voice. Everything in Sparta was dead—for that eminence was Sparta, and those stones disposed in a semicircle were the ruins of the theater, the only ruins of a city whose name still fills the imagination of all men!

Meanwhile, our aerostats were gliding in the direction of Alpheus, sometimes overlooking the plains where the women of the region were gathering olives, sometimes poor villages whose thatch sparkled in the sunlight. At the foot of a mountain, near a ruined aqueduct, beside large blocks of brickwork and stone, Stella pointed out in her turn empty tombs, then the scarcely-perceptible traces of a stadium, those of a hippodrome, slightly more visible although eaten away by the river, and finally, grottoes forming the sets of judges, and the debris of columns indicating the remains of a temple.

"Can that be Olympia?" I exclaimed.

"Olympia, Olympia…ympia…pia!" repeated an echo, quite distinct this time, but which faded away by degrees.

So that was all that remained of the vast theater of glory, whose palms were so sought after by the Greeks? The echo that had once repeated seven times the voice of heralds and the acclamations of the people…the wind.

An hour later, we were passing over some poor hovels near the sea when Naïs said in her turn: "Argos, cherished city of heroes and gods, nurturer of beautiful women and generous horses, you who were glorified by having had such princes as Phoroneus, Pelasgus, Jason, Agenor and the powerful Agamemnon, are you then reduced to the sad state of a miserable Morean pachalick?"[82]

Such was Argos, in fact: nothing of its primal splendor remained; even the least of its ruins had been used to built the modern shanty-town that people dared to name Argos!

---

[82] A pachalick was a province governed by a pacha; there were several in Greece while it was under the control of the Ottoman empire.

"Perhaps it will cheer me up, in a little while, to arrive at Athens," I said to the Lunians, "For I believe that we're getting close to it. Here, already, are the gulfs of Corinth and Saronica, which inform us that the Peloponnese is behind us and greater Greece has arrived. I recognize the isthmus, whose form is becoming clearer and less vaporous...and there's Corinth...what! Corinth, the daughter of Ephyrus, the sister of Athens and Sparta, the fatherland of Sisyphus and Helen, the kingdom of Jason and Medea, is no more than a miserable fortified town whose crown is formed by seven meager columns, the last debris of one of the temples that decorated it? Where can so much glory have gone?"

"*Cecidit sicut flos agri!*"[83] Stella replied. "It has fallen like the flowers of the field. But here's Attica and its mountains. There are the coasts of Salamis, the plains of Mantinea, Leuctra, Platea and Marathon, and in the air, a song repeating the names of Solon, Pericles, Alcibiades, Themistocles, Miltiades, Epaminondas, Philopoemen, Leonidas!

"We shall see the Acropolis, the head and heart of superb Athens, which gazed with pride at the diadem of rivals placed just as proudly around it: Megara, Corinth, Olympia, Sparta, Argos and many others.

"In fact, in a golden mist shining with opaline and reddish fire, the Parthenon is revealing itself atop the Acropolis, like a gigantic pearl set on the tip of a Pelasgic emerald—and from the Acropolis, descending to a charming plain at the confluence of the Cephisa and the Ilyssus, is a long cascading street, which, passing beneath the Dipylon gate, follows the long walls of Themistocles to reach the harbor of Pireus, facing us.

---

[83] This is not a direct quotation, but is improvised by Stella; the judgment was somewhat prophetic, as the last remains of ancient Corinth were destroyed by an earthquake a few years later, in 1858—but the modern city of Corinth was subsequently constructed on the site.

"Now, Athens was not built on a single surface. Its picturesque situation inspired in its inhabitants a taste for beautiful things, and caused them to place some rich monument on each of the protrusions rising from the ground within its boundary. Here the Propylaea, sumptuous colonnades constructed in white marble, serving as an entrance to the Parthenon; there the Erechteum, similarly in white marble; and then, descending with the long street I mentioned in front of the Acropolis, the theater of Bacchus and that of the Odeon; to the right and the left, the Ceramic, the Pnyx, with its tribune carved into the rock the seats of the secretaries; and then again the Agora, and below the Agora the Poecile, or picture gallery; and finally, on that platform, Andronicus Cyrrehestes' tower of the winds, the temple of Theseus, and on the other. The temple of Olympian Zeus with its hundred and twenty fluted columns sixty feet high. Plato's Academy, Aristotle's Lyceum, Antisthenes' Cynosarges and the Senate's Prytaneum.

"Seen from afar, this beautiful city smiles at us, still enveloped in the illusion of its memories—but when the golden mist of distance is effaced, when there is no more perspective and our balloons carry us brutally over the great Athens, the charm is entirely dissipated alas, for the Parthenon, Acropolis, Propylaea, Erectheus, theaters temples, Pnyx, Ceramic, Agora, Poecile, tower of the winds, colonnades, Lyceum, Prytaneum...are no more than ruins. And in those ruins, in the Agora, instead of the noble people of Themistocles or Alcibiades, there are only peasants with rheumy eyes, women with odious faces who display themselves, offering the fruits and vegetables from their gardens to passers-by...

"It is all gone; everything on Earth passes, and nothing remains; humans and objects, everything vanishes. And I feel my head bowing down under the weight of grief."

"Yes!" I exclaimed. "There is nothing stable under the sun, except loving God and serving him!"

"That is a profound truth, my dear Terran," said Mikaël, "and I urge you to draw similar conclusions from every eventuality; you will be the greatest philosopher in the world. In the meantime, look at Pireus, which has fallen a long way from its original grandeur. Dies it not say anything to your imagination?"

I looked—and imagine my astonishment! There, tranquilly anchored in the harbor were five ships carrying the flag of France. Oh, it was certainly the French tricolor...and besides, on the deck of each of the vessels, there were troops on parade in familiar uniforms, dear to my heart, and a military band hurled into the air and to the echoes of the shore the joyful strain of "Partant pour la Syrie."

"Vive la France!" I shouted. "They're allies of right who are going to the Crimea to extract Sebastopol and the Black Sea from the claws of the vulture of the north. Vive la France!"

It's necessary to believe that my cry was vibrant enough to reach the ears of our soldiers. Since we had been traveling in that manner, the inhabitants of the Earth had very rarely raised their gaze our aerostats, but this time, suddenly, in response to that cry of patriotic love, the eyes of all the soldiers fixed themselves on our vessels, and there were salvoes of applause and clamors of joy, which informed us that we had caused a sensation. But how far they were from suspecting that one of those balloons came from the Moon!

As our aerostats began to draw away, Mikaël steered us toward the narrow plateau of Lycabettus, which rises up like a cone in the Athenian plain, and which the traveler only seems to be able to climb with the aid of asperities in the rock. There, he pointed out a little chapel which was, he told me, consecrated to St. George.

"How the humble Christian temple in which some poor priest is praying contrasts, by virtue of its paltry appearance, with the magnificence of the ruins that surround it!" I exclaimed.

"Isn't it so?" Mikaël replied. "But it dominates, as much by the sublimity of the mysteries of which it is the witness as by its lofty location, the most celebrated monuments that human hands have built. The temple of Zeus and the Parthenon are at its feet, and in the very places where Socrates taught the immortality of the soul, it surpasses, by virtue of the pure idea that it represents, all the glories of the past, and all the grandeurs of ancient wisdom."

What immortal memories were surrounding us! The horizon had broadened out again; we could embrace all of Attica with a single glance: to one side, the immensity of the ocean; in front of us, Pireus, Phalera and Munychia, Salamis and its gulf, the isle of Egina, Megara and the sacred territory of Eleusis; here, the summits of Citheron and Parnes; there, the chain of Hymetta; behind us, the abrupt slopes of Pentelicus.

The scenery was arid, the mountainsides bare. The Ilyssus so dear to the Muses scarcely amounted to a trickle of water at present, but Mikaël told me that in winter, laurier-roses grew on its banks and anemones displayed their brilliant colors everywhere. Socrates and Plato, walking barefoot along the bed of the torrent, could have lauded the coolness of its waters, the mildness of the air, the delightful shade of the plane-trees protecting them against the heat of the day.

Further away, in the valleys and the slopes of Pentelicus, which limited the horizon, the terrain became greener and more uneven. In the depths of rustic gorges steams ran that never dried up; clumps of myrtle offered respite to sight wearied by the sad foliage of olive-trees, and beautiful forests of cedars extended from one chain to another al the way to the plain of Marathon. It was in those beautiful valleys that the Cephisus had its source.

That privileged corner on the Earth is restricted everywhere between the mountains and the sea, but under that pure sky, resplendent with light, the view extended beyond the ordinary limits, simultaneously embracing the snowy summits of Parnassus and Oeta, the mountains of the Peloponnese and, beyond the Cyclades, Samos and the coast of Asia Minor. Was that not the image of the ancient genius of Greece, which, delivered to ideal contemplations, possessed a grandeur so disproportionate to its real power, and which, in the world of intelligence, has conquered an empire that it was unable to conserve in the world of action?

Already, our rapid flight was taking us away from Greece, and carrying us over the Adriatic Sea, and then over Italy. Soon, we could even see Vesuvius smoking!

"Do you know," Mikaël said, "that that is one of the most talked-about of volcanoes? It got up to its old tricks very recently, frightening the neighboring regions with an unparalleled eruption. It goes without saying that it covered the country with lava, leaving not an inch of ground untouched—and when, that lava having cooled completely, it revived, heating up again, becoming incandescent, fiery red. What do you say to that mystery?"

"I can only explain it by subterranean heat, which increased in such a manner as to communicate its flames to the external crust of the volcano," I replied, "but I will also add that Vesuvius not yet said its last word, while earthquakes are furrowing Europe in every direction, destroying villages here, like Brousse, the residence of Abd-el-Kader in Asia Minor, and entire plains there, with their flocks and crops. Besides, volcanic eruptions and earthquakes are all one, the cause being the same—to wit, the alimentation of interior fires, and the destruction and fall of enormous blocks of the material entertaining those fires."

"What is certain is that, if you listen carefully, as I do, you will recognize the ordinary signal of the volcano, which does not lack courtesy, for it issues warnings to the world when it is meditating and eruption. That signal is nothing other than certain discharges of artillery—but an artillery of its own. Many people have concluded from these alarming noises that Vesuvius, having devoured all its sticks of ammunition, will crumble and collapse, or at least case to vomit flames and lava, and that one of these days, instead of its crater, one will find nothing but a pretty little lake next to which picnics will be held on the grass while cooling the wine in its waters...but people have already been living with that hope for two thousand years, and it has shown no sign of realization."

"Similar results have already been produced, though?"

"Yes, at Agano in your Auvergne, and elsewhere. Vesuvius itself does not have such a benign and obliging character."

"Braggart as it is, it's not the greatest volcano is the world, is it?"

"No. Kerovia, on the largest of the Sandwich Islands, is much more corpulent. The gulf that we call the latter's crater is no less than five leagues in circumference. That doesn't matter, though. The key to the enigma, with regard to volcanoes, is knowing at what depth the agent might be placed that is capable of such terrible effects. Now, for Vesuvius, for example, by estimating the approximate mass raised up by the volcano, and restoring to it the form it ought to have in the Earth's interior, the position of that matter is estimated to be at least three leagues below the surface of the Mediterranean. What must be the force of projection, therefore, that elevates above the volcano the immense flaming sprays that escape from it? And with what activity must the central fire be endowed to cause such eruptions? That's one of God's secrets. It was in vain that the intrepid Lazzaro Spallanzani descended into the depths of Etna's crater, and, suspended above an abyss of fire, supported by a thin layer of lava ready to fall back into the gulf, leaned over to observe the opening through which so much liquefied stone had passed, to cool outside. The naturalist could not see anything, and the stones he dropped did not return any sound—so human curiosity remained unsatisfied."

Mikaël was still speaking as we passed over the towns of Herculaneum, Stabiae and Pompeii, which Vesuvius—that time without warning—had buried under heaps of ash and lava in 79 A.D.

Then there was Rome coming toward us, and after Rome, whose eternal walls saw us floating above their enclosure for a long time, admiring the beautiful ruins of the Coliseum, Hadrian's Aqueduct and the Appian Way, our rapid progress was taking us toward northern Italy and the shores of France when I felt anxiety grip my heart...

At the same time, Naïs' and Stella's expressions darkened. They looked at me with tears in their eyes and spoke to one another in hushed tones, as if to say: "Poor Terran; he'll soon be abandoned to himself. What a sad fate! And yet, we can do nothing for him."

As for Mikaël, he was gazing at the horizon in the far distance with his finger extended and his eyes fixed on Constantinople, whose minarets, cupolas, cemeteries, mosques, harems, palaces, gardens—the most picturesque Oriental constructions—were glittering, becoming verdant or paling in the sunlight: the sunlight that throws golden dust into the air, which turns horizons blue, inflames sands and silvers mists. He showed us the English and French fleets heading toward Sebastopol, ships arriving at full steam, bringing our brave French regiments and the English Grenadier Guards, Scots Guards and Royal Artillery, in order to disembark the at Gallipoli, where Turkish armies were defending the key positions against the Russian armies that were incessantly moving into the Crimea in order to fight our battalions.

"The finger of God is there," he said, "and his eye is not closed to the events in preparation there. He will doubtless give triumph to justice, while he will humiliate the reckless and pitiless despotism of a man who is sacrificing an entire world to his ambition."

"So be it!" I added.

"We shall not pause at another port of call now," Mikaël added, a moment later, "for our fatherland is reclaiming you, and ours is similarly recalling us."

"Alas, my heart told me as much," I replied, melting in tears, and I'm very unhappy to leave you, dear Lunians. Although rendered very imperfect by sin and rebellion against God, the heart of a Terran is nevertheless susceptible to tender and pure affections, especially when it is inspired by beings who...that..."

"Yes, yes, I know what you mean. Come on, old chap, don't try to finish your sentence. Be calm..."

"It's just that you have been so good for me, Mikaël, since our meeting! I have had such kind attention from your beautiful Naïs and your dear Stella! As the angel Raphael once did for young Tobias, you have guided me and brought me home. How would I ever be able to thank you? Oh, yes, I'm suffering, for it is necessary for me to be separated from you, whom I love..."

"Come on, your lamentation is infecting us all," Mikaël interjected. "We have taken you to heart too, and for the first time we feel unhappy, for we are going to leave you on the accursed Earth—but God's decrees are inflexible, and no one can escape them..."

"Yes," said Naïs, in the middle of a sob, "return to the place where your mother is waiting." Then she added, with a sigh: "But always remember that you have friends up above."

"Will you conserve a memory of the poor Terran, benevolent Naïs, and you, indulgent Stella?" I asked. "Will you remember the Frenchman who sailed the skies with you? Will you recall that his gaze has contemplated your abode? That he has drunk your beverages, eaten your food, received your instruction?"

"We'll remember all of that," said Naïs.

"And many other things as well!" added Mikaël.

"Not to mention that we'll look at you often, from our Moon," Stella concluded, mischievously.

Diavolo! I thought. *I must be careful, in view of their terrible lens! For how can I, a poor imperfect creature, avoid shocking the gaze of immortal creatures?*

"As to that," said Mikaël, who had divined my thought, "you have only to practice virtue, always and everywhere..."

I shook my traveling companions' hands as a prelude to more tender farewells, while saying: "That I will do, venerated Master, not only to please you, but above all to please the sovereign who reigns in Heaven, from whom I await my destiny..."

"In that case, my dear chap," Mikaël said, "we may hope to see you again one day. "For my part, I would like that, for I'm interested in you, especially because of the religious sentiment flowering in your soul. It's a compass, a torch that will enable you to see clearly in the pathways of life. Conserve it preciously, therefore—otherwise, you might get lost..."

"Above all," said Naïs, beware of the vices of the century: indifference to moral and religious matters; monstrous egotism, which causes the sublime recommendation of Jesus—love one another, and do not do unto others as you would not have them do unto you—to be trampled underfoot."

"You'll follow this good advice, won't you, my friend?" said Stella in her turn. "And as we worship the same God, one day you will have the same recompense for your fidelity that we have. Then we shall reign in the same Heaven..."

"I swear it!" I cried. "my conduct will be such that you will never have to blush on high for the poor Terran who will suffer and die down here!"

I had scarcely finished my sentence than Mikaël, doubtless in order to prevent the explosion of our common grief, imparted an impulse to his aerostat, which suddenly rose into the sky with lightning rapidity. Except that four phrases were heard simultaneously ringing in the air, in four different tones:

"Adieu, dear Terran!"

"Adieu, Friend!"

"Adieu, fine young man!"

"Adieu, dear Lunians!"

And then it was over.

To say that I resigned myself to that abrupt separation would be false, but I dried my tears nevertheless. That was, admittedly, in order to be able to see the Lunian balloon more clearly—but I could no longer discover the slightest trace of it.

I was in France, however, sailing toward Paris. My heart leapt in my breast then; how long had I been absent? I could not calculate it, having forgotten to interrogate Mikaël as to the number of days that we had spent in our explorations. However long it was, I felt hungry for terrestrial alimentation, having lived for several days on nothing but lunar nourishment. I needed to eat. Alas, my provisions smelled bad…they were no longer fresh. That was annoying.

But another adventure was beginning!

Did it not seem to me that, as on my departure, a storm was brewing in the heavens. Large coppery clouds were piling up. The firmament was becoming black…

How I missed Mikaël!

In fact, lighting flashes were streaking the clouds; thunder resounded; a tempest burst. I found myself in the very heart of that tempest. Thunderbolts threatened my balloon at every instant. Great danger was suspended above my head.

I commended my soul to God; I made the sign of the cross; I thought about my mother; I…

Alas, what I had foreseen occurred. Electricity passed through my aerostat. The gas immediately caught fire…

I thought about Rozier, Zambecari, Gale, Emma Verdier! I was about to perish, like them. Indeed, there was a terrible turbulence in my gondola. It was falling, dragging its ropes after it, with the shreds of my balloon…

Imagine that fall, that tangled descent, dear readers…

It's all over! I thought. "My God," I cried, receive my spirit and protect…my mother!"

I waited to be flattened when I reached the ground.

The impact was, indeed, horrible. It seemed to me that I was reduced to the condition of cardboard; my back was broken; a frightful and unique pain weighed upon my reduced being. My head must have been crushed to pulp…

In sum, though, I was not dead.

I opened my eyes to take stock of my situation and to find out what village, town or département I was in…

Imagine my surprise!

I was in my bed, in my own bed, in my bedroom, the bedroom that I share with my mother!

My mother was in the next room; I heard her talking to the chambermaid.

It was daylight; a beautiful May sun was tinting my closed curtains pink.

The day before, while going for a walk in the Bois de Boulogne with my mother, she had talked to me about the necessity of choosing a profession, and had even expressed the desire that I should be a civil engineer. I had put up some opposition to the idea.

When we had passed the Hippodrome, an aerostat carrying passengers at five hundred francs a head—which is a little dear for that kind of curiosity—had risen into the air under the guidance of Monsieur Godard.[84]

That evening, after dinner, while chatting in the drawing-room, I had drawn balloons rising to the utmost heights of the sky, and I had written on their floating banners the legend: *Adventures of Parisian Aeronauts.*

Then I had gone to bed.

Now, dear readers, it was a dream that I had just had, and which I have related to you.

"You're awake at last!" said my mother, coming into the room. "You've had a turbulent night, my ear child. Your bed must be damp with sweat. I had to come to you several times during the night: you cried out, you laughed, you wept, you even appeared to be eating..."

"I dreamed that I was on the Moon, Mother," I said, laughing.

"Good—now get up, and let's make preparations for your new studies," said the angel that God has given me.

---

[84] Eugène Godard, the founder of an aeronautical dynasty, made over 2500 balloon flights and was much fêted by Napoléon III, whose support he repaid—to no avail—by using his aerostats to carry dispatches during the siege of Paris in 1870.

SF & FANTASY

Henri Allorge. *The Great Cataclysm*
Guy d'Armen. *Doc Ardan: The City of Gold and Lepers*
G.-J. Arnaud. *The Ice Company*
Cyprien Bérard. *The Vampire Lord Ruthwen*
Aloysius Bertrand. *Gaspard de la Nuit*
Richard Bessière. *The Gardens of the Apocalypse*
Albert Bleunard. *Ever Smaller*
Félix Bodin. *The Novel of the Future*
Alphonse Brown. *City of Glass*
André Caroff. *The Terror of Madame Atomos; Miss Atomos; The Return of Madame Atomos; The Mistake of Madame Atomos*
Félicien Champsaur. *The Human Arrow*
Didier de Chousy. *Ignis*
Captain Danrit. *Undersea Odyssey*
C. I. Defontenay. *Star (Psi Cassiopeia)*
Charles Derennes. *The People of the Pole*
Georges Dodds (anthologist). *The Missing Link*
Harry Dickson. *The Heir of Dracula*
Jules Dornay. *Lord Ruthven Begins*
Alfred Driou. *The Adventures of a Parisian Aeronaut*
Sâr Dubnotal *vs. Jack the Ripper*
Alexandre Dumas. *The Return of Lord Ruthven*
Renée Dunan. *Baal*
J.-C. Dunyach. *The Night Orchid; The Thieves of Silence*
Henri Duvernois. *The Man Who Found Himself*
Achille Eyraud. *Voyage to Venus*
Henri Falk. *The Age of Lead*
Paul Féval. *Anne of the Isles; Knightshade; Revenants; Vampire City; The Vampire Countess; The Wandering Jew's Daughter*
Paul Féval, *fils. Felifax, the Tiger-Man*
Charles de Fieux. *Lamékis*

Arnould Galopin. *Doctor Omega*; *Doctor Omega & The Shadowmen*

G.L. Gick. *Harry Dickson and the Werewolf of Rutherford Grange*

Nathalie Henneberg. *The Green Gods*

V. Hugo, P. Foucher & P. Meurice. *The Hunchback of Notre-Dame*

Michel Jeury. *Chronolysis*

Octave Joncquel & Théo Varlet. *The Martian Epic*

Gustave Kahn. *The Tale of Gold and Silence*

Gérard Klein. *The Mote in Time's Eye*

Jean de La Hire. *Enter the Nyctalope; The Nyctalope on Mars; The Nyctalope vs. Lucifer; The Nyctalope Steps In*

Etienne-Léon de Lamothe-Langon. *The Virgin Vampire*

André Laurie. *Spiridon*

Gabriel de Lautrec. *The Vengeance of the Oval Portrait*

Georges Le Faure & Henri de Graffigny. *The Extraordinary Adventures of a Russian Scientist Across the Solar System* (2 vols.)

Gustave Le Rouge. *The Vampires of Mars*

Jules Lermina. *Mysteryville; Panic in Paris; To-Ho and the Gold Destroyers; The Secret of Zippelius*

Jean-Marc & Randy Lofficier. *Edgar Allan Poe on Mars; The Katrina Protocol; Pacifica; Robonocchio; Tales of the Shadowmen 1-8*

Xavier Mauméjean. *The League of Heroes*

José Moselli. *Illa's End*

John-Antoine Nau. *Enemy Force*

Marie Nizet. *Captain Vampire*

C. Nodier, A. Beraud & Toussaint-Merle. *Frankenstein*

Henri de Parville. *An Inhabitant of the Planet Mars*

Georges Pellerin. *The World in 2000 Years*

J. Polidori, C. Nodier, E. Scribe. *Lord Ruthven the Vampire*

P.-A. Ponson du Terrail. *The Vampire and the Devil's Son*

Maurice Renard. *The Blue Peril; Doctor Lerne; The Doctored Man; A Man Among the Microbes; The Master of Light*

Jean Richepin. *The Wing*

Albert Robida. *The Adventures of Saturnin Farandoul; The Clock of the Centuries; Chalet in the Sky*
J.-H. Rosny Aîné. *Helgvor of the Blue River; The Givreuse Enigma; The Mysterious Force; The Navigators of Space; Vamireh; The World of the Variants; The Young Vampire*
Marcel Rouff. *Journey to the Inverted World*
Han Ryner. *The Superhumans*
Brian Stableford. *The New Faust at the Tragicomique; The Empire of the Necromancers (The Shadow of Frankenstein; Frankenstein and the Vampire Countess; Frankenstein in London); Sherlock Holmes & The Vampires of Eternity; The Stones of Camelot; The Wayward Muse.* (anthologist) *The Germans on Venus; News from the Moon; The Supreme Progress; The World Above the World; Nemoville*
Jacques Spitz. *The Eye of Purgatory*
Kurt Steiner. *Ortog*
Eugène Thébault. *Radio-Terror*
C.-F. Tiphaigne de La Roche. *Amilec*
Théo Varlet. *The Xenobiotic Invasion*
Paul Vibert. *The Mysterious Fluid*
Villiers de l'Isle-Adam. *The Scaffold; The Vampire Soul*
Philippe Ward. *Artahe*
Philippe Ward & Sylvie Miller. *The Song of Montségur*

MYSTERIES & THRILLERS

M. Allain & P. Souvestre. *The Daughter of Fantômas*
A. Anicet-Bourgeois, Lucien Dabril. *Rocambole*
A. Bisson & G. Livet. *Nick Carter vs. Fantômas*
V. Darlay & H. de Gorsse. *Lupin vs. Holmes: The Stage Play*
Paul Féval. *Gentlemen of the Night; John Devil; The Black Coats ('Salem Street; The Invisible Weapon; The Parisian Jungle; The Companions of the Treasure; Heart of Steel; The Cadet Gang; The Sword-Swallower)*
Emile Gaboriau. *Monsieur Lecoq*
Steve Leadley. *Sherlock Holmes: The Circle of Blood*

Maurice Leblanc. *Arsène Lupin vs. Countess Cagliostro; Lupin vs. Holmes (The Blonde Phantom; The Hollow Needle)*
Gaston Leroux. *Chéri-Bibi; The Phantom of the Opera; Rouletabille & the Mystery of the Yellow Room*
William Patrick Maynard. *The Terror of Fu Manchu*
Frank J. Morlock. *Sherlock Holmes: The Grand Horizontals; Sherlock Holmes vs Jack the Ripper*
P. de Wattyne & Y. Walter. *Sherlock Holmes vs. Fantômas*
David White. *Fantômas in America*

SCREENPLAYS

Mike Baron. *The Iron Triangle*
Emma Bull & Will Shetterly. *Nightspeeder; War for the Oaks*
Gerry Conway & Roy Thomas. *Doc Dynamo*
Steve Englehart. *Majorca*
James Hudnall. *The Devastator*
Jean-Marc & Randy Lofficier. *Royal Flush*
J.-M. & R. Lofficier & Marc Agapit. *Despair*
Andrew Paquette. *Peripheral Vision*
R. Thomas, J. Hendler & L. Sprague de Camp. *Rivers of Time*

NON-FICTION

Stephen R. Bissette. *Blur 1-5; Green Mountain Cinema 1; Teen Angels & New Mutants*
Win Scott Eckert. *Crossovers* (2 vols.)
Jean-Marc & Randy Lofficier. *Shadowmen* (2 vols.)
Randy Lofficier. *Over Here*

HEXAGON COMICS

Franco Frescura & Luciano Bernasconi. *Wampus*
Franco Frescura & Giorgio Trevisan. *CLASH*
L. Bernasconi, J.-M. Lofficier & Juan Roncagliolo Berger. *Phenix*
Claude Legrand, J.-M. Lofficier & L. Bernasconi. *Kabur*

Franco Oneta. *Zembla*
L. Buffolente, Lofficier & J.-J. Dzialowski. *Strangers: Homi-cron*
Danilo Grossi. *Strangers: Jaydee*
Claude Legrand & Luciano Bernasconi. *Strangers: Starlock*

ART BOOKS

Jean-Pierre Normand. *Science Fiction Illustrations*
Raven Okeefe. *Raven's L'il Critters*
Randy Lofficier & Raven OKeefe. *If Your Possum Go Day-light...*
Daniele Serra. *Illusions*